'Think *Jurassic Park* meets *The Walking Dead*'   Brad Thor

'Arachnophobes, move on. This is not for the likes of you'

We hope you enjoy this book. Please return or renew it by the due date.

You can renew it at www.norfolk.gov.uk/libraries or by using our free library app.

Otherwise you can phone 0344 800 8020 - please have your library card and PIN ready.

You can sign up for email reminders too.

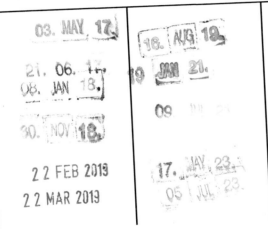

THE HATCHING

EZEKIEL BOONE

First published in Great Britain in 2016 by Gollancz
an imprint of the Orion Publishing Group Ltd
Carmelite House, 50 Victoria Embankment
London EC4Y 0DZ

An Hachette UK Company

1 3 5 7 9 10 8 6 4 2

A CIP catalogue record for this book is
available from the British Library.

ISBN 978 1 473 21518 4

Printed in Great Britain by Clays Ltd, St Ives plc

www.ezekielboone.com
www.orionbooks.co.uk
www.gollancz.co.uk

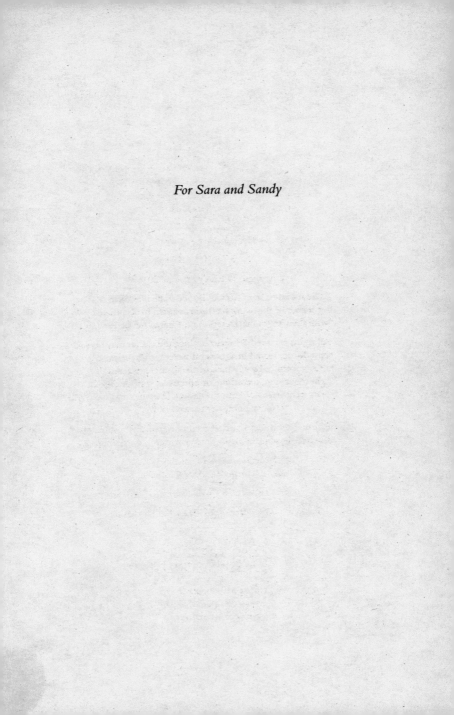

For Sara and Sandy

PROLOGUE

Outside Manú National Park, Peru

The guide wanted to tell the group of Americans to shut up. Of course they weren't seeing any animals: their constant complaining was driving them away. Only the birds remained, and even they seemed skittish. He was just a guide, however, so he said nothing.

There were five Americans. Three women and two men. The guide was interested in how they were paired off. It seemed unlikely that the fat man, Henderson, had all three women for himself. No matter how rich he was, shouldn't two women at one time be enough? Perhaps the tall man had one? Perhaps not. As far as the guide could tell, the tall man was there to act as Henderson's bodyguard and servant only. He and Henderson did not act like friends. The tall man carried the fat man's water and snacks and did not let his eyes linger on any of the women. There was no question that he was in Henderson's employ. As was the guide.

The guide sighed. He'd see how the women were portioned off at camp, he thought. In the meantime, he would do what he was paid for, which was lead them through the jungle and point out things that were supposed to impress them. Of course, they'd already done Machu Picchu, which always left tourists feeling as if they had seen everything Peru had to offer, and now there were no animals to show them. He glanced back at Henderson and decided it was time for another break. They'd had to stop every twenty minutes so that the rich man could run into the brush and move his bowels, and now the guide was worried Henderson might be overexerting himself.

It wasn't that Henderson was grossly fat, but he was definitely large and clearly struggling to keep pace with the rest of the group. The tall man and the three women, though, were all in good shape. The women, in particular, all looked embarrassingly athletic and young, twenty or thirty years younger than Henderson. It was obvious the heat was getting to him. His face was red and he kept mopping at his forehead with a damp handkerchief. Henderson was older than the women, but looked too young for a heart attack. Still, the guide thought, it wouldn't hurt to keep him well hydrated. After all, it had been made abundantly clear to the guide that if things went well, Henderson might be persuaded to make a sizable donation to the park and the scientists working there.

The day wasn't any hotter than normal, but even though the group had come directly from Machu Picchu, they didn't seem to understand that they were still at elevation. They weren't actually inside Manú National Park, which they didn't seem to understand either. The guide could have explained that they were technically allowed only in the larger biosphere area, and that the park itself was reserved for researchers, staff, and the indigenous Machiguenga, but all it would have done was disappoint them even more than they already were.

"Any chance we'll see a lion, Miggie?" one of the women asked him.

The woman next to her, who looked as if she had come from

one of the magazines that the guide had kept under his bed when he was a teenager, before he'd had access to the Internet, swung off her backpack and dropped it on the ground. "For God's sake, Tina," the woman said, shaking her head so that her hair swung around her face and her shoulders. The guide had trouble not staring down her scoop-neck shirt as she leaned over to unzip her bag and pull out a bottle of water. "We're in Peru, not Africa. You're going to make Miggie think that Americans are idiots. There aren't any lions in Peru. We could see a jaguar, though."

The guide had introduced himself as Miguel, but they had immediately taken to calling him Miggie, as if Miguel were just a suggestion. While he did not think all Americans were idiots—when he wasn't leading expeditions of tourists on "eco treks," he often worked with the scientists inside the park, most of them from American universities—he was beginning to think that, despite the presence of Henderson, who was by all accounts a genius, this particular group seemed to have more idiots than normal. They were not going to see a lion, and no matter what the woman said, they weren't going to see a jaguar, either. Miguel had been working here for the tour company for nearly three years, and even he'd never seen a jaguar. Not that he was truly an expert. He had been born and raised in Lima, and the only reason he was there, instead of back in the city of more than eight million, was a girl. They'd gone to university together, and when she landed a plum job as a research assistant, he managed to squirm his way into helping out inside the park occasionally. Recently, though, things hadn't been going so well; his girlfriend had seemed distracted when they'd been together, and Miguel had begun to suspect that she'd started sleeping with one of her coworkers.

He watched the Americans take water or little bars wrapped in plastic out of their backpacks, and then he walked a few paces farther down the path. He glanced back and saw the lion woman, Tina, smiling at him in such a way that he wondered if maybe that night, when Henderson went into his tent, she might be available for him. He'd had chances with tourists before, though the opportunity presented itself less often than he would have expected, and he'd always turned them down. But maybe tonight, if Tina offered, he wouldn't say no. If his girlfriend was cheating on him, the least he could do was return the favor. Tina kept smiling at him, and it made him nervous.

He was made more nervous by the jungle, however. The first few months after he'd left Lima to come here he'd hated it, but mostly he was used to the closeness of it by now. The constant buzz of insects, the movement, the heat, and the life that seemed everywhere. It had all become background noise eventually, and until today, it had been a long time since he'd been scared to be in the jungle. Today was different, though. The background noise was gone. It was unsettling how quiet it was aside from the nattering of the group behind him. They had been complaining about the lack of animals, and if he had been honest with them—and he hadn't, because that was not what a guide was paid to be—he would have told the group that he was bothered by it as well. Usually they would have seen more animals than they could have asked for: sloths, capybara, brocket, monkeys. God, they loved the monkeys. The tourists could never get enough monkeys. And insects, of course. They were usually everywhere, and when all else failed to keep the tourists entertained, Miguel, who had never been scared of spiders, would often pick one up on the end of a branch and surprise one of the women in the group with it. He loved the way they shrieked when he brought it close for them to see, and the way the men tried to pretend as though the spider didn't bother them.

Behind Tina, he saw Henderson bending over and grabbing at his gut. The man may have been very rich—Miguel had not recognized Henderson the man, though he had certainly heard of Henderson's company; the researchers all did their work on Henderson Tech's small silver computers—but he did not seem particularly special. He'd been complaining the entire morning. He complained about the roads, about the lack of access to the Internet at the lodge, about the food. Ah, the food. He complained and complained about the food, and as Miguel saw Henderson bent over and making a face, it appeared that at least as far as the food was concerned, Henderson might have had a point.

"You okay, boss?" The bodyguard was ignoring the three women, who were still arguing with one another about where it was exactly that lions lived.

"My gut is killing me," Henderson said. "That meat from last night. I've got to take a shit. Again." He looked up at Miguel, and the guide motioned with his thumb for Henderson to head off the path.

Miguel watched him disappear into the trees and then turned to look ahead again. The tour company kept the path well enough maintained that it was easy to move tourists along when there wasn't somebody like Henderson who needed to keep stopping. They'd bulldozed a strip and then tasked the guides with staying on the path so that nobody would get lost. As with any other human encroachment in the rain forest, the jungle was trying to reclaim the trail, so the company ran the machine out every few weeks. For the most part, the path made Miguel's work much easier. He could look ahead and see clear to where they would be going for close to a hundred meters. It also meant there was a break in the canopy, and when he looked up he could see the blue sky. There wasn't a cloud anywhere, and for a moment

Miguel wished he were on a beach instead of leading this group of Americans.

A bird flew over the breach in the canopy. The guide watched it for a second and was about to turn back to the group to see if Henderson had made it back from his bathroom break when he realized something was wrong with the bird. It was flapping its wings frantically, moving erratically. The bird was struggling to stay in the air. But there was something more. The guide wished he had a pair of binoculars, because the bird's feathers looked wrong. They looked like they were rippling, like there was—

The bird fell from the sky. It stopped struggling and simply plummeted.

Miguel shivered. The women were still chattering behind him, but there were no other animal sounds in the jungle. Even the birds were quiet. He listened more closely, and then he heard something. A rhythmic pounding. Leaves crunching. He'd just about figured out what it was when a man burst around the bend in the path. Even from a hundred meters away, it was clear something was wrong. The man saw Miguel and screamed at him, but Miguel couldn't make out the words. Then the man glanced at the path behind him, and as he did so, he tripped, falling heavily.

It looked to Miguel like a black river rushed up behind him. The man had only managed to get to his knees before the dark mass rolled over and around him.

Miguel took a few steps backward, but he found that he didn't want to turn away. The black river stayed on top of the man, roiling and building, as if it were dammed by something. There was a lumpy movement, the man underneath still struggling. And then the lump collapsed. The black water splashed out to cover the path. From where Miguel was standing, it looked like the man had simply disappeared.

And then the blackness started streaming toward him, covering the path and moving quickly, almost as fast as a man could run. Miguel knew he should be running, but there was something hypnotic in the quietness of the water. It didn't roar like a river. If anything, it seemed to absorb sound. All he could hear was a whisper, a skittering, like a small patter of rain. The way the river moved was beautiful in its own way, pulsing and, at certain points, splitting and braiding into separate streams before rejoining a few paces later. As it got closer, Miguel took another step back, but by the time he realized it wasn't actually a river, that it wasn't water of any kind, it was too late.

Minneapolis, Minnesota

Agent Mike Rich hated having to call his ex-wife. He fucking hated it, particularly when he knew that her husband—and he fucking hated that he was her *husband* now—might pick up the phone, but there was nothing he could do about it. He was going to be late, and if there was one thing that annoyed his ex-wife more than his being late to pick up their daughter, it was when he knew he was going to be late but didn't call. Hell, if he'd been better about both those things in the first place, Fanny might still be his wife. He stared at his phone.

"Just get it over with, Mike."

His partner, Leshaun DeMilo, was divorced himself, but didn't have any kids to show for it. Leshaun always said he'd made a clean break of it. Not that he seemed to particularly enjoy being single again. He'd been going about dating with a grim determination. Mike also thought Leshaun had been hitting the bars a little hard recently, and had come into work looking rough around the edges more than once since the divorce.

"You know the longer you wait the worse it's going to be," Leshaun said.

"Fuck you, Leshaun," Mike said, but he thumbed his phone on

and hit his ex-wife's number. Of course, her husband answered.

"I assume you're calling to say you're going to be late again?"

"You got me, Dawson," Mike said.

"I prefer to be called Rich, Mike. You know that."

"Yeah, sorry. It's just that, you know, when I hear Rich, I think me. Agent Rich. All that. It's weird calling you by my last name. How about Richard?"

"As long as you aren't calling me Dick—at least to my face—I'll live."

That was another thing that pissed Mike off about his ex-wife's new husband. Rich Dawson was a defense lawyer—which was reason enough—but he was also kind of a great guy. If Dawson hadn't gotten rich keeping the very douche bags out of jail that Mike spent his time arresting, and if Dawson weren't laying the wood to his ex-wife, Mike could have seen himself having a beer with the guy. It would have been easier if Dawson were just an unrepentant shit-bag, because then Mike would have had an excuse to hate him, but Mike was stuck with knowing he had nobody to be pissed off at but himself. Mike couldn't decide if he should look on the bright side of things because Dawson was terrific with Annie, or if that was something that made his ex-wife's new husband even worse. It killed Mike that his daughter had taken to Dawson like she had, but it had been good for her. She'd been quiet for the year or so between when he and Fanny had split and when Fanny had hooked up with Dawson. She hadn't been sad, or at least hadn't admitted she was, but she hadn't talked much. In the year and a half since Dawson had come into the picture, however, Annie had seemed like herself again.

"Just let me talk to Fanny, okay?"

"Sure."

Mike shifted in his seat. He never complained about having to sit in the car for hours on end, the stale coffee, the thick, fetid smell of socks and sweat that filled the car when they had to bake in the sun. The temperature was in the mid-eighties. Unseasonably warm for Minneapolis in April. There were years that he remembered snow still on the ground on April 23. Except for in the dead of summer, mid-eighties was *hot* for Minneapolis. He and Leshaun used to keep the car running and blast the air-conditioning—or, in the Minnesota winters, the heat—but Mike's daughter had been turned into one of those young environmental crusaders by her elementary school. She'd made both him and Leshaun promise not to leave the engine running if they were just sitting there. Left to himself, Mike probably would have caved and turned on the AC, but Leshaun wouldn't let him. "A promise is a promise, dude, particularly to your kid," Leshaun had said, and then he'd even bought reusable metal coffee cups for them to keep in the car. At least he hadn't gone so far as to make Mike wash and reuse the piss bottle on the days they were on surveillance but weren't parked close enough to a McDonald's or a Starbucks to hit a bathroom. They didn't actually run surveillance that much anymore. Days like this, though, when they *did*, were something Mike sort of missed. It was supposed to be part of the gig. There was a certain romance to the sitting and waiting. And waiting. And waiting. But his back was killing him today. They'd been in the car for nine hours already, and he'd spent the day before at the YMCA with Annie, swimming and throwing her in the air and chasing after her. At nine, Annie was getting to be a load, but what was he going to do? Not roughhouse in the pool?

He arched his back and stretched a little, trying to get comfortable. Leshaun held up a bottle of Advil, but Mike shook his head. His stomach had been bothering him, too—coffee and donuts and greasy burgers and fries and all the crap that made it harder and harder every day for him to stay in shape and run the miles and do the pull-ups he needed to do to keep passing his physical—and

popping a couple of pills to help his back seemed like a bad idea.
Fuck, Mike thought. He was only forty-three. Too young to be
getting old already.

"How late, Mike?" Fanny came on the line already swinging
for the fences.

Mike closed his eyes and tried to take a cleansing breath. That's
what his therapist had called it. A cleansing breath. When he opened
his eyes, Leshaun was staring at him. Leshaun raised an eyebrow
and mouthed "Apologize."

"I'm sorry, Fanny. I'm really sorry. We're on surveillance and relief
is running late. It will just be half an hour. Forty-five minutes at most."

"You're supposed to be taking her to soccer, Mike. Now I have
to do it."

Mike took another cleansing breath. "I don't know what else to
say, Fanny. I'm really sorry. I'll meet you at the field."

He wanted to be there. There was something about the smell of
the cut grass and watching his little girl run around chasing a ball.
The crappy wooden bleachers reminded him of what it was like to
be a kid, of looking over to the sideline at baseball or football games
and seeing his own dad sitting there, watching solemnly. Seeing
Annie goofing around with the other kids, or scowling and concen-
trating while trying to learn a step over or some other new skill, was
one of the best parts of his week. He never thought about his job
or his ex-wife or anything, really. It was a different world out there
on the soccer field: the sounds of the kids yelling and the coaches'
whistles all functioned like a reset button. Most of the other parents
chatted with one another, read books, tried to get work done, talked
on their cell phones, but Mike just watched. That's it. He watched
Annie run and kick and laugh and for that hour of soccer practice,
there was nowhere else in the world for him.

"Of course I can take her, but that's not the point. The point is that you're still doing it. I mean, I can leave you. I can get a divorce. But she's stuck with you, Mike. As much as she loves Rich, *you're* her father."

Mike glanced over at Leshaun, but his partner was ostentatiously not listening. Leshaun was doing what he was supposed to be doing, which was staring at the alley. There wasn't much chance that the prick they were waiting for, Two-Two O'Leary, was going to show up, but given that he used as much of the meth as he sold, and had wounded an agent in a bust gone bad the week before, it probably wasn't the worst thing in the world to have one of them paying attention.

"All I can do is keep apologizing." He glanced at Leshaun again and decided he didn't care if Leshaun was listening or not. It wasn't like they hadn't talked about his relationship with Fanny—or Leshaun and Leshaun's ex-wife's relationship—more than he had ever talked about it with his therapist, or, for that matter, with Fanny. Maybe if he'd talked about things with Fanny as much as he had with Leshaun, things would still be okay. "You know I'm sorry. About everything. I'm sorry about everything. Not just being late." Mike waited for Fanny to say something, but there was only silence. He went on. "I've been talking with my therapist about it, and I know that I'm late saying this. I mean, I guess I'm late with everything, but I'm trying to say I should have told you I was sorry a long time ago. I didn't mean to let things fall apart, and even though I'm not really happy about it, I *am* happy that you're happy. And you know, Dawson—Rich—seems like he makes you happy, and I know that Annie loves him. So, you know, I'm sorry. I'm doing my best to be a different kind of guy, a better man, but there's always going to be a part of me that's just the way I am. And that goes for the job too."

"Mike." Fanny's voice seemed faint, and Mike shifted again. He couldn't tell if it was his shitty phone cutting out or if she was talking more softly. "Mike," she repeated. "There's something I wanted to talk to you about."

"What? You going to divorce me again?"

Leshaun straightened and then leaned a little bit out the open window. Mike sat up in his seat. There was a car pulling into the alley. A Honda, which wasn't really Two-Two's ride of choice, but it was the first action they'd seen for a while. The car stopped with its trunk hanging over the sidewalk, and then a black teenager, maybe fifteen or sixteen, got out of the passenger-side door. Mike relaxed, and Leshaun sat back. Two-Two was selling guns and meth, but he was also big time in with the Aryan Nations. There wasn't much chance he was rolling with a black kid.

"I want to change Annie's name," Fanny said.

"What?"

"I want her to have the same last name as me, Mike."

"Just a second." Mike put the phone down on his thigh and rubbed his face with his free hand. He wished he still smoked, though it wasn't as if Leshaun would have let him light up in the car. The car. The goddamned car felt so close and hot. With his bulletproof vest over his T-shirt, he was sweating. Couldn't they run the engine just for a few minutes, have a little fucking air-conditioning? He needed to stand outside for a minute, to stand up, to get some fresh air. He opened the door. He needed a blast of cold air like they had in those gum commercials, but it wasn't any cooler outside the car.

"Mike?" Leshaun was looking at him. "What are you doing?"

"Nothing man. I'm not going anywhere. I'm just going to stand outside, okay? I just want to take this call outside the car for a minute. Is that okay with you? Do you mind?" He realized his voice had gotten loud and hard, and he knew that when he was done talking to Fanny he was going to have to apologize to Leshaun. Leshaun was a good partner, a good friend, and he'd understand, but still, it made Mike feel like an asshole. Like more of an asshole. Leshaun nodded, and Mike got out of the car. He shut the door behind him, not that it mattered with the windows open.

He lifted the phone back up. "What are you talking about, Fanny?"

"Come on, Mike. You had to see this coming. Didn't you see this coming?"

"No, Fanny, I didn't see this coming."

"Oh, Mike. You never see anything coming."

He heard the brush of the phone against Fanny's cheek and then the low murmur of her saying something to Dawson. He pressed the phone hard against his ear. "You're not changing Annie's name. She's my fucking daughter, and she's going to be Annie Rich, not Annie fucking Dawson."

"Mike," she said. "Annie's my daughter too. It's weird, having her have a different last name from me."

"You didn't have to change your name to Dawson," Mike said. Even as he said it, he knew it was the wrong thing to say, but he couldn't help himself.

Fanny sighed. "We can talk about this later, but it's going to happen. I'm sorry, Mike, I am, but things have changed."

"I'm trying to change too," Mike said.

"I appreciate that. I do," she said, and then neither of them said anything for a few seconds. Mike could hear Fanny breathing. Finally, she said, "Do you want to talk to Annie?"

"Please," he said. He felt defeated.

Mike leaned against the car, facing the alley. He shifted against the side of the car, rolled his shoulder, and tugged down on his T-shirt under the vest. It was wet with sweat. Better to be uncomfortable than dead, though. The agent Two-Two had shot in Eau Claire probably would have died if he hadn't been wearing body armor: three shots stopped by body armor, one bullet clean through the agent's biceps. It was a hundred miles from Eau Claire back to Minnesota, though, and hell, nobody thought Two-Two— even hopped up on Nazi meth—was going to come back to his bar after the debacle in Wisconsin. He adjusted the strapping to loosen the vest. Normally he had a shirt over it, but when they were just going to sit in a car all day, he figured there wasn't much point trying to hide it. And of course, it's not like he wasn't wearing his badge hanging off the chain around his neck. He loved being able to wear it, loved the way people looked at him differently when he introduced himself as Special Agent Rich, but as he fingered the chain, he thought that there were times when it felt like something he needed to take off more often.

"Hey, Daddy."

"Hey, beautiful. I'm going to have to meet you at the field, okay?"

"Okay."

"How was school?"

"Good."

"Anything exciting happen?"

"Not really."

That's what talking with her on the phone was like. When they were together, he couldn't get Annie to stop talking, but there was something about the invisibility of talking to each other over the telephone that made it so she rarely said more than a couple of words at a time. It was like she thought there was some sort of evil magic at work, and if she told the telephone too much information, it was going to steal her soul. The thought made Mike smile. It sounded like a book Stephen King would write.

He was about to ask her what she'd had for lunch when he saw the car. It was a red Ford truck, big tires, tinted windows, and it was turning into the alley. "Beautiful, I've got to go."

"Okay. I love you, Daddy."

"I love you too, baby." He felt his stomach churning. He let his free hand reach up again to finger the badge hanging around his neck. "I love you so, so much. You remember that, okay? No matter what happens, you remember that."

The truck stopped. Mike put the phone in his pocket. He felt the car move as Leshaun opened the door and slid out. Mike moved his hand from his badge to his hip, until he could wrap his fingers around the handle of his gun. The metal was cool against his hand. He took a moment to look over his shoulder for Leshaun. His partner was starting to stand up straight, and Mike looked back toward the red truck. He realized too late that Two-Two had already seen him standing outside the car, had seen the bulletproof vest, had seen the badge hanging around his neck. Mike shouldn't have been standing outside the car, talking on the phone. He shouldn't have looked back at Leshaun. Mike should have been in the car with his partner, should have been paying attention, should have been a lot of things.

Two-Two's passenger, an undershirt-wearing dipshit with a shaved head who looked like he was barely twenty, came out firing a handgun. Mike wasn't even sure he heard the bang of the man's pistol, but he heard the *plink* of a bullet hitting the door of the car, heard the glass of the windshield shattering. He heard a grunt, and then the heavy drop of Leshaun's body hitting the ground. All this before Two-Two even got out of the truck.

Mike's mind went blank, and he watched the man from the passenger side of the truck pop the emptied magazine out of his gun, reach into the pocket of his baggy pants, and pull out another clip. Meanwhile, Two-Two's door opened, and Mike saw that he was also carrying a pistol. Two men, two guns, Leshaun hit, though Mike didn't know how bad, and he hadn't even pulled his own gun out yet. He knew he was supposed to be doing something, but he was just standing there as if he didn't know what to do, didn't know what to do, didn't know what to do.

And then he did.

He put the kid on the passenger side down first. Three shots clustered in his chest. Two-Two and his buddy weren't wearing vests. He'd heard some of the agents who were gun nerds bitching about the stopping power of the service-issued Glock 22, but judging by the way the kid went down like a bag of chicken parts, the .40 cartridges seemed to work just fine. He'd never actually shot anybody before, had fired his gun only once in the line of duty—it had been one bullet, one time, barely a year on the job, and he'd missed—and he was surprised at how easy and normal it felt. All three bullets went home, and as the kid left his feet, Mike pivoted so that he could aim at Two-Two.

Two-Two had the same idea, though, and Two-Two was pointing back.

Mike wasn't sure who fired first, or if they fired at the same time, because the push of the pistol in his hand was matched by a tug on his sleeve. But he was entirely sure whose aim was better. Two-Two's head snapped back in a mist of blood. When Mike looked at his arm, there was a hole in the sleeve of his T-shirt, but not in his flesh.

The kid from the passenger side wasn't moving, and neither was Two-Two. Mike holstered his gun and hustled around the car to check on Leshaun. There were two holes in Leshaun's shirt: one hole a bloody mess on his upper arm, the other on the chest, clean and clear, the vest doing its job. Leshaun's eyes were open, and Mike had never been happier to see that big black motherfucker staring at him, but as he called for help he realized he was also going to have to call his ex-wife again.

He was going to be really, really late.

National Information Centre of Earthquake Engineering, Kanpur, India

It didn't matter what Dr. Basu did; the numbers kept coming back strange. She had rebooted her computer twice, even called Nadal in New Delhi and made him manually check the sensor in the basement of his building, but she kept getting the same results: something was shaking New Delhi with a consistency that was puzzling. Whatever it was, Dr. Basu thought, it wasn't an earthquake. At least, it didn't act like an earthquake.

"Faiz," she called. "Can you please check this for me?"

Faiz wasn't exactly quick to respond. He'd gone to Germany the previous month for a conference and had apparently spent most of his time in Düsseldorf in the hotel room of an Italian seismologist. Her colleague's focus, since coming back, was on e-mailing dirty pictures back and forth with his new girlfriend and trying to find employment in Italy.

Dr. Basu sighed. She wasn't used to such behavior from Faiz. He was funny and charming, but also sloppy and inappropriate and in many ways a horrible man—he had showed her some of the photos the Italian woman had sent him, photos that Dr. Basu was sure were not meant for sharing—but he was also good at his job. "Faiz," she said again. "Something's going on."

He banged his keyboard with a flourish and then pushed his heels against the ground, sending his chair wheeling across the concrete floor. "Yes, boss." He knew she hated when he called her that. He looked at her screen and then ran his fingers across the monitor, even though he knew she hated that too. "Yeah," he said. "Looks weird. Too steady. Try rebooting."

"I did. Twice."

"Call New Delhi and get somebody to check the sensors. Maybe reboot those too."

"I already did," Dr. Basu said. "The data is accurate, but it doesn't make any sense."

Faiz took a toffee from the bowl of candy she kept next to her computer. He started unwrapping the cellophane. "Ines said she might be able to come visit the last week in May. I'm going to need that week off, boss, okay?"

"Faiz," she said. "Concentrate."

"It's hard to concentrate knowing that Ines could be here next month. We aren't going to leave my apartment. She's Italian, which means she's extra sensual, you know?"

"Yes, Faiz, I know. And why do I know? Because you keep telling me exactly how 'sensual' she is. Has it ever occurred to you that I might want to spend my time focusing on data rather than on the way your new girlfriend likes to—"

"She's never been to India before," Faiz interrupted. "We aren't going to do anything touristy, though. A week in the bedroom, if you know what I mean."

"It's impossible not to know what you mean, Faiz. You are a man who has never encountered subtlety, and if I were not such a wonderful and understanding person, I would have you fired and possibly imprisoned. Now, please concentrate," she said.

He looked at the numbers again. "It's low and strong, but whatever it is, it isn't an earthquake. Too steady."

"I know it's not an earthquake," Dr. Basu said. She was trying not to lose her temper. She knew there was something she wasn't seeing, and while Faiz might be acting like a lovesick fool, he really was a remarkable scientist. "But let's concentrate on what it is, not what it isn't."

"Whatever it is, it's building," Faiz said.

"What?" Dr. Basu looked at the monitor, but she didn't see anything that stood out. The rumbles were all low. Nothing that really would have worried her if it had been something singular. It was the regularity, the pattern, that left her feeling as if something was wrong.

"Here," Faiz said, touching the screen and leaving a smear. "And here, and here. See how there's a rhythm to it, but every tenth one's a little bigger."

Dr. Basu scrolled to the beginning of the pattern and then counted. She frowned, jotted down some numbers, and then chewed on the end of the pen. It was a habit she'd developed in graduate school and one that, despite having more than a few pens break in her mouth, she'd yet to kick. "They stay bigger."

"No, it's only on the tenth rumble that they get big."

"No, Faiz, look." Dr. Basu handed him the pad of paper and then pointed at the computer screen. "See?"

Faiz shook his head. "Nope."

"This is why I'm in charge and you have to get the coffee," she said, taking some comfort in Faiz's slow chuckle. She clicked the mouse and isolated the points, then drew a line to plot the changes. "Here. Every tenth event it amplifies, and though it doesn't keep the entirety of the amplification, each set of nine that follows is slightly stronger than the previous set, until, again, the tenth."

Faiz leaned back in his chair. "You're right. I missed that. If it keeps up, though, keeps growing like that, we're going to start getting complaints from New Delhi. They won't be able to feel it yet, but sooner or later somebody is going to call us and ask what's going on." Faiz lifted his glasses and perched them on top of his head. He thought it made him look smart. Ditto stroking his beard, which he did as he mused, "Hmmm, every tenth one."

Dr. Basu took the pen from her mouth. "But what's it mean?" She tapped the end of the pen on the desk and then spun the pen away from her. "Drilling?"

"No. Wrong pattern."

"I know, but sometimes it's just good to get confirmation that I'm as smart as I think I am."

Faiz snatched her pen from the desk and started flipping it. One rotation. Two rotations. Three rotations. On the fourth he fumbled it and had to reach under his chair to pick it up. His voice came out a little muffled. "Maybe the military?"

"Maybe," Dr. Basu said, but it was clear to both of them she didn't really believe that either. "Any other ideas?" she asked Faiz, because she had none of her own.

American University, Washington, DC

"**S**piders," Professor Melanie Guyer said. She clapped her hands, hoping the sound would carry to the top of the auditorium where at least one student appeared to be sleeping. "Come on, guys. The answer in this class is always going to be spiders. And yes, they do molt," she said, pointing to the young woman who had asked the original question. "But no, they aren't really that similar to cicadas. For one thing, spiders don't hibernate. Well, not that cicadas exactly hibernate."

Melanie glanced out the window. She wasn't about to admit to the class that she found cicadas creepy. One time she had a bat get stuck in her hair while she was looking for a rare beetle in a cave in Tanzania, and another time, in Ghana, she accidentally stepped into a nest of western bush vipers. She'd gotten stung by a tarantula hawk wasp in Southeast Asia, which she thought was the most painful thing there was until she got bitten by a bullet ant in Costa Rica—that felt like having a nail gun fired into her elbow followed by a dunk in acid—but none of that really scared her like cicadas did. Oh, cicadas. The clicking sound from their tymbals, the ones with the red eyes, the way they swarmed and fell from trees and littered the sidewalks. And the crunching. Jesus. The crunching. The live ones underfoot, the discarded exoskeletons. Worse, the sheer number of them. Predator satiation was brilliant from an evolutionary perspective: all the cicadas had to do was breed in such numbers that anything that fed on them just got full. The survivors got on with their business. And then, after a few weeks, they died out, and there was just a graveyard of husks, which was also totally creepy. Thank all fucking everything that she was going to have another decade or so before Washington had its next big swarm of cicadas. She was going to have to plan a vacation. It wasn't really an option for a biologist who specialized in the use of spider venom for medicinal purposes to admit to being so afraid of cicadas that she couldn't go outside when they were swarming.

"But we aren't talking about cicadas," Melanie said, realizing that she'd drifted off. "We're talking about spiders. Even though spiders seem to scare the hell out of people, there's really almost no reason for that. At least not in North America. Australia's a different matter. Everything in Australia is dangerous, not just the crocodiles." She got a low chuckle from the class. In Melanie's book, a low chuckle near the end of a two-hour morning lecture with fewer than three weeks left in the semester was a victory.

She looked at her watch. "Okay, so for Wednesday, pages two twelve to two forty-five. Again, please note that this is a change from the syllabus. And to that we say," Melanie held her arms up and conducted the class as they said it along with her, "don't let the bedbugs bite." She watched the undergraduates shuffle out of the auditorium. Some of them looked a little dazed, and she couldn't tell if it was because of the early start time of the class or if she'd been droning again. She was a world-class researcher, perhaps one of the best at what she did, but even though she'd been working at it, lecturing was not her strong suit. She'd been trying to make her teaching more dynamic, throwing in jokes like the one about Australia, but there was only so much she could do for a three hundred-level course. Mostly she just hunkered down in her lab and dealt with graduate students, but part of the deal she'd struck with American University was that every second year she'd also teach a lecture class for undergraduates. She hated tearing herself away from her research, but if the price of a full lab, research assistants, and a team of funded graduate students working under her direction was that every two years she had to tell a class of nineteen- and twenty-year-olds that the spiders that stowed along in banana shipments were rarely dangerous, she'd live.

She looked down at the screen of her tablet, which mirrored the pictures on the screen at the front of the room. She had a soft spot for the *Heteropoda venatoria*, the huntsman spider. Partly it was because she'd had her first huge research breakthrough—the kind that made her what passed for famous in her field and got her this appointment and the subsequent grants and funding that kept the whole thing humming—working with *Heteropoda venatoria*, but if she was being honest, it was also because the first time she'd encountered a huntsman spider, her first year of college, her professor, in his thick accent, had described the spider as having a "moo-stache." Melanie liked the fact that there were spiders out there in the world with mustaches. In grad school, she'd dressed as a *Heteropoda venatoria* for Halloween and it had gone over well with her friends who were also working on their doctorates. Nobody else had gotten the joke, though. Most people thought she was trying to be a tarantula or something and couldn't figure out the mustache. She'd given up on spider costumes two years ago at a Halloween party, when she'd overheard somebody referring to her as "the black widow." The joke, if it was a joke, hit home, because the truth was, despite her husband's job—her *ex*-husband's job—she was the one who hadn't been available to Manny, who had spent so much time in the lab that their marriage foundered.

She shut off the projector, slipped her tablet into her purse, and headed out of the classroom. As she opened the door she decided to stop on the way back to the lab and pick up a salad. Something fresher than the sandwiches she usually got from the vending machines in the basement of her building. You could taste the preservatives with every bite. Actually, Melanie thought, it was probably just as well that the sandwiches were loaded with preservatives, because she wasn't sure anybody other than her ever ate them. They needed to last awhile in the machine. Even her most dogged graduate students either brought their meals from home or took the extra five minutes to walk across the quad to get something that didn't have to be purchased with a fistful of quarters. Speaking of dogged graduate students . . . She came to a halt as the door closed behind her.

Three of them were standing outside the classroom, waiting for her.

"Professor Guyer?"

Melanie raised her eyebrows, trying to indicate something close to annoyance with Bark. His real name was something complicated and Ukrainian, so everybody, including Melanie, called him Bark. Despite his obvious brilliance, he drove Melanie batshit crazy. It was some sort of strange skill he possessed that all the other graduate students did not. It was as though he spent his free time thinking of ways to annoy her. For instance, this: "Professor Guyer?" Just the fact that he called her Professor Guyer when everybody else in the lab called her Melanie made her want to smack him. She had asked him, told him, ordered him to call her Melanie, but not only did he continue to call her Professor Guyer, he said it in such a way that it was always a question, his voice rising at the end as if he was not entirely sure it was her name, like maybe it was something other than Melanie, even after three years of being in her lab.

Plus, since February, she'd been sleeping with him.

And that was what drove her the most crazy. He wasn't just annoying; he was also her lover. No, Melanie thought. Not her lover. She hated that term. Though fuck buddy wasn't something she liked either. Sex partner? Something. Whatever it was, sleeping with him had not been among her best decisions. The problem, as Melanie saw it, was that even though she wanted to smash a beaker and use the broken glass to slit his throat every time he opened his mouth, when he kept his lips shut—or better yet, glued to her body—he was all she could think about. She'd never thought of herself as shallow, but after the divorce, she'd wanted a little fun. And despite all the ways in which Bark made her barking mad, he wasn't a little fun in bed—he was a lot of fun in bed. Manny had made her feel all warm and secure when they had sex, but in the wake of her marriage's dissolution, Bark's hot and bothered was a nice change of pace.

So if it hadn't been the best decision to sleep with him in the first place, in her defense, it was a decision that had been helped by several glasses of something the graduate students had cooked up at the Valentine's Day party they talked her into going to. They'd called the drink "venom," and it had packed a punch. When she'd woken up the next morning with Bark in bed beside her, it took her a couple of minutes to figure out *who* she was, let alone *where* she was, what she was doing in Bark's bed with him, and why neither of them was wearing any clothes. She slipped into the bathroom without waking him. By the time she was swishing some of his mouthwash and smoothing her hair in the mirror, she realized she'd already made the sort of practical decision that had worked

so poorly in her marriage to Manny: she'd made her bed by sleeping with Bark, so she might as well lie in it. Again and again.

The Valentine's Day party was still a blur to her, but she could
remember the morning after with stunning clarity. Bark was brilliant, but he was nobody's idea of what a scientist should look like.
He dressed nicely, but even if he'd been rocking a pocket protec-
tor and a slide rule, he still would have turned heads. He'd come
to American University straight from Cal Tech, one coast to the
other, and maybe out in California he fit in, but in Melanie's lab,
in the whole entomology building, he stood out. He was a different species entirely. Melanie was close to six feet tall, and despite
being nearly two decades removed from her undergraduate playing days at Yale, she still played basketball at least three times a
week and swam four mornings a week. But Bark had another six
inches on her and his nickname fit him, because he was as solid
as a tree. She knew he didn't lift weights, and as far as she'd been
able to tell, he'd never even set foot in a gym or played a sport, but
even with his clothes on he looked as if he were sculpted. If he
hadn't wanted to get his PhD, he could have made a living as an
underwear model.

When she came back from the bathroom, ignoring her clothes,
which were crumpled on the floor, she slid into the bed and waited.
And waited. And waited. Bark slept like the dead, but when he finally began stirring, when they picked up from where they had
evidently left off the night before, it was worth it. Even after two
months of hooking up with him three or four times a week, she
still couldn't get over the way he looked without a shirt. Melanie
couldn't stop herself from touching his chest, his arms, the muscles
on the back of his shoulders. So different from her ex-husband.
Manny wasn't short, but he was shorter than her, and though he
could be incredibly intimidating, he wasn't exactly a slab of mus-

cle. No, Manny was hard on the inside, mean and petty when he thought somebody was fucking him over with work or politics— which, because he was the White House chief of staff, were the same thing for him—and as vicious as a Sydney funnel-web spider when he was being attacked. As aggressive as he was in his professional life, however, Manny was a little too deferential in bed. A beefcake he was not.

The beefcake in question, Bark, was staring at her. "Professor Guyer?" he tried again.

"Bark." She glanced at the other two students. Julie Yoo, who was far too rich to be spending her time studying spiders, and Patrick Mordy, who was in his first year in the graduate program and not anywhere near as smart as his transcript and application materials had indicated, and was, Melanie suspected, profoundly unlikely to finish his degree. "What?" she said. "What's so important that you guys couldn't wait for me to get back to the lab?"

Both Bark and Patrick stared at Julie, who looked down at her shoes. Melanie sighed and tried to keep her temper. She liked Julie, she really did, but for a girl who had everything going for her, Julie could have used a dose of confidence. Her parents had a lot of money. A ton of money. Private jet money. A building on the American University campus named after them money. What the hell was Julie doing in a lab studying spiders money. And Julie was pretty, and not just in the way girls in the sciences could be pretty because there wasn't a lot of competition. Julie would have been pretty in business school or law school, Melanie thought. Now that's pretty. She smiled to herself as she thought this. She could think like that because she knew she looked the same way. She looked her age, but she looked good for it, the kind of forty-year-old woman who made men stare at their wives and wonder why they hadn't made better decisions. She caught

Patrick looking at her and starting to smile back and she jerked her mouth into a scowl. They weren't as careful with their lab work if she wasn't hard on them.

"You can tell me while we walk," she said, brushing past them. "I'm going to stop and buy a salad on the way, and if what you guys have is interesting enough, I'll buy lunch for you as well. If not, I swear to God, if you're here because another moron thinks he's found a poisonous spider in a crate of bananas, I'm making you play hot potato with a brown recluse."

She hung her bag off her shoulder and braced herself for the heat she knew would be waiting for her outside the air-conditioned building. It was only five minutes from there to her lab, and she'd be making a stop at the café for her lunch, but it was going to leave her sweaty and red-faced. The Washington heat was not something she enjoyed, and it had come early this year.

"The brown recluse won't bite unless—"

Melanie spun around and Patrick's mouth snapped shut. She nodded. "That's what I thought. Now what do you have for me?"

It was Julie who positioned herself at Melanie's elbow, Patrick and Bark at her heels as they went down the steps and started crossing the quad. There were soft clouds sleeping above the campus buildings, but no real hope that rain would break the heat. Maybe she'd quit early tonight, crank up the air-conditioning in her apartment, get some takeout, and watch a bad romantic comedy or two by herself. Or maybe she'd have Bark over for a night of activities that required no talking from him. Deep down, though, she knew she wouldn't leave the lab before she normally did. If she were the kind of woman who quit early, she'd probably still have a husband to go home to. That wasn't entirely fair, she knew, since it wasn't as if Manny had ever come home from the White House earlier than she came home from the lab. The difference was that when Manny was home with her, he was actually home with her, while when she was home with him, there was still a large part of her that was at the lab.

"You were right," Julie said at last.

"Of course I was right," Melanie said. "About what?"

She walked briskly, not bothering to look behind her to see if the boys were having trouble keeping up. She didn't worry about Julie. The young woman might have no confidence, but she was maybe the hardest-working scientist Melanie had ever met, and even a pair of two-inch heels—modest for a night on the town, but deeply impractical for the lab—wasn't going to keep Julie from staying with her faculty advisor.

"Nazca," Julie said.

"Nazca?"

"Nazca," Julie repeated, as if it were supposed to mean something to Melanie.

Melanie didn't stop walking, but she did glance over at her. Another hundred meters and they'd be inside and cool again, at least for the two minutes it took her to buy herself lunch and have it bagged up so she could finish walking to the lab. "Nazca? What the fuck are you talking about, Julie? Nazca? That's what you've got for me? The three of you waiting outside my classroom like a bunch of freshman, waiting to pounce, and that's what you're giving me? That's what can't wait for me to get back to the lab? Nazca?" She picked up the pace.

"Nazca," Julie said again. "As in Peru?"

Melanie stopped. "Is that a question or a statement?" She turned to glare at Bark, who didn't seem to understand why he was being glared at but was smart enough to edge behind Patrick. She wanted to smack him. His habit of ending every sentence with a question had rubbed off on Julie. "Nazca. Peru," Melanie said. She looked at her three graduate students and they stared back at her, slight smiles on their faces, as though they were waiting for praise. Melanie sighed. "Okay," she said. "I give up. You're talking about the Nazca Lines. So what? Can you please tell me what the fuck you're talking about so I can get myself a salad and head back to the lab?"

"Don't you remember the Valentine's Day party?" Bark asked. She couldn't tell if his face was already red from the heat or if it flushed with the realization of what he was saying, but he almost tripped over himself to keep going. "You kept talking about Nazca? The lines? The spider?"

Patrick came to Bark's rescue. "You said they were there for a reason. The markings on the ground. There are all kinds of markings. Lines and animals and stuff. I'd never heard of it before, but you weren't really interested in the animals. You were talking about the spider marking. You said you can see the lines from airplanes, and they aren't that deeply dug, but it would have taken a ton of work, and you were saying you thought the spider had to have been for a reason."

Melanie didn't remember talking to them about the Nazca Lines—though she had no real reason to doubt her students—but the truth was she'd been fascinated by them since the first time she heard of them. And going off on some theory or other sounded like something she would have done when she was drunk. Also, evidently, sleeping with a graduate student was also something she would have done when she was drunk. Which is why she didn't drink very often.

She'd been to Peru only once, with Manny, in the death throes of their marriage, a last-chance vacation in the hope of gluing together the pieces of their broken relationship. Manny had suggested Hawaii, Costa Rica, Belize, pale beaches and private huts, but she had wanted to see the Nazca Lines for years, even if he didn't. Really, if she was being honest, part of the reason she had insisted was simply because Manny hadn't wanted to go to Peru.

From the air, they were stunning. White lines in the reddish-brown earth. Glyphs and animals and birds. Shapes she couldn't understand. And there, the one she'd most wanted to see: the spider.

There were some scholars—crackpots, Melanie thought—who claimed that the lines were runways for ancient astronauts, or that the Nazca had made the designs with the aid of hot-air balloons, but the general consensus was that the Nazca had used earthly means. Archaeologists found stakes at the end of some of the lines, showing the basic techniques that had been used to make the designs. The Nazca had mapped them out first and then removed the darker colored rocks to the depth of less than half a foot, where the whitish ground stood underneath in stark contrast.

Even though she'd seen it before in pictures and drawings, the sight of the spider took her breath away. From the height of the single-engine airplane, the spider seemed small, though she knew it was close to one hundred fifty feet long, maybe longer, on the ground. She heard the pilot yell something and saw him circling his finger in the air, asking if she wanted him to stay over the spider for a few circuits, something they'd talked about in her terrible Spanish before taking off. She nodded and felt Manny's hand on her shoulder. She put her fingers over his and realized she was crying. She hadn't wanted to visit the spider out of a desire to see in real life what she'd read about. No, it was more than that, and the scientist in her cringed at the thought. She hadn't told Manny because he would have sighed and they would have had another one of those endless conversations about the limits of science and biology and the question of adoption.

It was really only at that moment that she realized exactly why she had insisted on going to Peru. Insisted over Manny's objections. Insisted that if they were going to go anywhere, it was going to be to see the Nazca Lines. She knew it was crazy. The rational, scientific part of her, the woman who had ground her way through her PhD research, who slept in her lab two or three nights a week and chased off graduate students who weren't willing to work as hard as she was, knew her desire to haul Manny with her to Peru was the last desperate grasping of a woman in her late thirties who thought she could put off having children until she was ready and then discovered that maybe it had never even been an option. The trip was the longest of long shots, but once she'd read the theory put forth by one Nazca academic that the lines were ritual images, the birds and plants and spider symbols for fertility, she hadn't been able to shake the feeling that maybe there was a reason she'd always been drawn to the image, that there in the Peruvian foothills, the spider had been waiting just for her.

Up in the plane, she'd wanted Manny with an urgency that had long been missing from their relationship. As much as she wanted to stay in the air, flying circuits over the image of the spider, she also couldn't wait to be on the ground again, in the privacy of their tent, doing what she hoped would finally lead to the baby she thought might save their marriage.

She'd been wrong about both the baby and saving the marriage.

After she and Manny divorced, she still remembered the trip fondly. While they circled in the air she'd hastily drawn her own rendition of the Nazca spider:

After the divorce was finalized, she'd torn the page from her notebook, trimmed it neatly, and framed it. It was on the wall near her desk at the lab. It didn't take her breath away as the actual lines carved into the earth had. There was something about the scale, the permanence, the way the lack of rain and wind had left the lines undisturbed for more than two thousand years that both rattled her and filled her with happiness. She liked thinking there might have been a woman like her, hoping desperately for a baby, pulling rocks from the ground nearly twenty-five hundred years ago.

Or longer.

"Ten thousand years," Julie said. "Not twenty-five hundred."

Melanie pulled at the collar of her shirt, but she wasn't really thinking about the heat anymore. She recognized the first stirrings of intellectual engagement, the way that she could become consumed with curiosity. The fact that it was the Nazca Lines made it easier for her to get engaged, but the truth was that it had never been difficult to pique her interest. She'd gotten better about remembering to do things like eat meals, shower, and change her clothes—having a private bathroom in her office helped—but at heart, she was still the same research geek who was happiest in her lab trying to find the answer to a question. "Who?" she said. "Who's telling you that the lines were made ten thousand years ago?"

"Not all of them," Julie said. "Uh, and it's a friend of mine, a guy I went to undergrad with." Normally there'd be a little part of Melanie that would be interested in the gossip, would pry until Julie admitted he was somebody she'd slept with when she was nineteen or twenty, a guy she still carried a torch for, but she was starting to get impatient with these three graduate students. "He's a grad student too, and he's working on the site. Archaeology."

"Of course."

"Right," Julie said, "so we e-mail back and forth kind of regularly, and I mentioned your theory to him."

Melanie started walking again. This was getting tiresome. "What theory?"

"About the spider," Bark said. He started to say something else, but Julie cut him off.

"One of the things they're trying to figure out with the dig is if the lines were made in a compressed period of time all together—over years or a few decades—or spread out over a few hundred years. How long did they take to make? They've been able to find wooden stakes near most of the lines that they think might have been used almost like surveyor's stakes by the Nazca when they were doing the designs. But he was working on the spider site and, sure enough, he found stakes. They had one dated."

"And?"

"The spider isn't a Nazca Line."

Melanie realized she was walking more quickly than was comfortable, but the café was in sight, and the thought of the temporary respite from the heat helped her to keep up the pace. "It sure looks like a Nazca Line," she said.

"No," Julie said. "The Nazca Lines look like the spider. All the other lines are about twenty-five hundred years old, as you said, but the spider's older. A lot older. It's ten thousand years old, give or take a little. It was there well before the other lines."

Melanie slowed down as she reached the café steps. "So what does that have to do with us?" She glanced over her shoulder and realized that all three students had stopped walking. Patrick, Bark, and Julie were standing on the ground, three steps below her, looking up expectantly. "Well?"

Julie glanced at the two young men and they nodded at her. "It wasn't just the stakes," Julie said. "When he was doing the dig, he found something underneath the stakes, buried in a wooden box. He had some of that wood dated, and it's the same age as the stakes. Ten thousand years. You'll never guess what was in the box."

Julie paused, and Melanie found herself getting frustrated. Pausing for dramatic effect, she thought, was overrated, and in the case of a gaggle of graduate students, annoying. But despite herself, she was fully curious and couldn't stop from blurting out, "What?"

"An egg sac. At first, none of them realized what it was, but when he did, he suggested to his faculty advisor that they send it to our lab to see if we could identify it. They thought it was fossilized or petrified, or whatever it is you call it when something like that is preserved. Since the wooden box is ten thousand years old, and the egg sac was inside the box, the sac is probably at least that old too."

"Huh," Melanie said. "Okay. Tell them to send it to us so we can take a look at it."

"He already sent it. It's back in the lab. I, uh, I told him they could use our FedEx shipping code, so he overnighted it," Julie said. The words came out of her mouth as though she expected Melanie to yell at her.

Melanie stifled her annoyance. Budgets had been tight, but not so tight that Julie couldn't charge the shipping costs of a package if it was actually lab business. Though, Melanie wondered, how much did it actually cost to overnight something from Peru?

"There's more," Bark said. He was standing straight and staring at her with an intensity he usually reserved for when they were alone.

"More?" Melanie glanced at Patrick and Julie and then back at Bark. All three looked nervous and excited, clearly unsure if what they had come to get her for was as big a deal as they thought it was. "Well," she said, hearing that her voice was sharper than she meant it to be. "Out with it."

Bark looked at his colleagues, then back at Melanie. "The egg sac," he said. "It's hatching."

The White House

"Nuke 'em," the president said. "Just launch the nukes and be done with it." She leaned back in her chair and looked at the young man hovering by her side. One of the new interns. Manny smiled. He couldn't remember the intern's name, but President Stephanie Pilgrim liked them young and handsome. Arm candy, of sorts. She was never inappropriate with them—thankfully, that wasn't one of Manny's many worries as White House chief of staff—but she definitely liked having them around. The president reached out and put her hand on the intern's forearm. "How about you go get us a big bowl of popcorn or something, maybe some chips and salsa. All this talk of war is making me feel a bit peckish."

"Come on, Steph," Manny said. "You're not taking this seriously."

"I'm the president of the United States of America, Manny, and you will address me appropriately," she said, smiling. "President Steph to you. And how am I supposed to take this seriously? It's an exercise. The other team is out there in the heat of the primaries. Pretty soon they're going to figure out which one of those clowns is getting the nomination, and they'll start aiming at me instead of each other. In the meantime, we're holed up in the Situation Room pretending that we're actually going to go to war with China. Can't I just order the nukes and call it a day? I've got more important shit to do than play war games to satisfy the army's hard-on."

"Technically, this one's primarily a naval situation," Manny said.

"How long have you known me, Manny?"

Manny didn't say anything. He'd known Stephanie Pilgrim long enough to know she didn't want an answer. Known her back when they were young and dumb and undergraduates. He was a freshman and she was a senior, and she went by Steph, not Madam President, and she liked to torture him in certain inappropriate moments by telling him she wasn't wearing panties under her skirt. Not that she was particularly promiscuous. Even then she was careful about watching her reputation. She was already planning to be in the spotlight. But they had clicked immediately, and she had not only been attracted to him, she had trusted him. They hadn't exactly dated, but before Manny met and married Melanie, he and Steph had had a sort of understanding that went beyond their professional working relationship. They'd come to that understanding again since things had imploded with him and Melanie. Well, not imploded. *Dissolved* was a better word. But finding himself free and uninterested in dating, and with Steph having to be careful about maintaining the illusion that she was in a happy marriage, it had been easy to fall back into their old pattern of occasionally sleeping together. For him, there'd been a bit of guilt. The guilt wasn't about Steph. They were attracted to each other, reasonably decent in bed, and loved each other, even if they weren't *in* love with each other. They respected each other and liked each other and didn't have any secrets from each other.

Neither of them was going to end up hurt. No, Manny felt bad about George. He genuinely liked Steph's husband. Dr. George Hitchens was a nice guy. He was certainly an asset when it came to electability. Handsome and well-spoken, content to let Steph do her thing in the political arena, content to be a politician's husband. He was blue blood, old money from Texas, smart enough to go to an Ivy League university and to graduate from medical school without having to pull any strings, or at the very least, without having to pull them hard enough that they unraveled in embarrassing ways. He'd practiced as a dermatologist right up until Steph won the big one. Since they'd gotten to the White House he'd jumped feetfirst into being "the First Hubby," as the press liked to call him. He could cut a ribbon with the best of them. He was as close to a dream husband as a female politician could have.

That was the problem, though. Stephanie loved George, but only in the way that you love somebody who is decent and good and whom you've known for fifteen years. She loved him, but wasn't *in* love with him. Never had been. The politician had married him, not the woman. Probably if she'd gone for a different kind of career, done something other than pursue law school as the shortest route to politics and then the presidency, she would have already divorced George. But that wasn't an option now.

Manny was not a modest man when it came to his talents: he was a straight-out fucking genius in the political sphere. And although Stephanie Pilgrim was a machine—effortlessly attractive and likable, smart and witty, good background, better luck, fierce and determined—even Manny knew there were limits. Nobody had given her a serious chance when she declared, but Manny had hit it out of the park, and here he was the White House chief of staff. If they wanted to stay in power, however, Stephanie was going to have to do what she'd gotten good at, and that was walking the razor's edge between being female and being president of the United States. The country might have been ready for a woman president, might have been ready for that woman president to be forty-two and the youngest commander in chief ever elected, beating Teddy Roosevelt by a measly four days, might even be ready to reelect that same woman after three solid years of economic growth and peace, but they sure as hell weren't ready to reelect a woman in the middle of a divorce.

Stephanie rolled her chair back from the table and rubbed her eyes. "You know as well as I do that these things are just a bullshit waste of time. Let the military run their exercises and war games, let them have their simulations, and the next time something happens we'll do what we always do, which is assess the situation— one that is certain to be different from this imagined clusterfuck with China—and deal with it. The only reason we're doing this, as far as I can tell, is for the military to figure out if I have the balls to order an attack. So let's give it to them. Let me just order a nuke. Bomb the whole fucking country. We'll call it a day and get some real work done. Besides," she said, "this is scheduled for what, three hours? We end now and we'll have an extra two hours in the day."

She didn't say it, couldn't say it in the room full of suits and uniformed people, but Manny knew she was hinting that they could take half an hour of that extra time to themselves. He remembered the way it was in college. She was three years older than he was, and he'd still been a virgin when they met. At eighteen, he'd always been more than content to spend an entire afternoon lounging in bed with her. Now, in his early forties, he'd still be content to spend the afternoon lounging in bed with her, but that wasn't going to happen. The most important commodity the president of the United States had now was time.

"Madam President, if I may." It was Ben Broussard, the chairman of the Joint Chiefs of Staff. Ben was the one man in the room guaranteed to rub Stephanie the wrong way. Manny tried to stop himself from cringing at the sound of Ben's voice, but it was hard. Things had been going downhill with Ben since the second he was appointed, and sooner or later—sooner was better—Ben was going to find himself neatly retired. "I know it can seem like we are wasting time with these regular exercises, but it's important to run through plausible situations so that we can react quickly when there is an event that does call for military response."

Stephanie glanced up at Manny, and he knew she'd already said as much as she was going to say about the matter. It was his time to speak. That was one of the reasons they worked so well together. As much as it was bullshit, they both knew the truth, which was that a woman, even if she was the president of the United States of America, was judged differently. Perception was reality, and she couldn't be perceived as a complainer. Of course, Manny didn't have the same worries.

"Come on, Ben," Manny said. "This simulation does seem a little outdated. Might it not make a little more sense to be running this in response to a mock terrorist attack, or a conflagration in a place that is more of a hot zone? Obviously there have been some serious tensions with China, but we all know we aren't even close to exchanging shots with them. Not like we are with a country like—"

"Somalia." The secretary of defense, Billy Cannon, never had a problem with interrupting Manny. Usually because he was right. "We should be running exercises with Somalia, because we're going to have to do the real thing there soon enough. The chances of us actually engaging in open warfare with China seem remote at best. It's about as useful as running a simulation of a zombie attack."

The intern returned with a tray and put it down on the sideboard behind the president. He'd brought both a bowl of popcorn and bowls of tortilla chips and salsa, and he took them off the tray to place them on the table in front of the president. Manny watched how discreet the young man was, the way he waited until all the attention was focused on Billy before sliding the snacks in front of the president, the fact that he remembered that Steph liked her soda in a can, despite the White House staff's determination to serve it to her in cut crystal. There was a particular skill in that, Manny thought, in knowing how to keep the people around you happy while still blending into the background. The intern's name was Tim or Thomas or something like that, and Manny made a note to himself to see about keeping the kid on after his internship was over.

Manny put a hand on Steph's shoulder, a familiarity he was afforded by both his position and the length of their relationship, and leaned over her to snag a handful of popcorn.

Billy Cannon and Ben Broussard were at it now, the chairman of the Joint Chiefs of Staff still arguing that this China simulation was useful, and Billy not backing down. Manny knew he should cap things, either move them past the exercise and get them out of the room, or go ahead and force Steph to go through the motions, but he enjoyed watching Billy Cannon argue. Billy Cannon came from money, but he looked as though he belonged in uniform. Unlike some of the generals who let themselves go once they'd gotten to the point where they could give orders instead of taking them, Billy was still trim, coiled, handsome, and dangerous-looking, with salt-and-pepper hair and a scar on his temple from hand-to-hand fighting when he was in combat. Billy's wife had died four or five years ago, of breast cancer, and he'd only recently started dating. Manny could understand why the women in DC were dying to be on his arm. There was even talk that *People* magazine was considering him for the sexiest man thing. Sooner or later, Billy would decide to retire and then he'd run for some sort of office and he'd be a shoo-in.

"Enjoying the show?" The national security advisor, Alexandra Harris, rose partially off her seat and snagged a few tortilla chips. She didn't bother with the salsa. Manny liked Alex, and even though they were often at odds on what to do with the information she brought to the president, he thought she'd been one of the best appointments Steph made. Alex was smart, fierce, and loyal, and whatever her opinion was going into a fight, as soon as the president made a decision, she was completely on board. You didn't get to these heights without an acute sense of political survival and the kind of driving ambition you could see from outer space, but as far as Manny could tell, Alex was exactly where she wanted to be. She never tried to subvert the president. Besides, Alex was seventy-three. Too late for a presidential run of her own. Assuming Steph was reelected, Alex would serve out the first year of Steph's second term and then retire to the countryside.

Steph finally spoke up, and there was a bit of an edge to her voice. Manny and Alex might both be amused by watching the secretary of defense and the chairman of the Joint Chiefs arguing over whether or not the simulation was even worth doing, but clearly the president was full up.

"Gentlemen," she said to Ben and Billy, "I assure you I understand the importance of these exercises. You're going to have to trust me when I tell you that in a time of crisis I will treat things more seriously. The next time we run one of these simulations I

will have a better attitude, especially if the exercise is more perti-
nent, but today is not a time of crisis." She rose from her chair, and
everyone in the room who was sitting snapped to their feet.

He'd made the transition from lover to friend and then back to
lover without difficulty, and he'd handled moving from the campaign trail to the White House with equanimity, but getting used
to the ceremony that attended having one of his oldest friends go
from "Steph, down the hall in my dorm," to Stephanie Pilgrim,
the first female president, had been hard. He'd never been one to
stand on formality, but more often than not, since the election, he
found himself having to actually stand as part of the formality.

"Madam President?" It was one of the uniformed officers at the
bank of computers and monitors on the side of the room. There
was a large set of monitors and screens on one wall so that the
president and the other advisors could track details, but this officer
was looking at something else. His voice was loud enough to cut
through the room and bring the president to a stop. Normally an
officer of his rank wouldn't address the president directly unless
asked a specific question.

"Madam President," the man said again, and this time he pulled
the headphones off his ears. "The Chinese."

Steph let out a sigh and Manny stepped forward. "I think we're
done for the day," he said. "Call off the simulation."

"No," the officer said, and there was something urgent and
harsh in his voice that stilled the small movement that had started
up in the room, something that kept the president's attention, that
left Manny waiting for more. "This isn't part of the exercise," he
said. "They, uh, it's going to be on the screen in a few seconds.
Ma'am?"

"Well, spit it out." Stephanie had stopped, but she looked bored.
Most of the other men and women in the room had already started

packing up again, and Manny realized nobody else seemed to see
the look of fear on the officer's face. He also realized that Alex was
still sitting, a look of alarm on her face as a uniform whispered
urgently in her ear.

Manny glanced up at the big bank of television screens and
computer monitors that lined the wall. Most of the information
was related to the simulation, but on the end, there were two large
screens showing close to real-time satellite images of China, the
information coming in with only a thirty- or forty-second delay.
The country was split almost in half on the screens, with one
showing the more densely populated portions of eastern China,
Beijing a web of roads, the other screen displaying the western half
of the country, a line indicating the upper borders, Kazakhstan and
Mongolia.

And suddenly there was a glow of light. A burning dot on the
upper-left-hand side of the western screen.

"Holy Jesus," somebody said, and then a moment later Manny
realized he was the one who said it.

"What the fuck was that?" The president was looking at the
screen as well.

Everybody in the room was now staring at the map of China,
looking at the bloom and fade of light near the northwest corner of
the country. That is, everybody but the national security advisor.
She was staring at the uniform who had been whispering in her
ear. "Was that it?" Alex asked. She turned to look at the officer by
the console. "Was it a missile? Whose was it? Are there any others
in the air? Was it just the one?"

The officer, who had one of the earpieces on his headphones
pressed back against his head, held his hand up to Alex, looked
at the screen, and then nodded. "That's it," he said. "It wasn't a
missile."

Manny realized he'd been drifting between watching Alex and the officer and looking at the burst of light fading back to darkness. "If it wasn't a missile, what the fuck was it?"

The room had gone weirdly quiet, a sudden vacuum of sound in the wake of Manny's question, and he knew he wasn't the only person who jumped when the phone behind them rang. It was not just *a* phone that rang. It was *the* phone. He remembered as a kid when they showed the president picking up the hotline to the Russians in movies, how it was usually a red phone, sinister and there as the last resort before nuclear winter, but it wasn't until he'd actually spent some time in the White House that he realized the phone was real. And the phone was ringing. There was no question that the person on the other end was going to be the Chinese general secretary, and it took only two rings before Steph stepped over to it, her hand on the receiver.

"Can somebody," she said, barking out the words to the room as she prepared to pick up the phone, "tell me just what the fuck that was on the screen?"

"That," said Manny, looking at the screen again, where the flare of light had already started to dissipate, "was a nuke."

Xinjiang Province, China

For a moment he thought he was going to throw up, but he didn't slow down. The truck had barely made it through the barricades, and even then he'd had to drive over two soldiers. The thought of the thump and the screams was enough to make him gag again, but no matter what happened, he wasn't going to stop driving. He'd wanted to get to his sister and her family.

He'd been too late for that.

No, he wasn't going to stop for soldiers and he wasn't going to stop to vomit. He wasn't going to stop until he ran out of gas, until he'd put as many kilometers between the area and himself as possible. The officials claimed the situation was under control, but the area in which they claimed it was contained seemed to grow every day. That, plus the original broadcasts, which featured local newscasters and party officials he recognized, had been replaced by people he didn't know, people from outside the province. There had been rumors at the factory, rumors at the market. He knew of at least two men who had been working in the mines who had not yet been allowed home. Worse than any of that, and what had finally prompted him to steal a set of keys for the truck and stow a water bottle and a little food in the pockets of his jacket—the most he could manage without calling attention to himself—was that three days ago all communications with the outside world had been cut off. No landlines, no cell phones, no Internet. Nothing in or out. Just the official television and radio broadcasts.

It had been only five days since the first incident at the mine. He had assumed it was just another accident, but it didn't take long for the whispers to start spreading. A virus. The army experimenting with chemical or biological weapons. The old woman who brought him his soup at the restaurant around the corner from his apartment insisted that it was ghosts, that the miners had disturbed some sort of supernatural force. The sister of one of his friends, a girl who spent most of her free time reading pirated copies of American novels for teenagers, claimed it was either vampires or zombies, and that was why the army arrived so quickly.

At first, he didn't think too much of any of it. People died in the mines. That's the way it was. At least he didn't have to work there. While he didn't love his job in the factory, at nineteen he made more money in a month than his parents were willing to believe. They kept insisting he was exaggerating when he told them his salary. He had a small apartment to himself. He had his own television, a cell phone, a computer, and he even had the occasional night alone with that sister of his friend. His own sister and her two children were only a short walk away from his apartment, and she had him over for dinner a few nights each week. So if he did not see his parents as often as he would have liked, the five-hour bus trip something of a hardship, it was hard to complain.

Five nights ago, when most people thought it was just an accident, he'd had dinner with his sister, and while he bounced his nephew on his knee, his sister's blowhard husband went on and on about safety lapses at the mine, about how this sort of thing was bound to happen with all the steps they skipped. Four nights ago, he'd been aware that there was talk, but it was one of those nights when his girlfriend—or whatever she was to him—had come over, and the two of them didn't do much talking.

But it was three nights ago that he really took notice. He'd cooked himself dinner and then tried to go online. His computer was having none of it. He wasn't concerned, because even though the village had a relatively fast Internet connection, it was sporadic. Then he pulled out his cell phone to call his parents and realized he didn't have a signal. And on the television, every channel was blank except for the official local channel, which was on a one-hour loop. He sighed, read for a while, and then went to sleep.

It wasn't until the next morning, on his way to the factory, that he noticed just how many soldiers had come to the area. Then he saw the coils of wire going up and realized that the boys in uniform, boys his own age, were clutching their rifles a little too tightly. He normally kept to himself at work, but during his lunch break he sat with a group of older men. He was shocked when he heard that the mine had been sealed off, that none of the men who'd been working when the incident occurred had been allowed to go home. Then, later, near the end of his shift, the foreman came on over the loudspeakers and announced that they were expected to continue on, that nothing was wrong, and they should keep coming in for their shifts.

His cell phone still wasn't working, and nobody else could get a signal either, but he was smart enough to know that when soldiers started flooding in and razor wire started going up, when the people in charge tried to reassure him that nothing was out of the ordinary even though, clearly, things were out of the ordinary, it was time to worry.

That was when he stole a key to one of the trucks. That was when he filled a bottle of water and tucked an apple and some

crackers into the pockets of his jacket. He thought about packing a bag, but on the way to work, only yesterday, he saw a man
beaten to death by the soldiers. The man was in a car with his
family, the trunk tied down to keep the bags from spilling out, and
he'd stopped at the new gate that had been installed after the army
fenced off the village. The gate was the only way out now. He'd
heard the man and the soldiers exchange sharp words, and then,
as he tried to glance over without being terribly obvious about it,
he saw the man pulled from the car and beaten down with rifle
butts. Even from a distance, it was clear the soldiers kept driving
the metal into the man well past the point it was necessary.

All of which was why he'd driven the truck right through the
gate without slowing down. He just plowed through the metal. All
during that night there had been the intermittent sound of gunfire.
At one point there was something from the direction of the mine
that must have been an explosion. He couldn't sleep, and then,
finally, just after four in the morning, he crept from his apartment
and snuck through the night. The streets and alleys were empty
and dark, and the factory was quiet. There was no fence around the
parking lot where the trucks were sitting, and the key was in his
hand before he even noticed something was wrong.

There was a single light on at the corner of the building, and
though the yellow bulb was strong, it wasn't enough to do more
than cast shadows over the parking lot. He suddenly wished it
were brighter but tried to bury the thought. He knew he was just
spooked from the stories and rumors and from the influx of soldiers and the new fence, from the sound of shots and explosions
in the night. He should really calm down, he thought, and then he
laughed to himself. Why should he calm down? Those all seemed
good reasons to be spooked. He took the last few steps to the truck
and had his hand on the door handle when he heard the sound. It

was a sort of scraping. No. Something quieter than scraping. Like the sound of a leaf being blown across pavement. Or several leaves. He looked around, but there was nobody there. And then he noticed there was something wrong with the light. No, not the light, but the shadows. Over there, maybe twenty paces away, one of the shadows seemed to be moving a little, pulsing. He watched it, fascinated, and it wasn't until a thread of black seemed to fall out of the shadow and unspool toward him that he broke from his reverie.

He didn't know what it was and he didn't care. Even though he'd dithered on it, he realized he'd already made his decision the moment he stole the key to the truck, and he didn't see any value in waiting to find out what exactly it was he'd decided to run away from. He pulled himself into the cab, and as he was jumping in, he felt something brush across the back of his neck and then his neck felt all icy. He swatted at it, and something small and solid banged off his hand. Then he was inside the truck, key in the ignition, foot on the gas, leaving whatever the shadow was behind him.

He drove carefully through the village, toward his sister's apartment. He hadn't told her about the plan. He knew she would have told her husband, and her husband wasn't the sort of man who could be trusted with a secret. But he also knew that if he just showed up at the apartment with the truck, his sister would be able to persuade her husband to make a break for it. He didn't like his brother-in-law very much, but the man was not completely stupid.

But as he turned onto his sister's street, it was clear that things were more wrong than even he had thought. He'd been so preoccupied that he hadn't noticed the glow from the portable lights, but once around the corner, the brilliance of the lights showed the street in stark relief. There were five or six army trucks already parked and dozens of soldiers running with rifles. He saw somebody down on the ground, but the artificial color of the lights meant that it took him a few seconds before he realized the black pool around the body was blood. And up ahead, was that a tank? Oh my god, he thought. It *was* a tank.

Without even thinking about it, he turned the wheel and took the truck through the alley, turned the wheel again until he was headed out of town, mashed his foot against the accelerator and smashed his way through the gate. He was lucky that the soldiers had expected him to stop. They fired at him—the back window was shattered—but the truck seemed to be running fine and he hadn't been hit. He was fine.

That had been an hour or two ago. He'd lost track of time. But if anything, now that he'd put some distance between himself and the village, he was more than fine. He was great. The back of his neck was bothering him where something had hit him in the parking lot, but he couldn't see what it was in the mirror. He could feel a small bump with his fingers, maybe a cut, but it was more numb than sore. The real problem was his stomach. He could feel it roiling. He supposed it could be the flu, but more than likely it was just anxiety. Who the hell knew what he'd just escaped from, but he was pretty sure he was never going to see his sister again, never hold his nephew or his niece. He had to choke down a sob, and then he had to choke down another round of gagging.

He wasn't fine.

But he was alive.

He dug the bottle of water out of his jacket pocket, fumbled with the cap, and took a swig. It felt good and seemed to settle his stomach for a minute, but then it happened again, another surge of nausea.

Maybe he would pull over, just for a couple of minutes. Give himself a chance to be sick by the side of the road. Then he'd feel better.

Suddenly, there was a brilliant light behind him. Like a camera flash. He glanced in the rearview mirror, but the light hurt his eyes. He looked forward again and realized he couldn't see much more than the echo of the light. He slowed the truck down and then stopped it so he could rub his eyes. The light outside was already fading, and whatever it had been hadn't damaged his vision. There were ghosts of the landscape imprinted on his eyes, but they were already swimming away. And there, again, the surge of nausea. This time he didn't think he could keep it down, and he scrambled out of the truck.

As his feet hit the ground he turned to look back toward the village, toward where the flash of light had come from. But it wasn't a flash of light anymore. It was a lick of fire lighting the heavens.

Marine Corps Air Ground Combat Center, Twentynine Palms, California

Lance Corporal Kim Bock checked her rifle. Again. She knew there wasn't any point, but this was the first time she was leading her unit in a live-fire exercise, and checking her M16 calmed her down. She'd trained with the M16A2 in basic, but she'd been issued the M16A4 once she made it out to California. There wasn't much of a difference between the two rifles as far as she was concerned, at least not when she was out on the range. She did like that she could remove the carrying handle when they were in the middle of exercises.

She was crouching and trying to relax. The sun was a mother-fucker, but it was okay in the shade. She'd played catcher on her high school softball team, and she could stay in a crouch for a long time without getting uncomfortable, but the three men in her unit were sitting down on the concrete slab. Private First Class Elroy Trotter had his eyes closed, and for all Kim knew, Elroy might actually be sleeping. He never seemed to get excited one way or the other. The joke was that even while having sex Elroy probably looked bored. The person who first made that joke, Private Duran

Edwards, was a black kid from Brooklyn who was a lot smarter than any of the other officers seemed to recognize, and Kim was glad Duran was in her unit. At first she'd had a bit of a thing for the third man, Private Hamitt "Mitts" Frank, but having him in her unit was like pouring water on a fire. Only smoke remained. She could see how the two of them might have ended up a couple in civilian life, but as part of a unit, it was different. They were a team. She was lucky. The whole crew was cool; none of them seemed to think it was a big deal that a woman was the fire team leader. She knew that early on, when the armed forces first started slotting women into combat units, there'd been some blowback. There'd been a couple of high-profile incidents in the army, but even in the Marines it hadn't been all sweetness. Kim had still been in middle school when women were given equal status, though it was recent enough that some of the older generation still clearly hadn't adjusted to Marines with tits in the line of fire. Elroy, Duran, and Mitts were her age, though, and they'd gone through boot camp with her. Maybe they secretly didn't love the idea of taking combat orders from a woman in general, but since it was her, they were okay with it. They were familiar with Kim, and that made all the difference. Familiar with the fact that she was physically fit, able to compete with most of the men, familiar with the fact that she was smart and good at making quick decisions. They'd probably have accepted a different woman as their lance corporal, but it really did matter that they knew her. They trusted her to keep them safe.

Kim heard her name being called over the loudspeakers. "Okay," she said to the unit. "We're up in one. Remember, rifles on burst. Live fire, so extra careful here. Take your time and make good decisions. Quick action isn't good unless it's the right action." The three men scrambled to their feet while Kim rose from her crouch and they all put their hands in, making a small pile of different shades of skin. "Be smart," Kim said, "be strong, be Marines."

She loved the sound of the four of them shouting "Oorah!" and the way their hands shot down and up. Loved the feel of the M16 in her hands, the click as she flipped the rifle from safety to burst fire. She loved the way she looked in her utility uniform, surrounded by other Marines, and as she felt the first hit of adrenaline spiking through her chest, loved the way it felt to be a Marine. Her parents had never understood her fascination with it, still didn't understand why she was in uniform while all her friends from high school were off at college, drinking beer in dormitories and getting date-raped at frat parties. Well, Kim was pretty sure that's not the way her parents thought her college experience would have gone, but for Kim, college was something she would do only as part of the Marines. She'd wanted to be a Marine since they first started letting women into combat units, and from the minute she first put on a uniform and laced up a pair of boots she understood the saying, "Once a Marine, Always a Marine."

They got the green light and funneled down the chute. Duran and Elroy split left, taking cover behind a concrete barrier, while she and Mitts went right, taking cover behind the corner of a building. This was supposed to be an urban environment, and she had to hand it to whoever had built the set. It felt like being in a city. The Marine Corps Air Ground Combat Center might be in the middle of nowhere—the going nickname for Twentynine Palms, the city adjacent to the MCAGCC, was Twentynine Stumps, for its wonderful lack of fun stuff to do—but the training was great. The talk among the other Marines was that there was a reason the training had been intensified: they'd be boots on the ground in Somalia sometime in the next couple of months. Kim believed the rumors. If the increased schedules of training had been just for her and the other green recruits, she might have dismissed the talk, but it wasn't just the new Marines. Everybody had been gearing up.

She signaled for Duran and Elroy to cover, and she and Mitts hauled ass to the next barrier. Two civilian silhouettes popped up, and though she started to squeeze, she laid off the trigger. Then, as she saw Duran and Elroy leapfrogging past them, a target showed in the window of a building up ahead. Mitts didn't see it—he was scanning low—but Kim swiveled and fingered the trigger. Set to "burst," her rifle sent out three bullets with a single pull of the trigger, and she saw the target splinter and fall. Ahead of them, Duran and Elroy were already crouching and raising their weapons, but as she and Mitts started to rise to run forward, there was a voice over the loudspeaker.

"Cease fire. All Marines, cease fire. Lower weapons. Exercise terminated. Cease fire."

Kim hesitated. Was this part of the exercise? She knew they occasionally liked to throw wrinkles in to simulate the unpredictability of real life in the field, but this seemed a little too self-referential for the Marines. Besides, the guys in her unit were already standing up and flicking their M16s to safe.

She rose, put her rifle on safe, and then looked at Mitts. "What the fuck?"

Mitts shrugged. "Who knows? I thought it was going well. We were moving nice. Good job with the shooting. Things were clean. Maybe somebody was still in the arena, one of the techs not all the way out before we started the exercise?"

Elroy and Duran wandered over, and though Duran had a dour look on his face, Elroy was his usual unflappable self. "Suppose we'll have to start over," Elroy said.

Kim sighed, because Mitts was right, they'd been doing a good job, and it was going to be hard to get themselves psyched up for another go. She started to tell the unit to head back to the chute when the loudspeaker crackled on again. This time it let out a long, piercing siren. This wasn't just for the arena. This was for the whole base. And then, when the voice announced that all units were ordered to report immediately, when it said "This is not a drill," she got concerned. Not because of what "This is not a drill" might mean or not mean, but because, for the first time she could remember, Private First Class Elroy Trotter looked worried.

Hindu Kush, Afghanistan-Tajikistan Border

She was tired of the prospectors. Occasionally they'd come to visit her and ask her for information about the area, though she wasn't sure exactly what they were looking to find. Other times they'd trade with her for one of her sheep, and once they invited her to share a meal. But they'd mostly left her alone. That had changed since she'd shown them the rocks that she brought down from the old cave she sometimes sheltered in if she was caught up on the pass.

Until they'd seen the rocks, the prospectors themselves did not seem to want to be there either. From what little language they had in common, she'd gathered that they found it cold and inhospitable. Which was not short of the truth. She had a good touch with the sheep, and she was more prosperous than some, but even when her husband and daughter had still been alive, it had been a difficult place to live. The prospectors made things easier in some ways—they'd given her a knife and a new jacket that she was quite happy with—but mostly they'd been an annoyance. They liked to play loud music at their camp, and they used explosives in some of their attempts to find whatever it was they were looking for. They were friendly but disruptive, and she would not be sad to see them leave.

Today, however, they were paying her. They seemed to have no concept of how much to offer, and for what they had been willing to pay, she would happily lead them wherever they wanted to go for as long as they wanted. And so she was taking them up the pass to help them find the old cave, to show them where she'd gotten the rocks. She wasn't sure why they were so excited about the rocks. There wasn't any gold or silver in them. But really, she didn't care. What she cared about was that they were paying her handsomely.

Despite being older than most of the men—she was nearly forty, and the men seemed much younger, though most of them were older than her husband had been when he died—she kept outpacing them. Every few minutes she would stop and wait for the prospectors to keep up. They carried small packs filled with electronic gear, shovels and picks, and other tools, but she didn't think the bags were so heavy. She carried one of the packs herself. They told her, best they could, that they were having trouble breathing so high up in the mountains, so she slowed down and took breaks for them to catch their breath.

By the time they reached the cave, it was late morning. The sky was still clear. The lead prospector, a man named Dennis, had told her the weather would be good all day, that they would have nothing to worry about. He had put her in front of his computer and showed her a map full of colors and said there was no snow coming until the next day. She was not so certain. She'd lived there long enough that she had respect for the suddenness with which the sky could burst. If they got stuck in a storm, it would be a difficult descent. They wouldn't have a choice, however. None of the men carried the kind of gear that would see them through the night. They were idiots.

She had no trouble leading them to the cave. A few times every year she ended up seeking shelter in it, guiding her sheep in there with her when the weather caught her out too far from home. It was large enough for the entire flock, and the entrance was narrow with a jutted lip that held the wind at bay. The cave was normally dark, but that had never bothered her. She would spend the nights huddled close enough to the entrance that she could see the stars, but far enough back so that she was sheltered from the wind and the snow.

It was different with the prospectors. The cave had high ceilings—the half-dozen men could stand easily—and they all had powerful lights that they splayed along the walls and the floor. She'd never seen the cave lit up like this. One of the men shined his light on the floor along the wall and picked up a rock similar to what she'd shown them the day before. They murmured excitedly, and Dennis took the rock and looked at it. He brought it over to her. "You weren't kidding," he said then nodded at her. "This could be very good. If we find more, we'll pay extra." He rubbed his fingers together in case she didn't understand, but she knew what it meant: more money for her, but also that the prospectors weren't leaving.

There was a slight wind outside, and she glanced at the sky again. It still looked clear, but even with Dennis's assurances, she didn't trust the clouds to stay away. She'd had too many close calls with the weather, and it was on a day like this that the snow had swept through the valley and the mountains and left her both a widow and a woman without a child. She moved farther into the cave, around the lip of the entrance and out of the touch of the wind. She bent into a crouch and leaned against the wall. She did not know how long the men would want to spend in the cave, but she settled herself in for a wait.

From her perspective, they seemed to be both hurrying and

doing nothing. They pulled small machines from their back-packs, some she recognized, and others she hadn't seen before, and proceeded to gather samples from the floor of the cave. One of them took something that looked like a wand and ran it against the wall. The wand had a series of lights and let out a regular pattern of beeps that seemed to speed up as the lights changed from dull yellow to a piercing red. When the beeps settled into a steady tone, the man lowered the wand and called Dennis over. All of them stopped what they were doing, and from her spot crouched against the wall, she watched. After a few minutes, one of the men went and sorted through the pile of tools and shovels, taking the long-handled pickax. He started banging away at the rock.

She lost interest, however, because she'd seen something illuminated by the lights moving around the cave. She walked over to the packs on the floor and took one of the lanterns. She held it up, searching for what she'd seen. The light flared against the wall, moving the shadows around her. It took her a moment to find it. There. Up on the opposite wall. Far enough back that she'd never been able to see it before when she spent nights huddled in the near darkness with her sheep. It was as high as she could reach. Coal-black smeared on the wall. It was ash, she thought, but then, no. She lifted the lantern up and knew it was something else. Something older. She'd seen pictures painted in the caves before, but this one was different. It was simple. The sight of it made her shiver. A spider.

Behind her, the sound of the pickax striking the cave wall was constant, the man breathing hard as he swung.

The woman let the light of the lantern play over the wall, but there were no more paintings, no more pictures. Just the single spider. It made her uneasy. She was not afraid of spiders. There was no reason to be afraid of spiders. But still.

There was a small cheer and some applause. She looked over her shoulder. The man with the pickax was smiling. He'd broken through the wall. There was dark space behind it. Another cave. A tunnel. She couldn't see. A different man took the ax and started swinging, and the hole widened rapidly. It would be only a few minutes before it was large enough to admit a person, she thought.

Outside the entrance of the cave she saw something float by. A flake of snow? She looked out anxiously. How long had they been in there?

The sky, which had been blisteringly clear, was littered with clouds. The temperature had dropped. She could feel the damp cold of a coming storm. Behind her, the sound of the ax against the rock had stopped, but there was something else. A rhythmic thumping. The men were talking, and she turned to find Dennis. To tell him they needed to leave. A storm was coming.

And then she was no longer sure if she was looking at the sky or at the roof of the cave. But it was dark. And she was screaming.

Desperation, California

Seven minutes.

Seven minutes from seeing the news about the nuke until he'd secured the entrance to the shelter. Gordo was sweating and had to piss, but he'd called Amy from his truck, and she and Claymore were waiting for him underground by the time he came down the stairs at full tilt. Amy looked grim but determined, and Claymore, who had spent a lot of time down in the shelter with Gordo—Gordo had gotten into the habit of watching baseball out here instead of in the house where it drove Amy to distraction, and usually brought the dog with him—seemed to notice nothing out of the ordinary. Claymore did what he always did when he saw Gordo, which was wag his tail and then roll over onto his back and wait for some tummy rubbing.

Gordo checked the shelter doors one more time—this was the real deal, and one mistake would be the last—and then pulled his T-shirt up to wipe the sweat off his face. He bent over and scratched the chocolate Lab's belly and then looked at his wife. "Say it," he said. "I want to hear you say it."

Amy's mouth puckered in a little smile. He knew one of the things she loved about him was his ability to lighten things up.

Even in a moment like this, less than twenty minutes before nuclear weapons were going to start raining from the sky, Gordo could make things feel better for Amy.

"You were right," Amy said.

Gordo straightened up and put one hand to his ear. "What was that? It sounded like . . . no. I didn't quite catch that."

He could see Amy trying to keep her face still, but it didn't work, and her small smile got bigger. She shook her head. "I said, you were right."

He stepped over to her and put his hands on her waist. He leaned down so that his chin was resting in the nook between her shoulder and her neck. "The score, my dear, is now eighteen million, six hundred and forty-eight thousand, three hundred and two for you," he said, "and eleven for me."

"Gordo," Amy said, and he could feel her relaxing into his body, "you are the strangest fool I've ever married, but I'll say it again. You were right."

"And what was I right about, my sweet little bride?"

Amy moved back so she could place her palms on his chest and then gave him a gentle shove. "Right about moving out to this godforsaken little town. Right about building a bomb shelter. Right about the fact that sooner or later things were going to go to hell." She walked over to the television and turned it on. "But you were wrong about it being zombies."

"Well, that still remains to be determined," Gordo said, but he figured he'd probably lost that one. No zombies. Yet.

He'd gone into town to pick up pizza, their weekly ritual. It was more for him than for her. To their mutual surprise, Amy had adjusted quickly to the move from New York City to Desperation, California, or, as Amy sometimes called it, "Desolation." She had grown up on a horse ranch in Wyoming, and went to college at Black Hills State in Spearfish, South Dakota. Compared with Desperation, Spearfish was a decent-sized city, with a population close to twenty thousand when the university was in session, but her upbringing meant she was a lot more ready for small-town life than Gordo was. He was a born and bred New Yorker, and though he'd been the one to push for the move, the change had been harder for him.

In terms of their jobs, it didn't make much of a difference. Amy was a technical writer, which she could do from anywhere, and Gordo was a day trader. He worked market hours, hunched in front of his computer and running the program he'd written himself to exploit minor variations in the currency markets. He was consistent in his returns, and he'd have made a lot more money if he'd let everything keep riding, but he didn't have any faith that the digital zeros at the end of his balances would be of any worth once the apocalypse came. No, he much preferred keeping at least two-thirds of their money in a form he could hold. Right now he felt pretty damn good about the safe in the back of the shelter: one hundred thirty-one pounds, four ounces of gold. At current prices, near eighteen hundred dollars an ounce, it was worth close to three million, eight hundred thousand dollars, and he figured that with the nukes coming down and the inevitable collapse of paper currencies, gold would skyrocket.

No, it wasn't the work that had been an issue. It was the day-to-day reality of living in Desperation. It was an aptly named town, and Gordo was afraid Amy was going to realize how relieved he was that the world as they knew it was finally coming to an end. He'd been so excited when she first agreed to leave New York City behind that he'd thrown himself into the planning. First, he'd researched all the places they could move to, trying to determine where they would best be able to ride out the apocalypse. Fortunately, the Internet made things remarkably easy. It was easy to rule out some places: anywhere too close to a military installation was sure to be hit if it was nuclear war, and anywhere too close to a major civilian population was going to be overrun if it was zombies. Their refuge had to be easily defensible, close enough to some sort of small town and basic infrastructure that they could build the house and the shelter, and ideally, have some like-minded folk already in place who could help mount a defense after things had collapsed and the ravaging hordes were at their worst. Gordo knew it would be every man for himself, but he also knew there were certain situations when it could be good to have allies. If he and Amy were going to rebuild humanity, it would be nice to have a few helping hands.

He had immediately ruled out survivalist places that were settled with some sort of philosophy that he or Amy found distasteful, like the white supremacist compounds that seemed to dot the mountain states, or even worse, the hippie, vegan, peacenik, environmentalist survivalists who built their shelters out of sustainable materials and refused to stock even basic weapons of self-defense. When he found Desperation, however, a place already popular with independently minded survivalists, he knew it was the place. Next, he'd thrown himself into building the house and the shelter. They'd found the plot easily enough, just three miles outside of town. Or, as Gordo still thought of it, outside "town," the quotation marks necessary for a town that consisted entirely of four bars, Jimmer's Dollar Spot—a business that served as convenience store, gas station, grocery store, gun shop, post office, hardware store, clothing store, and coffee shop all in one, and despite its name, sold very little for a dollar—and lastly, LuAnne's Pizza & Beer. Which, Gordo realized, meant you could also argue that Desperation had five bars instead of four.

Gordo and Amy had bought one hundred and twelve acres at three hundred dollars an acre, and immediately started digging. One of the reasons Desperation was so popular with survivalists was that the land around it was dotted with abandoned mines, and with a little bit of planning it was easy to make use of the already hollowed earth for building a shelter. Most of the work was already done for them. The passage into the mine was big enough to drive a cement truck through, and the hollowed cave they built the shelter in had enough leftover space for Gordo to park a backhoe, "in case we need to dig our way out," he told Amy.

At a full run, he could make it from their house into the shelter in less than three minutes, but he didn't have to run: he just drove his truck down the tunnel. The hardest part of the whole project had been getting the series of doors installed to specifications that would keep out radiation. Other than that, it was mostly a big shopping spree: shelf-stable food and water, iodine tablets, radiation tablets, a Geiger counter, a spare Geiger counter, books and manuals on building everything from windmills to basic firearms, knives and shovels, first-aid kits, medicine, handguns and rifles, ammunition, and, with the aid of the Internet and some of his reserves of gold, high explosives.

But then, once they were done with construction and moving, once Gordo had planned everything he could plan, he realized all there was left to do was wait for the worst to happen. And wait. And wait.

He and Amy had met when he was still working for the hedge fund and she had come in as one of the junior analysts right out of college, freshly moved to New York City. Despite their youth, they were married within a year. By the time Gordo was twenty-six, he was making plenty of money trading currency, but they were spending it just as quickly. Amy had given up the markets for writing technical manuals, and their apartment had been broken into four times in a year. That was the price of living in New York City, and for Gordo, it felt like the premium was too much. Whether or not Amy agreed with him, she'd agreed to leave the city. Before Gordo turned thirty, the shelter was finished, and they'd been living in Desperation, California, for more than four years. It was a perfect setup. The house was right next to the entrance to the mine, and they had clear sight lines in every direction. If it was nukes, they could disappear down the maw of the tunnel, and if it was zombies or biological weapons, they could wait in the house until they saw trouble coming.

But it was the waiting. Gordo had been living on high alert since they'd decided to skedaddle from the city, and after seven years of it—three building the shelter, and four waiting to use it—he was exhausted from being prepared at any minute. And Amy, who was a good sport, had been hinting that they couldn't wait much longer if they wanted to start having kids. He was thirty-four now, and though that wasn't exactly old, it wasn't exactly young anymore, and they'd been together long enough that it was time. Time for what? Gordo wanted to ask. Didn't she understand that the entire reason he'd made them move to Desperation was that he thought it *was* time, that it was actually well *past* the time that things were going to go to shit? He wasn't sure he wanted to bring kids into a world that he knew was about to be destroyed. And yet every novel he'd ever read about the end of the world included children. Sometimes they were there just to tug at your heartstrings, but mostly the children were there for a reason: to repopulate the world. So maybe it was his duty; maybe, he thought, he could make Amy happy and do the right thing as one of the few men who were prepared to outlast the end of the world.

Plus, trying to have a kid sounded like more fun than waiting for *it* to happen.

He was thinking about all this when he drove into Desperation and parked in front of LuAnne's Pizza & Beer. Amy had been feeling under the weather and was taking a nap, but she'd insisted they not cancel pizza night. Gordo was pretty sure Amy knew how much he depended on the excuse to head into town and have a beer or two while he was waiting for LuAnne's hairy-knuckled husband to make their pizza. He supposed he could have just gone to one of the bars instead, but he was afraid that option sounded too appealing. There were maybe forty or fifty couples and families like him and Amy, who'd come out here because they were expecting things to go to shit at any moment, regular folk who were just realistic about the state of the world, but there were also a lot of single men who were off their rockers, who thought the government was out to get them, or who claimed they'd been probed by aliens, and those were the ones who hung out in the bars. Them and the bikers. For some reason that Gordo had never figured out, Desperation was a regular stop on the motorcycle circuit, and there were always bunches of bikes parked in front of the bars. There was some sort of pattern, understood rules about which bikers went where, but Gordo had never bothered trying to figure it out. Motorcycles seemed dangerous to him. Nope, give him a good, solid truck any day of the week and he'd be happy.

Inside LuAnne's Pizza & Beer it was busier than he expected. He saw the Grimsby family sitting at the long banquet table, seven girls, four boys, the balding father, who always looked as if he had gone a few days without sleep, and the mother, who was impossibly good-looking for the mother of eleven homeschooled kids. The rumor was that Ken Grimsby had made a killing in computers before moving to Desperation, and had come, at least partly, because he was terrified somebody else was going to try to sleep with his wife. Gordo let his gaze linger on Patty Grimsby for a second, and realized Ken probably had good reason. There was something unaccountably sexy about Patty. It wasn't just that she'd been a model—nineteen years old and almost that much younger than Ken when they got married—but also something else, a sort of availability, and though she'd never done or said anything that had led Gordo to think she actually wanted to sleep with him, he couldn't shake the feeling that she did actually want to sleep with him. Pheromones. Something like that, he thought. Maybe it was just that with the eleven kids sitting at their table, there was something about her fertility that sparked lust in men. Or the appearance of fertility: two sets of twins, two single births, and five adopted. But whatever the provenance of her kids, she looked a lot more like an ex-lingerie model than the wife of a semi-crazy survivalist and mother of eleven. And while her sexiness might be an interesting question, it was not one he could really talk with Amy about. He knew there were lots of men who, even if they didn't cheat on their wives, liked to fantasize about it. He wasn't one of those men. He'd never wanted anybody other than Amy since the moment he first saw her sitting in her cubicle at the hedge fund in the heart of Manhattan. But that didn't mean it was a good idea to talk to her about the perceived sexual availability of Patty Grimsby.

He could talk to Shotgun about it, though. Shotgun wasn't much into women, but despite his being gay, his marriage, to Fred Klosnicks, was a heck of a lot like Gordo's, and the two couples had become good friends the last couple of years. Gordo supposed that Shotgun probably had a real name, something benign like Paul or Michael or even Eugene, but nobody in Desperation had ever heard Shotgun called anything else. Actually, as Gordo looked at Shotgun sitting at the bar, for the first time he realized how appropriate the name was. Shotgun was tall and thin, several inches taller than Gordo, who was not a short man himself. Shotgun reflexively ducked when walking through doorways and constantly banged his head on the light fixture hanging above the pool table in the corner. He was lean and hard, like the barrel of a shotgun, and even the prematurely gray hair interspersed in the thick coat of black hair on Shotgun's head gave the impression of gunmetal. Shotgun was probably in his late thirties, and like a lot of the survivalists out here, an autodidact. There were three kinds: the plain old morons, who hadn't learned much of anything anywhere and seemed to blow themselves up on a regular basis; the guys like Gordo, who'd gone to good universities—in his case, Columbia—and trained as engineers or in some other field that leaned toward problem solving; and those like Shotgun, who were just smart as hell and able to teach themselves anything they needed to know. Shotgun was always building something new up at his ranch or working on some new project that sounded impossible and quixotic and always worked out. A lot of the families and men in and around Desperation were broke, jury-rigging houses out of discarded plywood and plastic, making survival shelters out of buried culverts and construction debris, but some of them had money. Gordo and Amy were relatively wealthy, and would be considered rich in most places other than New York City, and the Grimsby family had to have ten or twenty million in the bank, but of all of them, Gordo was sure Shotgun was the only one who was, without question, rich. As in *rich* rich. Wrath of God money. Shotgun held at least twenty-seven patents that Gordo knew about, and a couple of those were for high-use devices, kicking back serious money to Shotgun on a regular basis.

You wouldn't know it from looking at the man, however. Every time Gordo saw him, Shotgun was dressed the same way:

sneakers, a pair of dark cargo pants, a black T-shirt, and a Chicago Cubs baseball cap. He drove a beat-down truck, and his house, from the outside, looked like it could be blown down by a stiff fart. Of course, once you got to know Shotgun, everything was a little different. First of all, once you passed through the front door of his house, you realized it was built on top of an abandoned mine. What you saw from the outside was just a shell. While Gordo had built a shelter near his house, Shotgun had done one better and built his shelter *as* his home. From the outside, it looked like a Sears kit house with an extra-large garage, but underground there was close to twenty thousand finished square feet of living quarters and workshops. The living space consisted of four bedrooms, and an open kitchen and living room/dining room combo that would have looked at home in a swanky New York City high-rise, but it was the workshops that left Gordo drooling. High-tech stuff as well as every power tool you could think of. If Shotgun didn't want to wait for something to be delivered—or if it didn't exist yet—he could machine it himself. And in the garage, bigger than a basketball court, aside from a few toys like a Maserati and a vintage Corvette, Shotgun kept a couple of heavy-duty pieces of construction equipment, and, most impressively, a six-seater airplane.

Of course, none of that was as truly surprising to Gordo as the simple fact that there were gay survivalists. When the two couples got together, while Gordo and Shotgun talked about engineering problems or the quality of a certain kind of knife, Amy and Fred talked movies and books and cooking. In New York City, Gordo wouldn't have thought twice about being friends with a gay couple, but out here in Desperation, it was a little odd. There just weren't that many gay survivalists that Gordo knew of. Not many people of color either. Mostly it was white, crazy, straight single guys or families. He supposed he and Amy fit into that category.

Well, Gordo corrected himself, Shotgun and Fred were married, so they were a family, and they were white, and you had to be a little bit crazy to move to Desperation. But no kids. He'd asked Shotgun about it once, said he figured he and Amy would go about repopulating the world while they were shut away in the bunker, but that he wasn't sure what Shotgun was in it for.

Fred and Amy were sitting in a booth, but he and Shotgun were at the bar when he'd said it. Shotgun had tilted the bottle of lager back and finished it before speaking. He wasn't pissed off, but he was taking his time answering. They'd known each other long enough and had enough goodwill banked that Gordo knew he could say something stupid and Shotgun would take the time to explain why it was stupid. And right then and there, he was pretty sure he'd said something stupid.

Shotgun had put the beer back down, held up his hand to LuAnne to order another, and then stared at Gordo. "Well, buddy, what do you think I'm in it for? I *could* give a shit about humanity as an abstract concept, about repopulating the world and all that. But I don't. Not really. I'm here for Fred and me. I'm here because when the nukes start falling"—and Shotgun was sure it would be nukes, not zombies or a flu pandemic—"I'd like to live out the allotment of my natural life span."

Unfortunately, it looked like Shotgun was right about the nukes.

Gordo took a seat at the bar and ordered his pizza, shooting the shit with Shotgun while he drank his beer. Turned out Fred was feeling under the weather, same as Amy, and had sent Shotgun on a pizza run of his own.

"We should just put Fred and Amy on a couch together so they can be miserable with company, and you and I can be nerds together," Gordo said.

"Speaking of which, I wanted to show you this." Shotgun had

been working on a new sort of water filter, and he pulled out one of the drawings of a piece he'd come up with to bypass some of the constriction in the pump design. It was an elegant solution, and Gordo suggested a small modification. They were going back and forth, ignoring the television and the table behind them as Patty and Ken Grimsby tried to feed their eleven children. It wasn't until the young woman behind them had spoken twice that they stopped talking and looked up.

"I said, do either of you know anybody looking to rent out a piece of land around here? We're new to Desperation," she said, as if the fact that Gordo and Shotgun had never seen her or her boyfriend before wasn't enough of a clue. She was young, barely twenty, if that, and the young man standing behind her was only a few years older. Gordo didn't have to glance for more than a second to take a dislike to the guy. He recognized his type. Angry hippie. Pretending to be in it for love of the environment and all that sort of stuff, but really he was just too scared to give real life a go. Plus, angry hippie men always ended up with idealistic hippie girls like this. And sure enough, her name?

"Flower," she said. "And this is Baywolf. Spelled like it sounds."

"Ah," Shotgun said. "The kings who ruled them had courage and greatness . . ."

"No," the man said, cutting Shotgun off. "Not like the poem."

Gordo tried to smile, but he could feel that his face had turned sour. He'd had to read *Beowulf* for a class when he was an undergraduate at Columbia, and it had immediately turned him off English lit, but still, there was something undeniably dickish about this guy. "So, like bay and wolf," Gordo said. "You come up with that on your own?"

"My parents named me Flower," the girl said. "They were hippies." She smiled and had the good sense to be embarrassed about it, even though she'd clearly had to explain it her whole life.

"They aren't hippies anymore?"

She shook her head at Gordo. "No. Mom's an investment banker and Dad's a tax attorney. They aren't exactly thrilled that I dropped out of school, but you know, they did it and then went back, so they don't have a lot to really complain about."

Gordo decided Flower might be okay. And then, when Baywolf spoke, it reinforced his opinion of the young man.

"The old man's an asshole. Won't help us out with cash at all."

"You try working?" Shotgun said. "That tends to help out with the cash situation."

"Hey, fuck you," Baywolf said, and he grabbed Flower's wrist. "Come on."

She shook him off and looked at Gordo again. "So, you know any places to rent?"

Gordo finished his beer and glanced at LuAnne. She flicked her hands twice. He'd already been there for twenty minutes, and it was going to be twenty minutes more for the pizza. Her husband was slow as shit in the kitchen, but particularly since it was the only restaurant in fifty miles, the pizza wasn't bad. He nodded for another beer then looked at the couple. Baywolf was glowering, but it was clear he was going to follow Flower's lead. Fair enough, Gordo thought. She was cute and this airhead thing seemed like it was a bit of an act.

"What brought you and Mr. Wolf to Desperation?"

Baywolf scowled harder, but Flower didn't seem to mind the question. "Same as all of you, I guess. Just wanted to get away from the cities and camp out for a while somewhere that seemed like it might not bear the brunt of things."

Shotgun raised an eyebrow. Gordo couldn't tell if Shotgun was trying to be funny or if he was actually attempting to display skepticism, but it was amusing either way. For a man who had carved out a virtual doomsday palace, Shotgun was surprisingly critical of most of the other survivalists.

"Let me guess," Shotgun said. "Vampires?"

"Of course not," Flower said, patting Shotgun on the arm. "Vampires aren't real. It's zombies we're worried about." She paused for a second and then smiled. "Just kidding." She waited a minute for Shotgun to smile back then made her face look dead serious and said, "I believe in vampires."

Gordo decided he liked this girl. She had some nice spirit, and if she was already willing to tweak Shotgun, she might do okay out in Desperation. Her boyfriend was another matter, but that wasn't much his problem. "Shotgun is more of the nuclear apocalypse school of thought," he said.

"Shotgun?" Flower's boyfriend said with a scoff. "That's your name?"

Gordo had known Shotgun long enough that he recognized the curve of Shotgun's lips as something other than a smile. "Yes, *Baywolf*, my name is Shotgun."

Gordo stuck out his hand to Flower. "Gordon Lightfoot, but everybody calls me Gordo."

"Gordon Lightfoot? Like the singer?" Flower shook his hand. She had a firm grip.

"Yep, like the singer," Gordo said. "But no relation. You might want to ask Burly over at the Lead Saloon if you need a place to stay. His brother's place has been empty for a while. He'd probably let you rent it cheap. An old trailer over by the Grimsby homestead. Not much to look at from the outside, but if I know Burly, it will be clean and weatherproof."

He turned to take his beer off the counter and stopped. The television. He banged Shotgun on the arm. "Holy fuck. You see this?"

Up on the screen, the game show was gone, replaced by a

newscaster from the network. Gordo didn't recognize the man on-screen, but it was easy to tell he was harried. On the bottom of the screen were the words "nuclear explosion."

"Burly?" the girl said behind him.

"Just a minute. Hey, LuAnne, can you turn up the sound for a minute?"

LuAnne lumbered over and obliged, and Gordo realized it had gotten quiet behind him, the eleven Grimsby children shushed by their parents.

". . . minutes ago. According to the White House, the Chinese premier has confirmed that the explosion was an accident during training exercises. Again, we apologize for cutting away from your regularly scheduled program, but in breaking news, a nuclear bomb exploded less than twenty minutes ago in the northern Chinese province of Xinjiang. While the scope of the destruction is not clear, the White House has informed us that this was an isolated incident. The Chinese government is reporting it as a military accident. At this time we believe a military aircraft carrying a live nuclear weapon crashed during a training mission. We don't have much information, but we'll go now to the White House where—"

Gordo didn't wait to hear what the reporter from the White House did or did not know. He and Shotgun glanced at each other then scrambled out the door, followed closely by Patty and Ken Grimsby and their brood. His last image of the inside of LuAnne's Pizza & Beer was LuAnne tossing her white towel on the bar and spinning toward the kitchen while Flower and Baywolf looked around in confusion.

All thoughts of the hippie girl and her angry boyfriend disappeared as he pounded the gas pedal against the floor of his truck. He saw Shotgun's truck take the corner too fast, tearing up a cloud of dust, but he was too busy dialing Amy to worry about Shotgun. When he turned into his driveway, he hit the dip fast enough that he was pretty sure he got all four wheels airborne. He could feel his heart jackhammering as he slammed on the brakes and ran to get the shelter doors down.

And then, after all that, it was just the three of them inside the shelter, doors secured: Claymore wagging his tail, Amy telling him he'd been right all along, and Gordo feeling a hollow nervousness in the pit of his stomach.

He was ready for the end of the world.

Marine Corps Air Ground Combat Center, Twentynine Palms, California

One little nuclear explosion and everybody goes batshit. The newscasters had been jabbering all night, talking heads talking out of their asses, but nobody seemed to have anything to add to the initial reports that it was a military plane crash during training except that the Chinese government was now stating that the nuclear blast had been part of "an internal matter" and they were "securing the affected area." Not exactly comforting, Kim thought, but probably not worthy of this level of alert. They were locked and loaded and ready to be boots up at any minute, though she wasn't really sure what she was supposed to do in the event that nuclear missiles started coming down. Duck and cover? Probably better to be on a plane headed somewhere when mushroom clouds started growing. But then she remembered she'd read somewhere that a nuke could cause electromagnetic pulses that shut down electronics. Being aboard a plane when the electronics were fried seemed like an unpromising way to spend a morning.

Kim yawned and shifted in her bunk. Gunnery Sergeant Mc-Cullogh had spent the rest of the evening barking at the company until everything was as ready as it could be, and then Gunny did what good leaders do, which was allow them to get some rest. That was one of those military maxims that proved to be true: sleep when you can. Kim knew Mitts probably spent the night awake and overthinking the day to come. She wasn't sure about Duran, but Elroy never seemed to have any trouble sleeping. Even though Kim had her nightmares—the usual one of making a decision that got one of the men killed, plus a new and not unexpected nightmare of having the flesh melt off her body as she was enveloped in a nuclear blast—she'd gotten some solid shut-eye. An hour of lounging in bed after waking up would have been nice, though. That was one of the things she missed most from civilian life. She loved the order, the discipline, the uniform, the weapons, the promise of violence, the sense of belonging to something bigger than herself that came with the Marines, but she sure as shit missed lolling around in bed on Sunday mornings and taking her time getting ready.

She gave her head a quick scratch, sat up, slipped the elastic off her wrist, and pulled her hair back into a ponytail. She'd actually worried for a little while that she was going to have to shave her head as part of enlisting. Kim knew she would have been able to pull the look off. She wasn't vain, just honest about the fact that she had a pretty face. She'd always been athletically built, but as a softball catcher, she sometimes veered more toward solid than sleek. Three months in the Marines had erased all the extra padding. It felt as if she'd gone through a metamorphosis, turning into the woman she always wanted to be. Even though there were times she was terrified about being a lance corporal, about being responsible for her unit, she was also the most confident she'd ever been. Of course, that didn't mean she was in any hurry to cut her hair.

She double-timed it to the mess and sat down with her unit,

Duran sliding down the bench to make room for her. "What's the scuttlebutt?"

Mitts glanced up but didn't slow down in shoveling his scrambled eggs. Kim took note of the dark circles under his eyes. The part of her that had wanted to sleep with him and could imagine dating him under different circumstances felt bad, but the part of her that was adjusting to having command over her unit thought that she had to make sure he was on top of his game. If he fucked up, at least in the eyes of their squad leader, it meant Kim had fucked up too.

Elroy shook his head and took a sip of his coffee. "Heard a bunch of things. One of them is that it wasn't an accident. The Chinese dropped a nuke on purpose."

Kim felt her mouth drop open and snapped it shut. "Wild-ass guess?"

"Nope," Elroy said. "Honky Joe, and if Honky Joe says it wasn't an accident, I'm willing to believe it's more than a WAG. Said he was online and there's talk about the Chinese trying to cover something up. He said a lot of it sounds like the kind of stupid bullshit you'd expect, like a zombie outbreak, but he thinks it's credible. Said it feels like there's something real underneath it. He thinks it might have been something bio."

Kim toyed with the eggs. Mostly they'd been getting real eggs, but these were rubbery and specked with something pink. She hated powdered eggs, but sometimes they were extra funky because of cheese. The pink specks were probably supposed to be some sort of meat. Ham? She put off taking a bite and nodded at Elroy. Honky Joe was a weird dude, but he was smart as shit. Too smart by half. He'd either wash out or end up wearing brass. Despite his name, Honky Joe was actually a black kid out of Washington, DC. His dad was some sort of something important up on the Hill—Honky Joe wouldn't say what—and Honky Joe said that after he'd been busted hacking into the Pentagon, his father arranged to have him join the Marines instead of joining the fine folks at one of the federal penitentiaries. Early on in boot camp Honky Joe had started a gambling syndicate that pooled money on bets at a local racetrack, and before it was shut down, everybody involved had turned their initial hundred-dollar kick-ins into something closer to two grand. That's the kind of kid he was, and even though he usually ended up getting his black ass handed to him in the end, they'd all figured out he was worth a listen when he decided to speak.

"Anything else?"

Elroy shook his head. "No official word beyond what you already know, but if I was a betting man, and you better believe I am, I'd put a ten-spot on us being on the move by nightfall."

Kim offered her bacon to Duran and he pinched the greasy pieces off her tray. "Any idea where?"

"Outside the continental United States. Bet on that."

Mitts put down his fork and wiped his mouth with his napkin. He really did look like shit, Kim thought. She hoped that if Elroy was right about them getting shipped out, there'd be a chance for Mitts to get some sack time before they left. "I think they're all freaked out over nothing," Mitts said, then crumpled the napkin and put it on his tray. "Not that a nuclear explosion is nothing, but it's not like they launched one on us. Maybe Honky Joe is right, that it's something more than a training accident, but whatever it is, we're not talking shots fired. Wherever they send us, we'll be spending most of our time waiting for the brass and the general public to untwist their underwear. Same shit, different day."

Kim saw Gunnery Sergeant McCullogh hurrying across the mess and stopping to huddle with the company staff sergeants.

Whatever he said had the effect of making the staff sergeants hop to their feet.

"Might be you're right, Mitts," Kim said, nodding her head so that the three men looked across the mess to where she had been looking. "But judging from the way Gunny and the staff sergeants are starting to haul ass, it will be same shit, different day, *and* different country. I think Elroy's right. We're going OCONUS."

Henderson Tech Falcon 7X, over Minneapolis, Minnesota

Henderson couldn't tell if he was asleep or awake. Since he'd stepped off the trail to take a shit in the jungle, everything had the gauzy quality of a dream. A bad dream. Neither of the pilots nor any of the flight attendants said anything to him to indicate that they thought he was acting funny, but then again, when you owned a Falcon 7X, you could expect a certain amount of discretion from your flight crew. At first, Henderson had felt guilty about spending more than $50 million to buy his own jet, plus another $27 million to customize it. It felt wasteful. But in the scheme of things, it just wasn't that much money, and it was a lot easier to pay for it himself than to deal with the bullshit of doing it through the company. No matter that he'd founded the business, built it from the ground up to a market cap of more than $250 billion; once he'd gone public, he had to follow the rules. Not that he minded. Last year he'd been fourth on the list of wealthiest Americans, and with no wife, no kids, and no siblings, what the hell else was he going to do with his cash? Until recently he hadn't given a shit about that sort of stuff, but he'd started the company when he was fifteen and had been going nonstop for more than thirty years.

Now he wanted to spend some of his time and money *not* working. Until recently he'd just used one of the company's jets, since all he did was business, but he figured if he was doing stuff for himself, one of the things he could do was buy his own plane. Frankly, though he'd been wildly successful for most of his adult life, he still thought it was cool that he could own one. He'd thoroughly enjoyed the process of customizing it, though he burned through five designers in the process, but the Falcon 7X was well worth the money he spent. The inside was gorgeous. At least, it was gorgeous when it wasn't covered in spiders.

He was pretty sure it was a nightmare, but it was too close to what had happened in Peru for him to be sure. He'd spent the last morning in Peru on the toilet, but he'd been game for the hike through the jungle. You didn't become the fourth-richest American without having the fortitude to fight through the squirts. But it was embarrassing. The guide, Miggie, had been cool about it, but for Henderson, having to keep stopping to shit in the greenery while the women and his bodyguard waited for him was kind of awkward. He wasn't deluded. He wasn't a bad-looking dude. A little heavy. A lot heavy. Okay, kind of fat, and obviously on the wrong side of forty, but if he'd been just a doctor or something, he'd have been able to have a perfectly decent-looking wife. With billions in the bank, however, he rated three super-hot models. That still didn't make him feel any better about having to cope with diarrhea. He'd been trying to drink water and get some salt into his system, but it had been hard going with the heat and the elevation. He could have canceled the hike, could have done pretty much anything he liked and nobody would have said anything. The rules were different for people like him. Money, at least on the scale he had, changed things. But for Henderson, it didn't change the fact that he didn't like excuses. Didn't like to hear excuses—"Own your mistakes and move on, or pack your shit and get out," was one of the company's mantras—and didn't like to give them. But man, his stomach had been killing him.

He'd gone off the path for what must have been the fourth or fifth time, and he'd just finished wiping himself with some sort of foliage that he prayed fervently was nontoxic and was pulling up his pants when he heard the screaming. He took a dozen steps back toward the path, just close enough that he could see the guide being swallowed by a black tide. The three women clutched at one another and shrieked. His bodyguard turned to run but got tangled up in the women and fell to the ground with two of them. Henderson looked back to where the guide had been standing, but the man had disappeared. And then he saw the black wave wash over the body of the woman who was still standing. Tina. Her name was Tina.

There was screaming, but there was more than that. There was a rustling sound, a sort of clicking and flicking. It sounded both lush and creepy. The bodyguard lumbered to his feet, but there were patches of black over his back, his arms, on his head. Henderson couldn't figure out what the patches were, but then he realized they were moving, splitting and swarming, re-forming on the bodyguard's body no matter how much he swatted and brushed at himself. And then Henderson felt his stomach go liquid again, because from where he stood in the woods, even with the foliage fracturing his view, it looked as if the bodyguard's face was melting, the skin sloughing off to show flesh and muscle and then bone. The man was still standing, screaming, thrashing at the air, at his head, at his body, but the blackness only grew more solid.

That had been enough for Henderson, and he turned and started to run. He had no idea where he was going, and with the thickness of the plants and the trees he couldn't do anything other than crash blindly. He was sure he was moving at the speed of a slow walk, but however little speed he carried, he knew he needed to get out of there. At first, all he could hear was the sound of his breathing, the push and rattle of his hands and legs against branches and leaves, but then he heard the sound again, the clicking and flicking. If he thought he'd been moving hard before, he was desperate now. There was something sharp and then numbness on his ankle, a scrape on his arm that could have been a branch or could have been something worse. Henderson kept moving, swatting at his body, cursing and crying and barely able to stand. He tripped and rolled on the ground, knocking his elbow and waiting to be swallowed, but as he lay there, he realized that other than his ragged breath, the jungle was quiet.

He scratched at his arm, and then at the numbness on his ankle, his hand coming back with a smear of blood. Something tickled at the back of his neck and he swatted it, feeling something solid burst under his hand. He grabbed whatever it was and held it in front of his face.

Ew. He shuddered. He was afraid of spiders, and this one was black and hairy. Even though it was squished from his slap, it had been big. And then he had to clamp down on a scream as he realized this spider was part of the black wave that had washed over the guide, his bodyguard, and the three models. Jesus. A swarm of them.

He'd gotten to his feet and done his best to walk in a straight line, hoping that sooner or later somebody would come looking for him. Billionaires didn't just disappear without people noticing. After a period of time that he thought couldn't have been more than an hour, he stumbled out of the jungle and found himself standing on a paved road. "What the fuck?" He looked around, but there was no indication of which way he should go. He turned around a couple of times and then just chose a direction. Miracle of all fucking miracles, within three minutes he was waving down a Jeep carrying two scientists from the research center in the preserve. He'd offered them thirty thousand dollars to drive him directly to the airport, no questions asked.

By the time he was sitting in one of the leather seats on his Falcon 7X, he thought he'd already started having a fever. He'd made the scientists stop twice on the way to the airport so he could go to the bathroom, and the first thing he did upon boarding the jet was take some Imodium. That had done the trick with the diarrhea, but now he had the sweats and a pounding headache. His ankle was throbbing and he thought that maybe the cut was already infected. Fucking jungle. Fucking bugs. He couldn't wait to get back to the USA for some good old American antibiotics. He was more than done with being an international adventurer. Who was he kidding? Why would he bother with hardship? He was sticking to nice hotels from now on. Hot water and gourmet food. If he was going to seek the company of super-hot models, he wanted to get his blow jobs while lying on six-hundred-thread-count sheets. That, Henderson thought, was a good way to spend some of his fortune. Screw the jungle.

He knew there'd be some questions when he landed, though. No matter how many billions he had, there was the little matter of the missing guide, the bodyguard, and the three models who'd flown to Peru with him. Well, the guide probably didn't matter much, and the bodyguard's death had been an occupational hazard, but even he couldn't just make three semi-famous models disappear. Fortunately, he wasn't prone to drugs or violence and didn't exactly have a history of leaving bodies in his wake. When the questions came, he'd direct them to his lawyers and simply tell the truth: some sort of animals had attacked them, and sick, injured, and disoriented, he'd panicked and fled. For right now, what he was most concerned about was whether the spiders he saw swarming over the interior of his jet were real or part of a nightmare.

He could hear a steady drone and see the spiders growing like black moss on the walls and ceiling of the jet. He could feel them crawling on him. His skin itched and he jerked and swatted. He sat up with a start and blinked hard. He'd been dreaming. A nightmare. A dark speck floated across his vision and he rubbed his eyes to clear them. Nothing. He saw one of the flight attendants, a brunette named Wilma or Wanda or something like that, staring at him, and he tried to straighten up in his seat. He knew he looked like a mess. The movement made him wince. His head, his stomach, his ankle, the fever. He felt like hell. Screw it, Henderson thought, and he stayed slumped in his chair, not even bothering to try to give her a smile.

She walked down the aisle and over to him to touch his arm. "We'll be touching down in about ten minutes, Mr. Henderson. Can I get you anything before we land?"

He thought he saw something moving in the corner of his vision, another black spot, but when he flinched and turned, there was nothing there. Just his reflection in the window. He rubbed his eyes again, and that seemed to chase away the floating specks that teased him. "A tonic water would be good," he managed. "And see about turning down the temperature. It's hot in here." She started to turn, but he called her back. "And get my assistant on the line. I feel like shit. Tell her we're going straight to my doctor."

She nodded and retreated to the galley. Henderson closed his eyes for a moment and then snapped them back open. The tonic water was on the table in front of him in a heavy cut-glass crystal tumbler. He must have nodded off for a few seconds. He shook his head. He didn't want to fall asleep again. As lousy as he felt, sleeping meant dreaming, and right now dreaming meant those goddamned spiders. He had been scared of spiders even before his trip to Peru, even before he watched his bodyguard's face dissolve. At least here, on his jet, he knew that the only spiders were the ones inside his head. Which was killing him. The headache was a pressure that seemed as though it was centered in the middle of his forehead. He'd ask for some aspirin when Wilma or Wanda or whatever her name was came back.

He could feel the jet descending, and out the window were the first real outskirts of Minneapolis. He usually liked coming back to town, looking out over the city where he'd been born and raised and where he'd started one of the largest technology companies in the world. Today, however, when he tried looking out the window the light made him wince. It was like something pushing on his eyeballs. He could feel each beat of his heart like a hammer blow to his temple. Worse, he could feel something tickling inside his skull, a sneeze building up, and with this headache he knew that a sneeze was going to feel like the worst thing in the world. The pain in his head was suddenly enough to make black dots swim in his vision.

He sneezed. He saw a fine spray of blood coat the wall. Snot dripped from his nose. It felt like something was skittering around in there, and when he wiped at it, he realized something *was* skittering out of his nose. He felt the hairy, hard leg and pulled it. Holy fucking shit. It was a spider.

He just pulled a fucking spider out of his nose.

He had one of the spider's legs pinched between his fingers. The bug swung and clicked at him. It was making an actual clicking sound with its mouth or its mandibles or whatever the hell they were, and then the spider turned itself so that it was against his hand, biting into the flesh. It was a sharp pain, worse than a pinch, but oddly icy. He swore, and flung the creature away from him.

And then whatever pain was left in his head, the bite from the spider, the fact that he'd even had a fucking spider come out of his nose, was written over by the burning in his leg. It was worse near the cut he'd gotten in the jungle, as if somebody were holding a lit candle to his skin, and it radiated up and around his calf. He stared down at it, and for a moment he thought he might be having another nightmare, because he could actually see his skin bulging and rippling. He heard himself grunting and then screaming, and though he knew it was from the pain in his leg, it was both similar to and completely different from a dream: he was outside himself, watching. There was part of him that was writhing in his leather seat, straining against the seat belt, clutching at his calf and both shrieking and crying, and there was a part of him that seemed to be watching calmly as the flight attendant ran down the aisle toward him, followed by the copilot rushing from the cockpit. He wasn't sure what part of him watched the skin around his ankle split open, a zipper of blood and blackness, as spiders spilled out onto the floor, swarming over Wilma or Wanda, over the copilot, leaving all three of them screaming and thrashing at the pain and the biting, and he didn't even try to figure out what part of him watched as a thin line of blackness rolled toward the open cockpit door. And then he couldn't see anything at all, but he could feel it when the plane pitched steeply forward.

Minneapolis, Minnesota

Mike flashed his badge at the uniform sitting by the door of Leshaun's room. "Agent Rich. Mind if my daughter sits out here for a couple of minutes while I say hey to my partner?"

The uniform, a young Asian kid who looked fresh out of the academy and bored out of his mind at having to sit outside a hospital room all day, looked at Mike's suit and badge.

"What's she doing out of school?"

"She had a fever last night. She's totally fine, but school protocol is for her to be fever-free for twenty-four hours. I'm off today, so we're trucking around. You know how it is," Mike said. The cop raised his eyebrows. "No, I guess you probably don't know how it is. Just part of having kids."

The cop nodded and motioned to the seat beside him. Annie didn't even glance up from the game she was playing on Mike's phone, sliding into the chair and continuing to make her little duck eat pellets or whatever it was the duck was supposed to be doing. The cop looked over Annie's shoulder and crinkled up his brow. "Hey, how'd you get past level eight?"

Mike stepped into Leshaun's room and closed the door behind him. He could see Annie through the glass door. He knew the hospital wasn't the best place to take his daughter, but he also knew that if his partner was up for it, he'd be pleased to see Annie. He wasn't sure that Leshaun *would* be up for it, however. Two bullets. One to the vest and the other to his arm.

Mike hovered for a minute, watching Leshaun sleep, and then decided against waking him. The doctors had said Leshaun would be out of the hospital tomorrow, back on the job in a week or two. He was lucky as shit. The first bullet had gone clean through his biceps. Even though it had been a bloody mess, the bullet missed anything of real importance. It was probably going to take Leshaun longer to get over the second bullet, however. He had two broken ribs from where the vest caught the round, and those were going to nag for a while. Mike put the magazines he brought on the nightstand next to Leshaun and pulled out one of his business cards from his suit pocket so he had something to write a note on. As he clicked open his pen there was a loud sound from outside the hospital, a big *whomp*, and then the floor shook slightly. He looked out the window but couldn't see anything, so he scrawled a quick note on the back of his card, telling Leshaun to give him a call and that he'd stop back later.

Outside the room, Annie was watching the cop play the duck game on the phone, giving him pointers on how to eat the most pellets.

"You hear that sound, Officer?" The cop looked up from the phone and sheepishly handed it back to Annie.

"No sir. I've been stuck on level eight for a while, and your daughter was showing me how to get past it."

"She's a smart kid, that one," Mike said. "Thanks for watching her." He reached out to take Annie's hand. "Come on, beautiful. Uncle Leshaun's still sleeping. I'll come back later, after I drop you off at your mom's. What do you say we go get some ice cream, see if it cuts the heat a little?" He shook his head. "Crazy weather for April, isn't it?"

In the parking garage, he was already starting to back the car out when his phone rang. Annie knew the drill and handed it up front without complaint. Mike didn't recognize the number, but it was a DC area code, so he picked up.

"Is this Special Agent Rich?"

"Yep, but I'm not on the clock today."

"You are now. This is the director."

"The director of what?"

"*The* director."

Mike had to stop himself from blurting out, "Bullshit." Not that Annie had never heard him swear before, but if it was really the director of the agency, it wasn't in his best interest to sound like a moron.

"There's been a plane crash," the director said. "Happened maybe five minutes ago. You're the closest agent in the vicinity, and we need you there."

Mike cradled the phone between his shoulder and his ear and shifted the car into drive. "I heard it. Didn't know what it was."

"Well, you do now. You know Bill Henderson?"

"Of Henderson Tech?" Mike said. The phone Mike was talking on was an HT model, and the computer he had in his office was an HT as well. And even if Mike hadn't known what kind of phone or computer he had, there probably wasn't a single person in the entire country who didn't know who Bill Henderson was, let alone in Minneapolis, where Henderson was the success story to end all success stories. Henderson employed more than forty thousand people on nine campuses on the western edge of the city. And that was just in Minneapolis. "Yeah, I know Bill Henderson. I mean, I don't know him personally, but I know who he is. Why?" Mike asked, then immediately said, "Oh."

"Right now we don't have any reason to suspect it was anything other than an accident. You'll get more details on-site, but when a billionaire falls from the sky, particularly a billionaire who was the president's largest donor during her last campaign, all bets are off. If anything—anything—looks like terrorism or like it was something other than just a plane crash, I'll expect a phone call directly. And I mean anything. If I find out from the television that there was something suspicious and you haven't already told me about it, your career will look less promising. You can let the locals set up a perimeter, but we've got a team ready to be wheels up within the hour and on the ground by midafternoon. Make no mistake: the agency is going to be on this one. You call this number, the one I called you from. Keep me tight in the loop on this one, Agent Rich. You got it?"

"Uh, yes sir," Mike said.

"Good. Here's my assistant. He'll give you the details."

Mike took the address from the assistant, hung up the phone, and then turned to look at Annie.

"Sorry, beautiful, but this is a big deal. We're going to have to take a rain check on the ice cream, okay?"

Annie scowled, but he could tell she was faking it, and she didn't raise a fuss when he said he had to call Fanny.

The phone clicked through to voice mail. "Fanny," Mike said, "it's me. Something came up. I need you to come get Annie. I wouldn't be doing this if it wasn't a big deal, but trust me when I tell you this, I really can't get out of it." He left the address for Fanny and asked her to call back as soon as she could, resisting the urge to tell her to follow the plume of smoke. The gray ribbon was thick in the air, and even though he knew the address he had been given was more than ten blocks away, the smoke looked closer. As he drove, he tried Dawson's number, but Annie's stepdad was evidently away from his phone as well. Mike had to step hard on the thought that the reason his ex-wife and her new husband weren't answering the phone was that they were naked and in bed.

"Okay, beautiful," he said over his shoulder. "Mommy's not answering, so you're going to be stuck with me for a while. I've got to do some work."

He flipped the cherries on even though he didn't drive faster than the speed limit, conscious of his daughter sitting in the back. There wasn't much in the way of traffic, though he could already see the strobes of emergency vehicles up ahead.

"Daddy?"

"Yeah, beautiful?" he said, distracted by her voice and by what her voice meant: that he'd have to figure out what to do with her once they got to the crash site. Annie wasn't sheltered. She knew that he worked for the agency, knew he carried a gun, knew that occasionally there were guys like Two-Two who might shoot at him, knew why Leshaun was in the hospital, but that didn't mean Mike thought it was the best idea to walk around with her near the smoking crater the plane would have left in the ground. Or, oh hell, he thought, it was probably worse than that. Almost certainly the plane hit a house or a building or something.

"Daddy," Annie said, and there was something measured and hesitant in her voice. "I think I'm getting too old for you to call me 'beautiful' all the time."

"Oh." Mike slowed down at a red light and then, after checking both left and right, cruised through the intersection. He could hear sirens growing closer, and wondered how big of a clusterfuck this was going to be. Ambulance, fire, police. City workers, utilities, probably county and state everything. Likely to be feebies or other federals too. "Okay, beau—Annie. Annie."

He glanced in the rearview mirror, but Annie was looking out the window, watching the buildings pass by. It was something he knew she must have been thinking about, and even though the expression was overused, it broke his heart. It was too soon, he thought, too soon for her to be negotiating the passage from being a child to being an adult. She was only nine, for Christ's sake, not even into the double digits yet. Of course, that wasn't what really bothered him about it. He called her "beautiful" because she was beautiful, and she was his Annie and would always be his Annie no matter what he called her, but he couldn't shake off the conversation from the day before, the way Fanny had insisted that she and Annie had to have the same last name. Mike hadn't asked Fanny to change her last name to Rich when they got married but she'd done it anyway, and he hadn't fought when Fanny changed it to Dawson when she remarried. He understood that when you married a guy whose first name was Rich, you probably didn't want your last name to be Rich, particularly when it was a name you'd brought along from your first marriage. Still, it stuck in him that Fanny thought it wouldn't be a big deal to change Annie's last name. Fanny had never been the kind of woman to use their kid as a pawn, and he was sure she didn't mean it that way, was sure she meant exactly what she said—that it was too weird for her to have a kid with a different last name—but he didn't understand why it was *now*, months after Fanny Rich had become Fanny Dawson, that it suddenly mattered so much. Why now? What had suddenly changed in his ex-wife's new marriage?

Oh.

Now he understood.

"Hey beau—Annie?" he said. It was going to take some getting used to. "How's Mommy been feeling? Everything okay at home?"

"Fine," Annie said.

A fire truck came barreling through the intersection ahead of them, and Mike slowed down to check both ways before turning. They were close enough that he could see people standing on the sidewalk and pointing. A block away, maybe two.

"She been sick at all or anything like that?"

"She's been sleeping a lot," Annie said. "She's been going to bed earlier than me. Rich has been reading to me before bed."

Mike brought the car to a complete stop and closed his eyes. He thought he might puke, which was kind of funny since he'd basically been asking Annie if his ex-wife was suffering from morning sickness. She hadn't been sick when she was pregnant with Annie, but she'd been tired the entire first trimester.

There was a burst from a siren behind him and he opened his eyes and then pulled out into the intersection, turning the corner. He was about to ask Annie another question, but then he saw the building.

It was a school. "Oh fuck," he said.

"Daddy! You owe me a dollar!"

"Sorry Annie. I'll get you later, okay?" The street was choked with ambulances, police cars, and fire trucks, and in his rearview mirror he saw something that looked like it might be a SWAT truck rolling after him. The building was old and faced with brick, and he saw that the sign out front read BILL HENDERSON ELEMENTARY SCHOOL. He wanted to laugh. Henderson's plane had evidently crashed on the property of the elementary school named after him, but the sight of two or three hundred children milling around on the front lawn stopped him from finding it funny. "Fuck."

"Daddy!"

"Right. Sorry. It's just. Okay." He tried calling Fanny again, but once again, it went to voice mail. He pulled the car to the side of the street, angling it in next to a police cruiser, and then just sat there for a moment considering his options.

"Daddy?"

He sighed. He didn't really have any options. He'd never even seen the director of the agency before, except on TV when he was going through congressional hearings. If Mike fucked this up, he was going to find himself transferred out of Minnesota and working the ass end of the worst posting in America, wherever that was. He looked back at Annie and saw she was staring at him, waiting for an answer. "It's my boss," he said, though he didn't really think he could explain to her. It didn't matter. He couldn't leave Annie in the car, but if he didn't get out of the car—he couldn't ignore a direct order from the director of the agency—he wouldn't be living near Annie anymore anyway. "Okay. Okay. Okay. Let's do it," he said. "How do you feel about helping me out today, sweetheart?"

Annie shrugged, but she got out of the car when he did. She tagged along as he walked past the spectators and the gathering camera crews, kept with him as he held out his badge and ducked under the yellow tape that had already gone up. He turned the corner of the building and stopped with a sudden surge of relief. "Thank. Fucking. God."

"That's three dollars now, Daddy."

He glanced at Annie and then looked back at the field behind the school. The building was untouched, but there was a deep gouge in the dirt on the soccer field behind the school, starting from one goal and reaching almost all the way to the other, where the thick beam of smoke spiraled from a bundled mess of metal. There was a crew of firefighters hosing down a small section that was still burning and seemed to be giving off the majority of the smoke flooding the sky, but two other trucks already seemed to be packing up, and the ambulance crews, as far as Mike could tell, were just standing around. If there had been children playing on the field when the plane hit, it would still have been a circus of fevered activity.

A uniformed policewoman walked past them. Mike stopped her. "No kids?" he asked.

"Nah," the woman said. "I guess they'd just gone inside for lunch or something. According to one of the teachers, they missed being out there by about three minutes. The people on the plane weren't so lucky. Not much to do but hose it down and clean it up." She looked down at Annie and gave a little smile. "What's up with the munchkin?"

"She had a fever last night, so no school for her. I was going to take the day off and make it a daddy day," Mike said. "You know how it is, though. Sometimes you don't have a choice about working. Tried calling the ex-wife, but . . ." He stared at the cop.

She figured it out. "Nope. Sorry, man. I'm on the clock, and I can't play babysitter, especially for a suit."

Mike shrugged. "Can't blame a guy for trying."

"Actually, it's some kind of sexist bullshit." She glanced at Annie again. "Sorry about that honey."

Annie shrugged. "Daddy swears a lot."

"Not that much, honey."

"You said the F word three times already."

"Yeah," Mike said. "Sorry." He looked back at the cop. "And you're right. I probably wouldn't have asked a man. Not cool."

"I don't like it, but I get it," the cop said. "Good luck with it all. You might not want to take her too close to the scene. It's, uh, it's maybe not age appropriate."

"Grisly?"

"Half the plane disintegrated, and what's left has been worked over by the fire." She started to walk away but then stopped and touched Mike's arm. "Try one of the ambulance crews. Look for a short, thick blond woman. Tell her Melissa asked if she could lend you a hand. At least until your ex-wife shows up."

Mike nodded and made a beeline to the ambulances, Annie's hand in his. It turned out that the thick blond woman was the only female among the EMTs. Mike went through his song and dance about Annie having to stay home from school because she'd had a fever the night before and how he had to work unexpectedly, but he might as well not have bothered: at the mention of the policewoman's name, the EMT lit up with a smile and beckoned Annie to come sit in the ambulance. "I've got a daughter about her age," she said. "We'll hang out. You cool if I give her a little bit of candy?"

Mike would have been cool with a whole bunch of candy if it meant he didn't have to take his daughter into the wreckage. He texted Fanny to tell her that Annie was hanging with the EMTs and added the address again in case she missed it on the earlier voice mail. By the time he was ten steps away from the ambulance Annie had gum in her mouth and was playing a video game on the woman's phone and lounging on a gurney as if it were a couch.

Near the plane, the grass was wet from the firefighters' hoses, and he felt mud sliding under his shoes. He wished he were wearing a pair of good boots. As he stepped past a piece of metal the size of a car's hood—part of a wing?—a tall, olive-skinned man in a suit held up his hand. "Sorry pal."

Mike held up his badge. "Agent Rich. Just need to poke around a little."

"Moreland," the man said. "And sorry, but you aren't going to be poking around at all. PD. We got the scene."

Mike felt the phone resting in his pocket and resisted the urge to pull it out. The director had said he'd get the support he needed, but he was pretty sure it would look better if he could show some initiative. "Look, Moreland, I don't want to come in here like a dick. I know how it is when the feds step in, and I'd like to play nice. Today was supposed to be my day off. I've got my daughter with me"—he pointed to where Annie was now sitting on the bumper of one of the ambulances and evidently telling some sort of story to a crowd of EMTs—"and I was just at the hospital visiting my partner, who got shot yesterday. You hear about the shooting in the northeast?"

"Yeah. That you guys?"

"Yeah, that was us, and after shooting two Aryan Nations motherfuckers, watching my partner get hauled off to the hospital with a gunshot wound and a couple of broken ribs from where his vest took a hit, and supposedly having today off to visit my daughter, the same daughter whose soccer practice I missed last night because of the aforementioned shooting, well, I'm not too thrilled to be here. But the thing is, I got a phone call ordering me to be here. A phone call from somebody so high up it scares the shit out of me. If I needed to, I could phone him back and make it rain suits from here to Sunday. I could have your asshole designated a federal case if I need to. But I don't want to do that. And why would that be?"

Moreland couldn't seem to decide if he wanted to smile or scowl at Mike's rant, but he played along. "Because you don't want to come in here like a dick."

"That's right. I don't want to come in here like a dick. So all I'm asking is to poke around a bit, and if I can do that and reassure the same person who called and told me I was working today, that I was working regardless of my partner getting shot, regardless of me downing two Aryan Nations chumps yesterday like a regular hero, regardless of the fact that I had to ask the fucking EMTs to babysit, if I can reassure that same person there is nothing to worry about, that would be great. I would very much like to avoid making it rain suits down like spring showers, and I am sure you would very much like to avoid having your asshole designated something that needs to be investigated by the federal government."

Moreland didn't say anything for a few seconds, but Mike saw the man's eyes flicker in the direction of Annie and the ambulances. Finally, Moreland relaxed and moved to the side a little. "You been practicing that speech?"

Mike grinned. "Little bit. First time I've ever had to use it. Pretty good, huh?"

Moreland shrugged and then pulled a pair of nitrile gloves from his pocket and handed them to Mike. "The 'rain suits from here to Sunday' thing wasn't bad, but I'm not sure about designating my asshole a federal case."

"Improvised that one. I'll work on it." Mike took the gloves and worried them onto his hands. "We'll have a full team out here in a couple of hours, but in the meantime, anything I need to know?"

"That small section over there, where they're still hosing things down, was probably the engines. There are parts of the plane scattered all over the field. If there had been kids out here, it would have been a bloodbath. But mostly what you'll want to look at is in here. A couple of bodies, pretty burned, but that's about all there is to see until the techs get through with it. Haven't heard from the tower yet, but near as I can tell the plane came down in one piece and then split apart once it hit. Nothing to make me think it was more than an accident. Doesn't look like a bomb or anything. That's not exactly my specialty, though. FAA guys should be here within the hour."

"Anything else?"

"Yeah," Moreland said. "You go in there, you'll never want to eat barbecue again."

Mike was careful working his way up into the body of the jet. The plane wasn't flat, but it felt close enough. Water from where firefighters had hosed down the wreck dripped from the ceilings and pooled on the carpet. Mike's shoe skidded on something, and when he reached out to steady himself he felt the sharp tear of metal slicing through the skin of his hand.

"Fuck." He balled his hand into a fist and then opened it so he could see the cut. The impact of the crash had torn open the jet as if a giant cat had worked its claws through the plane's metal body, and the seams of metal were jagged enough that they'd opened a flap in his hand. The nitrile glove was shredded; he peeled it off and stuffed it in his pocket. He realized that, despite everything looking like an accident, he was already treating it as a crime scene. That phone call from the director had gotten into his head.

He could feel the blood leaking from his palm and running down his arm, so he worked his tie off his neck and wrapped it around his hand. He didn't want to get blood all over the place. He pulled a mini Maglite from his pocket. There was some natural light coming in through where the metal had been peeled back, but when he came to the first body, he was glad he had the flashlight.

It was a woman. Or it *had* been a woman. There was still enough fabric left of her skirt for Mike to be clear about that, but the rest of her body was destroyed. Her legs were bent, one of them broken and turned at an angle that probably would have made him gag had he been a newbie, though that wasn't as disturbing as the burns. She was charred and damaged beyond expectations. On her head there were a few tufts of hair, burned short but still showing some color, but her face and torso were shredded. Her skin was a mixture of black flakes and pink ooze, pitted in places and disturbingly raw. Clearly she'd been thrown through the cabin, and Mike figured that when the autopsy was done they'd find that chunks of metal had torn away at her body. Regardless, she wasn't Henderson, and the skirt, with the few scraps of white fabric that had been her shirt, looked like some sort of uniform. One of the stewardesses. No, flight attendant, he thought. Flight attendant.

He shined his flashlight at what had been the front of the plane, but there wasn't much to see other than a gaping hole. Everything forward of the galley had been torn off. What a mess. He debated just ducking out of the plane and getting himself some stitches for the cut on his hand. The director said that another agency team was coming to take over, but as much as he wanted to just wait for them to come, the director had also been clear that this was a live wire. Waiting was not an option.

Mike tried flexing his hand. Fuck. It stung like a motherfucker. He grimaced and then put the flashlight between his teeth so he could use his good hand to peel the blood-soaked tie from the cut on his other hand. As he pulled the tie away from the wound, the fabric stuck to the skin and the flap raised a little, blood pooling freely. Well, Mike thought, that was stupid, and he pulled the tie tight back against the palm of his hand. He should have just left it covered. At least it was his left hand, he thought, because once he was done here, assuming Fanny hadn't shown up yet, he might have to head back to the hospital with Annie to get himself a few stitches. Shit. He was going to owe that kid ice cream *and* a trip to the toy store.

As if she knew he'd been thinking about her, Mike's phone rang, and he pulled it out to see Fanny's number.

"Come on, Mike," she said. "Really? And you left her to play in an ambulance?"

"I didn't have much choice, Fanny. She's okay. Just do me this favor, okay, it's important, and get here as soon as you can."

He hung up, knowing that he'd pay for it later, but yet another uncomfortable conversation with his ex-wife seemed preferable to having the full weight of the agency come crashing down on him. Even if, as seemed clear, it was just an accident, he needed to make sure it looked like he had given the maximum effort. Maybe, if he handled it right, he'd come out ahead on this, looking good, but he knew for sure that if he fucked it up, the director would bury him. Cutting his day with Annie short wasn't ideal, but it was the way it would have to be. Ice cream, the toy store, *and* the bookstore, Mike decided.

He couldn't decide if his hand was throbbing or burning where he'd ripped it open, but it hurt. He was careful not to touch any more sharp edges as he shuffled to the opening and looked out at the circle of ambulances. Annie was still sitting on the bumper, and she happened to look up and see him. He waved at her, and she waved back. She'd be okay with it, Mike thought. She wouldn't complain about Fanny picking her up. She was a good kid. An easy kid. She understood his job could be demanding. The divorce had been tough, but she never made him feel shitty about it. It was funny, he thought, how quickly kids adjusted to new situations, how whatever was happening in their lives was what they thought was normal. He wished he'd been able to adjust to the divorce as quickly as Annie. Or, for that matter, as quickly as his ex-wife. He'd had a couple of casual things, but hadn't really tried dating seriously, and yet Fanny was already happily remarried. And, evidently, expecting.

The blond EMT caught his eye and called out across the grass that they were good, and Mike yelled back that Annie's mom would be there in about ten minutes. The EMT gave him the thumbs-up—at least he hoped it was the thumbs-up and not the finger—and Mike turned back to the guts of the plane.

He stepped past what was left of the flight attendant, mindful of the debris on the cabin floor. He couldn't stop from stepping in the ashes, however, and was unsettled by the crunching and popping sounds beneath his feet. Like walking on peanut shells. He tried to be careful in case it ended up being a crime scene after all. At least it hadn't been a passenger jet. That was one saving grace. He'd known friends who worked disaster sites or mass graves, and they all said the sound of bones breaking underfoot was not something you got over.

The inside of the jet was hot, much hotter than it was out in the sun. Mike couldn't help but think it was residual warmth from the fire that had burned in the cabin. He was sweating already, his shirt sticking to his back, and he wished he'd thought to take off his suit coat outside. He glanced at his watch. It was less than half an hour since the jet had crashed. As his flashlight beam came to rest on the charred body buckled into a seat in the middle of the cabin, Mike thought that for all the good it did Bill Henderson, the director was right: when a billionaire fell from the sky, it was handled a little differently.

He felt something tickle his left wrist and realized that despite the tie wrapped around his hand, the cut was bleeding through. He wiped the blood on his suit coat and then stepped closer to the body.

It was Henderson. No question.

The bottom half of his body was a mess of burns and exposed bone. The flesh and muscle and fat were completely stripped on one of his legs, and more than fifty percent gone on the other. Oddly, Mike realized he was more disturbed by Henderson's torso: from waist to neck, other than a few flecks of ash on the long-sleeved T-shirt, Henderson looked as undisturbed as a mannequin in a department store. Thankfully, what natural light came in through the windows and the rent in the side of the plane left the man's head hidden in the shadows. Mike played the beam of the flashlight on the wall and ceiling around Henderson. It must have been hell in here, he thought. The plastic was melted and buckled, scorched from the flames. Mike was just guessing, but he thought that probably fuel from the engines had spilled into the cabin. If they were lucky, they were dead from the crash before the flames reached them.

He stepped closer, the ashes crackling under his feet again, took a deep breath through his mouth—the smell of burnt plastic and flesh was too much for him—and fixed the flashlight on Henderson's head. The sight made him gag.

The flesh above his right ear, stretching close to the middle of Henderson's head, had been burned pink and deep, black ash mixing with blood and exposed fat, hair singed and curled back. That wasn't what made Mike feel sick, however. It was Henderson's left eye, his nose, his mouth, and his cheeks. Mike swallowed the sick down and closed his eyes for a few seconds so he could prepare himself to look again. He realized he was sweating, and he wiped at his forehead with the back of his injured hand. He opened his eyes when he felt something trickle down his wrist again: more blood soaking through the tie. He hoped to Christ it wasn't dripping on the floor. He pulled his jacket off and wrapped it around his hand too. That ought to hold it for a bit.

He steeled himself and looked at Henderson's face. The left eye was dangling from the socket, the impact of the crash popping it loose, the rest of the whole side of Henderson's face just a dark cave, gone to the bone. Mike thought perhaps a splash of fuel had fallen on it. Worst of all was the mouth, which hung open, a dribble of blood and char at the corner, his tongue out and half-chewed. Jesus fucking Christ. Mike hoped the FAA showed up soon so they could find the black box, because if this wasn't an accident, he didn't want to know what had happened. It did not look like Henderson had died peacefully. This was certainly proof that even billionaires couldn't escape death. Taxes, maybe, with the right accountants, but not death.

Weirdly, miraculously, there was an unbroken crystal glass on the floor next to Henderson's chair. Mike picked it up, half wishing there was still booze in it. He took a sniff. Whiskey? He put the glass down on the table in front of Henderson and then looked at his face again. He almost screamed.

It looked like something was moving. No, Mike thought, something really *was* moving. He knew that couldn't be right, but it looked like something was coming out of Henderson's face.

He shined the beam directly on Henderson's ruined head, and then he *did* let out a scream, because something *was* coming out of Henderson's face.

Mike stepped back and stumbled, and without thinking, he reached out with his jacket-wrapped hand to steady himself against the exposed wire frame of what had been a seat. "Fuck!"

That hurt.

"Everything okay in there, Agent Rich?" It was Moreland, the cop in the suit. He shined a light in, and Mike had to squint to look back.

"Yeah, just cut my hand pretty good. I'll be out in a minute."

"Pretty nasty in there."

"No shit," Mike said back, but he'd already turned to look at Henderson's body again, hoping that whatever it was he'd seen coming out of the corpse's face would turn out to have been a trick of the shadows.

It wasn't.

Mike could see it clearly. It was a spider, three-quarters of its hairy, golf-ball-sized body digging itself out from the flesh on the upper part of Henderson's right cheek. Mike's hand was throbbing and it was dripping blood freely now. The only noise in the plane came from Mike's breathing and the spider making its way out of Henderson's face. It sounded like . . . Oh shit. It sounded like chewing. Mike gagged again, and then couldn't stop himself. He rushed back to where he'd entered in the opening of the jet, held on with his good hand, leaned out, and let loose what was left of his lunch. Most of it splashed on the ground, which was good, but some got on his pants, which was still better than puking right in the heart of an investigation. When he straightened up his nose was running and his eyes had teared up. He had to wipe at his face with the sleeve of his shirt. Ugh. He was going to submit his dry-cleaning receipt to the agency as a legitimate business expense. Fuck the director and fuck this, he thought.

"Gross, huh?" Moreland looked pleased with himself.

Mike didn't reply. He walked back down the funnel of the plane and splayed the beam on Henderson's face again, and that's when he wished he hadn't puked already, because right *now* was when he really needed to puke: the spider was gone.

Frantic, he ran the light on the wall and then the ceiling, then across Henderson's face and torso and down the burnt flesh and exposed bones of Henderson's leg. And there. Relief. The spider. On the ground.

It was moving slowly. Mike knew it wasn't the right word for an eight-legged thing, but it looked as if the spider was limping. He squinted and leaned over. There was clearly something wrong with the bug—two of its legs weren't moving and it was dragging its body along the ground. Maybe it had been injured in the crash or gotten burned too? Mike shook his head. Who cared what happened to the spider? The only question that mattered was, how the fuck had it gotten into Henderson's head?

Except, Mike realized, as he watched the spider dragging its body across the floor, the question that was bothering him the most was, why in all of the angels of mercy was the spider coming toward him? Because it was absolutely headed toward him. It wasn't trying to get away or hide or even oblivious of Mike. It wasn't doing any of the things that to Mike, in his limited experience with creepy crawlies, seemed natural. No, it was clearly moving in his direction. Mike tried stepping to the side, and the spider changed its line, angling toward him again. Mike took another step to the side and banged into the table that was next to Henderson's chair, and again, the spider changed its bearing. Mike started to reach for his gun, but he quickly realized that shooting a spider might be overkill. He started to psych himself up to just squash the thing with his foot—it might be big and hairy and incredibly creepy what with the eating its way out of Henderson's face and then making a beeline for Mike, but it was still something he could stomp on—when the spider stopped moving on a dark spot on the floor.

It took Mike a second to understand what the spider was doing. The dark spot on the floor was blood. He looked at the suit jacket wrapped around his hand and saw a drop of blood fall to the floor. He had been bleeding on the floor.

The dark spot on the floor was *his* blood.

And as near as he could tell, the spider appeared to be feeding.

Mike wanted to shriek. It took everything in him not to run screaming, but then he felt the table against the back of his thigh again and he remembered the crystal glass he had picked up off the floor. He put the flashlight between his teeth again, then, trying to be careful but quick, he flipped the glass over and slammed it down on top of the spider. He grabbed the flashlight again and pointed it at the glass. The bug didn't seem to notice at first, but

then, after a few seconds, the thing went absolutely fucking ber-
serk. It flung itself at the sides of the glass, hitting it hard enough
that Mike could hear the ping of its body. He was glad billionaires
had serious, heavy cut-glass crystal on their planes instead of the
flimsy plastic cups he got when he flew coach.

A light hit him in the eyes and he realized it was Moreland
training his flashlight on him. The cop had come into the plane.
"Is that a spider?" he said.

Mike nodded and looked down at the glass. The bug had
stopped thrashing and seemed as though it had gone back to working on the blood. "I don't suppose you've got any big jars lying
around? Something with a metal lid that we can poke holes in?"

Moreland squatted next to the glass and tapped on the top. The
spider started flinging itself against the glass again. Its legs made
a disturbing skittering sound, like leaves blown across pavement,
and when its body hit the glass it made a clear ringing sound that
would have almost been pleasing—like wind chimes—if it weren't
coming from some sort of flesh-and-blood-eating creature that
was a quarter of the size of Mike's fist.

"Yeah," Mike said. "How about you don't do that?"

Moreland stood up and turned to walk out of the plane. "I'll see
what I can find. I bet the EMTs or the firefighters have some sort
of container that would work."

Mike kept his flashlight trained on the glass as the sound of
Moreland's footsteps disappeared. There was something niggling
at him. Something more than just having a spider eat its way out
of Henderson's face, something about the plane. Reluctantly, he
moved the beam of the flashlight off the spider so he could look
around. He splayed the light across the wall and the ceiling, but it
was just scorched metal, melted plastic, marks from the fire. On
the floor, bits of ash stirred whenever the wind cut through the

hole in the plane, but the larger lumps of charred materials stayed settled, held down by weight or simply melted to the floor. He extended his leg and poked at one of the lumps with the toe of his shoe and watched it collapse into a pile of loose ash. Were there more of these spiders around? Maybe they'd burned up in the fire? He took a few steps toward the front of the plane and caught what was left of the flight attendant's body in the beam of the flashlight.

"Oh." He said it aloud, though it was just him in the plane. He leaned over her body to get a closer look at the flesh that was pitted and chunked out. Some of it was just burns, but there, where he'd thought she'd been torn by shards of metal, he was no longer sure. The flesh bulged and looked raw, and suddenly he felt his skin go clammy. Had spiders been eating at her too? He looked out of the rent in the plane and saw Moreland coming back across the field toward him, some sort of jar in his hand.

Mike turned to glance at the crystal glass, suddenly worried that the spider wouldn't be there, but he was relieved to see the creepy thing was still under the dome. "Fuck," he said, and pulled out his phone. He wasn't sure exactly how he was going to explain this to the director, but he was pretty sure flesh-eating spiders didn't fall into the category of "anything other than an accident" that the director had been hoping for. Before he dialed, he looked around. Was there anything else? Was he missing something? This was Bill Henderson, not some anonymous housewife or corporate drone caught up in a drug deal gone poorly. Five minutes from the time the plane went down until the director was calling him as the nearest available agent. This was not something Mike could afford to fuck up, and if it turned out later that, oh, by the way, there had been something really obvious, some clue or thing that he should have seen that was what really caused Henderson's plane to crash, Mike was going to be eating buckets of shit for the rest of his career. So he took another look at the plane, at the burnt and ravaged bodies, at the scattered ash that was starting to blow and lift in the hot breeze. The metal tube was like an oven in the unseasonable spring sun, the sharp edges of the walls and exposed wires a diagram of disaster. At his feet, there was the pinging of the spider again, beating at the glass with its legs or body or whatever the hell those things were called. Mike decided that, no, there was this single crippled spider and nothing else. He wasn't missing anything.

But he was wrong. Near the back of the plane, in the gloom and ash, there was a small stirring.

The Indian Ocean

He slid the two rifles onto the deck of the boat and climbed up the ladder. The .40 cal Smith & Wesson was tucked into his waistband.

"Okay," he said, picking up the rifles and carrying them over to his wife. "They still coming?"

She shook her head. "Something's wrong."

He handed her the .22 caliber rifle. She couldn't handle the Winchester. Maybe a .22 wasn't ideal for stopping power, but he'd made her practice with it until she could put three bullets in an inch circle from fifty feet out. He was hoping it wouldn't come to that, but he didn't have a good feeling. He put the binoculars up to his eyes. Two years of sailing and they'd had only one close call with pirates, off the coast of Africa. They'd been lucky.

Until today.

No question that's what this boat was. You don't see a Zodiac where they were, out in the middle of the ocean, unless it was working from a mother ship. And this was a big one, stripped down for speed, with a bunch of men hunkered down in it. As soon as his wife had glassed the boat with the binoculars and then shown it to him, he'd put out a Mayday and run belowdecks for the rifles and his pistol. He knew how it worked. They both did. It was part of the risk of sailing in certain parts of the world. Help would come. Eventually. Maybe. They were on their own for now, and what people read about every now and then in the news was only part of it. Best-case scenario, they'd end up being held for a ransom that they couldn't afford to pay. Worst-case scenario, he'd end up dead, and his wife . . . Well, that was a thought he would hold on to when his finger was on the trigger and he was trying to figure out if he should fire. But his wife was right: something was off.

When he first saw the Zodiac, the eight or nine men in it had been leaning forward, as if their bodies could make them get to the sailboat more quickly. But now, as the boat cut across the calm water, the men were rising from their seats.

He hadn't even bothered trying to outrun the Zodiac. In the small community of sailors who had cashed in to retire early and spend their time at sea, their boat was neither the most ostentatious nor the most threadbare. In Madagascar they'd made friends with a couple who had been in technology whose boat was almost entirely custom-made, and off the coast of Sri Lanka they'd had dinner aboard a vessel that was so threadbare his foot had gone through a rotten plank on the deck and he'd needed to get ten stitches. Their sailboat was in good shape, but they'd bought it used and hadn't been able to afford to spend much on cosmetics. It was fast, though. Sure, it wasn't a racing boat, but for a cruising sailboat, it could move. Not that it mattered now. With the high buzz of the Zodiac coming at them, he'd known right away he and his wife couldn't outrun the pirates.

It was weird though. The men weren't even looking at them anymore. They were scrambling away from the bow, and one of the men was flailing around. It looked as though he was having a fit and the other men were scared. Wouldn't that be something? If they were saved from pirates because one of them was an epileptic and the rest were superstitious? That would be a funny story, he thought, certainly funnier than he and his wife being kidnapped or killed. Or worse.

He lowered the binoculars and turned to his wife. "Remember what we talked about," he said. "If you've got to shoot, shoot. We're not in Charleston." What he didn't say was that, if it came down to it, the reason he had the pistol was to make sure he had a bullet left for each of them, just in case.

He looked back at the water, and even without the binoculars, he could tell that something really was different about the boat. It had veered off course, no longer headed toward them. Instead of knifing across the water, it was arcing gracefully away from them, a large and gentle circle. And the men inside were . . . Fighting? It almost looked as though they were pulling some sort of a dark cloth from the body of the man who'd been having a fit.

He turned to his wife. She held her rifle tightly. He knew she was scared, and he reached out and cupped his hand around the back of her neck, kissed her, and then put the binoculars back to his eyes.

What the fuck? The boat was headed straight again, toward their sailboat, but there were no men left in the Zodiac. Instead, it was full of some sort of dark liquid. It looked like oil. He watched it for a few more seconds until he was able to understand that it was not a liquid at all, but something that seemed to move of its own accord. He dropped the binoculars and raised his rifle.

He took two shots, aiming for the air tubes, before he realized it was a bad decision. Even the smallest Zodiacs had three air tubes—one on each side and the bottom—and though he didn't know how many a big one like this would have, it was probably more than three. But even if there were only three to hit, the bigger problem was that he'd brought his Winchester Model 70. He loved his Winchester. It was accurate as hell, but it held only five rounds. Hunting deer? Sure. Hunting pirates or trying to sink a Zodiac? Not ideal. An AR-15 with a couple of thirty-round magazines would have been ideal. He could have sprayed the boat, changed the clip, and kept firing until the fucker sank. Instead, he had three shots left.

But he didn't have to sink it. With nobody left to steer, he just had to get it to veer off course, to turn away from them. If he popped an air tube on one side of the Zodiac, that would make it drag and turn. They wouldn't have to outrun the Zodiac, just outmaneuver it. He raised the rifle to his shoulder, looked through the scope then hesitated. The Zodiac was close. Maybe a hundred yards away now. It was headed straight at them, so the speed of the boat shouldn't be a problem with his aim—he'd always been a good shot—but he had doubts about popping the air tube. Maybe it wouldn't just deflate. Maybe it wouldn't drag into the water and turn the Zodiac away from them. Maybe he'd fire his last three bullets and then have to stand and watch the Zodiac crash into them.

The engine. Three shots to stop the engine, and then they could outrun the Zodiac all day. He moved the rifle fractionally, putting the engine housing in the middle of his sights. The boat was moving so goddamned fast, he had only a few seconds. The first shot was wide. He saw the plastic on the housing splinter. The second hit home, however. The buzz of the Zodiac's engine went quiet and he lowered the rifle, one bullet to spare.

His wife came up to his elbow.

"Where are . . . What is that? I don't understand."

The boat continued to glide toward them, the motor dead but its momentum still moving the Zodiac slowly through the water.

The black mound in the boat rising and falling in waves, as if it were an ocean unto itself, but in a different rhythm. Even from where the boat stopped gliding, nearly thirty feet from them, he could hear the sound of whatever it was scraping and clicking on the rubber and wood of the boat.

He turned to his wife. "I need to use the radio."

He turned and went belowdecks. His wife ran after him, peppering him with questions.

Neither of them saw the bloom of silk that started to rise from the mass of spiders, the white threads whispering and twisting in the gentle wind, spiders drifting into the air.

The White House

"**T**wo more to Germany. Wheels down in a couple of hours."
The chairman of the Joint Chiefs of Staff stabbed his thick finger against the map on the touchscreen monitor.

Manny was listening, but he was also looking at the press release one of his aides had prepared for him on the plane crash that had apparently killed Bill Henderson. The director of the agency had a man in place and a team on the way to make sure it wasn't anything other than an accident. Just another headache for Manny. Of course the nuclear explosion was the big news of the day, but the president was going to have to say something about Henderson, and she'd have to go to the funeral. Christ. Minneapolis. This was not what Manny needed. Bill Henderson had been a pushy asshole—which was one of the reasons he'd become a billionaire—but he'd also been an unabashed ally of their party in general and Steph in particular. Even if he hadn't rounded up his richest friends to donate, his own contributions to their campaign coffers had been what put them over the top. It wasn't that easy to replace a billionaire with deep pockets, and while the other guys each had a clown car full of buffoons driving them to the convention, sooner or later one of them would emerge. It was a miracle

121

they hadn't figured it out yet as it was. With the loss of Henderson's money and the fucking Chinese dropping nukes, Manny was suddenly thinking there might be a real race. He knew that's not what he was supposed to be preoccupied with right now. That was the lie of politics: that they were there to serve the common good. But it was a lie Manny believed—or maybe used to believe?—and that Steph believed. This wasn't the time for politics. There was a crisis and a real worry here. Nukes weren't something to be discounted. No. He had to think about the Chinese.

He sighed and watched Ben Broussard finish his presentation.

The chairman of the Joint Chiefs looked at the president and then at the rest of the people in the room. "We'll have them on the ground and operational by eighteen hundred tomorrow, and from there we can have a rapid response here and here as needed," he said, tapping the map again. "Any questions?"

There were none, so Ben took his seat. The president stared at the map for an uncomfortable second and then she turned and said, "Any comments?"

Manny saw that Alexandra Harris, the national security advisor, had slipped into the room sometime in the last couple of minutes, and at the president's question, she didn't hesitate. "It's the wrong reaction."

"You think we're overreacting? To a nuclear bomb?" Ben slammed his hand on the table. He didn't look pissed. He looked furious. For the first time, Manny considered that maybe the problem with Ben was simply that he was one of those old-guard military men who, no matter what he said, couldn't quite stomach the idea of having a woman as the commander in chief. Or, in this case, the national security advisor. Billy Cannon, the secretary of defense, didn't react like that when Alex challenged him, but that's probably because Billy looked at Alexandra Harris and saw the national security advisor, while Ben looked at Alex and saw a woman. The thought made Manny want to chuckle a little, because really, Alex looked like nothing other than a grandmother. She was sharp as hell, but there was always a part of him that expected her to pull some hard candies out of her purse.

Manny picked up his glass of Diet Coke and took a gulp. The burn of the carbonation helped a little, but what he really needed was that sweet surge of caffeine. He let his eyes shift to Steph then back to the group sitting around the conference table. A quick glance was enough for him to see that the president wasn't in a hurry to jump in. She was good that way, willing to let people talk and argue before she stepped in, and usually even then her first forays were to ask questions, so that when she did decide on a course of action she knew what she was talking about.

Alex took a cup of coffee from a staff member's tray with a polite nod and then, without raising her voice, looked directly at Ben and said, "I didn't say we were overreacting by scrambling troops and thinking about deployment. I said it was the *wrong* reaction."

Ben opened his mouth to speak but then stopped. It was actually kind of comical, Manny thought. Ben was not the kind of man to hold himself back or to second-guess, and the sight of him with his mouth hanging open would have been, at another time and under different circumstances, worth laughing at. But it wasn't another time and different circumstances. It was the day after China accidentally dropped a nuclear weapon on one of its own villages. Except the problem was they still weren't entirely sure if China had accidentally dropped the weapon or if they had "accidentally" dropped the weapon.

"That's what I'm trying to say." Alex put her cup down and pulled her tablet out and put it on the table. "I'm sorry for being late, and I'm sure Billy and Ben did an excellent job of explaining the rationale behind deployment decisions, but all those decisions are based on the idea that this nuclear explosion was either just an accident, as the Chinese claim, or part of some sort of wider, deliberate strategy. But the thing is, from the information I have, I'm willing to say it wasn't an accident, and that it wasn't planned either," Alex said. She tapped the tablet twice and brought up a picture. "The important thing is that the information we have leads me to believe that while this wasn't a strategic decision, there was a *reason* the Chinese set off the explosion. They were trying to cover something up. The images we have aren't great, but look here. There just isn't much going on in that part of China on a regular basis, and even though we have satellite coverage, it's limited. Frankly, this part of China isn't considered important, and it hasn't been a real priority with imaging. Tech has enhanced, but there's a limit to the resolution and to how much we can blow things up." She spun the tablet so that it was facing the president. The men— and everybody else in the room other than Steph and Alex was a man—leaned forward so they could see the picture. "Blow things up is maybe the wrong phrase given what happened, but this is from five hours before the nuke."

Manny had seen enough of these sorts of military satellite pictures that even if he didn't know exactly what he was looking at, he could recognize the pattern of cars and trucks in a parking lot, the layout of buildings. He turned to the aide behind him. "Get this up on the big monitor."

The young man nodded, took the tablet, tapped it a few times, and then the image was on the wall.

"Here," Alex said, standing up and tapping against the monitor. "This is the entrance to the main mine. Primarily rare earth metals, the kind of stuff you'll find in your cell phones and your tablets. They do most of the refining on-site, here, in this large complex of buildings." She tapped another spot. "As far as we can tell, all of this over here is just garages, maintenance, that sort of thing. I mean, it looks so damn regular it's almost comical. There are a couple of factories in the village, some chemical processing stuff, but basically, if this mine weren't here, the village wouldn't be here. The mine is the center of things."

Ben Broussard was standing now, leaning over Manny's shoulder and staring at the image on Alex's tablet instead of looking at the monitor on the wall. "Military? You're saying this is a hidden military facility?"

"Not exactly," Alex said. "That's the thing. If it were a standard military, chem, or bio research facility, we would have better pictures. I mean, obviously, it's possible we just whiffed. We all know how much we've struggled with getting agents on the ground in China, particularly in the rural areas, but I don't think that's what we have here. I think it's something small. Maybe biological weapons. Maybe chemical. But almost certainly only a couple of scientists, a few rooms, the sort of thing that could stay hidden because nobody, including the Chinese, think it's important. I mean, this is the ass end of China. The analyst for this region is young, uh," she looked over her shoulder at her aide who said something under his breath, "Terry Zouskis, but she's sharp. She knows what she is talking about, and, well, here's the thing. Something was going on, something that scared the shit out of the Chinese."

"Bioweapons?" Billy looked rattled when he said it, and Manny couldn't blame him. Conventions and treaties be damned, they all knew the Chinese were researching biological agents, and sooner or later there was going to be a breach. The only question was how big a problem it was to cause for the Chinese. And the world. Was it a "drop a nuke on it" kind of problem?

"We don't know what it is yet," Alex said. She walked back to her seat. "As far as we can tell, it looks like a mine and a refinery and maintenance buildings because, well, it *is* a mine and a refinery and maintenance buildings. But there is plenty of space to hide a few offices and a small lab without raising any eyebrows. There's no question there was something going on inside, out of sight of the satellites. If you look here, near the entrance of the mine," she said, and flicked her fingers on the screen, zooming in until they could all see that what had appeared to be simply part of the building was actually a group of figures. Maybe two dozen in all. "Soldiers. Or something to that effect. You can see here and here, automatic weapons, but the thing that made us start thinking this might not be a military or research facility that we'd missed is what the soldiers are doing."

"Their guns." The president sat up and gestured toward the screen.

"Yep," Alex said.

Manny didn't see it. "What about them?"

Steph pointed hard at the screen. "They've got their guns aimed *toward* the building, not away from it. The soldiers aren't trying to keep people out, they're trying to keep people in."

There was a buzz of voices in response to the president, but Manny saw that Alex wasn't trying to speak yet. She was sitting up straight and looking around the room, and as she did so, Manny watched her and saw the way Alex seemed to be counting who was in the room. She was hesitating. Manny looked around the room and tried to figure out who she was seeing that made her not want to speak, and then, after a moment, he realized it wasn't a single person, but the simple fact that there were too many people in the room. She looked at him and raised her eyebrows. Nobody else noticed, but he tilted his head toward the door and Alex nodded.

Okay, Manny thought. She wanted the room cleared. He had to trust her.

He stood up and clapped his hands twice. The room quieted. Steph was looking at him with a smirk, but she'd missed the transaction between him and Alex. She thought he was just trying to quiet the room down.

"Everybody out. Billy, Ben, Alex, you stay; everybody else out." He gave them only half a second to look confused before he yelled it. "Out! Get the fuck out of here!" The aides and staff scrambled, and suddenly it was just the president, the national security advisor, the chairman of the Joint Chiefs of Staff, and the secretary of defense, and all of them were staring at Manny and waiting for him to speak.

Alex looked at him calmly. Even if he didn't actually know the specifics of why he'd done it, why he'd cleared the room, it was what Alex had been waiting for: whatever it was she was about to say, he'd been right that she hadn't wanted to say it to everyone in the room. She turned to address Steph. Manny, just for a moment, thought that Alexandra Harris had arrived a generation too soon; she was somebody who could have held the presidency if she'd been born at the right time.

"Look, I don't have anything here," Manny said, "but Alex clearly does, and she can correct me if I'm wrong, but it is something she didn't want to say in front of a crowd." Everybody turned to look at Alex, and she didn't correct Manny. "You all know me, and you know I don't hold back, and if this was politics or whatever, fine, but the Chinese just dropped a nuclear fucking bomb. This is one of those 'history is going to look back and judge us' kinds of moments, and I, for one, think we better get it right. Or, maybe more importantly, we can't afford to get it wrong. I have no clue what the deal is, but there is clearly something Alex knows that she needs to share with us but doesn't exactly want to say."

Steph cleared her throat. "Just tell me it isn't zombies. Did you catch that asshole on the news saying there was a possibility that the nuke was to cover up a zombie outbreak?" Manny had watched the news with Steph and had actually been kind of amused at the earnestness of the commentators. He'd long ago gotten used to talking heads who made their livings bashing the administration. They were the ones who never seemed to let facts or journalism stand in their way. "I swear to God, if I hear the word 'zombies' out of anyone's mouth, I'm ordering the Secret Service to take you out to the Rose Garden to have you summarily executed." Ben Broussard and Billy Cannon both chuckled, but Alex's expression didn't change.

"Bugs," Alex said. Her voice was soft.

"Pardon me?" the president said, and she wasn't smiling anymore.

"I said bugs. It's not conventional, and we don't think it's chemical weapons. The Chinese used the word *bugs*, or *insects*, and we don't really know exactly what it is, so we've been calling the weapon 'bugs.' A nickname. Because the thing is, you're right about the guns. The soldiers are there to keep everybody inside the building. Zouskis, the analyst, pulled pictures from the satellite for the past six months, and until six days ago, there was nothing of note. Nothing. I mean, zip, zilch, nada. Malls in Lincoln, Nebraska, have more security than this place had. No men with weapons, no soldiers, no security guards. There wasn't even a fence around the mine. This was not a place that had any kind of priority for the Chinese government. There was nothing to protect. And then, six days ago, a couple of army trucks showed up. It's the sort of thing we wouldn't pay any attention to if this part of China hadn't just been turned into a radioactive crater. But we go from nothing to,

six days ago, a fence going up around the town and an entire fucking battalion, six or seven hundred troops, streaming into the area.
Most of the strength focused around the mine and the refinery
area, but it wasn't clear at first they were doing anything other than
guarding it. You know, making sure nobody got in. But there were
also enough troops left to keep an eye on the village as a whole, to
make sure nobody was coming or going except through the main
gate, and even then, as near as Zouskis could tell, it's only troops
coming in. No one leaves. The first picture where we figured out
they are worried about something coming *out* of the mine is this
one," she said, leaning forward and pointing to the photo on the
tablet, "five hours before the nuke."

Billy Cannon leaned back against his chair. He was looking at
Alex, not at the tablet. "Bugs?"

"I'm getting there," Alex said. "So we don't have satellite coverage again for two hours, but what we have next is video. Details
aren't great, but watch."

She closed the picture and opened a video file. There wasn't
any sound except for the five of them breathing. It was the same
buildings and parking lot from the satellite photo, though the
angle was slightly different. "So you'll want to look here," Alex
said, "near the entrance to the mine again. It's grainy, but here,
those pinpricks of light are muzzle flashes. The soldiers are firing
their weapons."

"They're running," Billy said. "They're running away."

"You can't really see much with all those shadows," Steph said.

Alex touched the screen and paused the video. "Madam President, those aren't shadows."

Steph went pale. She stood up and pointed at the frozen image.
"Right there. Not all of it, but the shadows covering where the
soldiers ran."

Manny felt his stomach hollowing. He was pretty sure he didn't understand everything, but this did not seem good. Alex, who tended to keep a neutral facade, never too hot or too cold, looked exceedingly grim. He stared at the stopped video, but all he was seeing were shadows.

Alex dragged the slider backward and Manny realized the shadows retreated with the video. "Those aren't shadows," Alex said again. "Watch here, where these two soldiers stop firing and start to run. See how they're in the lit area?" She hit the play button and the group watched the two figures move away from the building. A finger of shadow moved with them and then overtook them. The soldiers didn't emerge from the darkness.

"Bugs?" the president said, looking at Alex.

"Are you fucking kidding me?" Manny blurted out.

Alex sighed. "You can see why I was hesitant to say anything when there were more people in the room."

"Come on, Alex," Ben said. "How are you making the leap from this to bugs?"

"That's the word they're using. We ran it past three translators and they all agreed on some variant of *insects*. There isn't much." She pulled a sheet of paper from her bag. "Here. We caught 'No longer contained. The insects are,' and then it's cut off by static, and then we get another chunk that says, 'not stopping the insects,' before we lose it altogether." Alex put the paper on the table but nobody made any motion to pick it up. "I haven't lost my mind. I'm not trying to argue that we are faced with some sort of plague of flesh-eating locusts. I don't know what it is. Bio? Maybe nano? Whatever it is, it has some characteristic that is making the Chinese compare the weapon to insects. And whatever it is, it got out of hand. At this point, I'm pretty sure the Chinese nuked themselves to keep it under control."

Steph took a deep breath. "You're telling me you think China dropped a nuke on itself, on purpose, because of some shadows and because you picked up the mention of 'insects' a few times? Seems a little out on a limb. Are you sure about this?"

"No," Alex said. "And you should have seen Zouskis when she was telling me her conclusions. She might be smart, but she's still green enough that she was stuck on the ass end of a region in China. The sort of place she could learn the ropes without having to worry about dealing with anything of importance."

"Like China setting off a nuclear explosion," Manny said.

Alex nodded. "Like that. But the thing that really spooked her and made her stick to her guns even though her supervisor clearly thought she was killing her career, was the Internet."

Stephanie sighed. "I know I said I'd have anybody who said 'zombies' taken out to the Rose Garden and shot, but if this is some sort of crazy Internet conspiracy theory, if you tell me the message boards are full of chatter about bugs, I'll have you shot for that too."

Alex smiled, but everybody in the room knew she wasn't the type to screw around. "That's the thing, Madam President. There's nothing on the Internet."

Billy leaned his head back. "Oh, for fuck's sake, Alex, just spit it out."

"The Chinese government shut down the Internet for the province three days before the attack. Three days. All access to the Internet. Cell phone towers and all landlines too. Everything. Not just in the village. The entire province. I mean, if you could use it to spread information, it was shut off. They did a good job of it too—such a good job that we didn't even figure out everything was shut down until Zouskis went back to see if she could find any sort of chatter leading up to the explosion. I mean, an entire province?

All the communication shut down for three days? That would be like us shutting down phone and cell towers and Internet for Idaho, Montana, and Wyoming. Can you imagine doing that? Based on that alone, even if the Chinese hadn't set off a nuke, I'd expect a serious listen no matter whether the conclusion was insects or bugs or," she glanced at Manny and had the balls to wink, "zombies."

The president didn't rise to the bait. She leaned forward and pressed the play button on Alex's tablet. "So," the president said. "Bugs." They watched the pinpricks of light and the soldiers running from the shadows and then disappearing in the darkness. "What does that mean? Bugs? Insects? I mean, not like smallpox or other viruses you can't see, but what does it mean that they were calling the weapon, if that's what it was, insects?"

"We don't know," Alex said, "and I'm not trying to argue some sort of horror-movie answer. I think we can rule out blood-hungry cockroaches, but whatever was going on over there, it spooked the Chinese enough to drop a thirty-megaton nuke."

The president rubbed her eyes and then let her head hang. "Bugs?"

"Bugs," Alex said.

"Honestly," Ben said, standing up, "this seems kind of crazy. We should be focusing on the Chinese government and figuring out if this really was an accident, or if it was some sort of rogue thing. Or, and this would explain why they keep stonewalling us on information, the other plausible scenario, which both Billy and I believe, that this is a move toward something bigger."

Alex leaned back in her chair, and Manny realized she looked tired. Had she been up all night with her analysts? He hadn't gotten much sleep either. Part of the job, but even more so when there was the chance of nuclear Armageddon. Which he understood. Nuclear war was one of those remote possibilities you had to consider when you were the White House chief of staff and the president's closest friend and advisor, but he was having trouble coming to terms with the idea of Chinese military insects. Apparently, so was Alex, because she shook her head.

"I know, Ben." She looked at the president. "I know it sounds crazy, but Zouskis makes a really good case here. Our first impulse was the same as yours, but it doesn't add up. There has been no amassing of troops, no inflamed rhetoric, nothing to signal a political move or a territorial expansion, even when we look at it in retrospect. Things have been pretty good with China. So we looked at other avenues, all the things that come easily to mind like some sort of civil protest that got out of hand, but that's not the kind of thing that the Chinese would drop a nuke over, and unrest of the scale requiring nuclear pacification isn't really the sort of thing they could keep entirely quiet. We would have heard rumblings."

Alex sighed. "I suppose it's possible there was a full-scale secret military facility on the site and we just missed it, and it was a rogue faction of the army that had to be pacified with a nuke, but if that was the case, then we need to give the Chinese a hell of a lot more credit in their ability to hide themselves. No. As much as it sounds like a bit of a stretch, I think the most likely explanation is that there was some sort of a small lab. Really small. Just a scientist or two tinkering around. Off the reservation. I don't mean a lab that is completely off-the-books, but a lab that just wasn't considered important enough to be kept on a military facility site. Small-scale. A sort of boutique kind of shop with a mad scientist. Small enough that they weren't prepared for the kind of success they had in coming up with a new weapon. The kind of lab where they threw a couple hundred thousand dollars at the scientists and sent them off to go fail in peace. We do the same thing here. Do you know how many crazy, speculative projects we fund, both on and off the books? Nano parasites and sonic lasers and death rays and all that sort of crap? Look, I'd be really happy to come in here and say our information points to it being an accident or that the Chinese dropped a nuke out of political motivation, but that's not what we're seeing." She paused and looked at each of them.

And then she said, "I think it's something worse. I think it's worse than whatever we are actually thinking right now."

Alex stood up and pinched the touch screen, pulling back to a map that showed the entire province. "We aren't seeing soldiers fighting soldiers on the ground, and we aren't seeing the kind of troop movement that would indicate outward expansion. Maybe it's the use of the word *bugs* that's throwing you here, but when I say 'bugs' think of it as just a nickname for something. Our best bet—with what little intelligence we have right now—is pointing toward some sort of bioweapon that they lost control of. Right now, whatever it is, it's something we don't understand, and that something scared the shit out of them. It scared them enough that when trying to contain it they failed, and they were willing to drop a thirty-megaton nuke in order to clean up the mess they made. Whatever it is, I don't think we're looking down the barrel of a conventional ground war. I mean, Madam President, what would scare you badly enough that you'd be willing to nuke one of our own cities?"

"Okay." The president stood up and walked over to the monitor showing the map. "Bugs. A bioweapon. Whatever. The point is that our analyst . . . ?"

"Zouskis."

"Zouskis has given us information that shows something was going on. So can we agree, at this point, that we are ruling out the Chinese explanation, that it was simply an accident?"

"Maybe that's for the best," Manny said. "On some level the

idea that the Chinese just accidentally turned part of their country into a glowing wasteland is actually more disturbing than the idea that they did it on purpose."

The president nodded. "Okay. So we're already in the process of deploying troops outside the country based on the idea of containment if the Chinese are planning to use the explosion as a gambit to make a move for territory," she said. "But what if Alex is right? Because I have to be honest, as crazy as it sounds, and as much as there is no fucking way we can whisper a word of this to the press—can you imagine the civil unrest if word leaked that there was some sort of Chinese bioweapon experiment gone wrong that required a nuke to contain it?—I think there is a compelling argument here that this might have been pure panic on the part of the Chinese. So the real question is, what do we do?"

"Madam President," Ben said. He smoothed the folds in his uniform with his palm. "With all due respect to Alex and her little analyst, this is ridiculous. Two sentences that use the word *insects*, a couple of grainy photos, and a few seconds of jerky video? Based on that, we're going to assume there is some sort of new, virulent superweapon out there?"

Manny watched Steph stare at Ben. That was one of the things he liked about her. She wasn't afraid to make everybody wait on her if she needed to think about something. She looked away from Ben to the map that showed troop deployments and then back at Ben.

"Get them back," she said.

"Ma'am?" Ben looked confused.

"Get them back," Steph said. "All the troops we started shifting outside the country. Boots back on the ground."

Billy, who had been quiet for most of the past ten minutes, perked up. "You want us to pull all the troops who are OCONUS back home?"

"Not all of them," the president said. "Just the ones we sent in reaction to the nuke. And I want it done now. Immediately."

Manny saw Ben roll his eyes and struggle to keep from yelling. Ben looked like a teenager on the verge of throwing a temper tantrum because he had been told he couldn't get a new cell phone. The chairman of the Joint Chiefs firmly believed the only appropriate response was to keep the Chinese in line with a show of troop strength, and he'd spent most of the last twenty-four hours trying to make sure it happened. Interestingly, Billy didn't look too put out. The secretary of defense merely seemed curious.

"Madam President?" Billy said. "Let's say that we're wrong about the Chinese trying to expand their territory, and that Alex is right that they dropped the nuke to contain some sort of biological weapon. Okay? Alex is right. So why the hurry? Maybe Alex is right, maybe Alex is wrong, but either way, it won't hurt to let the deployment play out and then reel everybody back in with a little patience. If Alex is wrong, the smart play is to have our troops deployed, and if Alex is right, then we can order everybody back and start dealing with the shifting realities on the ground."

Manny sat up straight. He couldn't stop himself from blurting it out. "The flu."

Billy stared at him. "Pardon me?"

"The flu," Manny said. "If it is a bioweapon, maybe it's not contained by the blast. We act like it's a flu pandemic. The big one."

"Ding." Steph had a grim smile. "Three points for Manny. How quick can we get moving on this? Quarantine zones and soldiers in place? I don't want anything rolled out yet, but I want everything ready to move."

There was a moment of quiet in the room. Despite everything, Manny's first thought concerned the political ramifications. "This is going to be a disaster. You might get a brief bounce in the spirit of patriotism, but if we have to deploy troops at home, you are going to get killed in the polling."

Steph actually smiled at him. "Not my biggest worry right now, Manny. I think this might be the time where we have to ask if we care about doing what is right or if everything is about getting the political win."

"The latter. It's always about the political win," Manny said, but only because he knew Steph expected it of him. Despite her laugh, she looked as though she was feeling the weight of the presidency. He couldn't stop himself from worrying about the political ramifications, but if it was some sort of virus that had run amok to the point where the Chinese were willing to go nuclear, the *political* fallout—he almost laughed at the thought of fallout—of having to enforce quarantines and of billeting troops in the cities was going to be less of an issue in the next election than the problem of thousands, or maybe hundreds of thousands, of dead Americans. Fucking Chinese and fucking bioweapons. There was a part of him that longed for the good old-fashioned wars where men dug trenches and died in the conventional manner.

Still, the president and the others laughed at Manny's predictable reply. He started to speak again, but there was a knock on the door followed by the entrance of the president's personal secretary. "Excuse me, Madam President," she said. "I'm sorry for interrupting, but he's absolutely insisting."

"Who?"

"The director of the agency. He says he has to talk to you about Bill Henderson."

Manny couldn't see it, but he knew Steph was rolling her eyes. She certainly appreciated the fund-raising work Henderson had done on her behalf, but the truth of the matter was that the news of his plane crash was just swallowed up by the apparent willingness of the Chinese to break out the nukes. They'd release the statement, and at some point she'd answer questions about the crash, and she'd go to Minneapolis for his funeral, but with the Chinese thing, Henderson's funeral just wasn't the most important thing going on. He was about to tell the president's secretary that Steph would call back, but the president spoke first.

"What about Henderson?"

When the secretary hesitated, Manny got a bad feeling.

The secretary wasn't the sort of woman who hesitated.

"The director," she said, "insists that he has to talk to you." She paused as if picking her words very carefully. "He says that Mr. Henderson may have been eaten by spiders."

At that, the president's head lifted up and Steph stared at the secretary. Manny realized they were all staring at the secretary.

"Spiders?" Manny heard his own voice but wasn't actually convinced he was the one asking. "Spiders. As in, you know, bugs?"

"Spiders," the secretary confirmed. "The director seems quite . . . rattled."

The president stood up and pointed at Ben and then Billy. "Not just the ones we sent in response. Every fucking man and woman in the forces that we can pull. All of them. Boots back on the ground here at home. Ben, how quickly can we get ready to respond to this?"

"We've got the plans in place and everything is stockpiled, so probably twenty-four hours if we put a hellfire to it."

"Light the match," Steph said, "but don't put it to the wick yet. I don't want a single soldier outside the grounds of a single base, but I want trucks ready to roll."

"Steph," Manny said. "Madam President, I think . . ." He trailed off. He didn't know what he thought.

Steph walked to the end of the table that held a phone. "You think I'm overreacting, and you're probably right, but we know the Chinese nuked their own territory to keep something in check, something they are calling bugs, and now we've got a billionaire who crash-landed in Minneapolis and was eaten by spiders. I'm not exactly Mrs. Conspiracy Theory, but we better act on this. Worst case, what? We call it a training exercise?"

"A training exercise," Alex said. "We say we've had the plans in place for a year, but we didn't alert anybody because we wanted to really give it a test. That's the story we spin if we're overreacting."

"Okay," Manny said. "I don't like it, but I can live with it."

Billy raised his hand. Manny almost laughed. The man actually raised his hand.

"What?" Stephanie snapped.

"What if we aren't overreacting?" he said. "Near as we can tell, this started, what, six days ago? Six days from the start to China dropping a nuke? What if we're already moving too slowly?"

Stephanie looked at the secretary. "Put the director through," she said, and then she turned back to Billy. "If we aren't overreacting, then God help us all." She picked up the phone, but then paused and pressed it to her chest. "And Manny," she said, turning to look at him, "call your ex-wife. I've got some questions about spiders."

American University, Washington, DC

"**P**rofessor Guyer?"

Melanie snapped her head up from the desk. "I'm awake. I'm awake," she said. Her cheek and the side of her mouth were damp, and she wiped the drool off her face. Jesus. How long had she been asleep? As she turned to look at Bark, she could feel a sharp pain in her lower back. She had a couch in her office for this very reason, so she could sleep at her lab when she wanted, and yet she'd still fallen asleep at her desk. She glanced at her watch. Nearly four in the afternoon.

"Professor Guyer?" Bark said again, her name still a question.

She looked at him and then past him, to see that neither Julie nor Patrick was drafting behind him, and then she said, "How many times, Bark?"

"I'm sorry? How many times what, Professor Guyer?"

"How many times have I had your dick in my mouth? And you're still calling me Professor Guyer?"

Bark blushed, which, Melanie hated to admit, was kind of cute. He was really, really good in bed, though he seemed oblivious to it, always asking her if things were okay or if that was what she

141

wanted, and that was part of his charm. Of course, that same clue-lessness was what made her want to brain him with her desk lamp.

"You know it makes me uncomfortable when you speak like that," he said. He looked over his shoulder to make sure none of his colleagues had heard Melanie's remark, and then he shut the door behind him and came around her desk. He sat on the desk and put his hand on her shoulder. He'd been in the lab all night, as she had, but he still smelled good. A mix of soap and some-thing a little stronger. His hand was big and heavy, and despite herself, she could feel herself starting to sink into its weight. She turned her head and, very lightly, sunk her teeth into the edge of his palm.

She released his palm. "But my saying I had your dick in my mouth doesn't make you so uncomfortable that you'd stop me from doing it," Melanie said. "Spare me the old-fashioned 'deli-cate flower' bullshit, okay?" She yawned and stretched. There was something seriously tight in her back, and she really wanted to just put her head back down on the desk and close her eyes again. She felt as if she could sleep for days. She'd been dreaming about spiders—she always dreamed about spiders—and there was a nest of cobwebs in her head.

"It's time, Professor Guyer," Bark said. "It's happening."

That cleared away the cobwebs. There weren't that many eu-reka moments in science. Mostly it was just hard work, data col-lection, the slow and steady roll of progress. And she loved it. She genuinely liked spending time in the lab, in observation and no-tation. Back in high school she was the only kid who thought ti-tration exercises were interesting, and then as an undergrad and a grad student, even when she was bored by the grind, she'd been able to maintain her concentration. She was brilliant, there was no disputing that, but there had been a couple of other students in her graduate program who were equally brilliant. The difference was that they didn't carry the same level of discipline she did. She'd become famous in her field because she was able to make the logical leaps that pushed the science forward, but she knew that at the core, she'd been successful because she was a grinder. She didn't just come up with ideas; she was able to prove her theories through methodical research.

But no matter how much she was willing to grind, no matter how disciplined she was, there was nothing, absolutely nothing that compared with the excitement of a breakthrough. And if she was being honest, it had been a while since she'd done anything exciting in the lab.

Yes, discovering the medical use of venom from the *Heteropoda venatoria* two years ago had been a great follow-up to the work that had made her what passes for famous in the world of entomology in the first place, but as much as she was still fond of the huntsman spider, she felt as though she'd finished that avenue of research. It was time for something new.

Despite her annoyance at her graduate students yesterday when they'd ambushed her outside the classroom and reminded her of her drunken rambling about Peru and the Nazca Lines, she'd clearly been onto something. To say what was happening with the egg sac was interesting was an understatement. This was potentially one of those scientific moments that could define a career. There was an evolutionary ecologist in Oklahoma who'd started trying to resurrect dormant eggs back in the 1990s, and he'd had early success with eggs that were decades old. By the early 2000s, however, he was hatching eggs a hundred years old, and by 2010 he managed to get eggs more than seven hundred years old to hatch. Okay, admittedly, from what she remembered about the article, he'd been working with water fleas, which were quite a bit simpler than spiders, but still. The idea wasn't completely insane. So if it was interesting enough just to have found a calcified ten-thousand-year-old egg sac at the Nazca site, to have it hatch was at another level all together.

This could be huge. The cover of *Science* or *Nature* huge.

She gave her face a wash in the lab sink. She could have taken a quick shower in her private bathroom in her office—that bathroom, in and of itself, was reason enough to come to American University, forget the fact that she needed to get to DC for Manny or that American University made her the best offer—but if it was time, she didn't want to miss anything.

The three graduate students were huddled along the back wall of the lab. The insectarium was next to a cage containing a rat that Patrick had nicknamed "Humpy," for the cancerous growths on its back. On the other side of the insectarium, one of the students' laptops was playing a live stream of the news, the words a low mumble washing over them. Julie was bent over and writing something down in her notebook.

"All right," Melanie said. "What's new?" She reached over and snapped the lid of the laptop shut. She didn't need her lab to be silent, but she wasn't a big fan of background noise.

All three students stood up and looked at the laptop, making an array of distressed sounds. "We're kind of just keeping that going to listen to the news because of the nuclear explosion," Patrick said.

For a second, Melanie thought she had misheard him, but then she realized that no, Patrick had indeed said the phrase *nuclear explosion*. And yet, their reaction seemed more in tune with Melanie's having shut the laptop during the halftime show at the Super Bowl; it was something they wanted on in the background, but not their primary concern. None of the three looked particularly frazzled. No more frazzled than graduate students normally did, particularly after spending a night in the lab. There was nothing to indicate nuclear Armageddon. Patrick had some sort of smear on the corner of his lip, maybe chocolate, and Julie's hair was looking like it could use a good round of conditioning, but none of them seemed ready to set out for the hills, and as far as she could tell, none of them had been crying. Still, Patrick really had said that they were keeping the laptop open because of a nuclear explosion. She let her fingers fall back on the lid of the laptop and played them over the notch that opened it. "Uh, anybody care to fill me in? What the hell is going on? Exactly how long was I asleep?"

"We've been keeping the temperature steady and had video on the egg sac at HD resolution, and really there wasn't much of anything—"

"No," Melanie said, cutting Bark off. "Holy biscuits on a fucking stick. Are you serious? Not the spider. A nuclear explosion?"

"Oh, it's not really that big a deal," Patrick said. "It happened last night, but we just found out about it a little while ago. I mean, I guess it was a big deal, because it was a nuke, but it was an accident. It was a large nuke, but it wasn't a super-populated area. At least that's what the news is saying. It's not like it's the end of the world or anything."

"It happened in China," Julie added helpfully.

"Like a meltdown?" Melanie didn't open the laptop. Their blasé response to this nuclear thing had already turned her away from it and toward thinking about the egg sac. The way the three students were standing made it difficult for her to fully see the insectarium, but a piece of the egg sac was in her vision, and she could see it was moving. No. Vibrating, really.

She walked to the other side of the students and slid the cage containing the rat, Humpy, down the counter a bit so that she could have a clearer view of the egg sac.

"Oh, no," Patrick said. "Not a meltdown. An actual nuclear bomb. Or a missile. I'm not actually sure which. But either way, it was an accident. Maybe a training mission or a crash or something?" He looked at Bark. "Were you listening?"

Bark shrugged. "I mostly tuned it out after the president made her comments." He lightly touched the glass of the insectarium with the tip of his middle finger. "This thing has been really interesting. It's humming," Bark said.

That was enough for Melanie to take her hand off the laptop and turn fully to look at the egg sac. It was big. That had been the first thing that struck her the day before. Just how big it was. There was no question it was an egg sac, but she'd never seen one that size before. Bigger than a softball. The size of a small melon. And it was hard. Calcified. Or something else. She wasn't sure what had happened to it, and that was one of the things they were going to have to figure out once the spiders shucked their shell and they could analyze some of the pieces. It didn't have any give to it, and the feel of it was almost chalky. She realized what it reminded her of: those hard, sour, knobby candy balls she used to get from the quarter machines at the mall when she was just a kid. It looked chalky too, and they noticed the egg sac left a gritty white powder behind, something that looked like baking soda but was textured and grainy, like sand, when she rubbed it between her thumb and fingers.

It was, as Bark so unpoetically put it, really interesting.

Melanie realized Bark was right about the humming. Or, not humming exactly, but something like that. Maybe buzzing? Whatever it was, it wasn't steady. It seemed to be cycling, low and strong and then moving into a higher pitch but fading, and the vibrating of the sac seemed to alternate with it. She reached through the open lid and put her hand over the sac, and at her first touch she almost snatched it back. "It's hot." She looked up at Julie.

"Yeah, the temperature has been going up consistently. I didn't even notice at first. We tracked it," Julie said, nodding at the screen on the other laptop on the bench behind her, "but it wasn't super obvious initially. It was so gradual that at first I didn't really register that I was adding a degree, adding a degree. If you look at the data, there's clearly a pattern."

Melanie let her fingers wrap over the top of it, palming the egg sac just as she used to wish she could palm the ball back when she was in college and still thought there was a chance in hell she could dunk a basketball someday. Maybe if the hoops had been at nine feet instead of ten. And if she'd been able to go off a trampoline. Six feet was tall for a woman, but she'd never had great hops.

She realized that was what the egg sac felt like to her. Even with the small protrusions, the little knobs, it felt like a basketball. It was smaller, of course, small enough that it nestled in her hand. She wouldn't have used the words *sticky* or *tacky*, as she might with the kind of basketballs she preferred, but there was something to it that kept it from feeling slick. She could imagine that before it became calcified it had been woven against a wall or inside a crevice somewhere, the silk spun into a cradle to hold the bundle of spiders waiting to be born. And it was hot. Not so hot that she had to take her hand off it, but warm, like a loaf of bread fresh out of the oven.

It was amazing to think the egg sac was ten thousand years old, that it had been buried for so long. And that it was part of a Nazca Line. That giant spider was like a message just for her, a sign for Melanie to pay attention. Yes, she'd write articles about it—this egg sac's resurrection and what might be inside was the sort of thing she could run with—but more than anything, it reminded her of the fun her job as a scientist was, and of how truly amazing the world could be.

The egg sac gave a jerk under her hand. They were waiting to come out. How long had those eggs been in there? How long had they been waiting to hatch? And what was that sound? Something rising above the hum of the egg sac, a sharp tone. The tone was mechanical, it sounded like . . .

Oh. Melanie took her hand out of the insectarium and stood up straight. It was her cell phone.

She fished it out of the pocket of her lab coat. Manny. She thought about answering it, about talking to her ex-husband, and then she dug her thumbnail into the mute button and put the vibrating phone back in her pocket.

Bark was leaning down now, bent over almost comically, his chin pressed against the table so that he had an eye-level view of the sac. His mouth was open a little. "Yeah," he said. "Here we go."

"Where?"

"Here," Bark said, and he motioned for Melanie to bend over. As she did, Julie and Patrick crowded in. "There, on the bottom. See the seam?"

Melanie didn't at first, but then the egg sac gave another shake and she saw that what she had taken to be a difference in color was actually a crack, the beginning of an opening. She swung into action.

They double-checked that the video was recording, that the temperature streams were flowing through the computers. She sent Patrick running for the still camera and even took a few pictures herself to make sure they had enough light. In the few minutes that took them, the seam in the egg sac had already started to widen. Melanie was ready for it. Patrick was standing, but she and Bark and Julie were perched on stools, and Melanie had her hand resting on the top edge of the insectarium. It was still open, and she slid the lid closed, latching it shut from force of habit.

The egg sac went still, and Melanie realized she was holding her breath. All of them were so quiet Melanie could hear the ticking of the second hand on her watch. She wrapped her fingers around her wrist; the watch had been a birthday gift from Manny, the second or third year of their marriage, when things were still good. They waited. And waited. She unwrapped her fingers and looked at her watch. Thirty seconds. Forty-five. The egg sac was still. The humming sound had died down. One minute. One thirty.

Melanie felt the phone in her pocket buzzing again. She ignored it.

One forty-five.

Nothing.

Two minutes.

Julie cleared her throat.

Two fifteen.

"Maybe," Patrick said quietly, but he didn't say anything else.

Two minutes thirty seconds.

Three minutes.

Melanie shifted, and was about to look at her watch again when there was movement.

The egg sac pulsed. It pushed outward. The small, open seam puckered. There was something behind it. And there, on the top, to Melanie's right, a pinprick in the shell. The pinprick turned into a crack, zippering down the side and meeting the open seam. The egg sac pulsed again, the hum suddenly returning, a car engine idling in a closed garage. The egg sac jerked to the left, tilting, and then again.

"Jesus," Bark said. "They aren't coming out easily."

"Since the egg sac has calcified, it might be tougher than it usually is for them?" Julie had the camera to her eye, and the sound of the shutter opening and closing came to Melanie above the hum of the egg sac. She had to restrain herself from telling Julie to wait to take pictures until there was something worth taking pictures of. They could always delete any photos they didn't need, but better to have too many than too few. "I mean, I know it's scientifically possible, but I can't really believe it's hatching at all," Julie added.

The egg sac went still again for a few seconds, but the humming, if anything, got louder. And then, suddenly, it was both still and quiet.

Melanie's phone vibrated again. She ignored it. Goddamned Manny.

They were all quiet for a few seconds more, and then Melanie said, more to herself than to the room, "What the fuck?"

As if those were the magic words, the egg sac seemed to explode. Later, with the video slowed down, Melanie saw the way in which the spiders broke the sac open at its weak points, using the open seams for leverage, but in the moment, an explosion was the only word to describe their birth. One moment the egg sac was mostly intact, quiet and still in front of her, and the next moment spiders banged against the glass walls of the insectarium, scuttled across its floor and the underside of the lid, legs tapping against the glass and plastic, the sound like grains of rice spilling on the floor.

Patrick shrieked, high-pitched, like a child. Julie scrambled backward. Even Bark jumped.

But Melanie found herself drawn forward. She didn't know how many of them there were, but they were frantic. Dozens of them at least. They'd been packed in the egg sac, and they came out in a swarm, their bodies unfolding, alien and beautiful. Big and fast, black apricots thundering against the glass. Skittering. She put her palm against the glass of the insectarium, and the spiders flew to it. It was like the plasma ball she'd had as a kid, one of those globes with an electrical charge in the middle. She remembered the way she'd put her hand on the glass and the filaments of plasma would be drawn to her flesh. She could never feel the current, but she knew it was there. In the same way, the spiders flocked to where her hand pressed against the insectarium. Even though she couldn't possibly be feeling them through the glass, the vibrations went through her flesh anyway.

She pulled her hand back.

"Holy shit." Bark leaned forward and pointed to the corner. "They're eating that one."

Julie trained the lens toward the small group of spiders—three or four, though it was hard to tell given the way they crawled over one another—that were tearing into one of their brethren.

"Whoa! Do you see this?" Patrick pointed to the other side of the insectarium. A large group of the spiders—maybe half the number in the container—had gone to the other side. Some of them just seemed to be pushing against the glass, but several were actively throwing their exoskeletons against the glass. They wanted out.

"What the fuck?" Melanie stood straight up. "Are they trying . . . ?"

All four of them looked at the cage on that side of the insectarium. Inside, Humpy, Patrick's favorite lab rat, was oblivious to the arachnid swarm banging against the glass of the insectarium, desperately trying to get at his small body.

Metro Bhawan, Delhi, India

D r. Basu was not pleased. She did not like Delhi. And Faiz was exhausting her. Normally she found him mostly amusing, but he'd spent the entire drive from Kanpur to Delhi—which should have taken six hours, but instead had taken thirteen—in a state of despair. She'd already been dreading the drive with him because she knew he would be texting or e-mailing Ines constantly, and when he wasn't talking *to* Ines, Dr. Basu assumed he'd be talking *about* Ines. But literally five minutes into the trip, his Italian girlfriend had texted and informed him that she was now his Italian *ex*-girlfriend. Their relationship had moved too quickly, Ines wrote, and she was calling things off. Dr. Basu had a fleeting moment of relief—which made her feel immensely guilty—at the idea that she and Faiz could now talk about seismology instead of Ines, but of course, Faiz was distraught. Which was the lesser of those two evils, she thought, having to endure Faiz's misery or his ecstasy? The longer the drive took, however, the angrier she became at Ines. She hadn't even met this woman, but there was a part of her that wanted to fly to Italy just to give Ines a piece of her mind. How dare she break up with him by text? And worse, after an hour or so of Ines and Faiz texting back and forth, Ines dropped the bombshell: the real reason for the breakup was that she'd finally had a chance to read some of his work and she couldn't be with a man if she didn't "respect" his research. Saying she didn't respect Faiz's research was as good as saying she didn't respect Dr. Basu's research either.

Thirteen hours in that car, and most of that time spent reassuring Faiz that he was smart, which was true, and an excellent worker, which was mostly true, even if he occasionally—okay, often, well, always—made inappropriate comments, and that he deserved to be treated better. By the time they arrived, she had a throbbing headache. No surprise, then, that she was beyond annoyed that she could still not figure out what the hell was causing the odd seismic readings.

Faiz waved her over to where he was. He still looked miserable, but he was doing his best, holding his tablet and phone and talking with a man wearing a suit and tie. When she got closer, she saw that the man had a Delhi Metro Rail Corporation ID badge clipped to his jacket. He held up one hand.

"I'm sorry, but I'm not authorized to let you go any farther."

Dr. Basu pointed to the man's ID badge. "Are you not the supervisor?"

"I am, but—"

"There are no 'buts' to this. One of our sensors is below. We need to see it."

The man shook his head. "Yes, your assistant already told me that." Dr. Basu did not bother to correct the man about Faiz's status. "And you had a man go down yesterday. It's disruptive."

Dr. Basu stared at him and didn't say anything for a few seconds. She'd found that this tactic made men, in particular, uncomfortable. Sure enough, he started to fidget, and Dr. Basu decided to speak. "Is not the whole point of your having an earthquake warning system so that you can be warned if there are earthquakes? And is it not correct that you would like this system to be working properly?"

"That's correct, but—"

She cut him off again. She took great pleasure in doing that to men like this who didn't want to take her seriously. "Then we need to get down to the sensor to see if we can understand why we are getting these readings." Dr. Basu brushed past him. The man started to speak but then decided to just keep pace with her. She smiled to herself.

She was sweating too much to be comfortable, and they might not get an answer, but at least this area seemed to be where the activity was the highest. She pulled a tissue from her purse and wiped her forehead. She stopped in front of a large iron door.

"Open it," she said.

The man hesitated. "I can open this one, but I don't have the codes for the next two."

"But you brought our associate down there yesterday."

"Yes. Well, no, not exactly. Not me personally. I *am* the supervisor, after all. I sent one of the maintenance men down with your man."

Faiz leaned against the wall. "What's with all the doors?"

The man punched a series of numbers into the electronic keypad. "Water protection. For flooding. The doors are watertight, and they are set up in a series like on a boat or submarine. If one is breached, the next is designed to hold everything out. And if we know the water is coming, we can shut everything down, close the doors, and wait. Once the worst is over, we pump it out and are back up and running in just a few days. You only open one at a time, pass through, close it behind you, and then open the next. Like an air lock."

He opened the door and ushered them through. He had to push hard to get the door to open. It was maintained well, but the tolerances had to be tight, Dr. Basu thought, if they were meant to hold out water. The man closed the door behind them. The bolts shot home with a loud clank. The light in the hallway was fluorescent and shaky. Dr. Basu pulled a bottle of water from her purse. She unscrewed the cap and was about to take a sip when the ground shook and she stumbled a little. She spilled water on her blouse.

"Did you . . . ?" Faiz let his voice trail off.

"Yes," Dr. Basu said. "That was a big one." Ahead of them was another door that looked exactly like the one behind them.

She looked at the Delhi Metro man. "Get the codes. We're going to need to open all the doors."

Stornoway, Isle of Lewis, Outer Hebrides, Scotland

The plane was late. It was bad enough that Aonghas Càidh saw his girlfriend only every two weeks, but usually he was the one flying to her. Somehow it felt harder to have to wait for her plane from Edinburgh than it did to wait when his own plane was delayed.

It could have been worse, he supposed. He wasn't even sure how he'd managed to end up dating somebody like Thuy in the first place. He wasn't a bad bloke. He was smart enough to make a decent living—he'd taken over the writing of his grandfather's potboiler detective novels, a very successful series that had been in print for more than fifty years and seemed like it still had steam as long as Aonghas didn't make a bollocks of it—and he was generally considered good company. He was funny and had a lot of stories to tell, most of them involving being raised by his grandfather in the old castle on Càidh Island, their family castle and family island with their family name, an otherwise unpopulated rock in Loch Ròg, on the west side of the isle in the remote Outer Hebrides. His stories of being six and motoring from Càidh Island across storm-whipped waters so he could get to the Carloway Primary School—he was one of fewer than forty students on the rolls—or the time his grandfather knocked himself unconscious in the cellar and Aonghas had to wait two hours for him to come around, made him seem like an exotic creature to his friends.

Aonghas was in his early thirties, and until he met Thuy, he'd been the only one of his friends who wasn't in a stable, committed relationship, despite their repeated attempts to set him up. Sure, he was a little plush around the belly, but he had the kind of big frame that carried it well; if he'd been a little less lazy, he would have done well out on the fishing boats. He had an easy way of talking, and women seemed to like him. But he really couldn't believe Thuy was his girlfriend. She was athletic, gorgeous, and smart as hell: she'd just missed qualifying for the Olympics in the two hundred-meter freestyle, and had worked for a couple of years as a model before deciding to go to medical school. She was also unbelievably nice and thoughtful, the kind of woman who spent her free time volunteering at animal shelters and never passed a homeless person without dropping some money in their cup. All that, and she liked to cook. He was pretty sure it was a miracle she was his girlfriend. He knew the truth, which was that not being a bad bloke wasn't really enough to justify having a woman like Thuy fall in love with him. Still, who was he to question the vagaries of the human heart? Or, as his grandfather had put it: "Don't be such an ass. If the lass loves you, she loves you. Take what little gifts this life has to offer."

He met Thuy when she came to Stornoway for vacation. She'd walked into the Kenneth Street coffee shop he liked to write in. Three mornings in a row she'd come through the door with a backpack and hiking gear, and three mornings in a row he'd been sitting at a table in the back, hacking away at the newest Harry Thorton mystery, each word he wrote enriching his bank account ever so slightly. Finally, on the fourth morning, Aonghas worked up the courage to talk to her. It was the wrong time of year for tourists, and she would have stood out even if she hadn't been Vietnamese and ridiculously good-looking. Aonghas didn't admit it to her until they'd been dating for nearly six months, but he'd been surprised when she'd spoken to him and didn't have an accent. She was as Scottish as he was. They'd talked for a while about what she was doing there—she was in medical school and had a vacation and wanted to do some hiking—and he'd suggested a nice walk and a couple of places she might like to eat, and then he'd given her his phone number. They'd gone hiking together the next day and had hit it off.

They had five more days together before she headed back, but he'd already had a trip to Edinburgh planned for three weeks later, and ended up staying at her place. Somehow, it worked out. Even with writing the Harry Thorton books and motoring over to Càidh Island to check in on his grandfather every couple of days, Aonghas had enough free time that it was easy to take the one-hour flight to Edinburgh every other weekend. And here and there, when she could, she'd sneak away to the Isle of Lewis for a few days: she preferred coming to him, she said, and he believed her. She seemed to love the island as much as he did, and arranged to do her residency in Stornoway when she graduated. Two months, Aonghas thought. Two months and he'd get to see her every day, wake up with her every morning.

And with any luck, he thought, as he saw Thuy's plane come bursting through the clouds that hung over the ocean, two months from now would be the beginning of always.

He fingered the box in his pocket. He'd brought the ring with him the last time he'd gone to Edinburgh, two weeks ago, but it hadn't felt right, and he'd finally realized why he was hesitating: she'd never met his grandfather. Even though they'd been together for a year, Aonghas had never taken Thuy out to Càidh Island. At first, he'd hesitated because he wasn't sure it was serious, and then he'd hesitated precisely because it was serious. Padruig could be intimidating, and while Aonghas didn't want it to be true, he knew that if Padruig disapproved of Thuy, it would signal the death knell of the relationship. So there was a lot riding on this weekend. And he had to admit, he was scared shitless at what would happen when Padruig and Thuy came together.

The drive to the coast on the other side of the isle took only an hour, and he'd never seen Thuy so excited.

"You think he'll like me?"

He pulled her bag out from the backseat and then picked up his own bag, shutting the door of the Range Rover with his hip. "He doesn't really like anybody, Thuy. God, I've told you enough stories about how cranky he is. He can be a bit of a cunt at times."

She smacked him on the head. Not hard. But still. "Don't talk about him like that. He raised you."

Aonghas stepped over the rail of the boat and tucked their bags in the cabin. He'd loaded his grandfather's boxes already: three coolers full of milk, dairy, and fresh produce—more than usual, because he and Thuy were staying—plus mail and two boxes of books and magazines. He held Thuy's hand to help her on board, and then pulled her tight against him. He could feel her pressing against the ring box in his front pocket.

"He didn't have much of a choice about raising me, Thuy. He wasn't going to let his grandson go to the orphanage, and after my parents died . . ." He shrugged. "But you're right. He's a good man. He's a tough bastard, and he has his ways, but I love him, and he'll love you, Thuy. I promise. I love you, and I love him, and love's the sort of bridge we can all cross over."

"You say pretty things sometimes," Thuy said, and then she kissed him and went forward while he started the boat.

That was one of the other things he liked about her. He could say stuff like that—that love was a sort of bridge. He could read poetry and good books, and she never, ever, tried to tell him that he should write a "real" book, that he was wasting his time on the Harry Thorton novels. He'd had girlfriends before who pushed him, and in the end, he had to admit he loved those damned mysteries more than he'd loved any of those old girlfriends. He'd grown up with the books, helped his grandfather come up with new plots for them—two books a year, every year, for as long as Aonghas could remember—and taking over the writing of them was all he'd ever wanted to do.

He looked at the way Thuy sat near the bow and marveled again at his luck. She should have been a painting, the way she looked against the water. The weather never seemed to bother her, and even though it wasn't that cold, there was a bit of spray coming off the water. He liked watching the way she leaned into the wind, how she zipped her jacket but let the hood stay down, catching the mist on her face. Two more months. Two more months. He said it over and over in his head like a mantra. Two more months and she'd be doing her residency in Stornoway. The idea of living with Thuy, of having her on the Isle of Lewis all the time, not just for a long weekend every couple of months, was enough to make Aonghas almost burst with happiness. He patted the ring again.

She was going to say yes. She had to. He couldn't think about her saying anything else. He felt sick and knew it wasn't the waves or the water: they'd never bothered him. It was the gauntlet of facing his grandfather.

They rounded the eastern edge of Càidh Island, and he saw the familiar harbor and the castle standing on the bluffs. Thuy gasped, and he smiled. He'd tried to tell her, but nobody ever believed it until they saw it. It wasn't a big castle, as castles go, but it *was* a castle. His grandfather could never quite figure out how many centuries it had been in the family, and there was no real record of why it was there, but it was beautiful. It was home. And as far as castles went, it was actually fairly comfortable. Aonghas's grandfather had spent quite a bit of money to make it more livable: there was solar power connected to a bank of batteries and a generator for the many times there wasn't enough sun to keep the batteries charged, and a ten thousand-gallon diesel tank to keep the generator running; three large propane tanks kept the castle heated, since Càidh Island was almost bare of trees; two deep-freeze units were stocked with meat, ice cream, and frozen fruit, and the dry storage room was stocked with flour and grains and other dried goods; the furniture and linens, though a little outdated, had all been expensively furnished by a London decorator when Aonghas was still a little boy; and it had a wine cellar. Oh, the wine cellar. Even if he had been lonely at times as a child, Càidh Island, this barren rock in the waters of the Outer Hebrides, had been a good place to grow up, and it was an even better place to visit as a man.

He looked to the dock, but there was nobody there. Aonghas didn't mind. His grandfather, a man whom Aonghas had always thought of as having almost supernatural strength, was finally showing his age. Padruig had been forty-two when his daughter and Aonghas's father died in the crash, and at seventy-four, he wasn't quite as quick as he'd been. He was still a tough old man. There was no questioning that. Except for four years in the military, Padruig had lived his entire life on the island. He claimed he'd never seen a doctor or a dentist, and as far as Aonghas could tell, that was true enough. He spent most of his time reading or writing—even though he had handed the Harry Thorton novels over to Aonghas, Padruig was still hacking away at his typewriter, supposedly working on an autobiography—and when he wasn't doing that, he was out on the water fishing or back in the castle fixing things. Still, there was no reason for the old man to come down to the dock if he didn't need to. Besides, if Aonghas was being honest, it was good to have a little room to breathe. He was really, really nervous about Thuy and his grandfather meeting. Really, really, really nervous.

Aonghas tied the boat to the dock. He helped Thuy out of the boat and then started piling their bags and the groceries on the wooden planks. He heard a soft *ding* and turned to see Thuy pulling out her cell phone.

"Wow," she said. "I can't believe I get reception here."

He wrapped his hands around her hand and the phone. "You'd better turn it off. I wasn't kidding when I told you that he'll go batshit if he sees that. He is not a fan of technology."

"I thought you said he had the castle wired for electricity and that he likes to listen to BBC Radio nan Gàidheal."

"He does, but it's the same radio he's had since before my ma was born. And the electric is only so that he can power the freezer and fridge and the pumps for the septic system. No, other than the radio, it's books or walking or staring at the water. I tried talking him into buying a television and DVD player once. This was back when I was ten or eleven, and even then he'd have none of it. Basically, he hates the idea of having to rely on anything he can't fix himself. Just trust me, honey. Turn off the phone."

"Well, at least we'll be able to get the news from the radio. I still can't believe about China."

"China?" The sound of Padruig's voice startled them. The old man was standing on the rock path above them, hands stuffed into the pockets of his shooting jacket. With his flowing beard and the shadow from the clouds and the tree behind him, he looked practically biblical. "China is only the beginning," he said. "There's never just one of that sort of thing, is there?"

He walked down the steps until he was on the dock in front of them. He stuck out his hand and nodded. "Aonghas."

Aonghas shook his grandfather's hand. The grip was still strong, but it didn't crush his fingers the way he remembered early hand-shakes doing. It wasn't that his grandfather had been trying to pun-ish him, Aonghas knew, but rather that there was only one way he knew how to hold on to things: hard.

"Good to see you, boy." His grandfather gave him a wink as he said it, and that was when Aonghas realized his grandfather was wearing the hat.

Padruig was a bit of a hermit—he didn't leave Càidh Island that often, and rarely for more than a few days—but Aonghas's grandfa-ther was not an ascetic. His books had been bestsellers in the 1960s and 1970s, and they'd enjoyed a resurgence since Aonghas started writing them. His grandfather had plenty of money, and if there was something he cared about, he didn't mind spending money on it. The wine cellar in the castle was proof enough of that. And the old man's library had something in the neighborhood of ten thousand books. He'd also spent a fortune to make sure Càidh Island was close to self-sufficient: it was a fortress with the cistern and the diesel stores and the food stocked away in the cellars. While Aonghas always brought fresh produce and perishables, the castle could go for a year, maybe two, between deliveries of water and fuel and dry goods. But really, more than anything, Padruig was a clotheshorse. He'd had his jackets and shirts and trousers made to order in London for as long as Aong-has could remember, and his bootmaker was actually the grandson of the man who'd made boots for Padruig's father. Aonghas had never been all that particular about clothing himself, and once, when he saw his grandfather's bill from the tailor, he'd almost fainted. The man was, to borrow an old girlfriend's expression, always well-turned-out. The problem was that it made it hard to figure out if Padruig was dressed for a special occasion, since he was *always* dressed impeccably. But the old man had a tell: the houndstooth newsboy hat.

The hat had been a wedding present to Padruig from Aonghas's grandmother. He'd never met the woman, but when she died it had broken his grandfather's heart. Even though Aonghas was only seven when his parents died in the crash, he still remembered the way his mother described his grandmother's death: "For Da, it was like all the color drained out of the world."

Aonghas had seen his grandfather wear the hat on only a few occasions: his parents' funeral; Aonghas's graduation from college; each of the three times Padruig had won a Gold Dagger Award from the Crime Writers' Association, which, after Lionel Davidson's death in 2009, left him as the only living author with that hat trick; and the day, when Aonghas was fifteen, when they'd both been invited to Balmoral Castle to go hunting with the queen, who was a huge fan of the Harry Thorton series.

So it was the hat that made Aonghas relax. The ring had been his mother's, and he'd had to ask his grandfather for it, so both of them knew what was coming this weekend, but seeing that houndstooth newsboy hat on his grandfather's head made Aonghas realize that if he was nervous about introducing Thuy to his grandfather, and if he was nervous about asking Thuy to marry him—and the Lord knew he was nervous—well, his grandfather was also nervous about meeting his girlfriend.

If anything, however, it almost went too well: Aonghas was left to carry the bags and boxes by himself while his grandfather took Thuy on the five-minute tour that Càidh Island warranted and required, and then showed her around the castle itself. And then, Aonghas was left by himself in the living room to listen to the BBC Radio nan Gàidheal and look out over the water while Thuy showed his grandfather how to make curry.

The news was still dominated by China and the nuclear explosion, but Aonghas found himself tired of it. There was nothing new to report, and it seemed as though nobody really knew anything. By the time dinner was on the table, he was relieved when his grandfather turned off the radio.

"It's a shame, that sort of thing," his grandfather said. "I'd like to think we're at the edge of the world out here, but there are some things that are too big to hide from."

Thuy poured some more wine and leaned against Aonghas. She smelled of garlic and lemongrass, and he kissed her on the top of the head. Her parents had raised her strictly Scottish, except for cooking, and for that he was thankful. He'd never realized how much he loved Vietnamese food until they started dating. Of course, that was because he'd never had Vietnamese food until they started dating.

"I don't know, Padruig," Thuy said. "It seems like you could hide from anything here. You could whittle away a year without too much trouble."

His grandfather smiled and reached across the table to pat Thuy's hand. "A year's not so long, and not everything can be hidden from, dear. Do you know what Oppenheimer said after the first successful nuclear explosion?" Thuy shook her head. "He said, 'Now I am become Death, the destroyer of worlds.'"

Aonghas laughed. "You know that's not true. He said that later, but he didn't say it at the time. It was only years and years and years later that he said that."

His grandfather lifted both hands and then pounded them on the table with enough force that the silverware chattered and the wine sloshed in their glasses. Thuy jumped back, but Aonghas didn't move. He could see the smile on his grandfather's face. He was used to the old man's theatrics.

"But it makes for the better story," his grandfather roared. "The story. The story!" He picked up his knife and pointed it at Aonghas. "Never forget the story." With that, Padruig put the knife back down and looked at Thuy. "And he doesn't, you know. He doesn't forget the story. As much as it pains me to say it, I think the boy is doing a better job with the books than I ever did. Though," he said, dropping to a stage whisper, "he's not yet won a Dagger Award."

Outside, the light looked weaker. Clouds papered the sky, and the water had started to whip up a bit. Nothing to be worried about yet, but it hinted at a coming storm.

Since his grandfather and girlfriend had done all the cooking, Aonghas found himself exiled to the kitchen to wash the dinner dishes while his grandfather and Thuy relaxed in the living room, the radio on in the background. Aonghas was humming to himself, pleased at how well things were going, occasionally stopping to sneak the ring out of his pocket and take a look at it, when he realized Thuy was calling his name.

The urgency in her voice scared him. She said his name again, and instead of grabbing the towel, he just wiped his hands on his jeans. He hurried into the living room and came to a stop. They were just sitting there. Nothing was wrong. There had been a part of him that was sure he was going to come in and find the old man facedown on the floor, dead before he could see his grandson engaged and married, before he had a chance to see a great-granddaughter or great-grandson, the Càidh line carried on.

But both his grandfather and Thuy were up and alert. In fact, they were smiling.

Thuy stood up and walked over to him. "Is it true?" she said.

"What?"

Thuy looked at Padruig, so Aonghas looked at his grandfather as well. "Is what true?" he asked.

Padruig offered up something between a grimace and a smile. "I'm sorry, boy. It just slipped out."

"Yes," Thuy said to Aonghas. "Go ahead and ask me, because the answer is yes."

Desperation, California

"Well," Gordo said. "Waiting for the world to go boom is kind of boring." He tried changing the television station, but it was the same news everywhere: no news. China had set off a nuke and . . . and that was it.

"Fred called." Amy sat on his lap and put her arm around his shoulder. "He said if the world isn't ending today, we should go over and have dinner and drinks with him and Shotgun. We can play hearts."

Gordo sighed. "Sure."

"What's with the grumpy pants?" Amy tapped her finger on his lips. "You're all pouty."

Gordo kissed her finger. "Eh. You know. A nuke goes off and I'm thinking, okay, this is it. We're ready. I'm ready. Let's do it. I'm not saying I really want it to happen, but come on. I thought this was it." He wrapped his arms around his wife and pulled her tight against him. "Yeah, fuck it. Let's go over and play some cards. Beats just sitting around waiting for the bombs to start falling."

American University, Washington, DC

Oh, that private bathroom. Of all the things Melanie was glad that she negotiated for—lab space, funding, administrative support, reduced teaching—a private bathroom and shower in her office was what made her most thankful. There was the obvious plus of not having to use the public restrooms, but it was the shower that was the best. She could go out for a quick run and shower off without having to head to the Jacobs Fitness Center, or, on days like today, when she hadn't left the lab in nearly seventy hours, it meant she could take a shower and put on one of the changes of clothes she kept in her office. She could feel human again.

She tugged on her brown motorcycle boots and pulled her jeans down over them. She'd bought the boots at the same time she bought her first motorcycle, when she was eighteen, and even though she hadn't had a bike in a decade, she kept resoling the boots. They were scarred and had a deep patina of wear. She always felt like a badass when she wore them. She buttoned up her dark-blue blouse, gave her hair a quick brush, put her diamond stud earrings back in, opened the door of her bathroom, and crashed right into a big black man in a suit.

The man was rooted like a tree. Melanie bounced back a few steps, and he reached out and caught her arm.

"Sorry about that, ma'am," he said.

He didn't have to say anything more for Melanie to know he was Secret Service. She sighed.

"Where is he?"

"Ma'am?"

She straightened her blouse and slipped past him into her office. There was no one else in the office, though she could hear voices in the lab. "Manny. My ex-husband. Where is he?"

"He's in the lab, ma'am, with the others."

It was a pattern that was too familiar to her from their marriage: Manny wanted to spend time with her, she'd say she was busy, he'd show up anyway saying he hoped just to steal a few minutes, they'd fight about whether their marriage was failing because of how little time they spent together or because what little time they did spend together they spent fighting. It had been exhausting when they were married, and she didn't want to spend any part of the day doing a postmortem on a body that had long gone cold. She'd already taken the blame, already said it was her fault, even though there was a small part of her that thought Manny could have done more. No phone could be slammed hard enough, no door closed firmly enough to keep him out when it came to garnering support for a bill or getting money for Steph's campaigns, but he had never fought as hard for her as he had on Steph's behalf.

"All right, Manny," she said, pushing through the door to the lab, "I don't have the patience for . . ."

But it wasn't Manny.

Or, rather, it was Manny, but it was also Steph. The president of the United States. She was leaning over the insectarium with Julie, staring at the spiders.

At the sound of Melanie's voice, everybody in the room turned. And there were a lot of people in the lab besides her and Julie and Manny and Steph: Bark and Patrick, fussing over the computer and recording equipment, nearly a dozen Secret Service agents, and Billy Cannon, the secretary of defense.

"Madam President," Melanie said. She started to put out her hand and then nodded her head before turning it into a sort of half bow. It was embarrassing. She stood up straight and looked around the room. "Traveling sort of heavy today?"

The president waved her hand at the suited men. "Comes with the territory. It's hard to casually pop in anywhere." She stepped over and gave Melanie a hug.

Melanie hugged her back, reluctantly. She was never really sure how to feel about the president. She knew how she felt about Steph, but Steph, as the president, was a different matter. She'd known Steph for as long as she'd known Manny. Close to eighteen years now. She'd known Steph when she was still just Steph, before it was Governor Pilgrim or Senator Pilgrim, let alone President Pilgrim. Melanie had been one of the bridesmaids at Steph's wedding to George Hitchens, and one of the few people to really see what it was like behind the scenes during Steph's run for president. And she also knew that, since she and Manny had gotten divorced, her ex-husband and the president of the United States were fucking a couple of times a week.

She didn't begrudge it exactly. It was kind of hard to be pissed off at Manny for having a casual thing with Steph when Melanie was sleeping with Bark. At least Steph was the president and not a goddamned graduate student. The truth was they were divorced, and if Manny was going to be sleeping with anybody, Steph was probably the best bet as far as Melanie was concerned. It's not that she was still in love with Manny, but rather that there was a part of her that thought they might get back together. Someday. When they were older. Okay. Maybe she was still in love with Manny a little bit. They hadn't gotten divorced because they hated spending time with each other, but because Melanie hadn't loved Manny more than she did her work. At least if he was having an affair with Steph, Melanie knew that meant he might still be available to her. If she wanted. She wasn't sure what she wanted. Seeing Manny standing there, next to Bark, should have made it easy: Bark, tall and solid and muscular, looking even better with three days' stubble and his T-shirt wrinkled from camping out in the lab with her and Julie and Patrick; Manny, sporting ten more pounds than the last time she'd seen him, wearing a suit that was indistinguishable from every other suit he wore. Physically, there was no comparison. But just looking at Bark annoyed her, while seeing Manny, even though she wasn't happy to have him and half the White House intruding on her lab, brought a smile to her face.

She stepped out of the president's arms. "Good to see you. It's been a while."

Steph cocked her head at Manny, who offered a sheepish smile. "You know how it is," Steph said. "You don't mean to pick sides, but that's always how it works."

"I'm sorry," Manny said. He stepped forward and took her hand. He hesitated and then leaned forward to kiss her on the cheek. He had to get on his toes. Very quietly, so quietly that she almost missed it, he whispered in her ear, "You smell good."

Melanie touched her wet hair. She could feel herself blushing a little, and she took a quick glance at Bark. The oaf had a small sulk starting on his face. Ugh. Tonight. Tonight, she promised herself, no matter what else was going on, it was over. She'd meant to drop his ass the day before, but they'd spent the entire day working with the spiders, and there had never been a good time to bring him into her office and tell him she was done with it.

"Sorry to barge in," Manny said. "We need to talk."

"About what?"

Manny looked around. "Can we clear the students out? It's important, Melanie."

There was a part of Melanie that wanted to say no. It was that same impulse that had torpedoed their marriage: there was just too much to do in the lab, too many things to study. It was hard to do to his face, always had been, and it was impossible to kick him out while the president of the United States, the secretary of defense, and a gaggle of Secret Service agents were wandering around the lab. It didn't take somebody with a PhD to figure out this was something serious. So she found her purse, dug some cash out and handed it to Julie, telling her to take Bark and Patrick to Tara Thai on Massachusetts and get them some lunch.

As her students left the lab, Manny hustled the Secret Service guys out as well. He shut the door and attempted to smile at her. It was weak. "Sorry," he said. "I tried calling but you didn't answer your phone."

She couldn't stop herself. The words came out sharply: "I was busy."

It just felt too close to every argument they'd had about their marriage. When he wanted to talk to her, she wasn't available. Except this time, Manny did something different. He apologized.

"I'm sorry, and I know, but this isn't personal. It's official." He motioned to Steph. "We needed to talk to you. I was going to send somebody to get you and bring you to the White House, but Steph thought you wouldn't come unless they arrested you. Seemed counterproductive if we wanted your cooperation."

Melanie leaned against one of the lab tables. She looked at Manny and then at Steph. She didn't say anything. She liked watching Manny fidget.

"Look, the truth is that I, that we, me and Steph and Billy . . .

I can't remember. Have you met Billy before? Billy Cannon. Secretary of defense."

Billy's handshake was firm, but before he let go of her hand, he nodded at the insectarium that was behind her. "Ma'am, if I can ask, what the hell is that spider behind you?"

"That one?" Melanie turned and gently touched the glass wall. She was so used to the spiders in the lab that she forgot how much they freaked people out. Particularly the bigger, hairy ones like the one Billy was looking at. "*Theraphosa blondi*. Or, more commonly, a Goliath birdeater, though they don't really eat birds. Usually."

"Jesus." Billy leaned forward and tapped at the glass.

Melanie grabbed his wrist. "Don't do that."

Billy stood up straight again. "Why not? Is the thing going to kill me?"

"They don't like it. That's why. You wouldn't like it if somebody sat outside your house banging on the window. They're sensitive to vibrations. And no, it won't kill you, though it hurts like a fucker if it bites you. Like getting stung by a wasp. And they have urticating hair. It gets on your skin and stings and itches, and if you inhale it, you'll be coughing and unhappy. It's obnoxious. But they're like most spiders. You leave them alone and they'll leave you alone."

"Most spiders?"

"They hunt," she said. "Bugs. That sort of stuff." She turned to Manny. "Okay. What's the deal?"

Manny ran his fingers through his hair. It was a familiar gesture, something he did when he hadn't had a lot of sleep and when he was feeling overwhelmed, and the sight of it made Melanie smile a little. But only a little.

"This might sound crazy," Manny said, "but are there spiders that eat people? I mean, giant swarms of spiders? Does even asking the question make me sound like I'm out of my fucking mind? If there are, it seems like the sort of thing you would have brought up at a dinner party." Melanie smiled for real this time. She'd been to so many boring political dinners, and her one solace had been scaring the shit out of whoever was sitting next to her with stories about all the dangerous creepy crawlies out there. "Are there?" Manny said. "Are there spiders like that?"

To Melanie's right, Billy had drifted over to a shadow box on the wall that held a mounted spider. For a second he looked as though he was going to tap on that glass too, but then he saw Melanie watching. She glared at him and he lowered his hand. Melanie looked back at Manny. "You know how many phone calls and e-mails we get a month from people who think they've gotten bitten by a spider and are going to die?" she said. She stepped over to the smaller dorm fridge that was next to the larger lab fridges. She opened the door and pulled herself out a can of soda. She held one up to Steph and then Billy, both of whom shook their heads. Without asking, she handed one to Manny. She didn't have to ask. He never turned down a Diet Coke. She cracked open the can and took a swig. The bitter sweetness felt like an extra hour of sleep under her belt.

She hesitated. She wasn't sure if she wanted to share her new spiders with anybody outside the lab yet. She'd never seen anything like them, and she knew the discovery was going to be the next big step in her career. The ten-thousand-year-old egg sac hatching, the spiders themselves, and then the way they interacted? How many papers would she get out of this? And then she looked over at Steph and remembered again that she wasn't just Steph. She was the president of the United States. "May I ask what this is about?"

Manny glanced at Steph. Steph gave a small shake of her head. Manny sighed and popped the top on his soda. "Take my word for it," he said. "We wouldn't be here if it wasn't important."

"Honestly, Manny, you know what I always tell people about

spiders: there's really no reason to be afraid of them." Melanie walked to the back bench. "But that was before a couple of days ago, because these things scare the shit out of me."

She put her Diet Coke down next to a stack of cages holding lab rats. The rats were mostly quiet, huddled against the sides of their cages, moved as far away from the insectarium—which was already nearly three meters away—as possible. She picked up one of the cages. As Melanie carried the cage closer to the insectarium, the spiders started launching themselves at the glass. The thud of their bodies was rhythmic and desperate.

"They just came out of the egg sac yesterday, and it was something to see. Like an explosion. I haven't pulled one out for dissection yet, but I've never seen a spider like this. It's something new."

She held the rat cage above the insectarium.

"Are these—"

Melanie cut off her ex-husband. "Just watch."

Julie had rigged it so there was a double-chambered entrance; they could keep the spiders enclosed, add a rat to one compartment, and then close up the whole thing before dropping the rat in with the spiders. For a second, as Melanie dumped the rat in, she felt bad for it: the little thing was squeaking and clawing at the glass, trying to climb away. Below it, even though they couldn't see the rat in the top chamber, the spiders were frantic. They could smell it.

Melanie hit the lever, and the floor below the rat fell away, dropping it into the tank with the dozens of waiting spiders.

This was the fourth rat she'd sacrificed.

The sound of chewing hadn't gotten any easier to tolerate.

Clearly, the sound bothered somebody behind her too, because she heard retching.

"Holy crap." It was Manny, at her elbow.

Among other things—he was funny and smart as hell, maybe

even smarter than she was—the fact that he had never been afraid of spiders was one of the things she loved about him.

"No shit. Spiders aren't supposed to chew. Normally they liquefy their food and sort of suck it in. I have literally never seen anything like this."

"Where did these spiders come from?" he said.

"FedEx," Melanie said.

The president moved next to them as well, staring down and looking through the glass. The spiders had eaten half the rat, and one of them detached itself from the dead animal's flesh and started trying to get through the glass to Steph. "What are these things?"

"I'm serious," Manny said. "Where did you get these spiders?"

"I'm serious too," Melanie said. "FedEx. From Peru. Remember the Nazca Lines? A friend of one of my graduate students was on a dig there. He found it and he shipped the egg sac to our lab. Probably ten thousand years old."

"Sorry?" Steph said. "Did you say the egg sac was ten thousand years old?"

"Give or take. And you'd think there'd be no chance of anything alive in there, right? That it would be fossilized? But nope."

"How on earth could they still hatch if they're that old?"

She gave them the simplified version, the way that certain eggs could, essentially, enter a state of suspension, waiting for the right set of conditions. She told them about the evolutionary ecologist from Oklahoma who'd been getting seven-hundred-year-old water-flea eggs to hatch. "Or, maybe it's easier to think of cicadas. Some cicada swarms are annual, but others are on thirteen- or seventeen-year cycles. Nobody really understands how it works, why they're dormant that whole time, but our not understanding doesn't stop the cicadas from coming out."

Melanie shrugged. "I've got years and years of research ahead of me. There are only so many questions I can answer. All I can tell you right now is that once we realized they were hatching, it felt like it took forever. Twenty hours of staring at the fucking thing, but then, bam. And before you ask, no, I've never seen them or heard of anything like them before. As far as I can tell, it's a new species. Or, probably more accurately, it's a really old species. Totally extinct except for this egg sac. It's kind of a miracle. That they were found, that they were shipped here, that they've been sitting around for ten thousand years or so just waiting for the right time to hatch. I've got to be honest, there's a lot I'm not understanding here. I've never seen anything like this."

She frowned and leaned into the glass. All the spiders, save one, had gone at the rat. But one of the spiders was moving listlessly near the corner. It looked undamaged, but there was something wrong with it. As if it didn't have the energy to feed on the rat. She found herself about to tap on the glass but then stopped herself and turned to glance back at Billy Cannon. The secretary of defense had taken a paper towel from the rack by the sink and was wiping his mouth. She looked back at Manny, but he was staring at Steph. Steph was staring at Melanie and looked like she was about to say something when there was a knock at the door.

The Secret Service officer whom Melanie had banged into stuck his head in. "He's here."

Manny nodded, and the door opened wider. A white man in a suit came in. He was good-looking, Melanie thought. He had that first hint of softness around the stomach that comes with middle age, but he was only a couple of years older than she was. Even in the presence of the president and all the Secret Service agents, he looked sure of himself. He looked, Melanie thought, like what she wanted: a man. Certainly he was more appropriate than a graduate student. Even with his suit, he looked like a cop, though

Melanie had been in DC long enough to peg the guy for FBI or CIA or some agency other than plain old PD. He was carrying what looked like . . . yeah. It was a pickle jar. Except that wasn't a pickle.

Melanie took the jar out of his hands, noticing that the guy's left hand had a bandage wrapped around it. There were holes punched into the lid, and other than the spider inside, the jar was empty.

"Madam President," the man said to Steph. "It's an honor. Agent Mike Rich. From Minneapolis."

Steph shook the man's hand, and without letting go, she looked into Mike's eyes. "And this is the same one? This is the spider that came out of Henderson?"

Melanie looked up from the jar. "Wait. What? Came out of . . ." She put the jar down next to the insectarium. "Where'd you get this?"

"It came crawling out of a man's face, actually," Mike said.

Melanie stared at him. "No." She said the word slowly then said it again. "No. I mean, where in the world?"

Manny sighed. "You know how you asked me a few minutes ago if you could ask what this is about?" Melanie nodded. "The spiders you've got here," Manny said, pointing to the insectarium, "aren't the only ones. When you say you think they are totally extinct except for the ones you've got here, I'm pretty sure you're wrong. We think there are more of them."

Melanie looked at the spider in the jar and then at the ones in the insectarium. "I can't guarantee that these are the same spiders. At least on the surface, there is an apparent match, but I'd have to look a little more closely—"

"Melanie." Manny's voice was sharp. "When I say we think there are more of these spiders, I mean we think there are *more* of them. A lot more."

Metro Bhawan, Delhi, India

He was not happy about having to work overtime. His supervisor had basically disappeared since those two scientists from Kanpur had come by. With the baby coming, he could use the money, but with the baby coming his wife expected him at home more often. At the thought, he hitched up his pants and then took his cell phone out of his pocket. She liked it when he remembered to text her regularly, to check in. She was due two days ago, and her temper had been rather short. He was a big advocate of trying to stop a fight before it happened, and dutifully, he tapped in a quick message saying he was thinking about her, asking how she was feeling. And then another one to apologize again for having to work but reminding her of the extra money it would bring in. The doctor said if she went another week, they'd induce.

He tucked the phone back into his pocket and walked down the corridor. The crew was already standing by the door. The scientists had raised all sorts of hell about the tremors, insisting they be allowed to go down, and presumably they'd gotten to see what the problem was, because he hadn't heard any more complaints. And he hadn't heard anything from his supervisor either. The man was probably out drunk somewhere again. He liked his supervisor, but the truth was that the man, even if he had not been a drunk, was not particularly competent. He was also not particularly demanding, so that was good.

He nodded at the men standing by the door. The meters in the tunnel were going nuts, but the crew couldn't get the door open to check. They'd tried everything, including a master reset of the code on the door, but it was stuck. He didn't know what the hell the scientists had done to it—or, more likely, his supervisor—but there wasn't really any other choice: they had to get in. He sighed. He really would have preferred for his supervisor to make the call, but it had to be done.

"Okay," he said. "Break the pins."

The men went to work on the hinges, and he watched for a few seconds before he felt his phone vibrate with a text: *Contractions. I think it's time. Come home*.

He hesitated, but then he typed back *leaving now*. It would take only another minute or two to get the pins out, and then he would head right home.

The first pin went, and the crew held the door in place while one man finished the second pin. He could see the door was heavy. They strained to pull it off and move it to the side, but once they had, there was a lot of talking.

At first he thought it was dust or dirt or even coal, but quickly he and the crew realized what filled the tunnel nearly to waist height: dead spiders.

The black bodies were so thick that it was like a single mass. They'd pushed up against the door, but farther back the volume dropped, and as far as he could see down the tunnel, before the bend, they seemed to fall to knee height. On the walls, high up, and hanging from the ceiling, he could see chalky, white bundles. Spider silk. Most of them were the size of footballs, but a few were larger. There was one close to the door, and while the crew stayed behind him, he shuffled forward a few steps, sliding through the spilled spiders as though they were dried leaves. He reached up to touch one of the bundles. It was sticky. And though he'd expected it to be cool, it was warm.

His phone pinged again: *I'll meet you at the hospital.*

He put the phone back in his pocket and turned around. The sound of the spiders crunching and popping under his feet made him feel sick. They were scary, but no more so than looking at a specimen pinned under glass. He toed one with his shoe. It was light, as if it were hollow. Dead. Dried out. Used up. Whatever these spiders were—thousands and thousands of them, tens of thousands—and however they'd gotten down into the tunnel, they were dead.

He knew what he should do: he should figure out where the hell his supervisor was and get the man down here. And if he couldn't reach his supervisor, call his supervisor's supervisor. Not only was this the stuff of nightmares, it was also clearly something that was beyond what he was supposed to handle on his own.

His phone again: *Hurry.*

But if he did what he was supposed to, it would be hours and hours. The prospect of making overtime was much more appealing when his wife was waiting to go into labor than it was with her actively *in* labor. If he didn't get moving right away, his wife would hold it against him for the rest of his life.

"Okay," he said. "For now, we leave it. You two stay here and keep everybody out of the tunnel." The men he pointed to muttered and didn't look at him, but he knew they'd do their job. "We'll see to this tomorrow."

He gave one last look at the mass of spiders and then turned to hurry to get to his wife.

Perhaps if he'd looked more closely, he might have seen the bones buried under the pile of spiders, three bodies stripped clean. He might have then realized there was a reason he hadn't seen his supervisor since those two scientists had come. And, perhaps, if he'd been alone, if it had been quieter, he would have heard the sound behind him, back in the tunnel. A skittering. A tearing.

If he'd heard it, he would have realized that all the spiders weren't dead. Perhaps then he would have yelled at the men to shove the door back into place, to hold it tight.

Perhaps.

But he didn't.

Delhi. Second most populous city on earth. Including surrounding towns and villages, home to twenty-five million people.

Mathias Maersk Triple-E Class Container Ship, Pacific Ocean, 400 miles from Los Angeles

With a crew of only twenty-two men, the four-hundred-meter-long *Mathias Maersk* Triple-E could carry eighteen thousand containers, and, at a slow steam, use about a third less fuel than older and smaller ships. Modern efficiency at its best, already outdated: the *Mathias* was going to be outclassed soon enough. Scale. It was all about scale. As long as a ship was full, the bigger it was the more money it made. And the *Mathias Maersk* Triple-E was full. They'd loaded up in China, shipping container after shipping container. The manifest included everything from textiles to rubber ducks, all packed tight in their individual metal coffins, ready to hit the streets of America.

Calm seas and fourteen days of routine logs. If he'd been a religious man, he'd have given prayers of thanks. A good part of their cargo came from northwest China, where the nuke had gone off. He felt bad for the captains waiting in port in China right now. Their schedules were going to be thrown off. Routine logs were not in the offing for those captains. They were not going to cross the ocean anytime soon. Not like him. With the autopilot locked in on the Port of Los Angeles, at a steady seventeen knots, he had about twenty hours to go. Or he'd had twenty hours to go. Unfortunately, it sounded like there was going to be a problem.

Even with only twenty-two men on board, there were nine languages spoken. The captain was a native speaker of Italian, but fluent in English. Which was more than could be said for the majority of the crew. Shitty pidgin English was the order of the day. It was difficult enough to get everybody to understand one another face-to-face, but with the noise of the engine and the normal static of the radio, the captain hadn't been able to understand a single word from the engineer on duty. It didn't help that the man had been screaming.

He double-checked the autopilot, glanced at the zoomed-out map showing Los Angeles dead ahead, and went to call the first mate. Whatever it was, they'd get it fixed when they hit the port tomorrow. With a little luck they'd be tied up in time for him to grab a late lunch in Los Angeles while the ship was being unloaded. He was ready for a day on the town.

The CNN Center,
Atlanta, Georgia

"**I** don't know if it's worth bothering yet," Teddie said to her boss. Teddie Popkins—Theodora Hughton Van Clief Popkins, but she'd been Teddie since her first week on earth, and using the Hughton Van Clief part of her name instead of sticking with Teddie Popkins was a good way to make sure the only men who hit on her were gold diggers—played the video back again. It was shaky, but the quality was first-rate. She'd be the first to admit that cell phones had made her life as a producer a lot better. A piece-of-shit phone could still shoot HD video. Sure, when she had reporters out in the field, there was nothing better than a cameraman with a $20,000 Panavision. But she didn't exactly have a crew just standing around in India waiting for . . .

What the hell was it exactly?

Part of her job as a producer, particularly on a boring weekday morning shift like this, was to fill time when things were slow. Okay. Associate producer. Not bad for somebody three years out of college. But the point was that on slow news days, part of her job was to help make news, and today was as boring as you could get during a week when China had set off a nuke.

That was the problem. The nuke had eaten all the news. For the first twenty-four hours, the entire building had been buzzing. She'd called an ex-boyfriend at FOX, and he'd said it was the same there: reporters and producers were all hands on deck, the same ten China policy experts on heavy rotation, total speculation, what little video they had on a constant loop. And then, nothing. The nuke story just fizzled out. Nothing new happened and it didn't seem like there was much beyond the story: China had accidentally exploded a nuke in a sparsely populated part of their country. Basically, whoops.

That was the other reason the story faded so quickly: it was in China. Teddie wasn't jaded. She'd graduated from Oberlin College, the kind of liberal arts bastion where you learn to care about everything. She'd been out of school long enough to start eating meat again and to learn to walk downtown without having to stop and talk to every homeless person, but despite coming from money and painfully conservative parents—Theodora Hughton Van Clief Popkins's father was William Hughton Van Clief Popkins III after all, the kind of lineage that meant she would probably have been a better fit at FOX if not for, as her father put it, "youthful naiveté about the way the world works"—four years at Oberlin had done their job. She hated that a story about some Hollywood starlet overdosing on Botox could push a nuclear explosion in China out of the headlines. She hated it, but she was also realistic. Americans just didn't care about foreign news very much.

Which brought her back to the problem of what to do about this footage from India. India was a hard sell. Every once in a while there'd be some sort of groundswell story they would pick up on, but they weren't going to be the lead on something out of India. Particularly during a week like this, when they'd already used up their quotient of foreign news with the China stuff. But still. The video.

"You might be right," her boss said, "but just play it for me." He leaned in over her shoulder so he had a better view of the monitor.

She had watched it slowed down and with the sound muted. At quarter speed, it was still barely a minute long, and it definitely lost the creep factor. A lot of sky and buildings and people running. In a few places, she could see what looked like black ribbons coming out of the train station, but nothing definitive. Near the end, there was a man stumbling out of a doorway and then falling down, the ribbons spreading over him, but even with a decent-quality cell phone camera, it was hard to tell what was going on. But at full speed, with the sound up? Even though the herky-jerky image telegraphed panic already, it was the screaming, the honking cars, something smashing, that really made it scary.

She played it at full speed and risked a glance at her boss. Don's mouth had actually dropped open.

"Whoa. What the fuck?"

"Yeah," Teddie said. "That's why I've been going back and forth. There really isn't much to see, but it's kind of terrifying, isn't it?"

"Okay," Don said, "but what is it?"

"It sort of looks like it might be bugs, right?"

Don crossed his arms. He was a good boss, Teddie thought, though it wasn't as if she had a lot to go by. She'd started at CNN right out of college as his assistant, and he'd been the one who'd given her her first shot as a producer. Associate producer. Once or twice she tried to imagine what she would do if he hit on her; her dad might be right that she had a youthful naiveté about the way the world works, but she wasn't completely stupid. She knew how certain things worked. He wasn't married and he wasn't gay and he was only in his early forties, young enough that it wouldn't have been inconceivable. So she didn't really understand why he never hit on her, never even hinted at it, except that maybe he was just one of those scrupulous people who didn't mix business with pleasure. Or maybe he just didn't do pleasure. Near as Teddie could tell, all Don ever did was work. So he was a good boss, in that he didn't seem to think of her as some young thing he could take advantage of, but he was also a bit of a pain in the ass in that he didn't seem to understand that she sometimes might want to do something other than work. He wasn't much for amusements, and right now he was clearly not amused.

"Come on Teddie. Don't waste my time. Bugs?"

"Don, I'm—"

She never got the chance to try to defend herself, which was good, because she was pretty sure she was going to say something lame. Instead, they were both interrupted by Rennie LaClair yelling at them across the office.

She followed Don over to the bank of monitors by Rennie's desk.

"Is that Delhi?"

Rennie didn't look at either her or Don. "Yep. NBC just put it up. They had a crew on the ground shooting B-roll, but now they've got a satellite linkup. Running it live. It's complete fucking pandemonium on the ground there, and they don't have an actual reporter working, just a cameraman, but man. Look at this shit."

It didn't matter that Teddie wasn't able to recognize the New Delhi Railway Station. What mattered was that the camera crew was shooting from some sort of elevation. Maybe on top of a nearby building. And what mattered was that there was enough of an open expanse that they could capture the panic. People were running everywhere. No. Not running. Fleeing. They were fleeing. For obvious reasons, none of the televisions had their sound on, but it wouldn't have made anything more clear. The headline read *Panic in Delhi—Possible Terrorism?* Whoever was running the show at NBC was thinking of the Mumbai attacks in 2008.

They had it wrong. Teddie knew that immediately. She knew it even before the camera zoomed in on one of the building entrances.

A black thread.

The thread turned into a ribbon.

A river.

A flood.

The White House

Manny didn't usually run. He walked with purpose, and he was often walking and talking, but running inside the White House wasn't normally part of the equation. Normally. But today was different.

If it had been anybody else going full sprint toward the Oval Office, he would have been, at the very least, tackled and pinned to the ground, but the agents on duty knew Manny, and they were alarmed by his alarm. He was already sweating and out of breath, a cell phone in each hand and trying to talk on both at the same time. He broke off his conversations to tell the agents and Steph's bodywoman—political jargon for her personal assistant—to clear the room, but Steph barely glanced at Manny.

The office was crowded. Two congressmen with seven or eight high-rolling donors, a young man who looked familiar to Manny, maybe an actor or singer, and several overwhelmed-looking parents chaperoning a quartet of Girl Scouts in full uniform. Steph, as always, under control, finished the grip and grin, leaning over and putting her arms around the Girl Scouts, grinning on cue for the *poof* of the camera flash. And then a quick thank-you, the full smile, and stepping back so the handlers could get everybody out.

Thirty seconds from the time he entered the room. The woman was a pro. Manny hadn't even caught his breath yet when the office was empty.

As soon as the doors were closed, Steph's smile dropped. "The Chinese?"

"No. India. Alex and Ben should be here any minute. Billy's on his way." Both of his cell phones started ringing at the same time, but he let them go.

"India? Shit. Has Pakistan retaliated?"

Manny looked at her for a second, confused, and then shook his head. It was an obvious conclusion for Stephanie. India and Pakistan had been at war or on the verge since the stroke of midnight on August 15, 1947. One of those brilliant British ideas, the partition of India. There hadn't been an outright conflict in a while, but both states were nuclear, and some years the governments were more stable than others. Right now, neither country was exactly led by a group of levelheaded people. But they had a playbook for hostilities between India and Pakistan. Scenarios sketched out by analysts. Backup plans and contingencies and coordinated lines of communication. Guns and bombs and jets and escalation were all things they had planned for. But they hadn't planned for this.

"No. Not Pakistan. Think China."

"China?"

"The fucking spiders."

"Okay," she said. "How bad is it?" No hesitation. No disbelief. Just a need for information.

That was one of the things Manny liked about Steph, one of the reasons he'd pushed her to go for it. Because, despite all his political manipulation, despite his thinking of politics as a game, despite his ability to read a poll and spin a message, despite the way he could work a phone and twist arms and his willingness to ruin somebody's life if they didn't deliver a vote, he was still a bit of a romantic. A realist, but a romantic one. And he believed in the idea of the president of the United States of America. He believed the president had to be the one to step up, that most of the time it didn't matter who was sitting in the hot seat, but those few times, those once-in-a-generation moments, it mattered, and with Steph sitting in the chair, with Steph's finger on the button, he knew she'd make the right decision. She had that knack of filtering out the noise, of letting go of distractions and cutting to the core, and as soon as she heard him say "spiders" she did the math. China. Nukes. Henderson's body in Minnesota. And now India. She wasn't going to waste her time thinking that it couldn't be possible, and she wasn't going to dither.

Something wicked this way comes, Manny thought. Any time for hesitation was gone.

"Manny, how bad?" she asked again.

"Bad," he said. "It's on television. NBC, but I think everybody's going to pick it up soon." He walked her out of the Oval Office and into the President's Study, where she did most of her real work. An aide looked up and Manny asked her for some Diet Cokes and to make sure that Alex, Ben, and Billy were brought in immediately.

He picked the remote control up from the coffee table and turned the television on. Or, he tried to. After a few pointless jabs at the power button, Steph took it out of his hand. "Seriously, Manny? You can't work a remote?" She got the television on and flipped it to NBC. They were playing the video in a loop: people running and screaming, then the black flood coming out the doors.

After about thirty seconds, she turned her back to the television.

"That's it?" Manny said. "You don't want to watch more?"

"Is there more to watch?"

"Not really."

"So let's get moving. And Manny?"

"Yeah?"

"Call your wife."

Manny couldn't stop himself. "Ex."

Steph waved her hand at him in frustration. "Whatever. Don't be an asshole."

"Very presidential."

"Manny, how about you go f—"

Steph stopped herself as the door opened. Alex Harris didn't bother coming all the way into the room. She looked at Steph and then Manny. "I think we're past the point of us sitting in the President's Study and chatting," Alex said. "Ben's already down in the Situation Room, and I went ahead and called everybody in."

"Come on, Alex, rein it in," Manny said. First one and then the other phone in his pocket started buzzing again. And those were the phones he handled himself. His aide must have been getting slammed. "The press is going to sniff this out and have a field day with us overreacting."

"Grow up, Manny," Alex said. "We're past that. The press is going to have a field day if we don't start overreacting. You want to think politics, think 9/11."

"Pardon me?" Manny said. "Are you saying this is terrorism?"

"No. What I'm saying is if we don't do something right away, Steph is going to look a hell of a lot worse than Bush did reading about a goddamned goat while planes flew into skyscrapers. You want to worry about how this looks to the press, well, those are the optics you need to worry about, Manny. Not some journalists figuring out we're moving into crisis mode." She took a step into the room and reached out to touch Stephanie's arm. "Because you better believe we're moving into crisis mode, Madam President.

When we were looking at China we figured we could treat this like the flu or any other pandemic, right? Quarantines and using the National Guard to help out in areas particularly hard hit. And as with the flu or any other pandemic, we figured we'd see it coming."

Alex took a deep breath and then turned back toward the door. "So, Manny, you can worry about the press all you want, but I'm worried about people dying. Come on. Let's go, Manny. Situation Room." Manny followed, not because he was summoned, but because he realized Alex was talking as much to the president as she was to him. And Alex was not that kind of person. Alex was well past caring about where her career ended up—she'd hinted about maybe an ambassadorship to Italy after she stepped down as national security advisor, because she was done with real politics after this—but she cared about the office of the president of the United States of America, and if Alex was basically calling the president in, it meant she was worried. Alex kept talking as they walked. "We figured we'd see it coming. Well, it's not coming. It's come. That's the takeaway from India and China. They've got it, and they are already overwhelmed. Best-case scenario is it's not already here and we can shut down flights and do our best to lock the country down. If it's an overreaction, we'll take a hit in the press." Manny started to speak, but Alex kept talking. "Not my problem, Manny, and you can figure it out later, but Steph, Madam President, if I'm your national security advisor, I'm advising you to understand that if this is bad enough to get the Chinese dropping nuclear weapons and now it's in India, we aren't overreacting."

Alex stopped walking and turned to look Steph and Manny full in the face. "I don't think this is an 'if' situation anymore. I think it's a 'when' kind of thing, and we're only buying ourselves time until it hits our shores."

Minneapolis, Minnesota

Agent Mike Rich wouldn't have minded a few extra days in Washington if it had meant a chance to maybe take that scientist out to dinner. The hotel the agency had gotten for him was crappy, he hadn't slept a wink, and he wasn't crazy about the spiders, but Professor Guyer was a good-looking woman. She was tall enough to look him in the eye and had that lean, athletic look he favored. There was something weird going on there with her relationship to the president's chief of staff, a schlumpy schlub of a man who nevertheless seemed pretty confident, but hell, there was something weird going on with everything. At the beginning of the week he was worried about homegrown Aryans and meth and drugs, and now suddenly it was cannibalistic spiders and President Stephanie Pilgrim and strict orders to keep his mouth shut. Wait. Cannibalistic? Was that right? Wouldn't that mean they only ate one another? Were they cannibals if they ate humans instead of other spiders? Fuck it, Mike thought, it didn't matter. What mattered was it was going to be a while before he could sleep without having nightmares.

He'd tried to sleep on the plane. Economy all the way home. They'd flown him to DC on a government jet and sent him back to Minneapolis commercial. He'd sort of been hoping he'd get a first-class upgrade, but nope. That was the federal government for you. He'd tried closing his eyes anyway, leaning against the window and letting the drone of the motor vibrate him to sleep, but whenever he'd get close to actually drifting off he'd imagine the feel of something crawling on him. His leg. His arm. The back of his neck. After the third jump of adrenaline, the third time he started swatting at himself, he decided it was better to just call it a day and watch some television. Not a comfortable trip.

He waited until the plane was mostly cleared out before he made his way up the aisle from near the back. He didn't have any luggage. The director had made it clear he was expected in Washington immediately, with "immediately" being code for "If you stop to pack luggage, you will find yourself reassigned somewhere unpleasant." Mike did take the time to have his hand stitched and bandaged and to put on a new suit that didn't have blood or puke on it, but all he was traveling with was his wallet, his cell phone, which was dead because he hadn't brought a charger, his identification, and his Glock. The gun was a perk of working for the agency. They still wouldn't let him bring a bottle of water through security, but the Glock wasn't a problem. He wished he had taken the extra minute to grab his shoulder holster instead of his belt holster. A shoulder holster did a much better job of keeping his gun hidden, even if it was shitty for any real fieldwork. The holsters were slow to draw, and when you did draw, it was hard not to unintentionally put somebody in the path of the barrel as you moved it to where you were going. They looked undeniably cool, though. He kind of wished he'd been wearing one in that professor's lab. His suit wasn't much, a shiny Men's BusinessDress special, but with his jacket off and a shoulder holster, he would have looked good. He did push-ups and chin-ups for a reason. But no. Instead, he was back in Minneapolis, getting off a plane after going nonstop for three days, the holster on his hip sitting against a patch of sweat. He'd showered at the hotel, but a change of clothes was in his near future.

He could hear the buzz of voices before he reached the end of the tunnel, but it wasn't until he popped out into the terminal that he realized there was something wrong. The normal unpleasantness of an airport was turned up. Way up. Instead of the boarding-area stasis of families clustered together in boredom, middle-aged consultants who thought they were important enough to warrant three seats when there weren't enough to go around, harried parents with car seats and juice boxes, instead of all that, there was a sense of mutiny. Crowds were clustered around the airline desks at the gates, a jabbering mix of yelling and pointing here, small groups of people crying there. More worrisome was that the people freaking out were only a small minority. The rest of the people were engaged in what looked like a mass exodus. A dispirited mass exodus, but a mass exodus all the same.

This, he thought, was what 9/11 must have been like.

Mike saw a uniformed TSA agent making like a traffic cop, and he stepped over to the young man, giving a flash of his ID. "Just got off a flight and my phone is deader than dead. What's the ruckus?"

"No ruckus. Flights are canceled."

"This is all just for a few canceled flights?"

The TSA agent stared at Mike with what looked suspiciously like a smirk. For a second, Mike indulged in the fantasy of popping the kid a quick one in the nose. It was a nice fantasy, but unwise.

"It's not a few canceled flights. It's all of them."

"All of them?"

"Yep. Every flight."

"Every flight from Minneapolis has been canceled?"

This time there was no suspicion. It was definitely a smirk. "Every flight in the country. Grounded all of them."

Mike didn't have a chance to admit that yes, he might have his head up his ass, because the man had already walked away. It didn't bother Mike, however. He was preoccupied with the weirdness of the terminal. He hadn't been traveling back in 2001, the last time flights were grounded, but he bet it had been like this. On 9/11, people would have been crowded around airport televisions watching the endless loop of the towers coming down. Now, Mike wasn't exactly sure what they were looking at; the screens were captioned with *Delhi, India*, and what he saw didn't make a ton of sense. And yet it did. The families and business travelers stranded in the Minneapolis airport might not understand what was happening, what to make of the brief snippet from India, but it took only a few seconds from Mike's hearing that flights were grounded to his putting the dots together. Spiders. It had to be. Nothing else really made any sense. Not that spiders made sense. But with what had happened to Henderson, with his trip to DC, meeting the president, that's what it had to be. And that meant that the president, the good-looking scientist, the people who got paid to tell agents like him what to do, were freaking out. Grounding the entire country? That was some serious shit.

He passed a magazine shop that was shutting down. Middle of the day, and the woman running it was dragging the metal gate across the entrance. Just past that, a waiting area was quickly emptying out. Annoyed men in suits packing up laptops, families with crying children loading up strollers. As Mike came to the signs telling him that once he exited he could not reenter, he pulled out his phone and gave it a click with his thumb, forgetting it was dead. It didn't matter: there they were, waiting for him. Annie was working on some sort of smoothie, and Fanny was typing something into her phone. They weren't looking up, and that gave Mike a chance to watch them as he walked up. Fanny looked good. She always looked good. She'd never been the fancy type, but she ran and had a nice eye for clothing. Even when she and Mike were together, before she remarried and suddenly had access to a whole different kind of shopping, she'd been good about picking outfits that worked to her advantage. And she'd done something different with her hair, something that gave a little more emphasis to her face. But even though he recognized that she was still beautiful, most men would have said sexy even, Mike realized that for the first time since he'd met her, he wasn't attracted to her anymore. Whatever it was—that spark, that little jolt he felt when he kissed her—was gone. Even more interesting, the disappearance didn't bother him. It was a relief, really. He didn't know if it was because he was sure she was pregnant and that meant she was finally, irretrievably gone, or that enough time had finally passed, or meeting that scientist, Melanie, had reminded him there were other women he might be interested in, but he didn't care. What it meant was that he could look at Fanny as somebody with whom he shared his daughter instead of somebody he was trying to win back.

As for Annie, it had only been, what, two, three days? Could she really look older to him? Older and younger at the same time. She had on a yellow sweatshirt with the hood up, her hair partly pulled from her ponytail, and from her profile, Mike could see what she was going to look like in a couple of years. And then she straightened up, pulled the straw out of her cup, and dribbled the smoothie into her mouth, looking very much like the kid she was.

"Hey, beautiful," he said, leaning over and hugging Annie.

"Daddy!" She wrapped her arms around his neck and squeezed as hard as she could. He kept wanting to tell her she had to take it a little easier, that she was getting big enough to hurt him when she hugged him that hard, but he didn't have the heart to do it. It was as if she thought squeezing him harder meant she loved him more. "Whoops," she said. "Sorry. I got smoothie on your suit."

"No worries, sweetie," he said, grateful she hadn't said anything about his slipping and calling her "beautiful" again. He
straightened up and gave Fanny a loose, one-armed hug. That
seemed best. There was a lot of history, and with his sudden realization that he was no longer interested in trying to win her back,
he wasn't sure what else they had. More than just a mutual interest
in Annie? Maybe a friendship? Could it be that simple? A friendship? "Thanks for picking me up," he said. "I could have taken a
cab, but this is nice."

Fanny did that thing that wasn't exactly a smile, and Mike understood why she'd offered to pick him up. She wanted to talk.
And sure enough: "I wanted to talk anyway," she said.

Annie jumped up and held on to Mike's hand. "Mom's having
a baby."

Mike actually laughed. Maybe because he was expecting it, and
maybe because he realized he could just be happy for Fanny, happy
that she'd figured out how to move past their marriage and try
again, happy that Annie had gotten the bad first deal of divorced
parents and somehow still ended up hitting twenty-one. For a
minute, it was enough to make him forget about the buzz of people heading out of the terminal. The weird sense that the entire
airport was shutting down in the middle of the day.

"Congratulations, Fanny," he said. He hugged her, this time
for real, with both arms, pulling her tight and holding on for an
extra second. "I'm really happy for you. For you and Rich," he said,
and he understood that he really meant it.

Marine Corps Base Camp Pendleton, San Diego, California

Lance Corporal Kim Bock didn't know what was going on, but she knew things were fucked. The day after China dropped the nuke they were told it was boots up, and then they were told to stand down. Yesterday there had been a hastily organized training session to review procedures for putting on bio suits and gas masks, and it looked like it was going to be boots up again. But then they'd been ordered back to barracks and after spending a couple of hours packing and repacking gear, they'd been left to their own devices. There wasn't any news, and even Honky Joe, who had been on and off the phone with his father, had no real information to add.

And then, all of a sudden, the radio and television and Internet were exploding with news and everything was all India and spiders and every goddamned airplane in the country was grounded and then everybody with any kind of ribbons or medals was yelling at them to clean their weapons and gear up and board a bus. Go, go, go!

So here they were. On a bus. A school bus. An honest-to-God yellow school bus. Mitts had looked at Kim and she'd shrugged. It didn't make a lot of sense to her either. They were good Marines, and so they had gotten onto the school buses, packs on their laps and M16s beside them. Elroy had his earbuds in and she could hear the music leaking out—the same old country shit he always listened to—and Mitts, Duran, and Honky Joe were playing cards with Goons. Kim squirmed around in her seat so she could talk to Sue.

To say that Private Sue Chirp came from a very different background from Kim was putting it mildly. Kim's parents had met at Howard University. Her mom was a pediatric oncologist and her dad taught ninth- and tenth-grade history at the National Cathedral School. He liked to joke that he—and Kim, when she'd been a student there, which was one of his perks as a faculty member—was a nice splash of color for the school. As far as Kim could tell, she was the only person in her graduating class who hadn't gone directly to college, and even though her parents had eventually come around to her desire to serve, they still expected her to go to college at some point. While Kim's family wasn't rich compared with most of her friends at the National Cathedral School, they were well-off, and that made them seem like billionaires compared with Sue.

Sue Chirp came to the Marines straight from the backwoods of West Virginia. Kim hadn't really thought there was a backwoods anymore, but meeting Sue had convinced her otherwise. Sue was smart and she was going to be a good Marine, but that was only because she didn't really have any other choice. She'd never met her dad, and her mom cycled through a series of boyfriends and was in and out of jail, usually for drugs. Once they'd gotten to know each other a bit, Sue told Kim that the scar on her arm was a burn from when she was six and her mom's meth cooking had gone awry. But the Marines were a great equalizer, and despite their very different upbringings, with Sue white, poor, and mostly neglected, with the armed forces her only way out, and with Kim black, relatively wealthy, and the focus of her parents' lives, choosing the Marines over the easier path that had been laid before her, the two of them had become very good friends. Maybe it was just that they were both women trying to make their way through what had always been a man's world, or maybe it was just that Sue was nice and smart. And funny.

"How long do you think we're going to be on these buses?" Sue asked. "Long enough for the brass to figure out that some of their Marines can't piss in bottles?"

Duran, who had a bit of a thing for Sue, leaned back, holding his cards to his chest. "I'll hold the bottle for you if you want to try."

"You into golden showers, Duran?" Sue said.

That got Sue a laugh, and it made Kim smile. She'd been trying to persuade Sue to give Duran a chance. He was a good guy, and from what Sue had told her about her dating history, a good guy was something she wasn't used to. Besides, with the Chinese dropping nukes and spiders eating India and this fucked-up deployment, why not?

Kim shoved her pack to the floor, turned all the way around, kneeled on the seat, and folded her arms on the seat back to make herself more comfortable. "Can't be that long, right? No way we'd be on school buses if we were going to be traveling more than an hour or two. That wouldn't make a lot of sense."

Sue unclipped the gas mask that was bouncing off the outside of her pack. She held it up to her face. "You see this thing? It's like three sizes too big for me, like they decided to make a gas mask that could fit a grizzly bear. If there's gas or bio, or whatever it is they think they're trying to get us ready for in such a hurry, it won't matter if my mask is on or not. The fucking thing doesn't fit." She clipped the mask back to her pack. "We fought a war with Humvees that couldn't withstand a basic blast from an IED, and we've

spent the last couple of days getting on and off planes, jumping up
and sitting down. And you're banking on something making sense
in the military? You're telling me that putting us on school buses
means we aren't going very far?" She shrugged. "Want to put some
money on it?"

"Yeah, but a school bus means—"

"A school bus means things are really fucked," Sue said. "You
know how people get about that sort of stuff. Armed troops of any
kind on US soil make citizens freak the fuck out, so what do you
think it's going to do to people when they see us loaded up in little
yellow school buses?" She reached down to touch her M16. "We
ain't exactly toting Scooby Doo lunch boxes here. If this is a big
enough deal that they're requisitioning school buses, something
is clearly fucked. So yeah, I'm a little concerned that my gas mask
doesn't fit."

"Come on. You know you're not going to need a gas mask."

Honky Joe held up three aces. Mitts swore, and Goons just
calmly handed his cards to Duran. Honky Joe gave his cards to
Duran as well, and then turned to Sue and Kim. "Gas mask?
Maybe. Maybe not. But I agree that this is fucked up. With the
nuke, deploying somewhere closer to China maybe makes sense,
but we're deploying stateside. That, my friend, is a big deal." He
leaned over Sue and tapped on the window. "You see that?"

They were driving past flatbeds loaded with chain-link fencing and posts. Each truck was loaded to the gills, the trucks themselves five abreast in a line that must have stretched close to a
mile. It took the school buses more than two minutes to pass the
trucks.

"You already know how big a deal it is to deploy troops on domestic soil," Honky Joe said. "But that's a bigger deal. What do you
think that fencing is for? We've got to be setting up internment

camps or something. Who for this time? Who we trying to keep locked up?"

Kim looked down at Sue's gas mask as it jiggled atop her pack. The glass eyes and filter canister made it look menacing, bug-like. "No," Kim said. "You don't deploy troops in the United States unless you're expecting an invasion. Or something. My bet is it's a something. Gas masks? It's not who. It's what. And the fences aren't for an internment camp. Think of it as a quarantine. The question isn't *who* are we trying to keep out, but *what* are we trying to keep out?"

Sue held the oversize gas mask up to her face again. "Fuck," she said, drawling the word out. "I'm going to die, aren't I?"

American University, Washington, DC

Bark was crying again. It was eight o'clock in the morning, Eastern Standard Time. Melanie had slept for maybe four hours, and Bark was crying again.

Unbelievable. Okay, Melanie was willing to admit that maybe she could have handled it with more tact, that given how little sleep they'd been getting and how hard they'd been working since the egg sac arrived, this wasn't the ideal time, but the minute she'd told him it was over she felt nothing but relief. Relief and annoyance. Seriously. Unbelievable. He started crying like she'd been his high school girlfriend. She was pretty sure Julie and Patrick weren't aware of her and Bark's affair before, but whatever hope she had of continued discretion had gone out the window because Bark just could not keep his shit together. The good thing, she supposed, was that neither Julie nor Patrick seemed judgmental about it. There was a time when they would have tsk-tsked her and called her a slut behind her back, but now they mostly seemed like they were annoyed by Bark's constant crying. If anything, Julie seemed as if she might be impressed that Melanie had gotten a little bit of what she wanted. Score one for feminism, Melanie supposed. The downside of feminism was probably right in front of her, though: instead of putting a brave face on it, Bark was just standing there, in the middle of the lab, dripping tears. Like a leaky faucet, not even bothering to wipe his face. Julie was drawing the venom from the dead spider, Patrick was prepping the solution, Melanie was headed to her office to give Manny a call, and Bark was standing around crying.

Even though she had been intending to end things with him for a while, the reason she finally went ahead with it was at least partly Agent Rich. He wasn't a dreamboat physically like Bark, but he wasn't as unimpressive-looking as Manny was either. Not to dump on Manny, who was a good guy, but he wasn't what Agent Rich was. Which was a man. Agent Rich was a true-blue man. With handcuffs. There was a real part of Melanie, even with all that was going on in the lab, that hoped he'd stick around DC and give her a chance to see what he looked like wearing nothing but his handcuffs.

There was only a part of her that had wanted Agent Rich to stay, however, because the bigger part of her wasn't sure she'd ever want to leave her lab. These things were fucking incredible. And she'd started calling them "things" because she wasn't sure they were really even spiders. At least not the way she'd come to think of spiders. There are thirty-five thousand species of spiders, and they've been on earth for at least three hundred million years. From the very origin of humanity, spiders have been out there, scuttling along the edges of firelight, spinning webs in the woods, and scaring the hell out of people, even though, with a few rare exceptions, they are no real threat. But these were something different.

Melanie had never understood the panic people felt about spiders. What was it that made people so afraid? Was it the eight legs, each limb both separate and a part of the spider? Or, with larger spiders, was it the hair? Was there something about seeing something as familiar as hair on something as alien as a spider that made people take leave of their senses? Even if you knew that the *Mygalomorphae* infraorder of spiders, which includes tarantulas, had utricating hairs, it's not as if utricating hairs were much of a threat to humans. At worst, they caused mild irritation. And the few species of spiders that could harm or even kill a human weren't always the ones that looked the scariest to people. None of it made sense to Melanie. Dog bites sent close to a million people a year to the emergency room for stitches, but spiders—unless a brown recluse bit you, and that was still pretty damn rare—didn't do much other than keep the mosquito population down. And yet, a spider in the tub was enough to make a grown man scream. Even as a kid, Melanie hadn't been scared. She distinctly remembered being five and trapping a spider for her mother. She'd popped a glass over the spider, brushed the spider in, and then brought it outside. Maybe that wasn't unusual; kids were taught to be afraid by their parents. But who had taught the parents to be afraid in the first place? No, Melanie had never understood being afraid of spiders.

Until now.

Finally, there was a reason for her to be afraid of spiders.

She'd explained all that to Manny when he called her yesterday, before Steph grounded civilian air traffic across the country, but she was going to her office right now and shutting the door behind her to call Manny, because after another night of studying them, she'd figured out that while one of these spiders was impressive, and the brood of them in the insectarium was kind of frightening, the way they acted together was scaring the shit out of her. She was beginning to worry that grounding the planes might not be enough.

Manny's phone rang through to voice mail, but before she even started leaving a message there was the beep of Manny calling her back.

"If it's about our relationship, Melanie, we need to do it another time."

"Fuck you, Manny. You called me on this," Melanie said. She wasn't really angry, though. She knew Manny. Knew he was making the joke because he was already worried about why she was calling. "It's about the spiders."

"Please tell me you've decided we're overreacting. We're getting killed on grounding the planes, Alex is freaking out, and we've actually deployed soldiers on US soil to get ready to enforce quarantine zones. The ACLU is pitching a fit, we're breaking a half-dozen laws, and we still aren't sure this is a real thing."

"What about India?" Melanie asked. Manny didn't say anything, so Melanie pushed it. "There's been more news out of India, hasn't there?"

"Not publicly," Manny said.

"But you aren't lifting the flight ban, and you aren't calling back the troops."

"No."

"So it's bad?"

"Melanie, why are you calling?"

"I think it's bad, Manny. Some of this is speculation, and I'm going to need to study them a lot longer, get more information, really spend some time—"

"Melanie," he said, cutting her off. "I get it. This isn't for publication. This isn't going into your tenure file or getting peer-reviewed, okay? Wait. Hold on."

She could hear the muffled sounds of talking in the background. Manny's voice distinct but the words unrecognizable, lost to ringing phones and a crowd.

Manny came back. "We've got other scientists and advisors and everybody and their mother telling us what they think is going on. None of it makes any sense, Melanie. This might as well be an alien invasion for all of what we understand."

"It is."

"What?"

"An alien invasion. I mean, not exactly," she said, "but sort of."

"Okay."

"Okay, what?"

"Okay," Manny said. "We came to you because Steph and I knew you'd be discreet and knew you were an expert, but right now what I need is someone I can trust. Which means you. So I don't care if you haven't done all the research you need to. I don't care if it hasn't been peer-reviewed or any of that other stuff. All I need to know is this: Is it solid?"

Melanie hesitated. She hated it. She was a scientist, and she wanted more information. She wanted proof. But it was solid.

"So spiders are basically hermits. Antisocial and aggressive toward other spiders. They like to be alone. But that's not true for all spiders. Social spiders are rare, but they exist. Any spiders, in captivity, will form small colonies. Even black widows will do it. But out in the field, in the wild, there are only a few species that do it. The most well known is the *Anelosimus eximius*. They'll have colonies of forty or fifty thousand spiders."

"Fifty thousand? Are you fucking kidding me? Fifty thousand of those giant things in your lab?"

"No, that's the thing. *Anelosimus eximius* are small. They work together to care for the brood—the babies—and to build webs that can catch bigger and better prey, but that only means large insects, the occasional bat or bird. It's a sort of cooperative. They don't really hunt together. Not in any real sense, or at least not in the way people usually think of hunting. And they are social, not eusocial. But these are different. I don't think they are just social. I think they are eusocial."

"Meaning? What's the difference?"

"Social means they work together, but eusocial means . . . Okay, so there's the initial definition and then there's the expanded definition that E. O. Wilson came up with."

The voices in the background on Manny's end suddenly got louder and then softer. "Melanie, I don't have time for you to be in professor mode. I need this quick. Give me a rundown on the phone and then do me a favor: hop in a cab and come over. I'm going to want you to give this to Steph directly and be ready to answer questions. So, in a nutshell, what are we looking at?"

"Ants," she said. "Ants and bees and termites. Two kinds of mole rats also, but really, think of them as ants. These spiders aren't like spiders. They're like ants."

"Like ants?"

"Eusocial groups are characterized by each individual taking on a specific role in their colony. Digging tunnels, laying eggs, all that stuff. And at some point, for some kinds of eusocial animals, they reach a point where they can't take on a different role. They become a certain kind of specialist, and all they can do is what they can do. Like a machine on an assembly line. They do one thing."

"So you're telling me that these particular spiders are specialized, that they've turned into little machines?"

"Look, we've dissected two, and they've been the same; neither one can lay eggs. So there's no question that there are more than one kind of these spiders. They have to be able to reproduce. But the ones we've looked at are specialized. Again, I can't say with one hundred percent certainty, or that all or even most of them are like this—"

"Melanie." He wasn't angry, but he was firm. "Enough. I get it. You might be wrong. But you might be right. What are we dealing with? People here are starting to panic. I'm willing to take the risk that you've got it wrong, because right now, right this minute, we don't know what the hell is going on. The spiders in your lab are the same as the one that crawled out of Bill Henderson's face, and we think they're probably the same things that are on the rampage in India and caused the Chinese to drop a nuke. As far as I know, you're the only person who's actually studied one up close. When I was in your lab, you told me they were scary, but they were just spiders. And now you're calling me to say maybe not. Maybe these spiders are something else. You're saying these spiders are like little machines that can do only one thing. So please, just tell me, Melanie, what's the one thing these spiders are designed to do?"

"Feed," Melanie said. "They're designed to feed."

Desperation, California

Yesterday had started off like a normal day. Well, other than that terrifying video from India and rumors that mutant spiders were devouring people in Delhi, followed by the grounding of all air travel in the United States, it had started off like a normal day. Gordo made pancakes and then he and Amy took Claymore for a long walk. Then, while Amy watched two episodes of *Buffy the Vampire Slayer*, Gordo worked out on the treadmill, showered, and scrolled through the Internet looking for information. There wasn't much, however. He spent most of his time wallowing in rumors. After lunch, Shotgun and Fred invited them over to play Catan. A normal day. And then: a coup d'état.

It was a peaceful coup d'état, but it was a coup d'état nonetheless: Gordo and Shotgun were no longer in charge. After Amy beat all three men at Catan, which was a standard occurrence, Gordo and Shotgun went down to the workshop to take a look at Shotgun's new band saw. When they came back up, the plans had changed: Fred and Amy had decided the two couples were going to ride out the next couple of weeks together, and that was that. One minute the plan was that, come the apocalypse—zombie, nuclear, environmental, or otherwise—the couples would retreat to their

respective homes for survival, and the next minute it had been decided survival was not something that should be done alone.

"Look," Fred said, his arm around Amy's waist, "if you both
are going to insist on going into lockdown mode, it's going to be
a lot nicer if we do it together. Face it. This idea is much more
fabulous."

Neither Gordo nor Shotgun objected, because they both realized the immediate truth: it *was* much more fabulous.

Gordo had to hand it to Fred. Shotgun was an engineer and
about the straightest gay man Gordo had ever met, and almost as
if in response, his husband, Fred, seemed to go as far as he could
in the other direction. It was as if the only way Fred knew how
to be gay was loudly and stereotypically. Which, frankly, was a
lot of fun. And Fred and Amy fed off each other's energy. Fred
was entertaining even by himself, but with Amy, the two of them
were like a superhero social-hour comedy team. While Gordo and
Shotgun could spend hours in the garage gapping spark plugs and
checking bearings, Fred and Amy could spend the same time in
the kitchen, whipping up appetizers and cocktails. Gordo loved his
wife, but fair was fair: Fred and Amy together made things better
than good. They made them, well, okay, fabulous. It was going to
take a little emotional energy to get used to, because Gordo had
always thought the end of the world as we know it to be a rather
gloomy proposition—ashes and fire and corpses and all that Cor-
mac McCarthy stuff—but with Amy and Fred running the show,
it was a really well-thought-out music playlist and artichoke dip
in an underground shelter that looked more like an incredibly hip
loft without windows than the sort of sad bomb-shelter bunkers
that were the standard fare for survivalists.

"So much of this is just waiting around," Amy said. She stepped
over and gave Gordo a kiss. "I'd rather wait around with company

than by ourselves. There's only so much time I can spend watching television while you clean your guns and double-check the radiation seals on the shelter. I'm sorry, but it makes sense and you know it."

"And we have the space," Fred said. "Somebody, and I'm not going to name names, but we all know I'm talking about my husband, has us stocked to live out five lifetimes down here. I mean, come on. The man even has tampons in storage, for God's sake. The only things we don't have that you'll need are clothing and dog food. Though, if Claymore doesn't mind canned peaches," Fred said, bending over to scratch behind the dog's ear, "he'll be fine."

So Amy and Gordo went home to pack. Amy filled two suitcases with clothes while Gordo loaded up the back of his truck with forty-pound bags of dog food—if the shit really did hit the fan, Claymore could transition to human food, but Gordo knew from experience that it gave the Lab some pretty bad flatulence—and tried to decide what things he might need that Shotgun didn't already have. By the time Amy was ready to go, Gordo had realized the genius of Amy and Fred's plan was that there *wasn't* anything other than dog food and their clothes that Shotgun and Fred did not have stocked. Ultimately, the only extra thing he took was his Cooper Arms Model 52 Western Classic rifle and a dozen boxes of twenty-round .30-06 ammunition. It wasn't his most expensive rifle, but it was his favorite. He could cluster three rounds in a three-inch circle from five hundred yards with it. If it really came to it, Shotgun's armory was loaded for bear with guns and a few other things that weren't exactly guns and weren't exactly legal, but the Cooper Arms 52, even if it had only a three-shot magazine, was a sort of security blanket. He wasn't going to take on rampaging zombie hordes with it, but if he needed to take out one person from a distance, it was the rifle he'd choose.

They were back and unpacked in one of the spare bedrooms in less than two hours. By seven they were eating dinner, by eight they were pleasantly drunk and playing Scrabble, by ten Gordo and Amy were in bed, and by six the next morning Gordo was getting himself a cup of coffee and feeling good enough about the decision to move into Shotgun's place that he was beginning to think maybe it had partly been his idea. Shotgun's setup really was sweet, and they did have a better chance of surviving the end of the world if they were working together. Plus, even though Gordo hated admitting it, it really was sort of more exciting being prepared *with* Shotgun. Survival was great, but it was even cooler to have somebody to gloat with. What was the fun of surviving if you couldn't take pleasure in being more prepared and smarter than everybody else? It was exciting to think that these years of getting ready, all this effort, were going to pay off.

Gordo poured some cream into his coffee, taking an extra moment to savor it. That would be the first thing to go: fresh dairy, fresh produce, fresh meat. Freeze-dried, frozen, shelf-stable. That's what would come as soon as they had to bunker up. But in the meantime, there was fresh cream and no reason he couldn't drink his coffee outside. Besides, Claymore was already dancing around his feet. He'd trained Claymore to do his business on a five-by-five piece of artificial turf, but it made sense to take the pup out for a run while he could. Gordo walked up the stairs, through the double set of blast and radiation doors, and into the shell house that stood over the shelter. As soon as he opened the front door Claymore darted out, down the porch stairs, and into the dirt yard. The chocolate Lab took a piss against a boulder and then started rolling around in the dust. He seemed pleased with himself. Gordo took a sip of his coffee and then turned at the sound of a scrape on the wood.

"Didn't see you there," Gordo said.

Shotgun nodded. He was sitting on the porch in a rocking chair, a cup of coffee on the small table next to him, a tablet in his hand. "Couldn't sleep. Just wanted to catch up on the news."

"And?"

"Nothing. Well, everything. Same as yesterday. I guess a little more news out of India. Giant spiders, supposedly. There are a ton of pictures, but I've got to be honest: it looks like somebody went to town with Photoshop. Hard to believe it's not a hoax. That being said, the AP reported at least two really big explosions, and people are panicking. Evidently almost all communication systems in Delhi are overloaded. Clearly, *something* is going on."

"And here?"

"Just rumors. Crazy stuff. A lot of reports that troops have been mobilizing. Conspiracy folks are freaking out: It's the first step to the government enslaving us all. Hope you slept with that pretty little rifle of yours," he said, "because according to the whack nuts, the president is sending the suits in to take away our God-given right to bear arms."

Gordo laughed. That was one of the things he liked about Shotgun. He knew there was something a little crazy about preparing for the end of the world, about moving to Desperation, California, and building a shelter, but you could drive a truck through the gap between the real estate of *a little* crazy that Gordo liked to think he and Shotgun occupied and the *lot* of crazy real estate that some preppers lived on. Most preppers seemed to inhabit a world where the government was always one step away from turning us all into slaves, one step away from a massive global conspiracy led by the Jews, a plot by the blacks, an invasion by the Chinese, another terrorist attack. Some of it was racist or anti-Semitic or paranoid, but most of it was just downright loony.

"The black helicopter brigade is out in full force," Gordo said.

Claymore got up from the ground and gave himself a full head-to-tail shake. A small dust cloud poofed off him.

"No kidding," Shotgun said. "Black helicopters everywhere. Somebody posted that—"

"Hey," Gordo said, cutting him off. "Do you hear that? It sounds like . . ."

They were both quiet for a second, but then Claymore started barking. His tail dropped down and curled between his legs. He was pointed at Gordo and Shotgun, but looking up, over the roof. Shotgun got to his feet and stood next to Gordo. The two of them glanced at each other and then jogged down the steps of the porch until they were out in the yard near Claymore. There wasn't anything to see. Gordo reached down, rubbed at Claymore's ear, and then wrapped his hand around the dog's muzzle, quieting his barking.

Both he and Shotgun heard it. A soft *thwap, thwap, thwap* getting louder. The sound bounced off the dirt and desert and rocks.

The helicopter came in low and fast, buzzing the house and leaving a swirl of dust. It was too quick for them to do anything but turn and watch it fly past.

"What the fuck?" Gordo let go of Claymore's muzzle. The dog sprinted twenty or thirty yards after the helicopter and then planted himself in the dirt, barking again.

"Okay," Shotgun said. "That wasn't just me, was it? That was a black helicopter."

"Yep," Gordo said.

"Huh."

"Shotgun," Gordo said. "How do you feel about taking your plane out for a spin, get a look at what we have around us?"

"Absolutely."

Shotgun went to get the six-seater ready, and Gordo brought Claymore back downstairs, putting him in the room where Amy was still sleeping. He took a second to kiss her on the forehead before grabbing a pair of binoculars. By the time he was in the garage, Shotgun had the doors open and the plane ready to go. They were up in the air fifteen minutes after the helicopter passed over.

And two minutes after that, Gordo was worried.

Desperation, California

Kim probably wouldn't have noticed the small airplane above them if Honky Joe hadn't pointed it out.

"Civilian," he said. "They better bug the fuck out of here or they're going to be eating a missile."

"Come on," Duran said. "They aren't going to shoot down some Cessna just for flying over us."

They'd driven the convoy through Desperation, a pissant town, if you could call a few bars, a gas station, and a pizza place a town, and been ordered to halt about a mile out on an open plain of brush, scrub, and dirt. The only thing within shooting distance was a shitty-looking trailer, and sure enough, they'd barely gotten out of the bus before some redneck on an ATV came barreling toward them. Kim had been close enough to catch bits and pieces, but Honky Joe, as was his way, had the whole thing.

"Guy just about had an aneurysm. All 'Get off my land this, and the Constitution that,' and all that shit. I pointed out to him that he was actually on state-owned land and shouldn't be there in the first place, and he started to argue against *that* until I also pointed out we had more machine guns than he did. Dude came pretty close to getting himself forcibly removed." They all laughed, but Honky

229

Joe shook his head. "You guys don't get it. This *isn't* right. Why the fuck are we setting up here? Why not on a base somewhere? This side of the road might technically be government land, but what's here? Why outside this town? It's the middle of nowhere. The only thing it's got going for it is it's kind of near the highway. I think we're here because it will be an easy place to redirect traffic. It's a holding pen."

"For what?" Kim asked.

"People."

Nobody said anything to that. They just looked at one another grimly and did their jobs.

They'd worked through the night, and the longer they'd worked under the portable floodlights, the more what Honky Joe said made sense to Kim. They unloaded fencing from the flatbeds and set it up in a great perimeter, and there was no getting away from it: it looked like a holding pen. No, actually, it looked like a clean version of a refugee camp. Trucks and troop transports kept coming in; support material, portable toilets, water trucks, and tents getting set up. There was a constant stream of traffic. Trucks with supplies and trucks that were mobile buildings. Kim couldn't help but wonder where it all came from. Los Angeles? San Francisco? Las Vegas? All three? By six in the morning it was a terrifying sight: the US military mobilized. Near as Kim could tell, there were in the neighborhood of four or five thousand troops, a full brigade. It was fucked-up. This wasn't some sort of make-work training drill.

She was tired, and grateful for the coffee. The food could be pretty bad sometimes, and the coffee occasionally tasted like it had been filtered through socks, but it was always full of caffeine. She looked up and watched the tiny plane doing a lazy circle around the small city they were building. A black helicopter was buzzing around maybe a mile away. There were a couple of AH-64 Apaches loaded with missiles and ready to be all badass, but they were on the ground, rotors stilled. The airborne helicopter wasn't marked, but as near as Kim could tell, it was the sort of bird that muckety-mucks in suits liked to play in. After a few minutes of the plane circling overhead, the helicopter, which had been lingering out near where flatbeds were still pulling in, peeled off hard and up toward the direction of the plane. Whoever was in the plane, whatever civilian it was at the yoke, wasn't curious enough to stay; the plane straightened course and headed out. The helicopter tracked it for a few more seconds then turned back to where it had been hovering, came in low, and settled.

The lieutenant gave a yell for the platoon to finish up. Kim drained her coffee, pulled her work gloves on, and looked at her squad, Honky Joe, Sue, and the few other soldiers around her. "Okay," she said. "Whatever the fuck we're doing, just look alive. Something's coming down the pike."

Point Fermin Park, Los Angeles, California

Sparky was going nuts. To be fair, Sparky was a twelve-year-old coonhound, so he was kind of nuts to begin with, but he was braying as if there were a monster around the corner. He yanked on his leash again, but this time Andy was ready for it and didn't stumble. Andy Anderson was rounding eighty years old, a retired entertainment lawyer and widower. With no grandkids and his friends dropping dead right and left, he had two things left that he cared about: baseball, and the damned dog. The two things intersected. He'd named the dog Sparky in honor of his favorite manager: Sparky Anderson, the man himself. Andy would have named the dog after one of his heroes anyway, but he liked the idea that Sparky Anderson was a Detroit legend who had grown up in Los Angeles. Not that many people knew Sparky Anderson had moved to Los Angeles as a kid. If they knew Sparky Anderson, they knew him only as the manager of the Cincinnati Reds or the Detroit Tigers. They sure didn't know him for his utterly forgettable career as a major league player. But Andy didn't hold that against him. Andy had never been much of a ball player either, blowing out his arm after only two years of mediocre pitching on a medio-

233

cre team at a mediocre college. But he was born and bred Detroit, and it was for Sparky Anderson's time in Detroit that Andy had decided to pay homage to the man. The year the Tigers won, 1984, had been the best year of Andy's life. And that was saying a lot, because Andy's life had been good. But the year the Tigers won the World Series had been the best of all those years; everything had swung his way, including the Detroit hitters. Never mind that Andy had lived in Los Angeles since 1971, he still thought of himself as a scrappy Detroit kid. He never tired of the joke of having a dog named Sparky Anderson.

But Sparky—the dog, not the deceased MLB manager—was giving him fits today. The dog had started by taking a shit right in the middle of the kitchen sometime during the night, a thing he was wont to do once or twice a month. Normally, it wouldn't have bothered Andy. The dog was old, and there wasn't much you could do about it other than make sure you had paper towels and spray cleaner at home. He was tired this morning, however. He'd stayed up late to watch the president's speech and then the endless bloviating on cable news backed by crappy, boring footage of empty airports, parked planes, and that stupid, shaky video from India. The president said nothing of any substance—the threat was dire enough that she was willing to take "unprecedented action in defense of the country and our citizens, shutting down air travel and closing the borders as a temporary matter" even if she wasn't willing to specify what the threat was beyond referencing "the recent events in China and India"—and the news people were left with nothing real. Just damned-fool speculation. Some of the talking heads were saying that China was setting itself up to try to invade Japan, and at least a few of the opinion pukers said it was some sort of virus, like the plague. But the consensus, if there was one, was that there were hordes of spiders on the loose. Or swarms of spiders. Whatever you call a bunch of spiders. What you should really call a bunch of spiders, Andy thought, was horseshit.

So he'd been up late, and then Sparky woke him up before 5:00 A.M. by starting with his coonhound's warbling bark, calling out with some real distress before taking a dump on the kitchen floor. Andy had cleaned it up and then parked himself in his chair to watch the same cycle of drivel on the news until, just before it was time for their noon walk, Sparky took another dump on the kitchen floor. Even if it hadn't been time for their walk, the smell, even after it was cleaned up, would have been enough to force Andy out of the house. He drove the two of them to Point Fermin Park. The dog howled the whole way. Sparky seemed intent on being a little prick all day long. He was an old dog, and normally content to sniff at things, lift his leg occasionally, and amble down the path, but today Sparky was yanking on his leash. It was giving Andy fits. Andy didn't have many worries left—he had had plenty of money, and he was healthy enough that he figured he'd be fine for a while and then just go ahead and die of old age—but breaking his hip was one of his few real terrors. It was one thing to grow old and lonely, but it was another to finish out his days bedridden and in pain.

Even with Sparky being a prick, the day was beautiful. But it was Los Angeles. It was always beautiful. The end of April meant it was cool enough for Andy to slip on his leather jacket, but by one or one thirty, it would be warm enough for him to sit outside with Sparky at the café. They went to different parks on different days, but most of the time he tried to go for their noon walks near the water. That was the other thing about Los Angeles. It had movie stars and palm trees and sunny skies, and it had the ocean. They'd started at one end of the park, and Andy had almost dragged Sparky the whole way to the other. The damn dog lunging against the leash and baying away. Maybe an earthquake was coming, Andy thought. He knew dogs did that. Predicted things like earthquakes and tornadoes. And wouldn't that be a ball of crap, if the big one came when he was walking in a park at the edge of the ocean. The whole thing would slide right in.

Sparky started to move toward Andy and then turned and yanked at the leash again. Andy figured he should just give up on the walk, but he didn't want the dog to think he could win. He reined in the leash and then leaned over and scratched the dog under his jowls. "Come on, boy," Andy said. "Can we just finish our walk without you turning me into a cripple? You walk like a good dog, and when we're done we'll stop for a burger and some French fries. How does that sound? French fries? Who wants French fries?"

Sparky, evidently, wanted French fries. It wasn't enough to suddenly turn him back into a good dog, but it was clear to Andy that he recognized the words. He should have. It was part of their routine. Hop in the car, a walk in a park along the water somewhere, Sparky taking a little nap while Andy sat on a bench and read or just stared out into space and let the time tick away, and then a stop for a burger and fries on the way home. They always stopped somewhere with outdoor seating and Andy would end up giving as much of his lunch to Sparky as he ate himself. It wasn't healthy for either of them. Andy didn't try to kid himself that their ambling walks made up for the greasy lunches he shared with his dog, but at this point, he wasn't sure he cared. There was nothing like a burger, and feeding Sparky French fry after French fry, the dog daintily nipping them from his fingers, was one of life's little pleasures. But first, they had to finish their walk. That was the way it worked.

Near the end of the path, Sparky started being a prick again. The dog stopped walking and pulled back on his leash hard enough to make Andy stumble. At the same time, Sparky started howling again. Normally, Andy thought of Sparky's noise as a sort of singing, but today he was through with it. He was about to just pack it in and let Sparky lead the way—he was sure pulling on his leash, in a hurry to get somewhere—when Andy noticed the ship.

It was one of those container ships. Not particularly remarkable here, overlooking the Port of Los Angeles. At least, not normally a remarkable sight. It was huge. One of those new superfreighters, probably coming from China. He couldn't imagine what the thing would look like up close. Given the size and where he was standing on the coastline, Andy figured it was maybe a mile out from port. A mile and a half at most. And it was really moving. The size of the ship wasn't what captured his attention. It was a behemoth, but there were other ships out in the water big enough that this one didn't really stand out as *that* much bigger. The difference was that this one was moving fast. Andy didn't know much about shipping, but it just didn't look right. Like a bus coming into a parking lot at full speed. Except this bus was loaded up with containers. Each metal cube was a different color, the ship a kaleidoscope, a beautiful puzzle.

Andy pushed his glasses up on his nose. There were some weird shadows on the boxes. They didn't look right to him. They were more like lines, or streaks of paint. No. Like some kid had scribbled here and there with a thick-tipped marker, leaving marks on top of the picture. Except . . . Were the lines moving?

Sparky was really howling now, almost crying, and pulling hard against the leash. Andy had to dig in to hold his ground. "Come on, Sparky," he said. "Give me a break, you little monster. I just want to see . . ." He trailed off, because he suddenly understood just what it was he was going to see. Shadows or lines or whatever they were, the ship was still bearing ahead. He had no real idea how fast it was moving. Fifteen, twenty miles an hour? Fast enough that it looked quick against the backdrop of the ships that weren't moving. Fast enough that it wasn't a mile offshore anymore. Fast enough that Andy knew there was no chance of the ship stopping in time.

The dog was still pulling him hard away from the path, toward where he had parked the car. After another quick look at the ship, Andy turned and let Sparky lead him away. The thing with the boat seemed bad.

It quickly went from bad to worse.

The *Mathias Maersk* Triple-E was loaded with goods from all over China. Electronics and T-shirts and kitchen knives. Eighteen thousand containers to fill America's malls and homes. But some of those containers originated in Xinjiang Province, and now there were no crew members left alive to stop the ship from smashing into the Port of Los Angeles.

It would have been basic back-of-the-envelope math for guys like Gordo and Shotgun. The ship was coming in at eighteen miles per hour with a total deadweight of near 160 million tons when it ran aground. To calculate the kinetic energy, they would have simply plugged in the numbers: $\frac{1}{2}MV^2$, or $\frac{1}{2}$ (160,000,000 kg $\times$ (8m/s $\times$ 8m/s)). Roughly 5,120,000,000 joules. Or, to put it more simply, when the *Mathias Maersk* Triple-E plowed into the port at 12:47 P.M. Pacific Standard Time, the impact was the equivalent of an explosion of 2,500 pounds of TNT.

But Gordo and Shotgun were back in the shelter, talking to Amy and Fred about what the army was doing setting up fences in their backyard. Neither of them was there to run the math or to see the *Mathias Maersk* Triple-E run aground. The truth was that almost nobody was watching. So many things were automated at the port that during the lunch hour, there was barely anybody there. The first person to die from the actual impact was Cody Dickinson, who was also the only person who should have figured out there was something wrong with the *Mathias Maersk* Triple-E.

But instead of doing his job, Cody Dickinson had smoked twenty dollars' worth of pot and fallen asleep in his seven-hundred-dollar Herman Miller Aeron chair. He had the cushy office job because he had seniority, and he had seniority because he was sixty and had been a longshoreman for forty-two years, and because he had been working as a longshoreman for forty-two years, he'd worked as a longshoreman when working as a longshoreman actually meant working, which meant his back was wrecked, which was why he had the seven-hundred-dollar Herman Miller Aeron chair, but his back still killed him, and smoking a ton of pot was the only thing that really helped. So he was asleep when the ship ran aground and the impact caused the roof to collapse and kill him where he sat.

The shock wave was enough to easily carry the eight hundred yards from the point of impact to where the P. Lanster Insurance Agency sat just outside the fencing securing the Port of Los Angeles. The P. Lanster Insurance Agency was a low-slung office building, and at 12:47 P.M. Pacific Standard Time, Philip Lanster Jr., the son of P. Lanster himself, was the only occupant of the office. Philip Lanster Jr. had been trying to get his dad to move the agency to a better location for years. The office was inconvenient for everybody, dingy and too big for them, since they had only five employees. The benefit was that there were windows everywhere, and they all had views of the ocean. This afternoon, however, Philip Lanster Jr. was glad the office was inconveniently located. It meant that when his dad and the other employees went out for lunch, he'd have more time to finish cooking the books. He'd skimmed off only six grand, just enough to cover what he'd lost in Las Vegas the weekend before. A little creative paperwork, and problem solved. He was feeling pretty good about himself and had just stood up from the bookkeeper's desk when the impact of the *Mathias Maersk* Triple-E's crash made the window beside him explode into the room. If he'd still been sitting, he might have been fine, but he was just tall enough that one of the shattered pieces of glass hit him in the side of the neck. He bled to death in sixty seconds.

He was lucky to bleed to death in sixty seconds. The first spiders were crawling through the broken window in eighty.

Up on the hill, Julie Qi was catching her breath when the ship hit. She fell on her ass. She'd just finished a hard five miles. She fucking hated running. What kept her going was the knowledge that the only thing she hated worse was the idea of her husband leaving her for somebody younger and fitter, and in LA, unless she busted her ass, that meant almost every woman out there. Well, the fitter part. She couldn't do much about being younger. Bradley was forty-seven, however, and Julie was only thirty, so she figured she had a little bit of a cushion with age, if not with cellulite. So it was morning aerobics, running before a late, light lunch, and then yoga in the afternoon. Bradley worked and she didn't, which meant her job was to look good.

It took her a moment to realize she hadn't just fallen over for no reason—the shudder of the ground was enough to make her stumble and end up on her backside—and another moment to realize it wasn't an earthquake. The ship was a mile away. It had run aground, but the weight and momentum were enough to drive it far enough out of the water that it almost looked comical. Julie got back to her feet and pulled her earbuds out, the music leaking into the air. "Jesus," she said. There weren't any flames or anything, but there didn't need to be: the thing was like a quarter of a mile long. It looked spectacular just mangled and eating the coast. There was weird black smoke, however, Julie noticed. It sort of spilled off the ship, but instead of floating into the sky, it rolled over the edges and across the pavement.

She unzipped her waist belt and pulled out her phone. She

thought about photos, but decided instead that she'd just shoot some video. The phone had a good enough camera that she could just pull a still from the video if she wanted, and she had a partially formed thought that maybe she could sell the footage to a news station. Not that she and Bradley needed the money, but you know, it was a fun idea. Through the screen, however, it didn't look quite as cool. The boat looked too much like some sort of toy. The image just didn't give the right sense of scale.

She looked up from the screen and noticed the smoke had mostly stopped coming off the ship. There were just a few tendrils dripping down the sides. But the smoke that had already come off the ship was still drifting across the ground. It had spread out a little, so it was less a single carpet of smoke than larger patches and fingers spreading out over the road and the hills, pieces taking in some of the smaller office buildings outside the fence, near where the ship had hit. She remembered from 9/11 that a lot of the workers ended up having health problems from breathing in all the bad air, and she wondered if the workers on the docks were going to have issues.

She didn't notice the finger of black crawling up the hill toward her.

In the parking lot of Cabrillo Beach, Harry Roberts was pissed. He didn't like blacks—sorry, African Americans—and if that made him racist, he was fine with that, and he didn't like cops either, even if he liked to think of himself as a law-and-order Republican, so being arrested by two black cops was the sort of thing that got him seething. Sure, his lunch had really been more of a liquid brunch consisting entirely of Bloody Marys, but who wouldn't want a few extra drinks with what was on the news with that crazy stuff in India, China getting ready to invade Europe, and that cunt president grounding the flights? Admittedly, he didn't really remember leaving the restaurant and driving his car over from Manhattan Beach, and admittedly, he sure didn't remember crashing it into the light pole, and, okay, admittedly, he could understand their initial concern, since the air bag had evidently given him a bloody nose, and his face and shirt were covered in blood, but he couldn't believe they cuffed him and put him in the back of their cruiser. Pricks. And then, worse, as they were writing something up, there was that incredible noise, some sort of an explosion across the water.

"Sit tight," one of the cops had said to him. They left the windows partially open for him, but they walked across the parking lot and headed out of sight through the brush. And then, nothing for the last few minutes. Well, nothing other than the sounds of sirens, car alarms, a few screams. Harry had no clue what was going on except that he was pissed.

Then he heard two gunshots. Two. That was all. And then one of the cops burst through the bushes, running toward the squad car but looking back over his shoulder. He made it maybe ten feet into the parking lot before he started getting covered in . . . Harry couldn't figure it out, but the cop kept running, closing the gap from thirty, twenty-five, twenty, fifteen feet. By the time the cop fell, barely ten feet from the cruiser, Harry had figured out the cop was covered in insects of some kind. No. Spiders. But that was all he had time to realize before they broke off from the body and came for him.

Five minutes from the time the ship ran aground, Cody Dickinson, Philip Lanster Jr., Julie Qi, and Harry Roberts were dead. Close to a hundred other people as well. None of them able to see the threads of silk starting to twist into the air, catching and colliding, the soft breeze lifting spiders above the sand and surf and concrete that was the coast of Los Angeles, wafting over approaching ambulances and fire trucks and squad cars, sending them into the gentle noonday sun, south toward Compton and Lynwood and Chinatown, toward the 405 and the 10.

Stornoway, Isle of Lewis, Outer Hebrides, Scotland

"**P**erhaps a phone call or an e-mail or—"

"Sir," the British Airways agent said, cutting him off, "it was not our decision to cancel your fiancée's flight, and there is nothing I can do about rescheduling her at the moment. Haven't you heard the news?"

Aonghas had not, in fact, heard the news that the prime minister had grounded all flights. While on Càidh Island they'd been listening to the BBC and following the news in China until that was eclipsed by the news out of India and the hysteria about spiders, and they'd heard about the American president's overreaction in deciding to stop air travel. Typically American, Padruig said. But it turned out the UK was following in America's panicked footsteps again. The plane that had just landed was the last one in or out until the ban was lifted. Normally, Aonghas would indeed have heard the news: in Stornoway by himself, he would have started the day as he usually did, by reading the news, and had he and Thuy still been on Càidh Island, Padruig would have had the BBC on the radio. But he wasn't on Càidh Island with his grandfather, and he certainly wasn't in Stornoway by himself: they'd left the island at the first hint of dawn. It was a flat-out lie to Aonghas's grandfather. They told Padruig that Thuy's flight was early, but the truth was her flight wasn't until the evening: they just wanted to spend the day alone together, in bed, without worrying that the old man would wonder what they were up to. Not that Aonghas's grandfather was a prude, just that Aonghas knew he wasn't going to see his girlfriend—no, his fiancée—again for two weeks once Thuy boarded her flight back to Edinburgh.

He was still sort of amazed at how well the trip had gone. Sure, his grandfather had accidently asked Thuy to marry Aonghas for him, but she'd said yes, so there was no real harm in that. And for all his worry that Padruig might not take to Thuy, by the time they said good-bye to him, his grandfather dressed impeccably even just for the early-morning trip to the dock, Aonghas had a niggling fear Padruig might like Thuy more than he liked Aonghas himself. And Thuy had fallen head over heels in love with Càidh Island and the castle. She loved sitting in the library reading by the fire, spent a full hour down in the wine cellar with his grandfather, sat on the rocks and looked out at the waves. The trip was an unqualified success. The only problem was that, after they had gone to the trouble of sneaking away early for a little private time, it looked as though Thuy wasn't going to be able to leave after all. Really, though, was that such a bad thing?

The good news was that at an airport as small as Stornoway's, it wasn't much of a walk to the parking lot, and even with the passengers getting off the last plane to land on the island, it was easy in, easy out. "We can pick up some pasta and vegetables, maybe watch a movie. I'm sure you'll be able to fly out tomorrow. I can't imagine the prime minister is going to swallow this spider bollocks much longer. The upside is that you'll never have a better excuse for missing a little school, and you won't exactly have a glut of free time once you start your residency. Plus, you know," Aonghas said, loading her bag back into the Range Rover, "there are worse things than being stuck with your fiancé for another day. Fiancé," he said again, rolling the word in his mouth. "I like the sound of that."

He got into the driver's seat, started the Range Rover, put it into drive, and then hesitated. There was a man throwing up in front of the doors to the airport. "Jesus," Aonghas said. "Must have been a bumpy landing. That Indian bloke's cleaning himself out."

The man vomited again, and then slumped against a pillar. Even from where Aonghas and Thuy sat in the Range Rover, it was clear the Indian bloke was doing poorly. He was starting to claw at his tie, as though he was having trouble breathing, and the few other passengers who had been able to make it to Stornoway on the last flight before the grounding were either giving him a wide berth or standing well away from him. Now the Indian man let go of his tie and started pulling on his shirt, untucking it and then ripping it open. Jesus. Aonghas saw a button pop off, tracing a gentle arc before bouncing on the cement.

Thuy unbuckled. "I should go help."

"You're not a doctor yet."

She rolled her eyes, but Aonghas grabbed her arm. "Just wait. Hold on."

"Aonghas. I need to help."

He kept his hand on her arm, but he was watching the man, watching the way people weren't sure if they should move forward or back. The skin on the man's chest and stomach looked shiny, as if it was stretched tight. "Just, I don't know. Just wait one second."

One second was all it took.

The man's front opened up like a zipper.

"Aonghas!" Thuy screamed.

Aonghas slammed his foot on the gas.

"Aonghas! We've got to help him."

Aonghas kept his foot all the way down, overriding the eco function that was supposed to improve the Range Rover's miserable gas efficiency, overriding the computer in the engine that wanted to shift to a higher gear. He cranked the wheel and passed uncomfortably close to a middle-aged woman wearing a floral dress that looked like it belonged in the museum of "things from the 1970s that you wouldn't ever want to wear in public." Thuy was turned and looking out her window, and Aonghas, wrestling the steering wheel, stole a glance over his shoulder. He couldn't see the Indian man anymore, but the people who were outside near the entranceway seemed to be screaming, flailing their arms. He could see the black balls—spiders, he knew even without being able to make out the details that they were spiders—moving and jumping and crawling on people. One woman's face was streaming blood and she was clawing at her cheek.

"Oh my god." Thuy turned back in her seat. "What the shit?"

"Buckle up," he said. He lifted his foot off the gas and tapped the brakes, dropping from fifty kilometers an hour to thirty so he could take the corner at the end of the row of cars. With his foot off the gas for that brief instant, the Range Rover shifted gears. The tires gave the beginnings of a screech before he straightened it out.

By the time he came to the exit he was doing seventy. He didn't even think of touching the brakes. He took the wooden arm off the exit gate.

As he turned right onto A866, Thuy spoke again. "Those were . . . those were spiders, right?"

"I think so," Aonghas said. "Yes."

"And they came out of his chest and stomach."

"Yes."

"The Indian man."

"I suppose he could have been Pakistani."

"He could have been Pakistani. Yes. I suppose."

"But probably not," Aonghas said.

"No. Probably not." She was quiet for a few seconds. "That really happened?"

"I'm afraid so," Aonghas said.

"And?"

"And I write mysteries for a living," he said. "All I'm doing is connecting the dots."

"Okay."

"Okay?"

Thuy scooted on the seat until she was turned to face him. He was driving the speed limit now, since he didn't want to get pulled over, and those things didn't seem like they could keep pace with a car. He risked looking at her. She reached out and touched his cheek.

"Okay," she said. "That was impressive. You just reacted."

"I'm not normally like that," he said. "In fact, I don't think a girlfriend has ever called me impressive."

"Well, I'm not your girlfriend anymore. So what are we doing now? Where are we going?"

"Back to Càidh Island," he said.

"What about my flight to Edinburgh?"

They passed a house with a small plastic toddler slide in the front. There was a part of Aonghas that wanted to stop and bang on the door and yell at the family to run, to get the hell out of there, but he didn't stop. He kept driving. "Thuy," he said, "even if your flight wasn't canceled, we're getting out of here for now. Think about what we've been listening to on the radio. That video they keep talking about. I mean, we haven't seen it, but if the video is anywhere near as bad as it sounds, and if the pictures they're talking about are real—and now this, well, this . . . It seems like . . ."

"And China."

"China?"

"You don't think they're connected?"

"Why would they be connected?"

"I don't know," Thuy said. "But don't you think?"

Aonghas was quiet for a second, and then he turned on the radio and tuned in to the BBC. They were talking about Los Angeles.

It sounded terrifying.

The CNN Center,
Atlanta, Georgia

Teddie had thrown up only twice today, which, she thought, was pretty good. At first, that deep feeling in her stomach had been excitement: now *this* was a news story. They'd gotten reports of the crash and she ordered a camera crew from the Los Angeles studio over to the port. It was the kind of story that could get her a promotion: great visuals, easy to summarize, and plenty of ways in which they could spin it off. She was already thinking of the "hidden menace of shipping" special. But those excited butterflies quickly turned into something else.

The crew couldn't get anywhere near the port. Traffic was snarled everywhere, which wasn't that unusual for Los Angeles, but she gave up on the ship story pretty quickly. The news was spiders. The cell phone videos and phone calls were terrifying. India was one thing—it was so far away you could convince yourself it might be a hoax or that it wasn't as horrifying as it looked—but this was Los Fucking Angeles. Some kid near Long Beach uploaded a six-second clip of spiders overwhelming a jogger and coating him like an oil slick, and they got a call-in from near the port from a woman who was yelling that she was watching spiders eat a mom and a baby before the caller herself started screaming and then the only sound was this weird crackling. That was the first time Teddie threw up, when she figured out the crackling sound was actually the spiders chewing human flesh.

The camera crew finally gave up on the traffic and set up on McCarthy Quad at the University of Southern California. It was the perfect shot for a reporter who couldn't get an angle on the real action. The dichotomy of reporting on fear and chaos from the middle of an ivory-tower oasis. Students walked past in the background as if nothing was going on twenty-five miles across town. The reporter blathered excitedly, filling time in the way that only a seasoned pro can fill time when the facts are almost entirely speculation.

And then, the spiders came gliding down from the sky.

At first, there weren't many. The camera caught a few black dots against the cerulean sky, cotton-candy trails of silk streamers looking like vapor trails. But then some of them started drifting down. For a few minutes, it was almost comical. The camera recorded one landing near the reporter who promptly squashed it with his shoe. There. What was so scary about that? If you've got a shoe, you're safe. Around the reporter, however, students were pointing and beginning to scream. And then the camera caught one student flailing her arms, five or six of the large black dots scurrying over her, and then a burst of blood oozed from her face, her shirt staining crimson. And more screaming. And more screaming. And more and more and more and more. And the camera suddenly dropping. All Teddie could see on her screen was pavement and shoes and socks and the alien movement of spiders, and then just the lower body of the reporter, his legs kicking and then kicking more weakly, and then not moving at all. And all of it, Teddie realized, running live because she hadn't ordered it cut away. That's when she threw up the second time.

Since then, they'd gotten a helicopter in the air, and they'd gotten an incredible money shot, at, of all places, Mann's Chinese
Theatre. It was too good to be true, the sort of shot that would have
made Teddie stand up and seek someone out specifically for the
purpose of giving and receiving high fives if the situation had been
just a little bit less grim. Some sort of early-afternoon opening:
the kind of movie that didn't deserve klieg lights and a nighttime
slot, which meant the A-list stars on the project were really B-list
and C-list famous, and the brigade of fans standing in a corridor
ten deep were filled partly with paid extras, and the photographers
calling names were themselves also B-list and C-list. But the shot
from the helicopter? That was A-list all the way. The cameraman
had been panning the area, one of the anchors talking about how
not all of LA seemed to be caught up in this catastrophe, when a
car barreling down Hollywood Boulevard punched through a red
light at North Orange, clipped a delivery van, and then swerved
left across three lanes to plow into the crowd waiting outside the
theater. That would have been enough on a normal day to cause
chaos and have Teddie make the call to break into the live news,
but this was already live, already in the middle of chaos, and it got
immediately worse: almost as soon as the car stopped moving, before the anchors could do more than yell, a blob of black rolled out
of the smashed front window of the car. The cameraman figured it
out before Teddie did, because he was already zooming in, and the
blob of black turned itself into a thousand individual parts.

There was a pattern to the way the spiders moved. Teddie
knew there was a pattern to it, but she couldn't figure out what it
was. At first, people ran away from where the car had crashed, but
then they turned to help, and almost as quickly, the tide turned
again, but it didn't matter: whether it was the crush of people or
the bugs themselves, the spiders were faster. Teddie watched as

people went down. A woman screaming, disappearing under a mass of writhing spiders. A young black man whose back was a weaving carpet of spiders made it thirty or forty feet before he too fell to the ground, a sick slick of blood around him. But here and there, Teddie saw the thread of spiders weave itself around people, passing them by as if they were magnetically repelled; she couldn't figure out the pattern, why some people were swallowed by the swarm of spiders and others were left alone. And also, where most of the spiders seemed to move together in a synchronized dance, like a single, connected organism, here and there a few individual spiders peeled off.

That had been a couple of hours ago.

The first reports had been of swarms, veritable rivers of spiders drowning the city, coming from the sky like little specks of death, but now they were scattered. The cell phone towers were overwhelmed, and close to two-thirds of the city was without power—trucks and cars crashing into utility poles, sketchy reports of the spiders chewing through electric wires—but where people had Internet and energy, they were uploading videos of single spiders coming up drainpipes or shimmying through open windows, racing across floors and countertops and leaping on people and animals. Teddie knew there must have been other videos taken, ones that ended with screaming and the phone dropping to the ground, a cracked screen left to show only an empty ceiling, but the videos that made it online all ended with the same conclusion: a squished spider. One spider, the videos all seemed to say, wasn't going to be eating anybody on its own.

What was it, Teddie wondered, that made these people pull out their cell phones in the middle of whatever it was that was going on? Anybody who was watching television or listening to the radio or, hell, had a cell phone, had to know what was going on. Sure, maybe at first there had still been people posting photos of pop stars and cute cats and self-aggrandizing Me tweets, but that had disappeared as soon as it was clear something horrific was going on. By now, you had to be living in some sort of bubble to not know about the spiders. And even if you were skeptical—Teddie could imagine herself as one of those people, she could imagine herself to be the kind of woman who would hear about rampaging spiders eating people and call bullshit until she'd seen it with her own eyes—you couldn't possibly be in Los Angeles and not understand there was something seriously messed up going on. And yet, there were new videos every few minutes, people who couldn't help but interpret this as an opportunity to be just a little bit famous, when, as far as Teddie was concerned, they should be interpreting this as an opportunity to get the fuck out of Dodge. Seriously. It was amazing to her that great swaths of Los Angeles seemed to think that the proper response to a full-scale catastrophe was to document it.

Now, though, it was 7:00 P.M. Eastern Standard, or 4:00 P.M. in Los Angeles. More than three hours since the ship ran aground and hell skittered into the city, and President Pilgrim was ready for another presidential address, her first since grounding the planes. The anchors were cutting over to the live view. Serious stuff. When she'd grounded the planes, the president had walked across the red carpet of the White House's Cross Hall and spoken from the entrance to the East Room, but now she was sitting at her desk in the Oval Office.

"America," the president said, "is under attack."

Teddie leaned in toward her monitor, but she realized she didn't have to. She'd never heard such silence at CNN. The only sound in the entire building, as near as she could tell, was coming from banks of television monitors and computer screens, the president's image and voice beaming in from six hundred miles away.

The White House

"**A**merica is under attack."

Manny, standing behind the cameraman, experienced that slight disconnect between watching the president speaking on a screen and in real life at the same time. She let those words sit for a moment. "America is under attack." They'd gone back and forth on the phrasing. So much was unclear. War and earthquakes, hurricanes and landslides, terrorist attacks and industrial accidents. Those were all things Manny knew how to handle. He already had words for them. They were all things the American public understood. But this was something different. That much was obvious. And that had led them, finally, to the decision to be as clear as possible. There had been some concern in the room about stoking panic, but after a few minutes of debate they all realized they were well past the moment of worrying about stoking panic; panic was already there.

"I don't use these words lightly," Stephanie said to the camera. "By now, most of you will have seen the horrifying images coming out of Los Angeles. While it may be hard to comprehend in an age of technology and terrorism, the threat we are facing appears to be a natural one. A little more than three hours ago, at approximately

3:45 P.M. Eastern Standard Time, a freighter ran aground at the Port of Los Angeles. The ship appears to have been carrying a very aggressive and dangerous species of spiders. We do not know for sure how the spiders got onto the ship, but we believe they must have been among the cargo, perhaps hatching inside a shipping container en route. At least some of the cargo containers came from the same province in China where the nuclear explosion occurred earlier in the week. The Chinese government continues to state that the nuclear incident was an accident, but based on our own intelligence reports, we believe it was a deliberate decision made by the government in an attempt to contain an outbreak of these same spiders. While we cannot confirm with one hundred percent accuracy that they are the same, I believe it is reasonable to conclude that the menace in Los Angeles is connected to the incident in China, and to the reports of the city of Delhi being overwhelmed. The Indian government has been much more helpful, despite their own crisis, and they have been sharing information with us, so we hope to have confirmation within the next twenty-four hours.

"As your president, I say this with a heavy heart: our country is under a real and immediate threat." Stephanie paused. She looked, Manny thought, both presidential and exhausted. The weight of the world on her shoulders. And he knew why she was pausing: because what she was about to say had been a brutal decision. "If you are in or around the Los Angeles area, you must shelter in place. I have issued an emergency order of quarantine inside a two-hundred-fifty-mile radius of Los Angeles. That means that if you live within two hundred fifty miles of Los Angeles, you are required to remain in that area. The National Guard, local police, and state police, with the assistance of the army, navy, Marines, and air force, will be enforcing this quarantine zone. Again, if you live in Los Angeles or within a two-hundred-fifty-mile radius of it—which means south of the city all the way to the border of Mexico, east to the state border, and north past Fresno—you are under an order of quarantine. No vehicles or citizens will be allowed to pass beyond this area. I say this with a heavy heart but with hope for the future; to those of you who are within this zone, I want you to understand that you are not alone. The country is with you."

Manny couldn't stop himself from grimacing. He'd written the speech, but he hated those two sentences. He hated them because he knew they weren't true. Maybe they'd get this figured out in the next few days and have soldiers and cops and first responders in there, but all they were doing right now was trying to keep it contained. They were scrambling to get crop dusters and firefighting planes over the city to spray insecticide, but that was going to take at least a few hours, and even then, they had no clue if it was going to work. The bitter truth was that the people in that zone *were* alone. The country was not with them in any sense other than as spectators. The National Guard and the police, the army and the navy, the Marines and the air force weren't lined up with their guns pointed out, to protect them from some invading army, but rather with their guns pointed in. But as much as he hated those two sentences, he was even less happy about what was coming. Yes, it made sense, and he reluctantly agreed with the national security advisor and the secretary of defense and pretty much everybody else who said it had to be done, but it was still going to be tough to swallow in the polls.

"The news channels and the Internet have been awash in speculation the last few days, and the truth is that the facts of this situation are not entirely clear." Stephanie leaned in toward the camera, and despite himself, despite knowing the words that were about to come out of her mouth, Manny found himself responding in kind, leaning toward her. "What I know for sure, however, is that Americans are dying, and my job is to protect this country." She paused to take a breath. Here it comes, Manny thought. It made him feel sick. He knew it was the wrong thought to have at a moment like this, but he was a political animal and he couldn't help himself. All he could think of was that she was going to lose the election with the next sentence. "I am declaring the states of California, Oregon, Arizona, and Nevada under martial law."

There was more. Curfews. Pleas for calm. A stern reminder to stay indoors with windows and doors closed, to try to seal any possible entrances. But above all, it was Stephanie sounding presidential. Authoritative. Manny was proud of the speech he'd written, particularly given how short a time he'd had to write it, but it was Stephanie who sold it. She did what the president is supposed to do, which is look into the camera, look into the eyes of the American people, and say, "We've got this under control."

But Manny knew she didn't believe it any more than he did.

Soot Lake, Minnesota

A quarter past midnight and there was still traffic on the 6. He'd figured there'd be cars and trucks for the two hours up 169 from Minneapolis to Crosby, but they were already twenty-five minutes past Crosby, and the traffic was constant. It worried Mike. He thought he was being overcautious, a little crazy, even, to make Rich and Fanny pack up and head to Rich's cottage with Annie, but it scared him a little that so many other people had the same idea, that he wasn't the only person who wanted to get his family away from Minneapolis. He'd fought about it with Fanny for more than twenty minutes before Rich finally came in off the sidelines to say he thought Mike was right. For that, Mike begrudgingly liked his ex-wife's husband even more than he already did.

"I've got the vacation time," Rich said, "and I don't have any cases coming up for a few weeks." Fanny started to protest again, but Rich shook his head. "Maybe he's wrong, honey, but if Mike's right, and things get worse?" He shrugged. "It's not like spending a week or two at the cottage is a real hardship."

Mike had been at home, already a little anguished, when the president declared martial law out west. And then, five minutes later, even though he was supposed to be off the next day, he got the e-mail that he was on duty, that everybody was on duty, starting from the moment they read the e-mail until further notice. He hadn't opened the e-mail. It was enough to read the subject line. Besides, if he opened it, there'd be a record of his reading it. Instead, he dropped his agency phone on the counter—he could argue he didn't see the e-mail until the next morning—took his personal phone, loaded his truck with all the canned and dried food he had, plus a few other odds and ends, and headed over to Fanny and Rich's. By the time Rich had come around to the idea and they'd loaded up Rich's Land Cruiser and hitched up the boat, Annie was asleep. She'd barely woken up when Mike moved her to his truck—he'd left the agency car at home with his agency phone, another step toward deniability—and he was grateful she hadn't asked why they were heading out of town in the middle of the week, late at night, why she was in Mike's car instead of with her mother and Rich.

The brake lights on the boat trailer glowed red and then the turn signal came on. Rich had said the BP station in Outing was the last place to get gas before his cottage. Mike turned the radio down a notch. There wasn't anything new anyway, but what was on the radio was enough: Delhi, Los Angeles, Helsinki, Rio de Janeiro for sure. Suspicions in North Korea, but who the fuck knew what was happening there? More unconfirmed reports in rural areas all over the place. Scotland, Egypt, South Africa. But Mike didn't care if they were confirmed or not. He'd seen that goddamned spider come crawling out of Henderson's face, and he'd walked that spider into a university lab to find the president of the United States waiting, and then he'd flown home to a country that was on lockdown. Even before Los Angeles and the president's speech he was feeling antsy.

Rich turned off into the gas station, and Mike pulled his truck up to the pump on the other side of Rich's Land Cruiser. He tried to be gentle closing the driver's door so that Annie could keep sleeping, but she didn't stir at all.

As Fanny went to get them all coffee, Rich said, "You sure about this, Mike?" His tone wasn't challenging.

Whatever pissing contest there was between them had ended for Rich about the same time he and Fanny got married. For Mike, it had been harder to let go of the animosity. Mike liked to think he was the bigger guy, but it just wasn't true. He still busted Rich's balls occasionally, but this wasn't the time and he knew it. It said something about Rich that he was the kind of guy who would do this, that when his wife's ex-husband showed up at their house past a decent hour of night and told them it was time to head for the hills, Rich was willing to let himself be swayed, was willing to take Mike's side against Fanny.

"No, Rich. If I'm being honest, I'm not sure. But I'd rather be wrong about going than about not going."

Rich nodded, and other than a quiet thank-you to Fanny when she came back with the coffees, neither man said another word. Mike got back into his truck and took a sip while he waited for Rich to also fill the tank on his motor boat and then the two spare gas cans Mike had made him take.

From the gas station, it was twenty-five more minutes of back roads and twists and turns and past one in the morning before they got to the boat launch. Once everything was loaded up, Mike came back to the truck. He thought about just scooping Annie up and carrying her to the boat, but instead, he gave her a gentle shake until she woke up.

"Listen, Annie," he said. "You awake?" She nodded, and even though Mike wasn't sure she truly was, he had to trust that she'd remember. "You stay where you are for a little bit, okay? Stay with your mom and Rich. I'll come to you. You don't worry about me. I'll be back."

"Promise?"

Her voice was small and full of sleep, and it almost killed him. Two years ago, when an agent was killed in the line of duty and Annie had found out about it, she'd made him promise to wear his bulletproof vest anytime he was out on the job, but it hadn't felt like anything big to do. Yet for some reason this request made him hesitate. Could he really promise he'd be back? He didn't really understand what was going on, and it was terrifying him. But he looked at the way Annie was looking at him and he realized none of that really mattered. What mattered was making her feel safe.

"I promise, beautiful. I promise I'll come back to you. Back *for* you. I'll come back for you, okay?"

Annie nodded again, and then he walked with her over to the boat.

It was all he could do to let her go.

"Anything else?" Rich said.

"Actually, yeah." Mike lifted a duffel bag. "My backup pistol is in there."

"Jesus, Mike. You think that's really necessary?"

"I hope not."

"I don't even know how to shoot a pistol."

"Fanny does. I taught her. The pistol is for her. It's a Glock 27. It's small. There's two boxes of rounds in there and a spare clip," he said. "There's also a shotgun. That's for you. Go out tomorrow and have Fanny show you how to load it and take a couple of shots to get the feel of it."

"Mike—"

"Rich." Mike stepped close, keeping his voice low. "There's a quarantine out west. Martial law. I saw one of those fucking things come out of Henderson's face. You've got my daughter with you. Do you understand what I'm asking of you here?"

Instead of answering, Rich looked back over his shoulder at the boat. Annie was leaning into her mother. The light from the truck's headlights cast odd shadows, but both men could see Fanny and Annie clearly.

"Yeah. Yeah, I do, Mike."

"It's a Mossberg 500. A twelve gauge. There are four boxes of ammunition in there. You learn how to use it. It will take out anything in front of you. Like spraying a hose. The loads will spread. Shit for distance with that ammunition, but for personal defense it will do fine. Just point and shoot."

Mike handed over the duffel bag. The two men shook hands.

Mike turned to walk back to his truck, but then he heard Annie calling for him. He went back to them.

"How come you aren't coming with us, Daddy?"

"I've got to work baby, okay?" He bent over the rail of the boat and Annie got up and came over to him. She leaned into him and pressed her nose into his neck. "Don't worry. Your mom and Rich are going to take care of you."

"I'm not worried about me," she said.

He tightened his grip on her. "I'll be fine, beautiful. I'll be fine. And I'll come for you soon enough. I promise."

American University, Washington, DC

Melanie lunged for it, but her fingers only grazed the glass. There was nothing she could do but watch it fall.

It was close to two in the morning, and they were tired. They were all so tired.

They'd gotten the spider into the container safely enough, but Patrick put it down too close to the edge of the table, and then Bark's hip banged against the side of the table. The container teetered. For a heartbeat, it looked as if it was going to be okay. One of those moments Melanie wished she could have back. But it wasn't okay, and the container tipped and started to fall, and Melanie's skin barely touched the glass before it spun off the edge, dropped, and smashed on the floor. The shattering sound woke them up. All four of them, yelling and fumbling and trying to catch the spider. It scrambled, alien and fast, up the table leg and across Julie's lab coat and onto Bark's shirt and then . . .

A thin split in Bark's skin. An ooze of blood. The spider gone. Inside him.

They'd picked that spider out from the others because this one, Julie noticed, had subtly different markings from the others.

They'd prepared and dissected three that were identical, plus the seven spiders that had died on their own, and those seemed to be the same as well. The only difference with the seven that had died—for no apparent reason—was that they were almost desiccated. As if they'd just sort of used themselves up. It didn't make much sense to Melanie. None of it did.

They'd started by feeding the spiders normally. All the spiders in the lab were fed on a strict schedule, crickets and mealworms and other insects, but these spiders didn't seem interested in insects. From the beginning, they'd been after blood. It was grotesque and fascinating. The way they overwhelmed a rat, stripping the flesh from the bone was amazing. It looked like a time-lapse video gone horribly wrong. They had assumed that the food needs of these spiders would correspond to those of the spiders they were already familiar with, and they'd been wrong. These spiders were voracious. And they weren't patient.

When they first burst from the egg sac, they turned on one another, eating several of their kin in the frenzy of hatching, but they were quick to turn their attention to the rats. But then, yesterday, they'd counted again and realized that, even counting the dead ones, they were three spiders short. After a few minutes of panic, Julie suggested spooling back through the video, and they found footage of the spiders in the tank attacking and eating one another. The spiders that died on their own, the desiccated, used-up spiders, were left alone, but when it was time to feed, every living spider seemed like it was fair game. So instead of dropping in a single rat, Melanie decided to drop in a bunch of rats at the same time to see what happened. The spiders seemed pleased. The sound was disgusting, but it wasn't long before there were a few more piles of bones.

And one untouched rat.

The surviving rat was pressed against the glass, huddled in the corner of the insectarium, radiating sheer terror. Melanie didn't usually ascribe much in the way of emotional lives to her rats. She couldn't afford to. They were things for testing, or, right now, for feeding, and she didn't want to have a moral crisis every time she wanted to get some work done. There was no other way to describe it, however. The rat looked scared. It was squeaking and shivering and pushing itself as far away as possible from the spiders. The spiders, for their part, were ignoring the rat, which was bizarre to Melanie. They'd positively inhaled the other rats. It had looked like an unruly arachnoid wrestling match as they fed. But this rat seemed as if it were almost invisible to them.

"Julie," Melanie said. "How many rats have we dropped in?"

"Today?"

"No. Total. What number is this?"

Julie scrolled through some notes on her tablet. "Nine. No. Ten. Counting the first one, and then the ones we just dropped in, we've fed them ten rats."

Patrick gently touched the glass on the other side of the rat's body. "You think these spiders are counting or something?"

"Or something," Melanie said. "Why are they leaving this one alone?"

"They didn't," Bark said. "Not exactly."

Melanie looked at him. He'd mostly pulled himself together since she told him she was ending things, but he hadn't been particularly vocal. "What do you mean?"

"He's got a cut on him. On his belly." Bark pointed through the glass.

"Wait," Patrick said. "We're short another spider."

"What the fuck?" Melanie tugged at her ponytail and then pulled out the elastic. Her hair felt greasy. She couldn't remember if she had even brushed it after her last shower. "Julie, pull the video back to when we dropped the new rats in."

They watched it on Julie's screen and then watched it again, slower. What had seemed almost instantaneous earlier was terrifying with the frame rate dropped to a tenth the speed: the spiders were already leaping before the trap door had fully opened. They met the rats' bodies mid-drop. The spiders were feeding before the rats hit the ground of the insectarium. Except for the one rat and one spider. It was so quick and there was so much chaos going on with the other spiders feeding that Melanie understood why they'd missed it. The spiders had swarmed over the other rats, but only a single spider had gone to the surviving rat. But that spider hadn't fed. It had . . . disappeared? No. The rat's body blocked the angle from the camera, but they could mostly make it out. The spider lunged forward, gave a sort of shiver, and then was gone. It had disappeared inside the rat's body.

"Scroll back again. Get me a clear frame of that spider before it burrows into the rat." Julie found the frame, froze it, and then Melanie pinched at the screen, zooming in. "Look at that marking on the abdomen," Melanie said. "Does that mean something?"

They spent several minutes watching the other spiders move around the tank before Bark spotted another with the same marking.

They were careful. They segregated the marked spider. They followed all the protocols. But something as simple as putting a container too close to the edge of the table?

There was always human error.

Sooner or later, but always.

And now the spider was gone. Smashing glass. Yelling. Blood. Gone.

Somewhere inside Bark's body.

Julie marked the time: 1:58 A.M.

Highway 10, California

Sometimes, Kim thought, being in the Marines meant just being along for the ride. First they'd been sent to Desperation, the shittiest town this side of, well, anywhere, to build what looked like an internment camp, and then suddenly, minutes before the president's address, the company was peeled off from the brigade at full scramble. The whole company, nearly 150 Marines leaving behind close to five thousand, loaded up in a mix of brand-new Joint Light Tactical Vehicles and old, sand-scarred Hummers. They'd heard the quarantine order over the radio as they busted down the road ten miles back to the highway. And when they got to the highway, there were already two M1 Abrams tanks—tanks!—blocking traffic. Nobody in or out.

The captain ordered them out wide, the two tanks on the road and the mix of JLTVs and Hummers bouncing off the shoulders of the highway out into the scrub, until they were nearly one hundred yards wide on either side, far enough out to discourage any drivers from getting cute and trying to glide past the blockade, because there was no question that somebody would have tried. The civilians were getting antsy. It was past two in the morning. By now, Kim figured, with the traffic piling up and piling up for hours and hours, it might reach as far back as Los Angeles, quarantine order or no quarantine order. Even out in Desperation, putting together fences and working their asses off, they'd started hearing about what was going on in LA. At first, it sounded as though things were confined to one neighborhood, and it seemed like crazy panic with nothing to it. Just people freaking out over the idea of freaking out. There hadn't been much in the way of video: shaky images with lots of screaming. But then, suddenly, all the news—Internet, television, radio—was spiders, spiders, spiders. Spiders swarming over the city, spiders eating some people and leaving others alone, spiders drifting from the sky onto rooftops, spiders coming out of drains and scuttling under doorways. Private Goons said he'd heard from a cousin that all Los Angeles was on fire. Nobody else knew if that was true. And then they were bounced from Desperation to the highway, and Kim was facing down American citizens with a fifty-caliber machine gun. Kim's fire team had landed one of the new JLTVs. They were all the way out on the farthest edge of the left side, in the brush and scrub and dust. At first she thought it was silly. There were tanks on the road. Who was going to try to get past those? Did they really need to be so far off the road? But as night came, Kim started to think that maybe a pair of tanks and a few Hummers and JLTVs might not be enough if all these people decided they weren't interested in obeying the president's quarantine. The towers of portable floodlights sent a white glaze a couple of hundred yards back, but past that, from her perch on top of the JLTV out at the wing of the blockade, Kim could see headlights for what seemed like forever. There'd been announcements on the radio and the captain had sent a couple of men out to a distance of two miles to make sure motorists knew the road was blocked off and to encourage them to turn around and go home, but it had turned into a clusterfuck—with the backup from the roadblocks, people started trying to drive the wrong way down the highway, so now it was backed up on both sides. Nobody could go forward. Nobody could go back. The only way out was past the tanks, past the Hummers and JLTVs, past Kim and her .50 cal, and they were under orders not to let anybody by. Not good.

Some prick in a black BMW Roadster three vehicles from the front of the line got out of his car and came to argue with Captain Diggs for what must have been the fifth or six time, and Kim couldn't help smiling when she saw the man frog-marched back to his car. She kept her hands off the .50 cal. She had wedged an old shell casing under the butterfly trigger as an improvised safety. But still. The Browning M2 could barf out five hundred rounds a minute, and while it was one thing to accidentally punch out somebody overseas in a war zone, she didn't want to be the one to accidentally light up some civilian.

"Gum?" Elroy stuck his hand up out of the truck. Kim reached down to snag a piece.

"Anything new?"

Elroy popped his head up and showed her his phone. "No signal, and then no battery, so no, no news. Just what you hear on the radio."

Ten yards in from where her tactical vehicle sat on the outside of the blockade, Kim could see Sue's Hummer. The Hummers weren't in the best shape—they'd seen heavy use in the desert, and the army was taking its time with decommissioning—but Kim wasn't worried about IEDs in Southern California. "Sue," she called across. "You guys got anything?"

Before Sue could answer, Kim heard the call on the radio.

"White SUV leaving containment. Fire team leader Lance Corporal Bock, on your side. Copy."

"Copy," Kim said.

Down the line, maybe five or six hundred yards away, at the edge of where the portable floodlights made themselves felt, she saw a white SUV that had crept out of line and drifted off the highway into the dirt. They were doing that here and there, mostly trucks and SUVs, feeling out the line, trying to see what the holdup was, and then popping back into place as soon as they realized they weren't going anywhere. Some people still had their cars running, and Kim occasionally caught the sound of music drifting from the distance, but most people had turned off their cars hours ago, which was good. That's the last thing they needed: cars running out of gas on top of everything else. It seemed that most people had resigned themselves to the wait. Earlier in the night, some people had gotten out of their cars to stretch, to sit on their hoods, and in one case, to toss a Frisbee, but now, at two in the morning, it was quiet. People were sleeping in their cars, seats reclined, a freeway slumber party. But the driver of the white SUV wasn't sleeping and he wasn't getting back in line. It was going wide. Fifty yards. Maybe sixty. And it was moving toward them. Fast.

"Fire team leader, if vehicle attempts to pass brigade, you are to engage."

She keyed her radio. "Sir? It's a civilian."

There was a brief pause. "Fire team leader, fire a warning volley in front of the vehicle."

"Now?"

"Affirmative."

Kim took a breath and then she tracked the white SUV. It was moving, kicking up dirt and heading at an angle. If it kept going, there was no question it was going to pass her. The SUV was maybe 150 yards in front of her now. She led it by ten yards to be safe, snuck the spent shell out from under the butterfly trigger, and let out a five-round burst. It had been a while since she'd qualified on the .50 cal, and she'd forgotten how loud it was. The flash from the muzzle looked like the sun, and one of the rounds was a tracer, but neither the light nor the sound seemed to matter. The SUV didn't stop. It didn't even slow down.

Kim hesitated.

"Fire team leader."

She had her fingers on the trigger.

"Bock. Take it out."

Kim didn't lead the SUV this time. She lined up directly on the engine block and pulled the trigger.

Desperation, California

Accurate facial recognition—picking a moving person out of a crowd—was still only the stuff of movies and television, but detecting the sound of a gunshot was something that had been solved years ago. When Lance Corporal Kim Bock pulled the trigger on her .50 cal, the aboveground audio sensors outside Shotgun's house sent a notice to the tablet he kept by his bed. Just a small ping. Not enough even to bother Fred on the other side of the bed, but enough to wake Shotgun up. He threw on a T-shirt and jeans and went out to the kitchen. Gordo was sitting at the table, a single light on above him, pooling over him.

"Couldn't sleep?"

Gordo looked up from his computer. "Not really. This is bad, Shotgun. Seriously bad."

Shotgun nodded. "Yep."

Gordo paused, considered it, and then shrugged. "I've got to say, I guess I'm glad we did this. Glad Amy and I came over. I think we're going to be riding this out for a while."

"Shots outside."

Gordo sat up straighter. "What? Seriously?"

"Something big. Military."

"That's what got you up?"

"Yeah," Shotgun said, but then he shook his head. "Yes, but not just that. I'm just going to check everything one more time. We're good down here. Anything other than a direct hit by a bunker buster, but you know."

Gordo did know, and together they double-checked the blast doors, double-checked that everything was shut down and sealed tight. From the outside, no casual observer—or member of the military thinking of trying to force civilians to evacuate—would realize there was an entire bunker under Shotgun's house.

They were safe and sound underground. They could wait awhile before they had to poke their heads back up.

The White House

Manny was slumped in a chair. There was a point, and he didn't want to admit he was at that point, where Diet Coke could do only so much. It had been a rough couple of days. He thought the fallout from shutting down all air travel was bad, but it had gone from bad to worse rather abruptly.

For a few minutes, just after Steph's speech last night, he thought it was going to be okay. The Indians reported that the spiders seemed to be dying out. No reason. They were just dying. There were dead spiders all over Delhi. Heaps and piles of them. Hundreds of thousands, millions of dead spiders, like waves washed to shore and frozen in place. He'd seen film shot from a helicopter: the wind from the rotors stirred up the piles, spider corpses drifting in the breeze. Manny had, just for a moment, allowed himself to believe it was going to be that simple. The spiders would just die out in the same way cicadas did. Melanie had brought up the idea of periodical cicadas as a potential comparison, and Manny hoped she was right. Around Washington, DC, the Brood II and Brood X cicadas hatched on seventeen-year cycles. They'd last come to the surface in 2013 and 2004, respectively. Maybe the spiders would do their thing for a few weeks and then melt away like the cicadas, leaving only their husks behind.

But it wasn't that easy. The spiders in Delhi might be dying, but now he had the spiders in Los Angeles to worry about, and then, in short order, reports from Helsinki, Rio de Janeiro, Lebanon, South Africa, and Russia. None of it made any sense anymore. Dawn was breaking in Washington, DC, and the entire world was falling apart. What was he supposed to do? They were treating it like a flu pandemic. A flu pandemic he would have at least understood. But spiders?

What he really needed was a nap. Five minutes. He just wanted five minutes to close his eyes, to let the din of the room drift away. Just five minutes to hit the reset button. Five minutes of sleep.

He got thirty seconds.

China.

Holy. Fucking. Shit.

China.

They all stood quiet watching the balloons of light on the satellite imagery. A roomful of colonels and generals. Two stars, three stars, four. The secretary of defense, the national security advisor, the secretary of state, the director of Homeland Security. The fucking president. Thirty or forty aides and attendants and all of them, including Manny, staring at the screen and watching what looked like a small field of beautiful flowers blooming in western China, a line of nuclear explosions stitching all the way down from Mongolia to Nepal. There were no human sounds in the room, just the constant chirp and chime and ring of e-mails and text messages and phone calls.

"What the hell?"

Manny didn't know who broke the language barrier, but it opened a flood of yelling. First: denial. No way those were nukes. Second: confirmation. Nukes. The Chinese had just deliberately erased a third of their country. Third: silence again. The silence came slowly and then all at once, everyone in the room turning to look at Stephanie. To look at the president of the United States.

Nobody needed to ask the question. It was in the air. The question was everywhere. What the hell were they going to do?

It was not a good time for Manny's cell phone to be buzzing, but as Steph started barking out orders—cabinet members to the conference room, military on full alert—and the room returned to noise and chaos, Manny snuck a look and saw Melanie's name.

He pressed the phone hard against his ear and cupped his free hand over his mouth. "I'm kind of busy right now."

"Manny," she said. "You don't understand. It's worse than I thought."

Manny rubbed his eyes. He wanted to believe he'd heard her wrong. Worse? How could it be worse? China was going to be glowing for the next thousand years, Los Angeles was a war zone, and his ex-wife was on the phone saying it's worse than that? He motioned for an aide to grab his stuff so he could follow Steph. "Okay."

"Okay?"

"Okay," he said. "Just tell me, okay, Melanie? I don't think you understand just how bad a time this is for me to talk. You've already told me these spiders are designed to feed. What's worse than that?" He caught a quick glimpse of one of the screens cutting to live satellite. The image was full of static, but it was panned all the way back so that most of China showed up, and even that far back, the dust or dirt or smoke or whatever the hell nukes left behind was terrifying.

"Okay. So stay with me. The timing doesn't make any sense, right? They come out and they're fully grown and eating like locusts. It's accelerated."

"What's accelerated?"

"Everything. They're like rockets. They feed until they burn themselves out. That's what's happening in Delhi. And it's going to happen in Los Angeles soon."

Manny perked up. He'd been right. "So you're telling me they'll just die out? How much longer?"

"No. You don't understand. I was wrong before. When I said they were designed to feed, I was wrong. They're colonizers."

"What do you mean?"

"I mean some of them feed. But some of them lay eggs, and those things are accelerated too. They'll hatch quickly."

"How do you know?"

"Because I'm looking at a new egg sac. I'm absolutely sure this thing isn't more than a few hours old, but it doesn't look like it. It looks like one that's going to hatch pretty soon."

"What? Where are you?"

"The National Institutes of Health. Bethesda."

Manny stepped into the hall, following the bustle of suits and uniforms. He saw Steph holding on to Ben Broussard's arm and talking at him as they walked.

"Why are you at the NIH?"

"You gave me carte blanche. And we needed a surgeon and a hospital with a biocontainment unit. There are only four places in the whole country with biocontainment units. The other three are at Emory University Hospital, in Atlanta, the University of Nebraska Medical Center, and St. Patrick's Hospital in Missoula, Montana. So Bethesda, Maryland, seemed like an obvious choice."

"Why didn't you call me?" Manny asked. "No, never mind. That doesn't matter. But why did you need a surgeon? Wait, what? Biocontainment? Please tell me these things don't also carry disease."

"No, they aren't infectious-disease carriers." She stopped. "Well, at least I'm pretty sure they aren't. Wouldn't that be something, though? If they carried the plague? No. I don't think that's the worry, but we didn't want to go to a normal hospital and then have the egg sac hatch and then have a spider, I don't know, slip out an air vent or something. We needed a place that had procedures and the facilities to keep everything inside. So, NIH."

"Do I want to know why you needed a surgeon? No," he said, answering his own question, "I probably don't want to know, but okay, I have to ask: why do you need a surgeon?"

"Because the egg sac is inside one of my students."

National Institutes of Health, Bethesda, Maryland

Melanie looked down at Bark lying unconscious and cut open on the operating table. At first, they'd been relieved: the surgeon had opened Bark's abdominal cavity and the spider flopped out. The thing was dead. Spent, really, as far as Melanie could tell. Like the ones that had died for no apparent reason in the lab. Like the spiders being swept up on the streets of Delhi. And soon, soon, she hoped, Los Angeles. The relief was short-lived, however, because the spider seemed to have spent itself on putting together an egg sac inside Bark. It was like the one that was shipped to her lab, except it wasn't calcified. The silk was sticky as hell, and the whole thing was warm and buzzing. The surgeon looked terrified, and one of the nurses had tried to run from the room before remembering they were in a biocontainment unit—it was built for guarding against the spread of the kinds of diseases that made Ebola look like a kids' game, and both entrance and exit required going through air locks and all kinds of decontamination— but Melanie couldn't stop herself from laying her gloved hand on the sac. She knew she should have been freaking out. She and Bark had been sleeping together regularly until this week, and here he was now, the spider playing a game of hide-and-seek in his body that left him put under and cut open. And there *was* a part of her that was freaking out. She could feel it. There was a little piece of Melanie that wanted to scream and try to run from the room like that nurse, but that little piece was being outvoted by the part of her that was trying to understand the puzzle.

Under the gloved hand, she felt the pulse of the egg sac, and in her other hand, the phone was warm against her ear. "Manny?"

"Sorry," he said. "I don't . . . Okay. Why is there an egg sac in your student?"

She gave him the quick brief. Dropping the container, the glass breaking, the spider slipping through Bark's skin as if it were barely there, the panic and then the resignation that the only thing to do was to get it out. The rushed trip to the NIH, the Secret Service agents flashing badges and yelling and cutting through the red tape as if they'd never heard of it. "Aren't you glad you left me with a bunch of suits and Steph's presidential orders?" she said, but the joke fell flat. Which made sense. It wasn't a time for jokes, but she wasn't sure what else to do.

"Feeders and breeders," Manny said.

"And there's a pattern," she said. She took her hand off the egg sac. Julie Yoo was suited up in scrubs, and Melanie watched Julie and the surgeon start to work through the cords of silk that connected the sac to the inside of Bark's body. They'd brought an insectarium from the lab, and the egg sac was going into it the second it was out of Bark. "We figured it out from the spiders in the insectarium and the rats. And then Patrick—one of my students—noticed it on the video out of Los Angeles. The feeders stay away from the hosts. They're marked somehow. This serves a dual purpose: the hosts are both places for the eggs and a way to spread the colony. The person, or, I guess, animal, can travel with the eggs inside them until they hatch. Whoever their host is will likely be able to travel farther than the spiders could on their own. Shutting down air travel was a really smart call."

Manny didn't say anything for a few seconds, and Melanie could hear noise in the background on his end. She realized that while they were working away in her lab dealing with a few of these spiders, Manny's job was to help Steph deal with *all* the spiders. She was an academic, but as much as Manny was a politician, sometimes that meant he dealt with the real world in ways she didn't.

"It's bad out there, isn't it?" she said. "We're not getting the full story, are we?"

"Melanie," he said. "Mel." And that's when she truly felt worried. He almost never called her Mel. The last time he'd called her Mel was when he told her he wanted a divorce. "I asked you earlier to come to the White House to answer some questions for us, but now I *need* you to come answer some questions."

"Okay. Like what?"

"Like how to kill them."

The CNN Center,
Atlanta, Georgia

Teddie scrolled the video back and watched it again and again and again. There was a pattern, she was sure of it.

Minneapolis, Minnesota

Leshaun looked like shit, but Mike was happy to see him. After he'd gotten back from dropping Annie off with Rich and Fanny at the dock, Mike went home, grabbed his work phone and agency vehicle, and headed in. He was the last one to the office.

The bureau chief gave an uninspired speech relaying the national orders and then telling them the arsenal was open for business. "Gear up," he said. "Urban unrest, basically. That's the model we're using. We've got nothing to worry about on the ground here yet, so we're just going to help local law enforcement keep the peace. Make sure nobody gets too panicked."

"Right," Leshaun said under his breath so only Mike could hear him, "because the way to keep everybody calm is to have us running around with machine guns."

But he and Mike did the same thing as everybody else: they slipped agency Windbreakers over body armor and took M4 carbines, Remington Model 870 pump-action shotguns, and spare magazines, clips, shells, and ammunition and then got into Mike's agency car and started driving around.

It was kind of boring.

"You sure you're up for this?" Mike asked. Leshaun had leaned his seat back and had his eyes closed, but was not asleep. "Nothing's really going on here. I mean, Los Angeles sounds like some incredibly dystopian nightmare, but good old Minneapolis? I guess rush hour is going to start soon, but let's face it. We're still in the Midwest."

Leshaun laughed. He was from Boston originally, and was always willing to laugh about how boring the Midwest could be. "I'm good. My arm's good. The ribs still hurt, but there's nothing I can do about it, so I might as well be out and about."

They didn't talk much for the next half hour. A stop for coffee. And then Mike's phone showed an incoming call from the bureau chief.

"If you saw that spider again, could you identify it?"

Mike shuddered. He didn't think he'd ever forget it. "Yes sir."

"We've got a report of a dead spider. There's actually been a ton of calls about spiders, but this one's maybe a little different. It's two blocks from where Henderson's plane went down."

Mike put his phone back in the cup holder on the center console and flicked the siren on. It was a quick ride across town, traffic still light and the cherries clearing the way.

The building was a warehouse for a plumbing-supply company. There were two black-and-whites outside, a pair of cops leaning against their cars and smoking. They gave Mike and Leshaun a wave as they passed. Inside the warehouse, Mike and Leshaun followed the sound of voices until they came to another pair of cops standing with a woman in her mid-fifties wearing civilian clothes.

"I called it in as soon as Juan called me," she said. "Juan's the night manager. We fill most of our orders at night so that our customers can be ready to roll out first thing in the morning. There it is," she said, pointing.

Mike reached out to grab onto the shelf so he could balance himself to get a closer look. The cut on his hand was still uncomfortable, but he had pretty good mobility. Actually, between the stitches in his hand and Leshaun's broken ribs and shot-through arm, he and his partner weren't in the best shape. But you worked with what you had.

There was no question this was the same kind of spider.

"But it's a warehouse." The woman was still talking. "We get spiders and mice and the occasional squirrel. If it wasn't for all the stuff on the news, I don't know if I would have called it in. And there's those awful-looking cocoon things too."

Mike looked up at her. "What?"

"Oh, around the corner. They look like cocoons."

Mike and Leshaun and the two cops followed the woman. She had a flashlight and pointed the beam near the rafters. There was a lattice of cobwebs. And from the ground, Mike could see at least three softball-shaped orbs. It took him a second, but then he realized what they looked like: they looked like whole versions of the split-open egg sac from the lab in Washington.

This was not good.

Highway 10, California

The SUV was still smoking a little.

Kim was hugely relieved that the two passengers, both young men, had jumped out of the car with their hands up, scared shitless but apparently unharmed. The captain had both men detained and then sent down the line to the temporary internment camp outside Desperation. Maybe ten minutes after Kim had fired her .50 cal, somebody noticed the white SUV was on fire, but the captain delayed the rush to put out the flames. "Let it burn," he ordered. "Maybe it will stop the next idiot from trying to get past the blockade, at least until we start moving everybody off the highway and to the camp."

It was morning now, and the rerouting of traffic had begun. Kim wasn't sure why they weren't just turning people around, but Honky Joe said that if Los Angeles was as bad as it sounded, they couldn't send people back, but they also couldn't let people just break the quarantine zone. Hence the wire fences and temporary holding pens. Or, as Honky Joe put it, not at all reassuringly, "Think of it as a short-term refugee camp."

The sun made an angry promise about the coming heat of the day. A thin wisp of smoke twisted out of the burning hulk of metal that had been an SUV just a few hours earlier. The Marines had opened the road toward the camp outside Desperation, and from where she sat in the driver's seat of the JLTV, Kim could see every driver and passenger take a look at the smoldering SUV as they turned off the highway. Kim's squad and all the other squads— including the two tanks—were ordered to hold their line; squads in Hummers and JLTVs lined the road to the internment camp, spaced out every hundred yards or so, but they barely seemed nec-essary. Once the traffic started moving, people seemed so happy just to be off the highway that nobody questioned where they were going. The American people, Kim thought, preferred to be sheep. They'd been funneling traffic toward the holding pens outside Desperation for close to an hour, and there had been only one report of a car trying to break the line. If anything, the civilians had an almost celebratory air. Sure, they looked a little startled at the sight of the smoking SUV, but for the most part, people were waving and smiling at the Marines as they passed. They'd been taught to see the military as heroes, even if, Kim thought, they were mostly acting as traffic cops right now.

She had the windows open in the tactical vehicle, but it was still pretty gamey, full-on FAN: feet, ass, nuts. Duran was in the passenger seat and had found a phone charger somewhere. He was reading the news, a frustrating endeavor given how shitty the signal was out where they were. Elroy was manning the .50 cal, and Mitts was taking a nap in the back. There wasn't much to do other than watch the traffic merging painfully onto the side road. What exactly did the military plan to do once all the cars were there? How long was this quarantine supposed to last? There had to be what, forty, fifty thousand people backed up on the highway? Maybe more? Kim glanced over at the wrecked hulk of the SUV again, looking at the pockmarks where the bullets had punched through the hood.

She still couldn't believe nobody had been killed. It made her feel sick. She'd been trained to open fire on hostiles, to take the shot before anybody could get close enough to detonate a car bomb. That was the world the military lived in now. But she'd never expected to have to operate on domestic soil. She was in the Marines to protect Americans.

"They're saying Japan now too."

Kim looked over at Duran. "Tokyo?"

He shook his head. "No. I've never heard of the place. Somewhere rural, in the mountains."

"What about Los Angeles? Anything new?"

"Nothing. Phones and satellites and all that shit are overwhelmed. I mean, there's stuff, but it all seems kind of sketchy. Guesses."

Kim turned to check on Mitts, but he was still sleeping hard, his mouth open and the low whine of a snore coming out. "So, basically, nobody knows what's going on?"

Duran put his phone on the dashboard. "It's the military. Somebody probably knows what's going on, but we're going to be waiting a long time before anybody shares that information with E-1s."

"Yeah, well, I'm an E-3. Since I wildly outrank you," she said, her voice droll, "they'll clearly tell me first." She was pleased to see him smile. "So," she said, "what's next? We just going to sit here and babysit traffic for the next few days?"

"Honestly? I haven't really thought about it."

"How can you not think about it?"

"Well, I figure, as you are so quick to remind me, you're the fire team leader, Ms. Lance Corporal, so it's your job to think about stuff. I just follow orders."

"Go fuck yourself, Duran." She smiled when she said it, but that didn't stop Duran from frowning and shaking his head forcefully.

"No, no. I'm not giving you a hard time, Kim. I'm serious. We trust you. There's a reason you're the fire team leader instead of one of us. I kind of figured if there was something to worry about, you'd think of it. That's not what I'm good at."

"Fine. Okay. But there are some real questions, right? I mean, if these spiders are all over the world, can we really expect them to stay put in Los Angeles? And what happens when the camp fills up?" She gestured out the windshield at the traffic. It was moving slowly, at the pace of a brisk walk, but it was moving. "Because there are a lot of cars out there."

"Kim, what's that—"

"No, seriously. We need to worry about—"

"Kim." He said her name sharply, holding up his hand. "Do you hear that?"

She was quiet, but the *pop-pop-pop* of a heavy-caliber weapon was easy to hear once she stopped talking. It was coming from her far left, toward the temporary holding area. She turned and gave Mitts a poke, waking him up, before opening her door and stepping out. Even with the heat, it was a relief to be out of the JLTV. The fresh air was good. She saw Elroy looking down at her from where he stood. He had spent shells under the triggers as safeties and his hands at his sides, but he didn't look relaxed. There was a moment of silence, and then one, two, maybe three of the .50 cals went off, plus small-arms fire. It sounded a ways off. At least a klick. There was nothing on the radio.

"What do you say, Kim?" Elroy pulled his sunglasses off.

"Somebody jumping the line?" she said.

Elroy shrugged. "Maybe. A few rounds on a fitty, if that's the case."

He didn't need to say that it was more than a few rounds out of a .50 caliber. Kim nodded. "Go ahead and pull those shells out from behind the triggers," she said, and then she walked around the back of the vehicle and over to where Sue's squad was parked. Sue was outside her Hummer, sitting on the ground and leaning against one of the wheels. She was staring glumly at her cell phone, and when she saw Kim, she held it up. "Shit signal," she said. "Shit phone. It's all shit."

"Could be worse, right?"

"Always," Sue said, and pushed herself to her feet. "Firing's stopped, yeah?"

"Yeah, but . . ." Kim trailed off. There was another sound, and it took her a second to figure out what it was. Honking? Down the highway this time. Far away. Far enough that she and Sue had to stand there quietly, straining to hear it. The beginning of a ruckus. Maybe screaming? It was hard to tell. And then whatever sound might have been coming from the highway was washed away by the sound of rotors. A pair of birds, AH-64 Apaches, missiled-up and moving like piss fire, roared overhead and down the straight shot of highway. Kim and Sue looked at each other for a second and then scrambled to get back into their vehicles.

Kim barely had the door closed when the birds started firing. The jackhammer retort of the guns—the AH-64s sported a 30 mm M230 chain gun that could fire three hundred rounds per minute from the chin turret—sounded almost dusty from a mile away.

"All units, all units," the radio barked. "Prepare for hostilities."

Kim started the JLTV, the thrum of the engine coming on just as the birds' chain guns went quiet. She'd seen the ammo the Apaches took: each bullet was about the size of her hand. Behind her, she could hear Mitts scrambling, and in front of her, she could see more cars breaking out of line. There was a column of smoke coming from where the helicopters had been firing, and then there was a small explosion. The birds split, drifting to either side of the road and spinning toward the center, dropping their chins so the pilots had a clear view of the road. And then, from the Apache on the right, there was the vapor trail of a missile and a much larger explosion.

There was a weird vacuum of silence following the missile, broken, a few seconds later, by Duran. "Okay," he said. "This does not seem good." He turned to look at Kim. "Well?"

"Holy shit!" From above them, Kim heard Elroy shouting, but she didn't need to hear him call out "Fast mover" because she saw the jet spear past them. And then. Holy God. The jet launched a missile.

Chaos.

A fireball fifty feet high.

The slow, orderly movement of cars and trucks onto the side road toward Desperation broke down immediately. In front of them, cars and trucks and SUVs pulled into the desert wherever they could, and Kim could see people getting out of their cars and running. A couple hundred yards in front of her, she saw a man running across the dirt get plowed down by a sedan that had left the highway. The sedan didn't slow down. The helicopters opened fire with their chain guns again. Kim could see more and more people getting out of their cars. They were running from the fury of the helicopters and the burning ash from where the jet had launched its missile. It was a sight she never thought she'd see: American citizens running from the might of the American military.

No. No. That wasn't right. They weren't running away from the gunfire and missiles. She grabbed the binoculars from the console and spun the wheel on the dial until the view came into a tight focus. "No," she said. She could see moving shadows, see the way dark fingers were reaching up and sucking people down into the maw. Men and women and children were running and screaming. The jet and the birds weren't firing on civilians.

"They're here," she said. She didn't scream it or yell. It was her normal tone of voice. Almost conversational. She felt . . . calm. She was scared. She was willing to admit that. How could she not be scared? But she also understood that she was where she needed to be. She looked at Duran and then at Mitts. She looked up and then at Elroy, standing with his hands on the butterfly triggers of the .50 cal. She'd never thought about deploying on US soil, but she'd wanted to join the Marines her whole life, and she was ready for this. She needed to be ready. Her men trusted her.

The radio crackled. "All units, you are cleared to fire. Do not, repeat, do not allow the quarantine zone to be breached. Fire at will."

She wanted to ask what the fuck they were supposed to be firing at, people or spiders, but the Marines had already opened up. She felt the truck shiver from Elroy firing the .50 cal, the dead heavy thump of the gun spitting bullets. A semitruck that had made it off the highway and into the desert exploded and then tipped over. There was a huge mess of cars moving and smashing and trying to get anywhere but where they were. To her right, Kim could see that Sue's Hummer was firing its .50 cal as well, and one of her crew, maybe Private Goons, was out of the truck and firing his M16. Next to her, she saw Duran reach for the door handle, but she grabbed his arm.

"Stay in the car," she said. "We can stop cars and we can stop civilians, but what's the point of shooting at spiders? I want to be ready to roll."

She picked up the binoculars again. Without the binoculars, the spiders were a black mass, four hundred yards out now, but through the glass, Kim could see a woman flailing her arms, her head shimmering with black beads. The woman dropped suddenly, and Kim wasn't sure if it was from the spiders or a bullet. At first, it seemed like there was no pattern to it, but Kim realized most of the people were running from right to left. And the firing Marines didn't seem to matter. The people were more scared of the spiders than of the guns.

"Kim?" Mitts leaned forward. He had his hand on her shoulder. "Kim? What are we supposed to do?"

She didn't know, but there was something bothering her. Something about the way the spiders were moving. It reminded her of a sort of dance. Liquid spilling forward and back, waves of black washing forward over certain people and then tucking back under, like the ocean pulling sand into the deeps. And some people, inexplicably, left standing, the bugs splitting around them, desert islands. Three hundred yards out now, and with the binoculars, she could see the spiders as individual drops, but without the binoculars, they were a single flood of liquid, moving together.

And then the radio came to life: "Fall back! Fall back!"

She didn't hesitate. She shoved the JLTV into drive and hit the gas. Because they were out on the wing, the last vehicle in the barricade, all she had to do was crank the wheel all the way to the left to spin a spitting semicircle of dirt, stone, and dust before she was turned in the other direction.

"What the fuck?" Elroy ducked down, holding tight to the edges of the turret. "We've got orders to—"

"They're calling for us to fall back. It's too late," Kim yelled. "They fucked up. This isn't the flu. We can kill as many civilians as you want, fire until you're in the black, but it isn't going to stop the spiders. We can't shoot our way out of this one." She kept the gas pedal tight to the floor, and the JLTV was picking up speed now that it was moving straight. On the highway, she could get the fourteen-thousand-pound beast up to seventy miles per hour, but on the sand and dirt, she'd be happy with thirty. In the rearview mirror she saw Sue's Hummer tracking behind her, the rest of the line in a mix of chaos. Mitts scrambled across the seat to the other side so he could look out the window and back at the barricade.

There was another explosion, bigger this time. The entire JLTV bounced and bucked, but the tires bit back into the sand and it kept moving forward. The fast movers screamed over them again, from the other direction, payloads emptied, and Kim risked a look in the mirror again. All she could see was smoke and fire.

National Institutes of Health, Bethesda, Maryland

Melanie figured she had another ten minutes or so before the helicopter got there. Manny had been insistent. Despite the president's speech and all indications that the infestation was only in LA, people were starting to stream out of DC to go . . . To go where? Where did people think they were going to run to, Melanie wondered, a hotel in the Hamptons? It didn't matter, though, because the end result was that the normally bad traffic around the DC area was even worse, and the half-hour drive to the White House was going to take a lot longer. So. Helicopter.

She leaned into the window of the isolation unit to try to get a better view of what the surgeon was doing. At first, she thought it was going to be a simple thing. They'd cut Bark open, the dead spider had flopped out, and the egg sac had presented itself. Snip some threads, pull the sac out and drop it in the insectarium, sew Bark back up, call it a day. But it wasn't so easy. The strands of silk weren't just tacked around the sac. They were literally sewn through Bark's body. And worse. The threads were dotted with eggs, like mini egg sacs on a highway throughout his body. Nasty little surprises, and the surgeon had to track each thread and make sure he caught each of the eggs. The big egg sac was still in there; the surgeon wanted to work around it, to make sure he didn't lose any of the precious threads. As an added bonus, the egg sac, all the spider silk, was incredibly sticky. It was nothing like the sac from Peru. That thing had been hard, designed to go the distance. But this egg sac was different, and the surgeon had to be careful to avoid getting tangled up.

Plus, as a final bonus, it was vibrating and getting warmer.

None of it made any sense to her. Normally it took two or three weeks for an egg sac to hatch, and the spiders that came out were hatchlings, growing slowly to their full sizes. But these things could lay eggs and have full-sized spiders popping out in twelve hours. Or twenty-four? She didn't actually know. She would have said twenty-four based on what was happening everywhere else, but this egg sac seemed as though it was moving faster. It would hatch within twelve hours for sure. Maybe even quicker. It was like they were speeding up. One generation burning out quickly and the next even more so. Maybe the way she'd described it to Manny had been the best: like a rocket burning itself up.

But that didn't make sense either. What evolutionary advantage was there in dying quickly? The parasitic part made sense. By laying eggs inside hosts, the spiders had guaranteed food sources once they hatched. But the fact that they could eat their hosts wasn't normal either. Most spiders dissolved their prey and ground it up with their pedipalps since they didn't have teeth. She'd described it once to Manny as having a broken jaw and needing to run everything through a blender before slurping it up through a straw. But these spiders? They had more in common with piranhas than anything else. Actually, Melanie thought, that might not be a bad comparison, though she didn't know much about the fish other than what she'd seen in a couple of bad horror films. The spiders were uncommonly social and coordinated, swarming together and almost organized.

There had to be a reason for it. There had to be more to it. She was sure of it. The answer was a sort of itch she couldn't reach. She knew she'd figure it out if she had enough time, but that was the problem. *Did* she have enough time?

Inside the containment unit, the surgeon was still bent over Bark's body, assisted by three nurses and an anesthesiologist. Patrick was in there too. He had the lab's expensive SLR camera plus a video camera, and he was alternating between taking pictures and shooting film. She tapped on the glass to try to get his attention. Video was fine for now. It was high-definition. She wished they'd brought a tripod from the lab. If they'd had a tripod, Patrick could have left the video camera running and bounced around with the SLR, but a tripod was another thing they'd forgotten. It was a miracle they weren't shooting video on a cell phone. Like idiots, they'd rushed Bark from the lab without thinking it through other than to get him to the biocontainment unit. Nobody brought a laptop or a tablet, which didn't seem like a big deal at first, until they realized that, with the egg sac starting to hum and heat up, it might be a good idea to look back at the data from the other egg sac. When Melanie stepped out of the isolation unit to get ready for her Manny-mandated helicopter pickup, she sent Julie scurrying to get on a computer to see if she could access their data remotely. The big question was: How hot was too hot? How soon was this sucker going to hatch? It was one thing to watch the egg sac in the lab hatch, another to actually have the numbers in front of you for comparison. Julie needed to get her ass back there as quickly as possible so that Melanie could crunch the numbers. She wanted to make sure that, if necessary, she could get Patrick and the medical team out of there with time to spare.

She leaned her head against the glass, suddenly exhausted. There was so much she didn't know or understand about these things, but it wasn't exciting anymore. It was just scary. She knew she could be detached sometimes, that she didn't always get upset the way some other people did, but in there, through that glass, lying on the operating table, his chest and abdomen split open, was a young man she'd been sleeping with—okay, dating—until a few days ago. And she was being called to the White House to tell a bunch of generals and cabinet members and the president how to kill spiders. A rolled-up newspaper? Would that joke go over? Probably not. She didn't know what she could say.

It would be different if there were just a few of them. If she had them in her lab and had the time to study them. There were so many questions. Just the egg sacs to begin with. Why were there two kinds? One for longer incubations and a softer, sticky one for immediate delivery. How could some of the spiders hatch so quickly? It was as if some of the spiders were on fast-forward.

"Doctor Guyer?" She turned, expecting to see a suit, but it was a man in full army combat gear. Or maybe navy or Marines. In their fatigues, she didn't know how she was supposed to tell them apart. She nodded. "Your ride's here, ma'am," the young man said.

"I'm sorry," she said, "I didn't hear the helicopter come in. Let me just . . ." She trailed off. She was about to say that she needed to tell Patrick she was leaving, but she caught sight of Julie coming down the corridor, running. *Running.*

No. It was too soon. Not twenty-four hours or even twelve hours yet. They should have more time! But Julie was running and screaming and Melanie knew it meant she'd gotten access to the data from the lab. Melanie turned back to the glass and started to bang on it with her fists, to get the attention of the nurses and the surgeon and the anesthesiologist and Patrick, to get them the hell out of there.

Too late.

Minneapolis, Minnesota

Mike knew he was out of his depth. But sometimes, when you're thrown in, the only thing you can do is swim. Or, phone a friend.

They cordoned off the whole block, cleared the warehouse of anybody who wasn't wearing a badge, and called in four more agents plus the bureau chief. But then, honestly, they just sort of stood around. Nobody knew what to do. They all stared at the egg sacs and made serious faces and serious sounds, but there wasn't really a protocol for it. One of the junior agents came back with a big glass jar and scooped the dead spider from the floor into it, but other than that?

And then Mike remembered the card from the scientist in DC. He pulled it from his wallet. Melanie Guyer. Dr. Melanie Guyer. She'd written her cell phone number on the back. It was 8:30 A.M. Minneapolis time, so 9:30 A.M. in Washington, DC, but Mike figured that with all that was going on and with a lab full of those suckers, she was probably out and about. What he didn't expect was for her to be on a helicopter.

He had to speak loudly, and with the hush in the warehouse— it was easier to look serious if you were kind of quiet—everybody turned to look at him. He held up his hand in an awkward apology and headed outside.

"Agent Rich—"

"Mike."

"Mike, listen, not really a good time right now."

"I found a few, well, I guess egg sacs? I can text you a picture." There was no response for a few seconds. He listened to the staticky chop of the helicopter blades. "Hello?"

"Sorry. I'm just . . . I just watched spiders hatch from a living human."

Mike pulled the phone back from his ear and looked at it. He knew it was a strange thing to do, but it was also a strange thing to hear, and he needed to make sure it wasn't something he'd imagined. He put the phone back to his ear. "In DC?"

"Maryland, actually, but it doesn't matter."

"They're loose in DC now?"

"Maryland. But no. He was in a biocontainment unit. There was an egg sac inside him. They were trying to get it out. It shouldn't have been . . . It shouldn't have hatched so quickly. None of this makes sense."

"Yeah, well, I'm hoping you can tell me what to do."

"I don't think anybody can tell you what to do," she said. "You're in Minnesota?"

"In a warehouse."

"Is it as bad as Los Angeles?"

The phone was muffled for a second and he heard her shouting something. Then she was back. "No," he said. "There's nothing. It's calm here. The only thing we've got is a dead spider and three pod things. As far as I know, there aren't any other spiders on the ground here. We're only a couple of blocks from where Henderson's plane crashed, so I'm sort of figuring there must have been another spider that survived, that came over here and made these egg things."

"Are the egg sacs warm?"

"I didn't, uh," Mike stammered, "I mean, nobody's touched them. We set up a few barricades and taped the area off."

"Like, with police tape?" She actually laughed. "That's not going to do much."

"That's funny? I guess it's a little funny. We're a federal agency. It's kind of what we do. But no, I don't know if they're warm or what."

"Okay. Listen, Mike, I've only got a couple of minutes before I land, but I need you to go touch one, tell me what it feels like."

"Give me a minute." He walked back into the building, ducked under the police tape, and walked over to the shelves. He tucked the phone between his ear and his shoulder and pulled a wheeled platform ladder over. He went up a few steps, reached out his hand, and then hesitated. "Just touch it?"

"What does it feel like?"

From a distance, it looked smooth and white, almost like an egg, but up close he could see the individual strands, the way the silk threads were wrapped in layer after layer to create the sac. He shivered and then let his hand fall on the orb. He expected it to be sticky, but it wasn't. It was a little rough, maybe a little bit tacky, but it was nothing like what he'd been afraid of. There'd been a part of him that was terrified his hand was going to stick to the thing. "It feels a little bit like one of those jawbreakers, after they've dried out again."

"What?"

"Yeah, I've got a kid. You know those big jawbreakers? My kid will eat one for a while and then stick the thing in a bowl and come back to it later. They're basically pure sugar and chemicals and don't go bad, but once they dry out, they're sort of smooth and rough at the same time."

"That's disgusting."

"Lady, you work with spiders," he said. Even with the sound of the helicopter and everything else, he imagined he could hear her smiling. Definitely, he thought. If they managed to survive all this, he was going to fly back to DC and take her out on a date. What the hell?

"It's not sticky?"

"No. A little tacky, sort of, I don't know—"

"Calcified?"

"Yeah. Good word. And it's not warm at all. Cool, really."

The White House

Melanie kept the phone pressed to her ear, her other hand covering her free ear. She was talking somewhere between loud and shouting. Below her, she saw the South Lawn of the White House looming up. They were landing.

"Keep track of the temperature. Far as we can tell, when it gets hot, it's ready to hatch. Don't touch them in the meantime," she said. "No. Wait. Scratch that. Find one of the local universities that has an entomology program and have them bring over some insectariums. Get the egg sacs in there, and then make sure they're somewhere contained. Somebody has to have a lab in the area that will work. I think you're safe for now, but I don't know."

She felt the jolt of the struts hitting the ground, and the battle-dressed soldier next to her grabbed her arm. "We've got to go, ma'am."

She ducked her head instinctively as she ran out from under the chopper blades. "Let me know if anything changes," she yelled into the phone. It was louder outside the helicopter. "And good luck."

The soldier handed her off to a pair of Secret Service agents, and they hustled her through the halls and toward the Situation

Room. It was overwhelming, and as they passed a bathroom, she stopped. One of the Secret Service agents tugged on her arm, but she shook her head.

"I've got to use the restroom."

The agent, a young Latino man, kept his hand on her biceps. "We're under orders to take you to Mr. Walchuck immediately," he said.

She gently peeled his hand off. "I'm forty and have a doctorate. I'm the one who gets to decide when I pee."

The hallway was buzzing with people moving back and forth, some of them running, all of them looking harried, and the bathroom felt cool and quiet. She ducked into the stall and peed. It was a surprising relief. For that matter, when had she last had something to eat or drink? She needed a coffee or a Diet Coke. She needed a few minutes to get herself together before she faced Manny and the president and a roomful of uniforms, she thought.

Dead spiders in the insectarium. Dried out. Used up. And the other spiders. Feeding machines. The egg sac in Bark, sticky and ready to hatch, and then the egg sacs in Minneapolis? Mike said they were cool. A little rough. She tried running the numbers in her head, thinking over the data. It was . . . something. There was something she was missing. She was so close. She needed her lab. She needed a nap.

She closed her eyes and then heard the door to the bathroom. She opened her eyes and stared at her knees, sitting on the toilet for a few more seconds, savoring the time to herself, before she finished up and stepped out of the stall. Stepped out of the stall to find Manny leaning against the sink and waiting for her.

"Jesus, Manny. Come on."

"We were married for eleven years," he said, and then shrugged. His version of an apology. "I needed to talk to you before you go in."

She brushed past him to wash her hands. "What am I doing here, Manny? This is way past me at this point. I'm a lab kind of girl. What do you expect me to do?"

"I expect you to do your job," he said. "You know spiders. That's all we need. Tell us, as best you can, what we're dealing with."

"Minnesota," she said.

"What?"

"They're in Minnesota now. You knew that, right?" Manny turned pale, and Melanie had the answer to her question. "Mike—Agent Rich, the one who brought the spider from Minneapolis—called me when I was on the way here. They found a dead spider in a warehouse near the crash site and some egg sacs."

Manny took a deep breath. "How many? How many egg sacs?"

"I think he said three. Three? But the good news is that they're cool, and we might have some time before they hatch."

"There's something you need to see," Manny said.

He walked her out of the bathroom and down the hall. As they passed the Situation Room, a young woman in army dress bounced through the doors, a cacophony of voices following her. Manny didn't glance in. He turned, four doors down, and took her into a smaller, quieter room. It was nearly empty. Just Billy Cannon, Alex Harris, and a couple of aides.

"Show her the footage," Manny said.

Melanie sat down in one of the chairs around the table. They all faced the same large screen on the far side of the room. One of the aides turned down the lights, and the screen lit up.

"We shot this forty minutes ago. Marines in Los Angeles."

"Don't worry," Billy said dryly, "we're not going to show you the Hollywood sign covered in spiders."

The video was shaky and poorly lit. There were dark shadows

and whoever was holding the camera kept moving it back and forth. She realized it must have been mounted on his helmet. Melanie caught a glimpse of someone in a military uniform—one of the other Marines, she assumed—and a shape on the ground that she realized was a body. The camera stopped moving, the light showing a dark carpet. No. It wasn't a carpet. It was a layer of dead spiders. A foot reached out and poked at the spiders, pushing them aside.

"They're dying?"

"Some of them. Most of them. But that's not the point of the video," Manny said. "This. Watch this."

The video moved forward again, out of the mouth of a hallway, opening out into a cavernous space. There were sections of seats. The camera panned over and she saw a Los Angeles Lakers logo.

"Is that the Staples Center?"

"She's a basketball player. I told you she'd recognize it," Manny said to Alex, but Melanie barely heard him. She was leaning toward the screen, reaching out with her finger.

"Oh my god."

The egg sacs closest to the light on the camera were white and dusty looking, casting shadows on the ones behind. What should have been the hardwood court was covered in white lumps, and there were more of them up in the stands on the other side, until the light gave way to darkness. Thousands of egg sacs. Maybe tens of thousands.

"Near as we can tell," Manny said, "the spiders are all dying out. There was a respite last night, late, and then a fresh wave with a break in the middle of the night, and then another wave, but they're dying. We've got boots on the ground, and we're getting the same report over and over. The spiders are just keeling over. Spider bodies everywhere."

Melanie's phone started ringing, but she ignored it. "All of them?"

"All of them," Manny said. "We've got a couple of coolers full of spiders on ice being rushed back to you now to take a look at. But right now, it's suddenly weirdly calm. Which means the question is: What do we do about this basketball stadium full of spider eggs?"

"For starters," Billy said, "we should probably cancel tonight's game. Though the Lakers probably would have lost anyway." No one laughed.

Alex touched her arm. "Are we fucked?"

Coming from the national security advisor, who looked as if she could be cast as the grandmother in some sort of feel-good Christmas commercial, the question was almost funny. Almost.

"It depends," Melanie said. Her phone stopped ringing, kicking to voice mail, but then it dinged with a text. And then another. And another.

"I'd say it probably doesn't depend," Billy Cannon said. "I can make all the jokes about the Lakers I want, but when those things hatch, we're talking how many? Millions more? And what does it mean that one day we have this swarm in Los Angeles, and the next they're all dying or dead?" He pushed his chair back and launched his coffee cup at the trash can, missing by a good two feet. "Fuck," he said. "What happened to regular war?"

Melanie fished her phone out of her pocket to read the texts, suddenly realizing they had to be from Mike in Minneapolis. If those egg sacs were getting warm, getting ready to hatch, then . . . But no. The texts were from Julie.

She'd left Julie a sobbing mess outside the biocontainment unit back at the National Institutes of Health. Not that she could blame Julie. To see the nurses and the surgeon go down under the swarm of spiders, let alone Bark, still opened up on the table, and Patrick. At some point, Melanie knew, the scientist part of her was going to get overwhelmed, and she'd be crying heaps too.

Spiders at NIH dying. The first text.

Call me! The second text from Julie.

And the third, longer: *The spiders behind the glass are all dying. Just falling over. Almost all of them. All at once. Called lab. Some dead. Some alive. But Melanie: egg sac at lab! Got to see it.*

"No," Melanie said. "We're not fucked. Or, maybe we are. Like I said, it depends. Manny, you're wrong. The problem isn't what to do about a stadium full of eggs. Though you're going to need to start searching to see if there are other infestation sites in Los Angeles. The question that really matters, however, isn't *what* you need to do, but *when* you need to do it. For now, you've got to get somebody into the Staples Center to take the temperature of the egg sacs. Before they hatch, there's a spike in temperature. Maybe this will give me a sense how much time we have," she said. "Oh, and I want somebody in Minneapolis."

"Minneapolis?" Alex Harris looked alarmed. "Why Minneapolis?"

EPILOGUE

Los Angeles, California

Andy Anderson never thought he'd be pleased to have his dog take a shit on the kitchen floor, but all things considered, he was happy not to take Sparky out for an early-morning walk. He'd spent the night huddled under the covers with the dog, listening to the sounds of sirens and gunshots and screaming. But for the past hour, it had been quiet.

He decided to risk it. He clipped the leash to Sparky's collar, gingerly opened the door, and stepped out onto the walk. The sun came down unfiltered, but there was a nice breeze to cut the heat. He took a few more steps until they were on the sidewalk. Sparky seemed unconcerned, so Andy decided to walk past a few houses. Nobody was out, though he could see a station wagon that had smashed against a tree partway down the block, and past that, two lumps in the middle of the street. He started to walk closer but then, realizing what the lumps were, stopped. The breeze gusted into a stiff wind, and he heard something skitter and bounce behind him.

He stumbled and twisted, trying to turn, knowing he'd made

a dumb mistake, that the spiders were still out there, but it was nothing. Just a few leaves skating across the pavement. One of them landed against his shoe and he realized it wasn't a leaf. It was a dead spider. A husk. He looked around him more carefully. There were carcasses everywhere.

Minneapolis, Minnesota

Mike had never seen so many uniforms in one place. As near as he could tell, every cop, fireman, EMT, National Guardsman, and federal agent in three states was painstakingly searching each and every inch in the two square miles surrounding where Henderson's jet had crashed. But so far? Zip. Nada. Nothing. Just the three egg sacs from the warehouse, and those were already in insectariums and winging their way to Washington and Melanie's lab.

He double-checked with the bureau chief that he was good to go, told Leshaun to head home and get some rest, and started driving north.

American University, Washington, DC

And there it was, in the insectarium at the lab. An egg sac. Chalky looking, a fresher version of the one that had been sent from Peru. She wanted to put her hand in, to feel it, to make sure it was as cool as she expected it to be, but there were still two spiders alive and moving around the insectarium. The rest were dead. The two live ones didn't have the markings, but they were big—bigger than the dead ones—and after what had happened with Bark, she was keeping the fucking lid closed. There were more egg sacs coming, from the microsite in Minneapolis and from the giant brood in Los Angeles, plus a sampling of dead spiders from all over the world. Manny promised he had jets scrambling everywhere to get her what she needed.

But it didn't matter. She'd figured it out.

It was worse than she expected. Much, much worse.

Alex Harris had called it: they were fucked.

Càidh Island, Loch Ròg, Isle of Lewis, Outer Hebrides

Aonghas put his hand on Thuy's shoulder. She was sipping a cup of tea and pretending to read a mystery. A rather inferior mystery, in Aonghas's opinion, but he knew he was biased. Not that Thuy was actually reading it. She was doing the same thing he was, which was keeping part of his attention on the BBC and part on looking through the windows at the old man walking circles around the rock.

Desperation, California

Gordo was pretty sure Amy had thrown the last round of Catan. Fred never won, and he seemed extraordinarily pleased with himself, but they were all glad for the distraction.

Shotgun tapped his tablet and changed the music to Lyle Lovett while Gordo filled a bucket with ice and beer. Amy and Fred reset the game. In the corner, Claymore let out small moans in his sleep, his legs twitching, running from something in his dreams.

The CNN Center,
Atlanta, Georgia

"**I** don't know, Teddie." Don played the loop again. "I don't think we can go with it yet. It's barely been twenty-four hours since Los Angeles got quiet, and it's time to start thinking about stories of the aftermath. We've got dead spiders everywhere. People want to see positive stories. Stories of survival. It's over."

"Come on," she said to her boss. "You can't tell me you don't see the pattern?"

He shook his head. "It's not that. It's just . . . What's it mean?"

She let her chair rock back. He was the only real boss she'd ever had, and he'd told her to go for it, but she knew this was a little out there. Still. She could feel it. She was right. "They aren't moving randomly. Like stupid bugs."

Don hit the button again, the loop playing across the screen once more. "Okay. But what does it mean?"

"They're hunting."

"We already know they're killing people and—"

"No," she said. "Watch the way this group moves to the side and this other string funnels them in. It's not just a bunch of spiders attacking people. They're hunting as a group. Like a pack. It's coordinated."

Marine Corps Base Camp Pendleton, San Diego, California

She couldn't sleep. Kim got out of her bunk and wandered outside. She figured she'd be the only one up that time of night other than the patrols, but Mitts was leaning against the side of the barracks, drinking a beer. He nodded at her, reached down to the six-pack at his feet, and handed her a bottle. The beer was warm, but it was good.

She took a few sips, neither of them saying anything, neither of them wanting to talk about how many empty bunks there were inside. After a few minutes, she leaned into him and he silently put his arm around her.

The White House

Not even twenty-four hours since the spiders started dying in Los Angeles and it was over. How many millions of people dead across the world? But it was over. Manny reached for his Diet Coke and realized his hand was shaking. He wasn't sure how long it had been since he last slept. Three days? Four? But what he knew for sure was that the reports everywhere—India, China, Scotland, Egypt—were that the spiders were all dead. All that was left was the cleanup. How come it couldn't be as simple as only having to deal with the fucking Staples Center?

"Sorry," Melanie said. "You know as well as I do the Staples Center is just what's obvious. You think because you kill one spider in your bathroom that there aren't others hiding somewhere else in your house?"

Steph was lying on the couch. Not exactly dignified behavior in the Oval Office, but it was just the three of them. She had her eyes closed, but she clearly wasn't sleeping. "Please tell me you didn't say that."

"But can't we just, I don't know, soak all of them in gasoline and then light the whole thing on fire?" Manny said. "Okay, so the whole idea of spraying insecticide over Los Angeles was a fiasco—"

"Honestly," Melanie said, "it wasn't the worst idea."

"Sure, if we had enough insecticide and planes to spray more than a few square blocks, and then if the insecticide we used had actually worked. But fire? Right?" Manny said. "Set the Staples Center on fire? That should take care of any we don't see."

"I'm not talking about the Staples Center."

"Then what are—"

"The spiders aren't all the same," Melanie said. "They just look the same because we're seeing them as a group. You get a mass of these spiders, a swarm of them, and it looks like a unified group. We've been thinking about it wrong, trying to figure out what kind of spider it is, and then thinking, oh, they're dying and all that's left is the egg sacs. But it's not just one kind of spider. There are spiders. Plural."

Steph sat up and put her feet on the floor. "I don't understand."

"The spiders display patterns of eusociality similar to *Hymenoptera* and *Isoptera*, and I think, in a similar fashion, these spiders have different castes too."

"Melanie," Steph said, "I know you think what you're saying makes sense, but please understand I've barely slept since this started, and nothing you just said makes *any* sense to me. We aren't scientists, okay?"

"Spiders are normally loners. There are about thirty-five thousand known species, and mostly they live by themselves, but there are about two dozen species that display eusociality. Which just means they work together. They all help care for the brood and share resources, all that sort of stuff. So when I say *Hymenoptera* and *Isoptera*, you should think ants and bees and termites. Colonies. They work together, and they take on defined roles. You know, worker bees and queens and that type of thing."

Manny leaned forward. "You're saying they have queens? That all we have to do is kill the queens?"

"No, I'm . . ." She paused. "Well, maybe. Fuck. Okay. I have to think about *that*. But that's not what I'm talking about. Just stay with me for a minute. We've got a kind of spider that isn't like any other we've ever seen, but it's not just one kind of spider. In the lab, we've already figured out how to differentiate between feeders and breeders, but it also looks as though there's more than one kind of breeder. There are the spiders that use hosts to carry their eggs, the ones that lay eggs inside people, and there are breeders who lay eggs in sacs in places they've cleared out. Some egg sacs hatch quickly, some seem to be slower. Maybe it's the same breeders and they just choose what kind of sac to make depending on the conditions, but I don't think that's it. It's like they are on parallel but different tracks. There are the ones that behave like normal spiders and seem to develop at a normal pace, and there are the lightning ones."

"Blitzkrieg," Steph said.

"What?"

"Not everything is comparable to the Nazis," Manny said.

"Lightning war," Steph said to Melanie. "Blitzkrieg. Fast, overwhelming attacks as a military doctrine."

"Yeah. I guess. They hatch and grow in this crazy accelerated fashion, and they die more quickly too."

She looked at Manny and Steph, but they didn't seem to get it. "I'm explaining it wrong. I'm talking about some of the spiders being feeders and some of them as breeders, but that's the wrong way to think of it. It's about timing. These ones, the ones we're seeing out in the wild, they're the colonizers." She leaned over, putting her hands flat on the table. "They're like pioneers, clearing the land."

Steph squinted at her. "Clearing the land? For what?"

Melanie felt sick. She didn't want to say it. "For the rest of them. Think of it as an advance team. These spiders, the ones we're seeing, they're just the first wave."

Steph put her elbows on her knees and let her head sink. "You're saying this is just the beginning?"

"It's part of their evolutionary advantage. They come out with a first wave and clear out any potential predators. They're designed to breed quickly and feed on anything that gets in their way, but the price of that fast growth is that they burn out. That's what we're seeing now. The first wave has hatched and cleared out space to set the table for the next stage."

"So, what's next?" Steph asked.

"More," Melanie said. "Worse. The next ones are the real ones. Those will be the ones that are in it for the long haul."

"How long?" Manny said. "How long until they come back?"

"Again—I can't stress this enough—I'm working by feel here. I've never seen spiders like this, and I don't have a lot of data. But looking at the egg sacs, looking at the variations in the spiders?" She stopped. "I'm not completely confident—"

"Melanie," Steph said. "Just give me a number. How long?"

"Two weeks," Melanie said. "Three if we're lucky."

Soot Lake, Minnesota

Every fifteen minutes or so, Annie would stick her foot into the lake. With the sun out, it was hot enough that she wanted to swim, but in April, in northern Minnesota, no matter how warm the air was, the water was barely different from ice. She sighed and went back to coloring. It was better to be out here, on the dock, than inside her stepdad's cabin. All her mom and Rich wanted to do was sit around the radio and read the news on their stupid tablets.

She waved her hand around her head. The black flies weren't bad yet, but there were already mosquitoes. Their whine was a constant part of cottage life. She whisked her hand back and forth a couple of times before she realized the buzzing wasn't the sound of mosquitoes. It was a motor. She jumped to her feet. She could see her daddy at the helm of a boat. He was coming to get her. Coming to tell them it was safe to go home.

ACKNOWLEDGMENTS

Writing a book is a solitary endeavor, but getting a book out into the world requires a great deal of help.

Emily Bestler at Emily Bestler Books / Atria Books is a terrific editor, smart as hell, and a joy to work with. And while most writers are lucky if they have even one editor like Emily in their whole career, I'm about as lucky as it gets, because I also got to work with the magnificent Anne Collins at Penguin Random House Canada and, in the UK, with the excellent Marcus Gipps at Gollancz, an imprint of the Orion Publishing Group.

Bill Clegg at the Clegg Agency is my literary agent extraordinaire. I can't thank you enough. I'll keep trying, though.

Erin Conroy at William Morris Endeavor Entertainment. Crushing it, as always.

At Emily Bestler Books / Atria Books, thanks to: David Brown, Judith Curr, Suzanne Donahue, Lara Jones, Amy Li, Albert Tang, and Jin Yu. At Penguin Random House Canada, thanks to: Randy Chan, Josh Glover, Jessica Scott, and Matthew Sibiga. At Gollancz, thanks to: Sophie Calder, Craig Leyenaar, Jennifer McMenemy, Gillian Redfearn, and Mark Stay.

At the Clegg Agency, thanks to: Jillian Buckley, Chris Clemans,

Henry Rabinowitz, Simon Toop, and Drew Zagami. Also thank you to Anna Jarota and Dominika Bojanowska at the Anna Jarota Agency, Mònica Martín, Inés Planells, and Txell Torrent at MB Agencia Literaria, and Anna Webber at United Agents.

You guys didn't actually do anything, but thanks to Mike Haaf, Alex Hagen, Ken Rassnick, and Ken Subin. Shawn Goodman, you actually did help, so thanks to you as well.

And, of course, thank you to my brother and his family, my wife's family, the friends who are family by choice, and to my wife and daughters. But no thanks to my dogs. You two are not super helpful.

It's not over yet . . .

Turn over the page and get a taste
of what's coming next

SKITTER

PROLOGUE

Lander, Wyoming

It was a big flipping spider. That was the only reason he screamed. He wasn't afraid of spiders. Really. But the thing had been the size of a quarter. Right on his cheek. He'd been backpacking solo for fifteen days, and he hadn't been scared once. Until his last day out, today, when he woke up with a scary, hairy, ugly spider on his cheek. Well, that wasn't entirely true. Fifteen days alone in the Wind River Range in Wyoming, not seeing another living soul the entire time? Fifteen days of scrambling across scree fields, traversing open ridges, even doing a little free solo rock climbing despite what he'd promised his dad? He'd have to be a complete moron not to feel a little twinge of concern here and there. And Winthrop Wentworth Jr.—nineteen, the son of privilege—was not a complete moron.

Win had been on the road nonstop for ten months. Biking through Europe, surfing in Maui, scuba diving in Bonaire, skiing in the Alps, partying in Thailand. His father owned a hedge fund and a significant stake in three different sports teams and family vacations had tended toward butlers and private jets and water that you could drink without worrying about dysentery. But Win's dad had earned his money the hard way and liked the idea of his son taking a gap year before he started Yale. He wanted Win to have the year off that he was never able to take as a young man. So Win had a pair of credit cards with no spending limits and instructions to check in every week. He had started off right after high school graduation with five of his private school buddies, biking across Italy and then driving through the old Eastern Bloc countries. Every week or two a couple of friends would take off and a couple more would join on. That lasted through mid-August, when all his friends had headed home to get ready for college. Since then, it had just been Win. He didn't mind. He never had a problem making friends along the way.

It wasn't that Win was a particularly good-looking kid. He was tall, which was good, but kind of scrawny, which wasn't. But he was confident, he spoke French, Italian, and a smattering of Chinese, and he was genuinely interested in other people. And he was rich. Smacking down a black American Express Centurion Card or his gold-colored but just as heavy-sounding JPMorgan Chase Palladium Visa to buy a round or three, to hire a boat for the day for the seven other backpackers he'd just met in Phuket, or to buy a new suit and pay extra to have it tailored while he waited so he could take a woman twice his age to dinner at a very small, very exclusive restaurant in Paris, meant that he made friends wherever he went. It also meant he got laid a lot. Not a bad way to spend a year between high school and college.

But by the middle of the following April, all this adventure had started to drag at him a little. Despite his father's seemingly inexhaustible supply of money, Win had always been a hard worker. He'd actually earned the As he'd gotten in high school. He wasn't the most talented player on the basketball team, but he ran until he puked and was the first man off the bench. So he called his dad from a hotel in Switzerland and said he was pretty much ready to wrap things up. He was going to come home and intern at the hedge fund until he started school in the fall. But first, he wanted to take a solo backpacking trip in the Wind River Range. Fifteen days of just him and his pack, a little something to clear his head.

And it had worked. As he hiked, he could feel the residues of booze and pot clearing out through his pores. By the third day, he felt fresh and sharp again, and by the fifth day, he was climbing some easy lines. His dad had made him promise not to rock climb solo, but Win didn't think it was much of a risk. Fifty-, sixty-foot climbs with ledges and handholds like ladder rungs. Just enough to get his heart rate up a little.

On the last day, he woke up at the same time as the sun. That was the devil's bargain of sleeping in a tent. He laid still for a moment with his eyes closed, hoping for a little more sleep, taking a few deep breaths, and that's when he felt the tickling sensation. He opened his eyes and it loomed. He couldn't help himself. He let out a scream and swatted the spider off his cheek. It moved quickly, scuttling away from him, into the corner of the tent. Win grabbed one of his hiking boots and smashed the living shit out of the spider.

Even now, with ten miles of trail behind him and maybe five more minutes to the trailhead and his truck, Win gave an involuntary shudder at the thought. He really wanted to believe he wasn't afraid of spiders. But this one had been so close. On his face. *Blech*.

Win had originally considered chartering a jet so he could fly in close to Lander, but in the end it had actually been easier to fly to Denver, even with the almost six-hour drive. All he'd had to do ahead of time was call the American Express concierge service. As a Black Card member, he'd arranged to have somebody meet him at the gate and take him right to a Toyota Land Cruiser, Win's age of nineteen be damned. When he got to the trailhead and his rental truck, Win dropped his pack to the ground. It was a hell of a lot lighter after fifteen days on the trail. He'd eaten all his food, for one, and for another, he was simply used to the weight. Still, it felt good to get it off his back. He fished the key out of the inside flap pocket and opened the trunk. He pulled out his cell phone and turned it on. While he was waiting for it to power up, he rooted through his other gear to see if he had any good snacks. He was starving. He struck out on the snacks, and he struck out on the cell phone: his battery had held its charge, but there was no signal up where he was parked. He sighed, threw his phone back into his bag, and then lifted his backpack into the trunk. Screw it.

Barely an hour later, just past two in the afternoon, he cruised into downtown Lander, Wyoming. The idea of calling it a downtown was a bit of a joke. The population was maybe six, seven thousand people. But the place did have something he really wanted: hamburgers and onion rings. He passed the Lander Bar and Gannet Grill, looking for a parking spot, and found one a block away. It was one of those rites of passage if you backpacked in the Wind River Range. Come back to town and stuff yourself full of fried food at the bar and grill. Maybe, after, he'd even get an ice cream. He half thought of grabbing a hotel room, but he liked the idea of hitting Denver tonight better, taking a suite at the Four Seasons and calling up a redheaded girl he'd met in Thailand who had been taking off part of her junior year of college. He could put down a couple of thousand calories, hit the road by three, be out of the shower by ten, and getting laid by midnight. That sounded a lot better than staying at some paper thin–walled motel in Lander.

He got out of the truck and paused for a second. He knew he should dig his phone out of his pack now that he could get a signal, but he decided it could wait. His dad didn't actually expect him off the trail for a couple more days. He could call him from the road. He'd call the redhead too. And get the concierge at the Four Seasons to book his room, make sure there was champagne for her if she wanted—he liked how clear he felt right now, and was done with booze for a while—plus some fresh fruit, and a box of condoms tucked away in the bedside drawer. If the redhead wasn't feeling as frisky as she'd been in Thailand that was okay, too. She was smart and funny, and it wouldn't be bad just to cuddle up on the bed and watch a cheesy movie.

He started for the bar but then stopped. What the heck? The store across the street was a fire-gutted shell. The sign was blackened and he could just make out the letters: THE GOOD PLACE. HUNTING. FISHING. CAMPING. GUNS. He'd bought most of his gear there before he'd headed out on the trail. Barely fifteen days earlier it had been a thriving outfitter store, but now it was empty. A ruin. No boards on the windows, no tape around it to keep people away. He looked up and down the street and saw it wasn't just The Good Place.

He hadn't been paying attention as he'd driven in, too focused on the idea of a good old American gut-busting burger, but Lander looked messed up. He knew The Good Place hadn't been like that when he'd hit the trail, but he couldn't remember if the rest of the town had been so similarly beat down. It was hard for him to imagine that Lander had a thriving business community, but still, this was weird. Empty storefronts were one thing, but these places were actively destroyed. A few stores down from where he'd parked, a pickup truck was lodged halfway through the front wall of a liquor store. It was a mess. Really, all of Lander seemed like

a disaster zone. It looked like a college town after they'd won—
or lost—some sort of championship. White kids rioting. But this
wasn't a college town, so maybe . . .

He let out a chuckle. Maybe the zombie apocalypse had finally
arrived while he was out in the wild. He *had* been gone just a hair
past two weeks. Long enough. He'd been in the mountains all
alone with no cell phone and no way to check in with the modern
world. Who knew what could have happened, but zombies would
be awesome. Still, it was pretty quiet out where he was standing.
A few blocks down he saw a pickup truck move slowly through
an intersection, but he was the only person on the street. The
smell of smoke hung heavy in the air. Melted plastic and charred
wood. He tried to remember the last time he'd seen the vapor
trail of an airplane overhead, and he realized that he wasn't sure
if he'd seen a plane above him even once while he was hiking.
September 11, 2001, wasn't part of his memory, but he'd heard
his dad talk about how weird it had been to see a sky clear of air
traffic. He glanced up. Blue sky with a few clouds. Another stunning day in Wyoming.

Ah, whatever. It was too beautiful out to worry. Zombie apocalypse or not, he needed some bar food after fifteen days of freeze-
dried chili mac and trail mix. He was ready for a basketful of fat
and salt.

He hit the lock button on his key and walked to the bar and
grill. Whatever qualms he had disappeared as he got to the door.
He could smell something grilling and the familiar odor of a deep
fryer. Oh man. A cheeseburger and onion rings, chicken wings
drowning in hot sauce served with a side of blue cheese for dip-
ping. A couple of cold Cokes so full of ice it would make his
teeth hurt even to take a sip. There was music playing and the
bar sounded like it was hopping. It didn't occur to him that a bar

probably shouldn't be that busy at two o'clock on a weekday until he was already through the door.

The talk died as he entered, and Win stopped. It took a second for his eyes to adjust to the dim light of the bar. When they did, he realized that an extremely large, extremely fat man with long gray hair and a beard that ended mid-chest was pointing a shotgun at him. Whatever impulse Win had to make a little quip died a quick death with the sound of the shotgun being racked. That sound. Was there a scarier sound on earth than a shotgun being pumped?

"Where did you come from?" the fat man asked.

Win hesitated. Had he walked into the middle of a robbery? But wouldn't the guy with the shotgun have locked the door or something? Or robbed a bank instead?

While Win was thinking, the fat man took a couple of steps forward and bopped Win on the side of his face with the shotgun. It didn't feel like a bop. It felt like maybe his cheekbone was broken, but Win thought of it as a bop, because that's what it would have looked like in a movie. He pressed his hand to his cheek and felt a tear in his skin. Slick and sticky blood. He couldn't stop himself from thinking that he'd just been bopped in the same spot he'd seen that damn spider perching when he woke up.

"Jesus frickin' Christ. What the hell?" Win had taken a shot like that, once, his sophomore year playing basketball, but it had been an errant elbow that left him with a broken nose and a black eye. It was clearly an accident. Hustle and vigor and athletic competition and all that, but even though the plastic surgeon had fixed his nose just fine, Winthrop Wentworth Sr. had been livid. Win's dad had gone so far as to have his hedge fund take a controlling interest in the bank where the kid's dad worked just so he could fire the poor guy. "Nobody," Win's dad liked to say, "messes with the Wentworths. Somebody hits you, you hit them back so hard they don't get up. You get in that habit, people stop hitting you."

Win's dad said all sorts of shit like that, but then again, Win's dad had grown up in Brooklyn back when Brooklyn didn't have hipsters or neighborhoods with twelve-million-dollar brownstones. He'd gotten in plenty of fights as a kid, and maybe one or two as an adult. There was a story that might have just been a legend, or might have been true, of his dad sealing his first billion-dollar deal by putting another man's head through the passenger window of a car. That wasn't Win, though. So he just stood there with his hand on his cheek.

The man had backed off, but the shotgun was pointed right at the middle of Win's body. He said, "I'll ask it again, and maybe you want to answer this time. Where'd you come from?"

"Whoa, whoa," Win said. "Wind River Range. I was backpacking. I got back to the trailhead maybe an hour ago."

He wanted to sound brave, but he knew he didn't. He didn't *feel* brave either. Having a shotgun pointed at him sucked away whatever courage he might have had.

"How long were you out?"

"Fifteen days." Win risked a quick glance around the room. Nobody was moving to help him. If anything, he thought he saw a couple of other guns in evidence. "I just came in here to get a burger and a soda before I start my drive to Denver."

"You were out backpacking for fifteen days?"

"Solo. Hit the trailhead an hour ago. I've been dreaming about a big hamburger and some onion rings." Win probed a little bit at his cheek. He winced. He could feel something sharp under the skin. Was it his cheekbone? Had this guy broken his cheekbone? So much for Denver and getting laid. He'd be headed straight to the hospital. Stitches at the least, maybe minor surgery.

"Look, I'm sorry for whatever I stepped into here, but if you can just—"

"Spiders?"

"What?" Win's hand was still on his cheek, but he couldn't stop himself from grimacing. That spider that he'd squished on the floor of the tent.

The man pulled the shotgun tight against his shoulder. Win didn't like the way the man's finger stayed on the trigger or how he'd started to squint down the barrel. "I said, did you see any spiders?"

"Spiders?"

"Are you deaf?" the man said. "Do you want another tap on the face? Did you see any spiders when you were out there?"

"Yeah. One. There was a spider on my cheek when I woke up this morning. Right where you smashed me with your—"

But Win never got to say the word *shotgun*.

It had gone off before he'd had a chance to finish his sentence.

ABOUT GOLLANCZ

Gollancz is the oldest SF publishing imprint in the world. Since being founded in 1927 Gollancz has continued to publish a focused selection of bestselling and award-winning authors. The front-list includes **Ben Aaronovitch**, **Joe Abercrombie**, **Charlaine Harris**, **Joanne Harris**, **Joe Hill**, **Alastair Reynolds**, **Patrick Rothfuss**, **Nalini Singh** and **Brandon Sanderson**.

As one of the largest Science Fiction and Fantasy imprints in the UK it is no surprise we have one of the most extensive backlists in the world. Find high quality SF on Gateway written by such authors as **Philip K. Dick**, **Ursula Le Guin**, **Connie Willis**, **Sir Arthur C. Clarke**, **Pat Cadigan**, **Michael Moorcock** and **George R.R. Martin**.

We also have a strand of publishing in translation, which includes French, Polish and Russian authors. Gollancz is home to more award-winning authors than any other imprint, with names including **Aliette de Bodard**, **M. John Harrison**, **Paul McAuley**, **Sarah Pinborough**, **Pierre Pevel**, **Justina Robson** and many more.

The SF Gateway
More than 3,000 classic, rare and previously out-of-print SF novels at your fingertips.
www.sfgateway.com

The Gollancz Blog
Bringing you news from our worlds to yours. Stories, interviews, articles and exclusive extracts just for you!
www.gollancz.co.uk

GOLLANCZ
LONDON